The New Shell Guides
Oxfordshire and Berkshire

Richard Lethbridge

Introduction by Robert Hardy

Series Editor: John Julius Norwich

Photography by Nick Meers

Michael Joseph · London

This book is for Dido

First published in Great Britain by
Michael Joseph Limited, 27 Wrights Lane,
London w8 5TZ 1988

This book was designed and produced by
Swallow Editions Limited, Swallow House,
11-21 Northdown Street, London N1 9BN

© Shell UK Limited 1988

British Library Cataloguing in Publication Data:

Lethbridge, Richard
    New Shell guide to Oxford and Berkshire.
    1. Berkshire — Description and travel — Guide-books
    2. Oxfordshire — Description and travel – Guide-books
    1. Title
    914.22′90458   DA670.84

Cased edition: ISBN 0 7181 2908 3
Paperback edition: ISBN 0 7181 2968 7

Editor: Mary Anne Sanders
Reader: Raymond Kaye
Cartographer: ML Design
Designer: Mick Keates
Production: Hugh Allan

Filmset by Keyboard Graphics Limited, Bolgoved House,
5-6 Clipstone Street, London W1P 7EB
Printed and bound by Kyodo Shing Loong Printing, Singapore.

A list of Shell publications
can be obtained by writing to:

Department UOMK/60
Shell UK Oil
PO Box No. 148
Shell-Mex House
Strand
London WC2R 0DX

*Front jacket photograph: Broughton Castle, Oxfordshire
(see p. 77)*
*Back jacket photograph: Memorial window to
Sir John Betjeman by John Piper, Farnborough Church,
Berkshire (see p. 181)*
Title-page: Inkpen Hill, Berkshire (see p. 186)

Contents

John Julius Norwich was born in 1929. After reading French and Russian at New College, Oxford, he joined the Foreign Office where he served until 1964. Since then he has published two books on the medieval Norman Kingdom in Sicily; two historical travel books, *Mount Athos* (with Reresby Sitwell) and *Sahara*; an anthology of poetry and prose, *Christmas Crackers*; and two volumes on the history of Venice. He was general editor of *Great Architecture of the World* and, more recently, author of *The Architecture of Southern England.*

In addition, he writes and presents historical documentaries for BBC television and frequently broadcasts on BBC radio. He is chairman of the Venice in Peril Fund, a Trustee of the Civic Trust, and a member of the Executive and Properties Committee of the National Trust.

Richard Lethbridge was born in 1934 and educated at Downside. Brought up in the Chilterns, near Henley-on-Thames, he has a passion for visiting old churches and out-of-the-way places. He lives with his family in the Evenlode Valley in west Oxfordshire.

Robert Hardy is a distinguished actor, perhaps best known for the part of Siegfried Farnon in the BBC television series *All Creatures Great and Small*. He has a son and two daughters and lives near Henley-on-Thames, Oxfordshire.

Anthony Quinton is an eminent philosopher and, until 1987, was president of Trinity College, Oxford. He has published several books on philosophy. Created a life peer in 1982, he has been Chairman of the British Library since 1985.

Peter Levi is a poet and classical scholar. He is a fellow of St Catherine's College, Oxford, and Professor of Poetry and is currently working on a book about Shakespeare. He is a keen walker and lives just south of the Cotswolds.

Hugo Vickers is best known as the biographer of Cecil Beaton. He gives occasional lectures and has appeared on television, normally in connection with royal events.

Christine Zwart lives in Charlbury in Oxfordshire with her husband and their four children. She has written several books.

Nick Meers was born in Gloucestershire in 1955, and gained a diploma from Guildford School of Photography in 1978. In 1986 he won first prize in the 'Events' category of the British Photography Competition organized by the *Sunday Telegraph Magazine* and the National Trust.

Author's Foreword and Acknowledgments

The biggest single change in Oxfordshire and Berkshire since my boyhood, spent on the borders of the two counties, has resulted from the Local Government reorganization of 1974, when Berkshire was reduced to a shadow of its former self. In the name of greater efficiency (not yet apparent to most people) the age-old boundary of the Thames was changed and Berkshire lost Abingdon, Wallingford, Wantage, the Vale of White Horse and, worst of all, much of the famous Berkshire Downs. The consequent discrepancy in size between the two counties is apparent in this book.

My thanks are due to many people: to the ever-helpful ladies of the Oxfordshire Mobile Library Service, to many church keyholders for their courtesy, to Sir Ashley Ponsonby for lending me his set of Victoria County Histories and to Mary Anne Sanders of Swallow Editions for her advice and help. I am especially grateful to Marilyn Dennis for typing the manuscript, to Henrietta and Denis Napier for their hospitality in Berkshire and to my wife and family for constant encouragement and support.

Note on using the Gazetteers

Entries in the two Gazetteers are arranged in alphabetical order. 'The', if part of the name, follows the main element: **Bartons, The** (alphabetized under B).

Entry headings consist of the name of the place or feature in **bold** type, followed by a map reference in parentheses: **Wallingford** (4/3C). The figure 4 is the map number; 3C is the grid reference, with 3 indicating the across and C the down reference.

If a name mentioned within the text of an entry is printed in capital letters – i.e. WANTAGE – this indicates that it has its own entry in its county Gazetteer.

Bold type is used for certain places, buildings or other features of interest or importance referred to within Gazetteer entries.

Every effort has been made to ensure that information about the opening to the public of buildings, estates, gardens, reserves, museums, galleries, etc., and details of walks and footpaths, were as accurate and up to date as possible at the time of going to press. Such particulars are, of course, subject to alteration and it may be prudent to check them locally, or with the appropriate organizations or authorities.

Introduction

ROBERT HARDY

No part of England brings into sharper focus man's thrust for power and for domination, as well as for a pleasant life, a thousand years ago or today, than Oxfordshire and Berkshire. Any view of their histories reveals the constant struggle throughout the centuries to possess the rich lowlands that stretch north and south from the Thames, and to gain control of the broad river valley and of the waterway itself, which gave easy access to London and the seat of southern power. In 1334 Oxfordshire and Berkshire were already assessed at £20 a square mile, two of the five richest counties in England.

My own point of view is from a parish in the very south of Oxfordshire, known by various names through the ages, and in the Domesday survey held by one Alfred from another Miles Crispin. In the church there is a brass to a knight who fought at Agincourt, and his lady. Less than five crow miles to the north lies the seat of Thomas, Lord Camoys, whence in 1415 another Thomas Lord Camoys went on campaign with Henry V, to command the rearguard, which became the left wing of the army at Agincourt, taking with him a personal retinue of 24 men-at-arms and 69 archers. A mile to my north lie the buried remains of an important Romano-British villa, now presumably sunk for ever beneath the pleasant slopes of a golf course. The Romans, like the present occupants, knew how to site themselves delightfully. A mile to the south-east the Thames runs a well-channelled course downstream towards Henley, just about where the Viking invaders, in a time when the unconfined river spread broad and shallow across the valley, found they could navigate no further upstream and abandoned their longships. My own house is on the site of a Roman steading, a farm that formed part of the estate of which the villa was the centre.

The shape and lie of the land

The very land shape was formed by the southward pressure of ice at the end of the last Ice Age – and hereabouts it reached its central southern limit. So, as in much of this part of the world, the layers of history lie thick upon each other. Oxford is some 20 miles away; Reading, the county town of Royal Berkshire, only 8 miles; and Buckinghamshire less than 4 miles away. Thus my viewpoint is from the conflux of three counties, where the tidal wash back from the English capital has filled the region with a combative and expansive mass of rural, or almost rural, dwellings and places of recreation from city congestion. The age-old flow of commodities towards the capital is well shown by the cluster of houses on the Thames a mile or so to my east, whose ancient name derives from two Old English words which together mean 'a landing place for bullocks', or in other words another ox ford. I have always supposed that beef on the hoof crossed the river there on its way to supply the London market.

No picture can be drawn without some vital statistics or some sense of perspective. The county of Oxford (*Comitas Oxoniensis*, hence the shortened Oxon

The Whispering Knights, Great Rollright (see p. 103)

Chalk path on the Berkshire Downs near Streatley

of its common naming) consists of over 750 square miles, and has a maximum length of 50 and a maximum width of about 33 miles. The rock underlay slopes gradually from the north-west to the south-east, consisting of Cotswold oolite in the bare, rolling, stonewalled uplands, yielding to the clay of the Oxford vale. Next comes the low Corallian ridge, giving way to clay again in the vale of Thame, and then the greensand terrace and the chalk of the Chiltern Hills; the chalk and the oolite are the more resistant formations that make up the high ground. The county boundary follows the escarpment of the lower Cotswolds from Chipping Norton to Edgehill. Down the gentle slope flow the many streams and larger tributaries, the Evenlode, Windrush, Cherwell and Thame, which feed the Thames. The Chiltern scarp is divided by deep combes and its slopes are thick with beechwoods dipping towards the rich cornlands, pastures and watermeadows of the river, and right to the water's edge in spectacular gorges cut through the chalk around Goring.

Nowadays smaller, but still comparable in size and, on the whole, in its gentle climate, Berkshire lies to the south, beyond the Thames, stretching west and east and exhibiting both similar and very different geological features. Its 500-odd square miles, with a maximum length of over 50 and breadth of 30 miles, comprise

the high chalk downlands of the centre, which rise in a trenched escarpment from the London basin, and connect with the Oxfordshire Chilterns across the Thames and the Marlborough Downs in the west. Northward lies the Vale of White Horse – mainly Kimmeridge and gault clay – then follows the Corallian ridge and the flat alluvial clayland of the Thames Valley. Further south at the foot of the chalk lies the valley of the Kennet with the Mortimer and Greenham plateaux of tertiary sands and clays. South of this valley the chalk escarpment rises again to over 970 feet at Inkpen Beacon. Then to the east, beyond Reading, the chalk gives way to the Waltham clay vale and the sandy plateaux of Wokingham, Bagshot and Windsor.

In both counties the air of the higher, barer lands is sharp and bracing, but once into the Thames Valley the moisture, and in summer the warmth, make for an enervating, lethargic atmosphere. Even in winter – the average winter temperature in Reading is below 40°F – the air tends to lack stringency, which is perhaps why stretches of the Thames Valley become more and more a dormitory area.

Settlement and early history

Over these broad and pleasant lands moved the hunter-gatherers and then in Neolithic times the prehistoric farmers, the Iberians who grazed their stock on the

Radcot Bridge, north of Faringdon (see p. 96)

chalk hills, and began to cultivate and clear the lowlands. The Celts came during the first millenium BC. Traces of Celtic field systems can be seen on the Berkshire Downs by Segsbury Hill fort; and the Wansdyke, running 50 miles from Avon into Berkshire, and still in places a formidable obstacle, is a noble monument to perhaps the last effort of the Romano-Celtic peoples to withstand the Saxon thrusts into the rich grain belts of the south chalklands. Both counties were in the region of the Atrebates when Julius Ceasar first set eyes on them. Under early Roman rule the Atrebates' name persisted, with an administrative centre just over the Hampshire border at Silchester, but by the 4th century AD the counties (not yet formed of course) were part of Maxima Caesariensis. Dorchester was a Romano-British town of importance, in close association with Silchester and Cirencester. An altar once in Dorchester was inscribed: 'To Jupiter best and greatest, and the divine Emperors, Marcus the second in command after the Governor erected this altar at his private cost'. By the 6th century, when the Saxons had settled in these areas, Berkshire was part of the kingdom of Wessex, while Oxfordshire belonged to Mercia. Dorchester was still an important centre, and as Christianity spread during the next 100 years it became one of the early bishoprics. Cynegils, King of Wessex, and Oswald, King of Northumbria, gave Dorchester to St Birinus, and its church was a cathedral. From then on Christian centres in the region proliferated, Oxford and Abingdon, Eynsham, Bradfield.

In 849 Alfred was born at Wantage, twice visited Rome, succeeded his brother as King of Wessex, and married into the ruling family of Mercia. By the time of the death of this acknowledged leader and overlord of all the English, Mercia and Wessex were divided into shires, so both Berkshire and Oxfordshire can date their foundations to before AD 900. Somewhere on the Berkshire Downs Alfred inflicted a great defeat on the Danes led by Halfdane and the charmingly named Ivar the Boneless, sons of the legendary Ragnar Leatherbreeches, who like the Romans and Saxons before them aimed at the rich lands of the Thames Valley. Their efforts were to continue long after Alfred's death, when because of the unifying strength of his policies, his victories, his legislation and his personal pre-eminence, the prize the invading Danes now sought was to all intents and purposes the Kingdom of England. Between 1009 and 1013 Thorkell fell upon Oxford from the north, then straddling Wallingford went south for Winchester. He was followed by Sweyn.

Not many years later William, another Norseman, from Normandy, after the bitter victory of Hastings, skirted London westwards on what became the Pilgrim's Way, from Canterbury, sending detachments towards the former and as far as Winchester. The main army went north to Goring, where William's infantry crossed the Thames by the west Ridgeway, and Wallingford, where the Icknield Way spanned the river. There he led his cavalry across and allowed them to pillage the countryside. William decided on a bold sweep eastwards, through Hertfordshire, before plunging down on London. In that same year, 1066, the energetic Conqueror founded a castle at Wallingford, the only major building of its kind in the area bounded by Cambridge, Canterbury, Winchester and Buckingham –though by 1086 the Normans in their exuberant military zest had built great castles at Oxford and Windsor.

In the civil wars of the next century Stephen attacked Wallingford and Oxford. Both those castles were held for the King in 1215, and until 1415 they remained royal castles. In Richard II's reign, in 1371, there was a fierce encounter at Radcot Bridge, north of Faringdon, between the forces of an aristocratic rebellion against the power of the monarchy, and those of the crown itself, from which the King's favourite, the Earl of Oxford, only escaped by swimming down the Thames. Radcot Bridge still stands.

One of the earliest and most ancient houses in Oxfordshire is Broughton Castle, outside Banbury, seat of the Fiennes family, the Barons Saye and Sele, strong supporters of Parliament and the Puritan cause.

In the early 1640s there gathered at Broughton with Lord Saye and his son Nathaniel Fiennes men of like persuasion who planned much of the political and military action of the conflict that was to come. There was never, in those early days, thought of a deposition, much less of a royal execution, but movements, rebellions, revolutions and wars have a habit of getting out of hand and away from their original causes and determined actions.

Broughton is eminent among the great houses that can be visited today. Soon after 1397, when Richard Gilkes, a master carpenter much employed by New College, Oxford, had been at work on the hall of Broughton, the place was described as being built round a courtyard, with a great gate, outhouses and farm buildings, a bakehouse, a slaughterhouse, well, stables, and a slow oven in the court for drying peas and for malting hops, and with a great barn 'the finest in Oxfordshire'. Much of that is still there.

The English Civil War

The Civil War raged across both counties. King Charles had his headquarters at Oxford, where the city became an armed camp, the streets echoing to the sound of soldiery, the clatter of hoofs, and quarrels after dark, though there were many Puritan-inclined colleges and most of the Town, as opposed to the University, declared for Parliament. But the King moved there in the winter of 1642 and after the partial Royalist victory at Edgehill, Charles with his sons and nephews came to Oxford in triumph and the fortifications were refurbished. Earthworks for the mounting of cannon were thrown up. You can see one of these mounds today in New College gardens, where several wars later, in 1914, VADs under canvas

Broughton Castle (see p. 13 and p. 78)

trained to nurse and cook and bottlewash before being sent off to France.

There were two major battles near Newbury. Hampden was killed at Chalgrove. An Oxfordshire man from Epwell suffered the sort of horrifying night shock that must have been common throughout the land. Soldiers came into his house and 'violently took away most of his household goods'. The man himself, who in his petition for redress described himself and his wife as 'poor and aged', was held prisoner for a week, and claimed the loss of money: '7 pairs of sheets, 3 brass kettles, pewter, clothing, candles, eggs, bowls, spoons' and whatever else the soldiers had been able to remove.

Reading in 1643 was for Parliament. Thomas Knyvett, a Royalist, wrote to his wife: 'The town is fiercely besieged and they as strongly defend. Much blood has been spilt there already and abundance of maim'd men carried to London in carts...t'will be a bloody business...God in mercy turn peoples' hearts in charity one to another...I fear I shall be lousy before I get any change of clothes, but 'tis all our cases.'

Prosperity and learning

But what of construction and progress? Oxford began to emerge as a centre of learning early in the 12th century, largely as a result of the exodus of English students from Paris. Defoe would place the origins earlier: University College 'was probably the University itself for about 345 years, being as they tell us founded by King Alfred in the year 872...after which viz. anno 1217, William Bishop of Durham formed it into a regular house and built the College, which however was for a long time call'd sometimes the University...there being at that time no other.'

In 1348 the plague, beginning at Bristol on 15 August, struck London on 29 September and, as Geoffrey le Baker, the Oxfordshire cleric, has it: 'at last it attacked Gloster, yea and Oxford...and scarcely 1 in 10 of cither sex was left alive...while the Scots rejoiced!'

'Some will have Woodstock', wrote Defoe, 'to have been a royal palace before Oxford was a University…ever since King Alfred…' Henry II merely rebuilt it and added the bower for his mistress, Fair Rosamund, 'of whose safety he was it seems very careful. Notwithstanding which the Queen found means to come at her, and as fables report, sent her out of the way by poison.' That palace is no longer to be seen, but the present charming town full of delightful buildings clusters at the park edge of Blenheim, one of the great palaces of Europe. It is the seat of the Spencer Churchills, Dukes of Marlborough, and the birthplace of Sir Winston.

Reading grew up around its important royal abbey, founded by Henry I in 1121. He is buried there, with Matilda, and William, son of Henry II. Parliaments were held there and all throve until Henry VIII sacked it and hanged its last Abbott, Hugh of Faringdon, outside the Abbey Gate.

The Oxford Canal at Cropredy (see p. 16 and p. 89)

By the time Defoe visited Reading he found: 'a very large and wealthy town, the inhabitants very rich and driving a very great trade...by the waterway to and from London.' In the late 18th century the building of canals, particularly the Oxford Canal, which made water travel possible into the Midlands and joined with the Thames and Severn Canal, enhanced the reliability of water transport, and reduced the dangers to purely river traffic of floods and shallows, mill and fishing dams. The railways superseded the waterways, and the frequency of trains, on the Reading line particularly, helps to turn much of Thames land into commuter land. The waterways now are pleasure ways, and in the summer the Thames is thronged with boats managed with every degree of skill. Trade roars along the M4, the M40 and the M25 motorways, which slice through the countryside, dividing and conquering.

Newbury, for Defoe, was 'an ancient cloathing town', and he tells of a Mr Kenwick, son of a Newbury clothier, who left £4000 to Newbury and £7500 to Reading to encourage the clothing trade. Henley and Maidenhead were remarkable for 'malt and meal and timber' for centuries using the Thames for transport to London. Now, Henley is thought of as the home of the Royal Regatta, packed to the gunwales each summer with visitors who come to watch the slim boats of the international rowing community. Henley is well known, too, for the ancient and still independent Brakspear brewery, run by a family that not only brewed well back into history, but also provided the only English Pope, Nicholas Breakspear, who as Hadrian, or Adrian, IV, wore the triple crown from 1154 to 1159.

At Windsor, Defoe noticed that on a clear day you could, from the round tower 'see St Paul's Cathedral in London, very plain'. 'Here,' he adds, 'we saw Eton College, the finest school for what we call grammar learning...that is in Britain, or, perhaps, in Europe.' Queen Victoria, contemplating the great castle at the start of her reign, wrote: 'Windsor requires thorough cleaning, and I must say I could not think of going in sooner after the poor King's death...it always appears very melancholy to me and there are so many sad associations.'

The counties today – and in the future

Today the counties are still with us, but altered. In the 1974 redrawing of county boundaries, Berkshire lost nearly a third of its ancient acreage. On 1 April 1974 the Queen granted permission for official use of the style 'Royal County of Berkshire' to be used, which may be some compensation perhaps. The title, unique among English counties, acknowledges the long Royal association with Windsor. The populations have climbed erratically, from something below 30,000 each according to the 1377 Poll Tax returns to very well over half a million each at the present time; and the tide of goods still flows into the capital, as the tide of humans flows out, seeking reachable rural retreat, comparative peace, cleaner air. That is the modern equivalent of the old invasions and military excursions – but now the threats to the counties are measured in acreage of concrete, dwindling countryside, vanishing birds and animals, insects, flowers, grasses.

Berkshire today has some 8 per cent woodland, 56 per cent arable (and falling), 36 per cent grassland (falling), 10 per cent fully built-up areas (growing), and 3 per cent gravel workings. About half the arable area is wheat, and a third barley. Oilseed rape has had only a 5 per cent, but none the less dramatic, effect on landscape; in May and June its virulent citric yellow has given rise to a new disease among motorway drivers, 'rape blindness'. The flowered meadows of the past have shrunk to tiny areas, on the whole confined to steep valleys where intensive cultivation is too difficult. Oxfordshire offers comparable figures, with some 5 per cent woodland (much of which is conifer), 65 per cent arable, 22 per cent grassland, 9 per cent built over, 1 per cent limestone and gravel workings. The river valleys of the Thames and its tributaries still show some hay meadows with rich flora, including the local speciality, the snakeshead fritillary, best seen in Iffley and Magdalen meadows. In both counties sensible, well-balanced conservation organizations struggle to resist the pressures of building development, roadmaking and, in some instances, modern farming. In both counties the Berkshire, Buckinghamshire and Oxfordshire Naturalists Trust (BBONT), which is affiliated to the Royal Society for Nature Conservation (RSNC), has woodland, grassland, old heathland and wetland sites, which are protected and worked quietly and efficiently, but rely for upkeep and expansion (as other threatened sites come on to the market) on public donations and charitable gifts. Without these protected sites the danger to wildlife would be even more fearful than it is – and it is grim.

In the last decade of the 20th century, these two historic counties will come under great pressure for change. In terms of landscape and wildlife, ten years of fixed agricultural prices led to an increase in arable and a loss of hedges, copses, and grassland. This process is now faltering, as European politicians rebel against the high cost of the Common Agricultural Policy, and the additional storage costs of the food surpluses such a policy has generated. In March 1987 the British Government published its first attempt at proposals for dealing with these changes, entitled *Farming and Rural Employment.* The two significant changes within the Government's present thinking that may have considerable effect upon the countryside are the releasing of agricultural land, up to 50 acres at a time, for development; and the offering of financial incentives for afforesting land at present under cultivation. The former proposal, linked with ministerial statements that the Green Belt policy will be preserved, suggests that there may well be pressure to add 50 acres of housing or light industry to our most rural settlements. That would have far-reaching consequences. The latter proposal, for forestry on agricultural land, could be very destructive to wildlife, partly because the financial incentive is not likely to be high enough to encourage landowners to plant on their arable acreage, but probably lucrative enough to induce forestry enterprises on more marginal land. This is the very sort of land that supports the orchid-rich meadows for which the counties are famous.

These are specifics: in general the choice is between allowing the uncontrolled destruction of what beauty still lies around us, and the determination to find a balance in future land use; a balance between the very real needs for profitable and efficient farming, for housing and roadworks, new factories, urban change and development, and the equally vital need to keep some vestige of natural, though organized, countryside, woods and fields, streams, lakes, hills, marsh and lowlands, with their natural wildlife, so that our children and their children can enjoy a little of the joys our forebears took so easily for granted. Every acre of Berkshire and Oxfordshire needs thought before it is sacrificed to the future: but then so does every acre of the whole countryside of Great Britain, now, before it is too late. We inhabit an island. We cannot enlarge it. We can only diminish it.

Overleaf: Sunset in the Kennet valley, Berkshire (see p. 186 and p. 197)

Oxford

You can live in Oxford for many years without realizing that it shares with Florence the property of being at the bottom of a shallow, but still quite undeniable, bowl. It is only when you get to the top of some high building – the tower of St Mary's Church, for example – that the circle of hills around it becomes evident. The hills are too modest to make themselves felt to anyone on the streets of Oxford, hemmed in by buildings.

Another fact of the same sort, but rather more interesting, is less elusive. A resident would have to be exceedingly imperceptive not to realize that the city has something of the shape of a four-pointed star, with thin points to the north, west and south and a more bulky one to the east and south-east. In between these built-up points or prongs, grass, fields, the open country penetrate right up to the ancient central core of the city.

North Oxford is kept long and thin by the constraining force of the river Cherwell to the east and of the canal and the railway line to Banbury and beyond to the west; and again, beyond them and the hummocky expanse of Port Meadow, by the Thames which has flowed down from its Cotswold source. The Botley road, which is the main way out of Oxford to the west, and the Abingdon road, the main exit to the south, are both long, thin strings of ribbon development, with some built-up chunks adhering to them here and there and, in the case of the Botley road, with an industrial park of an uninsistent kind. Between them are the gently suburbanized Cumnor and Hinksey hills with the marshy reaches of Hinksey proper at their base and plenty of open space in and around them. The railway to Didcot, Reading and beyond runs alongside the Abingdon road to the west. The Thames having passed under Folly Bridge, where the Abingdon road begins, runs along beside it to the east until, with Iffley and Littlemore, the city finally peters out in that direction.

Cowley, in a broad sense of the name, occupying the upper part of the south-east quarter of the city, bounded by Headington Hill and the London road at one side and by the Iffley road at the other, is the only large, continuously built-up mass of the city as a whole, apart from the considerably smaller old central core. The two are thinly attached at the Plain just east of Magdalen Bridge, the limit of the old city, where the Cherwell runs under the last stretch of High Street. As you head over the bridge towards the new, industrial Oxford, to the town Lord Nuffield made, you see to the left large parklike tracts of land belonging to Magdalen College and, beyond them, as far as Marston, a sequence of college sports grounds. To the right there are more of the same, starting with the playing field of Magdalen College school and on into a dank, reedy wilderness, adjoining Christ Church Meadows, where more or less formal walks contain a large, resolutely agricultural space.

The outcome of all this is that, although the centre of Oxford is relentlessly urban, with its one bit of open space, Radcliffe Square, for the most part paved and cobbled and with only a few severe enclosures of grass around the dominating central building, the Radcliffe Camera, it is always easy to get to something like

Canterbury Quad Gatehouse, Christ Church College

open country from anywhere in the centre. Wherever you are fields are only a few minutes' walk away: Port Meadow or the University Parks or Christ Church Meadows. The debris of the town's industrial explosion in the first half of the century has been squeezed in such a way as to preserve a good deal of the traditional environment of the old university city.

Intellectual life does not have to be carried on entirely in libraries and studies or rooms for lectures and seminars. The most humanly compelling of Plato's dialogues is his *Symposium*, in effect a dinner party, the ideal at which the common dinner of a college hall is hopefully aimed, even if it is only sketchily and intermittently realized. Aristotle's followers were known as 'peripatetics', walkers, because his disciple Theophrastus taught his master's doctrines in a covered walking place in his house. The Oxford version of that practice is the walk between lunch and tea. The idea is that while the undergraduates are occupied on the river or playing fields their seniors follow up lines of thought excited in a morning of tutorials or lecturing, then animate themselves for more of the same between 5 and 7 o'clock by a brisk trot or leisurely stroll in one of the rural spaces within easy reach.

Hidden spaces

Even in the central area there is in fact quite a lot of open space that does not at once strike the eye. Colleges vary considerably in numbers of resident members; they vary much more in the amount of lawn and path and garden they provide for their members to walk about in. Quite near the centre of this congestedly busy town there are several impressive tracts of more or less private open space to which the public at large is admitted, at least in the afternoons. The finest of these are to be found in colleges at the edge of the central area, in Magdalen above all, with its deer park and, near by, Addison's Walk and a string of gardens beyond it, along a branch of the Cherwell.

Nearer the centre is New College with its noble L-shaped garden enclosed in the largest surviving portion of the medieval city wall. The land was granted on condition that the wall was kept up at the college's expense. The agreement has been honoured; the wall is still defensible, at least in terms of 14th-century military technique. The colleges of Turl Street – Exeter, Jesus and Lincoln – are close to the central shopping area and are accommodated with rigid medieval economy on very small sites which allow for only ornamental or symbolic gardens (although Exeter's is surprisingly spacious). But opposite the end of Turl Street, on the other side of Broad Street and next to Blackwell's, is Trinity, one of the smallest colleges in numbers but with a substantial grove of trees, visible from the street through the iron gates and, beyond the north-east corner of that quad, a glorious expanse of grass, bounded by an old wall from the equally glorious, more richly planted and even more sizeable garden of St John's.

Three other colleges on the periphery should be mentioned while we are on this subject. Christ Church has a pleasant, but not very accessible garden. With the Meadows so near at hand it can afford to keep it to itself. Its main visible open spaces are its two fine quadrangles: the Great Quad, revealing Wolsey's plans, and Peckwater quad – a magnificent Augustan ensemble, made up of a three-sided range of buildings, which was designed by Henry Aldrich, then Dean of the college. On the fourth side is the vast library, designed by George Clarke, Fellow of All Souls. Wadham, which was not a very notable institution until C.M.Bowra

In the garden at St John's College

became its Warden in 1938 and put it audibly on the map, has a remarkable range of gardens, divided up between College, Fellows and Warden. It once had more: the large and strategic piece of ground now occupied by Rhodes House was sold by Wadham for that purpose in the 1920s.

Most remarkable of all, however, is Worcester, very much at the western edge of the University area. Beyond it to the west, on the far side of the Oxford Canal which bounds it, is the railway station. Inside Worcester, however, the railway is never seen, only heard. The ponderously splendid entrance to the college leads one towards a sunken lawn with a fine Augustan range (George Clarke again) to the north of it and a row of cells to the south, recalling the monastic origin of the college. Beyond this is a large, parklike area, some of it mown and planted, some rough. There is a considerable ornamental lake, the only body of water that could not be described as a pond in an Oxford college. The total effect is not at all academic and is most like a benevolently neglected (but not in the least derelict) Irish country house of the larger sort. So although Worcester is not rich, it is right that it should have the richest college library, much of the strength of the collection lying in two bequests from gentlemanly, book-collecting fellows of the college earlier this century.

The defining streets

Just as the city is divided into separate regions which are as distinct in character as they are disjoined in space, so the central University area is carved up by the principal streets. First there are the colleges south of High Street: Merton, University, Oriel, Corpus Christi, Christ Church and, tagging along, Pembroke on the far side of St Aldate's, where the main entrance to Christ Church is placed.

These might be called the Merton Street colleges, partly because they all have (or nearly have) an entrance on it; partly because Merton is Oxford's first real college. It was a going concern when University and Balliol, who dispute its primacy, did not even have their statutes. The large chapel is 13th-century; humble, introverted Mob Quad is 14th, the oldest college quadrangle, and almost Oriental in its minimization of windows. The library has its handwritten books chained to the desks but, like some of its users, is not as old as it looks. The Merton Street colleges look south in spirit, away from the town, towards Christ Church Meadow. Cobbled Merton Street attracts little traffic apart from people desperately seeking a place to park and anxious about the effect of the road's surface on their springs. This, and the fact that the obvious way to the river, for oarsman and spectator, is by a path between Merton and Corpus, imparts an air of Edwardian peacefulness to these colleges. It is entirely natural and reasonably safe to walk in the middle of the road.

To the north of High Street, up to Broad Street, with Cornmarket to the west and Longwall to the east, is the main central portion. From Broad Street to High Street runs Catte Street, passing Radcliffe Square and ending up at St Mary's, the University church, the original nucleus of the University, where the faculties met and the books and the money were kept. To the west of Catte Street are the three Turl colleges on their narrow, overshadowed sites and, rather more amply housed, Brasenose, college of Walter Pater and, for a shorter period, of his grateful pupil, Field Marshal Lord Haig. A fine piece of aesthetic agitation 20 years ago closed it to

The Cloisters, New College   *Opposite: Brasenose Lane*

The Radcliffe Camera from the Church of St Mary the Virgin

through traffic and all but a handful of privileged parked cars, to the advantage of nearly everyone.

The eastern central area is grander. All Souls, New College and Queen's are three of Oxford's noblest (and richest) colleges. At the eastern extremity of this region lies the sublime, palatial composition of Magdalen. Hertford and St Edmund Hall are in principle a little out of place in this company. In the early 19th century Hertford was in very low water. There was only a half-crazed fellow left, who declared himself Principal, and no students. The ruinous buildings were infested by squatters and some of them collapsed. But since its refoundation in 1874, with its remaining architectural bits and pieces ingeniously woven together by Victorian Oxford's favourite architect, Thomas Graham Jackson, it has progressed steadily upward. Unsmart enough to embarrass Evelyn Waugh in the 1920s, it has been one of the academically most successful colleges of the last decade or so. St Edmund Hall is really a college now, in numbers at any rate. But it still looks the much smaller thing a hall used to be, with its tiny quad, in which a well looms large, and its minute dining hall. The halls, of which it is the last, were the main containers of Oxford's students in the Middle Ages, consisting then simply of a house, with up to 12 of them in it, under the loose supervision of a Master of Arts.

Finally, to the north of Broad Street, are Wadham, Trinity, Balliol and St John's, with Worcester some way beyond them to the west. The four colleges bounded by St Giles' and Broad Street correspond in their interior spaciousness to the amplitude of those noble streets. Even Balliol, the only ugly one of them, has an attractive Garden quadrangle deep inside it.

Opposite: Encaenia Procession

North Oxford

At the north end of St Giles', where Woodstock and Banbury Roads begin, is north Oxford, a region of houses for the new species of Oxford resident, the married don, created by late Victorian reforms. Here high-minded don's wives, readers of the old *Manchester Guardian* and Kingsley Martin's *New Statesman,* brought up their precocious children, seeing them off, with a violin and Kennedy's *Latin Primer,* to the Dragon School and the Oxford High School for Girls, only a few streets away. It is a world affectionately embalmed in plays, novels (best of all Robert Liddell's *The Last Enchantments*) and poems (such as Betjeman's *Sudden Death at the Bus Stop*). Because of the rents the area has been invaded by schools of English for foreigners and A-level crammers, and the larger houses have been cut up into flats with inordinately spacious rooms and bedsitters. But some donnish families still hold out, east of the Banbury Road, above all, between Linton Road and the north end of the University parks. An excellent book for children – *The House In Norham Gardens* by Penelope Lively – catches the flavour of the neighbourhood perfectly.

How far north does north Oxford go? Geographically, to the roundabouts where the northern bypass marks the end of Woodstock and Banbury Roads, no doubt. Spiritually, not nearly as far. Certainly no further than the sequence of Frenchay, Staverton and Belbroughton Roads. True north Oxford shops in North Parade, a tiny little lane off Banbury Road that winds up behind St Philip and St James's church; not in Summertown, a long stretch of Banbury Road half a mile or so to the north.

Dotted around true north Oxford are straggling, late-coming elements of the University: new, or fairly new colleges, such as Keble, St Antony's and, remotest of all, Wolfson, finely sited on the Cherwell, and four of the five colleges founded for women (the fifth, St Hilda's, is far away, just out of serenading distance from Magdalen and, like the latter, making good decorative use of the river).

The central area

The central University area is about half a square mile, or some 300 acres, in extent. The city as a whole is much larger. The area within the encircling system of bypasses is something like 12 square miles. It has the shape of an elderly rugby ball, positioned for a free kick, with its base in the south-east, in the industrial muddle of Cowley, and its apex at Wolvercote and the big motel where the A40 sets off to Cheltenham. Visitors to Oxford usually give little attention to what lies beyond the central half square mile. Not very many residents seem to. If they are part of the University they work and, if students, live in this small space. If they are not they will come here to shop, to eat out, to go to plays and films and concerts.

The colleges are the main things to look at, but there are other handsome and interesting University buildings to be found in among them. They include the Ashmolean Museum and its 17th-century predecessor in Broad Street which now houses the History of Science Museum. Then there is Wren's Sheldonian Theatre, with a massive unsupported area of ceiling, emblematically adorned. Another place where a more or less practical aim has served to produce an even more significant aesthetic effect is the Botanical Garden, opposite the front entrance to Magdalen at the bottom of High Street. It has very great charm, combining formal dignity of walls, arches and urns with horticultural profusion and a good deal of delightful inconsequence, imposed by the peculiarities of the site.

Of the world's great universities, Oxford is the most oriented to the humanities. Its library, the Bodleian, is therefore very much more for use than for ornament. It is also spread about the place in buildings of very varied types and merit: the early 17th-century Old Library, a three-storey quadrangle, between the Clarendon Building (the main university administrative centre until the early 1970s) and the Radcliffe Camera, which is a reading room of the library. The New Bodleian lies beyond the Clarendon Building on the other side of Broad Street.

Non-academic Oxford does not have much to show for itself. The Randolph Hotel, opposite the Ashmolean, is in the rich Victorian Gothic of Ruskin's sublime University Museum (home of the scientific collections). The Covered Market, an 18th-century affair, hemmed in by Jesus and Lincoln Colleges, is a lively, glittering place. The Clarendon Centre is an indoor shopping plaza built after the demolition in the 1950s of the pleasant old, Christmas-cardy Clarendon Hotel. Not far away is another such centre, the Westgate, put up in what was a region of humble college servant's dwellings between Pembroke College and the Thames. Bits of it survive. There is more of the same kind of thing in Jericho – the 'Beersheba' where Hardy's Jude the Obscure lodged – to the north between lower north Oxford and the railway.

A fine place to live

For all its noise, congestion and damp Oxford is a fine place to live in. When the weather permits it is possible to lead something like the life of a Greek city state. A resident cannot walk in the streets for ten minutes without meeting several people he would be glad to talk to. It is remarkably well served by restaurants – astoundingly well served by comparison with Oxford 40 years ago. Parking can be difficult, but everything worth seeing is within easy walking distance. The exuberance of undergraduate self-expression leads to the putting on of plays never to be seen elsewhere: *Samson Agonistes* and *Comus* have been on at the same time, as if Milton were a kind of Andrew Lloyd Webber. It is a real town, but the inveterate rusticity of the English spirit is catered for by those great arms of green penetrating right into its centre.

The Ridgeway Path

PETER LEVI

What they now call the Ridgeway is an attractive promenade for hikers devised by planners. A Ridgeway Youth Hostel is just about to open. Wantage has a Ridgeway Garage with an agency to sell German cars: but this is no cause for alarm, because few cars venture more than a few yards on to the ancient track. Motorcycles are more of a menace, but on some days they come and go swiftly, in infrequent but adventurous swarms like gnats. It is hard to exclude them altogether, since the Ridgeway is one of the oldest highways in Britain: an extremely long green lane passing through four counties – Wiltshire, Berkshire, Oxfordshire into Hertfordshire and beyond.

The ordinary word 'ridgeway' just means a hilltop track. It occurs once at least a century before the Norman Conquest; it can be used in the plural; and has been employed in many parts of England as a local name for particular hill tracks. In Berkshire and Oxfordshire it was traditionally used in certain villages for the most spectacular part of the Icknield Way, the section that crosses the Marlborough

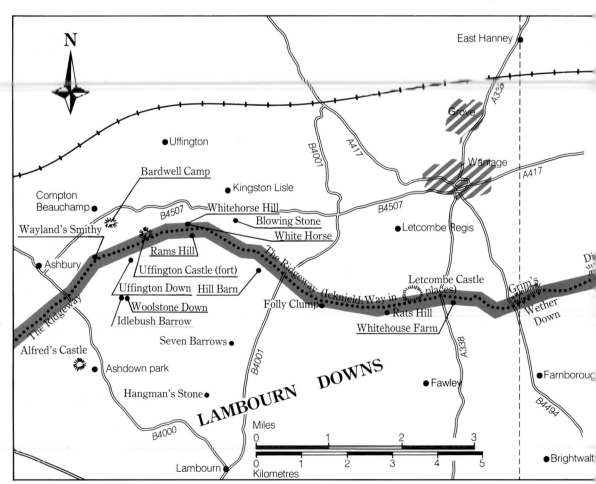

Downs and overlooks the Vale of the White Horse. Not all of the Icknield Way survives.

The Icknield Way starts somewhere near the Wash, and makes its way round the top of the Chilterns, then southwards along their western edge, to a crossing of the Thames near Streatley, where that mighty stream must once have been fordable, as of course it was at Oxford. The Thames is all that divides the Chilterns from the foot of the downs that extend to Marlborough and beyond. I have puzzled for a long time about where this prodigious track was going to. It bypasses Avebury Rings, crossing the Herepath not far east of Avebury, and dies out – although it can be traced along a trickling waterfall of lanes heading southwards, directly towards Stonehenge.

Fantasy might make a holy road out of this; or triviality might suggest a supply of salt herring for Stonehenge, since the Wash implies salt. It looks to me like a very ancient droving track, avoiding forest and moving between enclosed hill villages, now known as camps or castles, only because they are dramatic and defended by the ditches dug to make their walls. At times you can see from old maps and on the ground that the Icknield Way splits and joins up again, as droving tracks so often do, as if the drovers followed the whims of their cattle. This sometimes happens where the ancient track once led straight through what is now a modern village, and

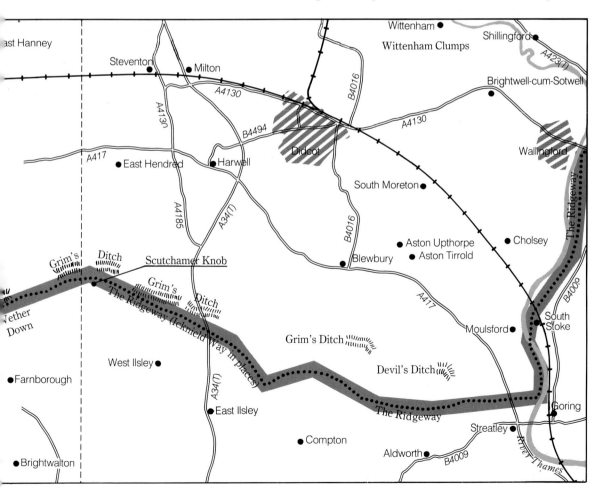

so a new track was devised that skirted the village fields and their cultivation.

Just south of the Thames the route becomes particularly entangled, with an important junction north of West Ilsley, further complicated by the training tracks of racehorses. But that is one of its finest stretches, above the part of the Oxford plain brought to life as a landscape only within my memory by the visually magnificent cooling towers of Didcot power station. (The same thing happened a few years later to the central plain of Arcadia.)

The important issue of where the old track was and why it went one way and not another is obscured by the modern planners, who have labelled the Icknield Way the Ridgeway from the north Chilterns north of Chequers to a point near Avebury Rings, and in places have distinctly rationalized its vagaries to make a continuous hiking path.

The Ridgeway Path by Seán Jennett (Long-Distance Footpath Guide No 6, HMSO for the Countryside Commission, 1976) follows the designated route from Ivinghoe Beacon to the old A4(T) Bath Road near Avebury. From there to Stonehenge the way is not certain and is barred by an artillery range, although only when the red flag is flying.

Beyond Ivinghoe Beacon, the Icknield Way crossed Watling Street at Dunstable. We have a furious letter written in 1285 from Edward I to the Prior of Dunstable about the repair of this crossing, where the highways were 'broken up and deep by the frequent passage of carts'. The Prior has to repair them, 'so that for your default in this part it shall not be necessary for us to apply a heavier hand to this'. Watling Street, Ermine Street, the Fosse Way and the Icknield Way were always considered in the Middle Ages to be under the King's special protection. Of the four of them, only the Icknield Way is pre-Roman.

The Ridgeway in Berkshire and Oxfordshire really is a ridgeway, and I am still as excited by it as a pensioned-off racehorse stepping on his old turf again. Of course it has a long history, and it no more belongs to one period of time than does the landscape that spreads out below it, so your mind wanders. You may choose the harebells and the larks, or watch the villages, or plot what remains of the long barrows and the camps. The Ridgeway can surely never have looked better than it did in the sunny and benign late autumn of 1986. The prehistoric burial places are richer along the Wiltshire section, close to Avebury. It is a strange thought that when they were built they were glistening white monuments, before the grass began to cover the chalk, just as the White Horse is still glistening white. That was scoured for centuries by the people of Uffington nearby. The scouring was the occasion for an attractively rowdy festival, described and it is thought revived by Thomas Hughes of Uffington, who wrote *Tom Brown's Schooldays*. He was a muscular Christian socialist, a disciple of F. D. Maurice and at one time an MP. The scouring festival lasted until 1875, I believe, which is a little longer than the Cotswold Olympic Games, old Whitsun games institutionalized by Robert Dover under James I. At Much Wenlock in Shropshire the games were organized by the local doctor, and the King of Greece visited them, and hence came the modern Olympics. That is what I thought about on the Ridgeway.

You could hardly get near the White Horse for barbed wire and general governmental spit and polish, and what with the approach roads and car parks and granny loos, but now things are better.

In the mid-1940s two little girls shared one bicycle and one pony between them, on which they took turns. They used to eat their sandwiches on the White Horse's eye, although they made no wish there, as books say people used to do. In 1958 I failed by pure bad luck to go by pony trap to have a picnic there. Those who went said it was an oasis of sun and silence. To see it like that today you would have to spend the night up there; which I am too old to do when the frost has started, and too fastidious in the tourist season.

> Before the gods that made the gods
> Had seen their sunrise pass
> The White Horse of the White Horse hill
> Stood hoary on the grass.

Sunrise is the right time, and the word hoary is right at that time, before it begins to gleam. But G. K. Chesterton was not quite right about its antiquity. The White Horse is only a century at most older than the Romans, and to find political and social conditions that explain the length and course of the track, you would have to go back closer to the age of Stonehenge. Some people date the White Horse by the horses on Belgic ritual buckets, others by the early coinage of Belgic tribes, in pursuit of whom Julius Caesar invaded Britain. It could well have been magnified from the figure of a horse on a coin. It is best seen from below, from the lanes south of Faringdon, but all the same to get close to it is to be thrilled.

The Ridgeway is older than many of the monuments on these hills, but Wayland's Smithy is older still. Like other early burial monuments, this one seems to have been constructed to house the bones removed somewhat at random from a cemetery of the ancestors or kinship group of settled farmers. The original barrow sheltered a stone and wooden house of the dead, then later a chambered tomb was added. The bones do not add up to complete skeletons, but at first there were bits of thirteen or so, some complete. At the second stage, the chambers with a fine façade of sarsen stones were added to the south end, and an outer ditch was dug to pile up a bigger barrow. The barrow drowned in grass, and a grove of trees grew up around it. Medieval iron bars have been found there, as if someone tried to dismantle it. I am not quite sure why the dead were buried or reburied in chamber tombs. The crasser archaeologists think they expressed economic triumph, but they are a strange way of celebration. They are landmarks and a claim to the land. The dead are grouped and subdivided, and the system expresses kinship; the chambers recall the chambers of a house, although no one has ever found such a house. Or could it possibly be that the dead are placated, because their first burial ground was disturbed and disease or a bad crop followed? Not all the dead are buried in such monumental tombs.

Wayland's Smithy is a legendary name: the legend is well enough told by Kipling in *Puck of Pook's Hill*. It was first recorded in 1738. Wayland the invisible blacksmith shoed horses on the Ridgeway. Walter Scott had a son who stayed with the Hughes family at Uffington, and Scott put Wayland's Smithy into *Kenilworth*. As a place name it is genuinely old; it is mentioned in a Compton Beauchamp land charter of the mid-10th century. Wayland as a character in Germanic mythology survives from the 7th century AD, carved in ivory on the Franks Casket in the British Museum. Down in Ashbury, one of the best starting places for an evening walk along the Ridgeway, with your back to the west and the sun behind you, there

Overleaf: The White Horse on Uffington Down

was once a standing stone called Snivelling Corner stone, which has been lost for forty years. Wayland threw it at his imp Flibbertygibbet for going bird's nesting when he was sent for some nails. Grim's Ditch, nearer to Streatley but just as close to the Ridgeway, is a prehistoric land division supposed to have been ploughed by the Devil in one night. Two round barrows beside it are the scrapings of his ploughshare, and a smaller mound is the clod he threw at his imp for not ploughing straight.

These stories are not completely lighthearted – they mask an anxiety. Evidence of witchcraft is supposed to have been found at Wayland's Smithy, as it has elsewhere among prehistoric stones: in the Channel Islands for example. Think of all the nonsense associated with Stonehenge! These monuments are vast, unexplained, and venerably old and weird. Stonehenge used to be called the Hanging Stones. In the case of the long barrows there is a sense that they are associated with the dead. To us, because we no longer fear the dead and can measure time easily backwards and understand prehistory, or hope to do so, the mounds are pleasant and symbols of human continuity. Even the loneliest thorn trees, and there are many on the Ridgeway, are only slightly disquieting, and that because for a moment we see them with the eyes of other generations. I am assuming someone who travels alone, whose reactions of pleasure and of fear are therefore a little intensified, as they would be among mountains. At the weekend, within a mile of a highway like the Oxford–Winchester road, or near a famous place like the White Horse or Wayland's Smithy, which lies just north of the Ridgeway, the track is frequented by people with dogs, families and other groups. At other times and away from the roads the only company is larks and hawks. On Lambourn Downs south of Stanford in the Vale I saw a great number of rabbits.

You need a map to explore the Ridgeway, although you can best enjoy it sensually without one. What you follow is an extremely obvious green lane as broad as a road and often bounded by hedges. In spring and autumn the thorn hedges are thrilling. The point of a map is to know how far you have got and what you are looking at, and what ancient monuments to expect. Crossing the M4 is a bit of a surprise, but that happens in Wiltshire. For our purposes we might as well start at Ashbury, not without a bow towards Compton Beauchamp, which is one of the most enchanting houses and gardens in this part of England. As late as October the roadside flowers stain the grass with their colours. From Ashbury you will climb into a purer, less luxuriant world. Ashbury has a 15th-century manor house with buttresses that captivated Nikolaus Pevsner, but I have never seen inside it, being always in a hurry to get up on the downs. Without a ridgeway the downs would be as pathless as the ocean. I have seldom been happier than on some trackless downs in Dorset, and have never seen anyone happier than a young man who had just walked home at night right across the Sussex downs, steering with his nose. He looked as if he had swum the Atlantic. The Ridgeway is tamer, but nevertheless it has its rewards.

There is a lot to be said for starting at the more exciting end. From Ashbury you reach the heights by the B4001, a tiny road leading towards Lambourn. Wayland's Smithy lies just above the Ridgeway, and in a mile or so east you see Bardwell Camp below you and then Uffington Castle on the top of White Horse Hill. Bardwell Camp is on the road near Compton Beauchamp. The Ridgeway route is an alternative, or deviation, of this but the lower way has been adopted as a modern

Wayland's Smithy

road. Nothing disturbs the upper route that would tempt a macadamizer; it is as grassy as a racetrack and the only buildings are solitary barns. Uffington Castle is empty and unexcavated: it was a hill village before the White Horse was cut. A track wanders away from it southwards across Uffington Down to Woolston Down past Idlebush Barrow and Hangman's Stone to Lambourn. But the Ridgeway follows the north edge of the downs. Beyond the White Horse one of those numberless small enclosures all called Alfred's Castle lies below you on the western edge of Ashdown Park. You have not travelled more than four miles. The ramparts of the so-called castle, which is much the same date as Uffington Castle and might be its lower village, were once lined with sarsen stones, but they were used as building material for Ashdown in the late 17th century.

The Ridgeway wanders gently up and down Rams Hill to cross the Kingston Lisle Road, which is called Blowing Stone Hill after a standing stone that once stood on the downs, although now it stands in somebody's garden on the edge of Kingston Lisle. The stone has holes in it and if you blow through them they say it brays like a conch. However, I did not blow nor did I hear it; I had no wish to lose height by climbing down to Kingston Lisle and then up again. I did not visit this amazing stone, and I greatly doubt whether King Alfred ever blew through it either, to summon his armies to battle. But it pleases the people of Kingston Lisle, and one sarsen less on the downs does not really matter. All the same, I am against their tendency to travel downhill, because once they get to the foot of the hill they run the risk of being broken up sooner or later.

The Kingston Lisle Road passes southwards to an amazing burial ground called Seven Barrows. The number seven in English place names like the Seven Sisters just means 'a lot', as nine did in ancient Greek (the Nine Springs of Athens and Nine Towers of the Acropolis), and the Seven Barrows include traces of at least forty large and small mounds. As a matter of fact nine is just as magical a number in English as seven is: there are at least four stone circles in Cornwall called the Nine Maidens, and Nine Stones in several places, but ninestones or ninepipes was a game like skittles. There are groups of barrows called Nine Barrows in the west of England, although Seven Barrows is a commoner name. Local stories about them, which are many, tend to be not about seven people but either three or nine. Today the downs are fertile ground, and ancient field systems can be traced here and there on the slopes below the Ridgeway; but in the case of a burial ground like Seven Barrows the dead must have been carried up there, probably from a lower village, Perhaps the attraction was a monument of white chalk. Perhaps it was important to bury the dead away from the village fields, in the upper grazing grounds. It is easier to theorize than to solve these puzzles. The Seven Barrows date from more than a thousand years before Christ. The skeletons were buried crouching, with pitifully poor pottery, though prehistorians value it.

The Ridgeway leads eastward past Hillbarn Clump, a name that speaks for itself. I like the clump, which makes a fine landmark. Clumps like that are sometimes planted by shepherds to shelter their sheep (the grove on the hilltop at Chanctonbury in Sussex is less than a hundred years old). A little further on the maps mark Collett Bush and then Wixen Bush. They are indistinguishable now among a profusion of bushes, but once they must have been shepherd's landmarks. The track around here is in a condition that Edward I would not have tolerated, being pitted and rutted into the chalk. It runs between thorn bushes, then at Hillbarn it flings them aside, and naked grass stretches ahead. A fence defines the Ridgeway. You can see the Cotswolds and the towers of Didcot puff their white smudges into the air. You have come to the training grounds of the racehorses, and the edge of some of the finest-looking country in the south of England. The galloping tracks are a deeper green than the Ridgeway path, and they run beside it for miles. But to see the horses exercising you would have to be up earlier than I was. How odd it is that the thunder of hoofbeats is such a thrilling sound, yet the clip-clop of horses walking down a lane is so tranquillizing. In the village where I live, people keep horses in their garages and happily let their cars stand outside. I am sure they even keep hens in their garages, for from the bus stop around dawn you hear the muted crowing of cocks. If you are lucky enough to hear a cock crow or a dog bark or a bucket clang from the Ridgeway, it carries with extraordinary purity on a still day, up from the Vale.

This section is a tramp of several miles, past Folly Clump to Rats Hill and Letcombe Castle, which is the first place I ever stood on the Ridgeway. It lies above the racing villages of Letcombe Bassett and Letcombe Regis. The castle is just a banked enclosure, with sarsens under the earth of its simple rampart. It was never really a castle I suppose, but just an upper village where people lived in summer. No legend attaches to it and it is not a dramatic place, although the view from it is dramatic. The Victorians thought all such enclosures were castles, because they

View towards Wantage from the Ridgeway

failed to notice the postholes of wooden buildings, and they thought more in terms of empires and wars than we do, and less in terms of the movements of cattle. But Letcombe Castle is the simple monument of a way of life. I would not have minded being a shepherd up there. A swineherd's life in a forest would be more exciting, but I like the clarity and the fine air of the downs. Nowadays, for better and (to my mind) for worse, there is a Youth Hostel and a picnic area at Courthill Quarry, but that was unfinished in October of 1986.

Hereabouts, the Ridgeway crosses the Wantage Road and you have to follow some mysterious dog's legs because the track has got lost. I suspect it was swallowed by Whitehouse Farm. The first dog's leg is southwards along the road then east again, then beyond Whitehouse Farm northwards on to a green lane which if you followed it in the wrong direction would take you down into Letcombe. The track comes into its own again between Ridgeway Down and Wether Down, beyond the B4494, a tiny road from Wantage leading nowhere in particular. The difficult bit of the Ridgeway is well signposted, but the roads it crosses and the easiness of car parking make it a less pleasant stretch. All the same it has some historical interest. Grim's Ditch crosses it, indicating an important land division at a period when no one moved freely along the whole length of the Icknield Way: not long before the Romans I dare say. The Victorians thought places called Grim's Ditch (Grim, originally an alternative name for the god Woden, came to mean the Devil) were like the Great Wall of China, or a prehistoric foretaste of frontier warfare, but recent work has related them to humdrum landholding in case after case. The Berkshire Grim's Dyke once ran 24 miles to the Thames, but now it can be traced only here and there. It goes without saying that no one is ever going to excavate the whole of this long barricade.

Harwell and Didcot dominate the plain, but the track still offers a fine walking surface and some surprising views of woods and groves of trees, a Victorian monument, and the training tracks of horses. Then the Ridgeway plunges into the shadow of a wood, private property, which was planted round a barrow called Scutchamer Knob. This barrow is reported to have been 77 feet high in the 18th century; it is thought to be the burial place of a king of Wessex called Cwicchelm who died in AD 593. The hill is called Cuckhamsley Hill. A small road leads downhill across Grim's Ditch to East Hendred, but the track stretches ahead north of West Ilsley to the Oxford–Winchester road, neck and neck with the empty gallops of the racehorses. I left it there, although it bounded ahead indefatigably, away for miles over downs tufted with wonderful clumps.

If you are going to walk so far, it is better to do it in this direction, rather than arrive late and tired at the White Horse and Wayland's Smithy with the descending sun in your eyes. The enthusiast will want to vary his walk on different days, perhaps by exploring southwards towards Lambourn and Ramsbury, by adventuring into Wiltshire or clambering up and down the gulleys that indent the north face of the downs. The short walker will develop a favourite stretch of the track, and the process of selecting that will be personal and enjoyable. The condition of the surface varies considerably, and on a shortish there-and-back walk it is easy enough to choose one along level turf. On a longer stint you need solid walking shoes and an eye to the weather, and if you want a pub you will have to climb down from the Ridgeway to a village.

I have not got to the end of understanding this track. The Danes used it, and

Looking north-west towards Oxford from Swyncombe

Alfred defeated them at the battle of Ashdown, but only as Harold used Roman roads to get to Hastings. This is not a Danish nor an Anglo-Saxon monument. The ramparted enclosures are not frontier fortresses or lookout posts, although they must certainly have controlled the Ridgeway track and had access to it. They are not a regular series of caravanserais, though they may have served as that too. The track was there before they were built, and it has outlasted them because of the modesty of its means. I believe it might now be technically possible to discover a more precise date for any individual stretch of the Ridgeway by subjecting it to a battery of tests, but substantially we know the answer. Its history is part of the history of the landscape, and that cannot be read off in terms of one period of time or a single line of development. Landscape history is a huge, entangled subject. It splits and joins up again just as the Ridgeway does. Nothing is harder to master intellectually than this simple track, nothing is easier to enjoy.

The Thames

RICHARD LETHBRIDGE

The first recorded reference to the Thames is in Julius Caesar's *De Bello Gallico*, where it was called Tamesis. The name is Celtic, going back to an ancient word meaning 'dark water'. In the Middle Ages the river was sometimes called the Isis and around Oxford it is still frequently known by that name.

Rising in a field in Gloucestershire near Cirencester, about 20 miles inland from the Severn Estuary, the Thames makes its gentle, meandering way for some 170 miles to the estuary beyond London where it meets the open sea. Southern England is almost cut in half by it. Throughout its long journey it is continually fed by tributaries with charming names like Windrush, Evenlode and Glyme in Oxfordshire; and Kennet, Pang and Loddon in Berkshire. Fed by these and countless other streams from the hills, the Thames imperceptibly widens from 150 feet at Oxford to 750 feet at London Bridge.

There is a peculiar Englishness about the Thames: understated, gentle, with no great waterfalls or gorges. Only in the Goring Gap (7/1A), where it cuts through the hills, and divides the Chilterns from the Berkshire Downs, is there a hint of the mighty power of a river that can deliver 20 billion gallons a day across Teddington Lock in the rainy season. But for most of its course it seems a sleepy giant, preferring to take the easy way around the obstacles in its way as it gently falls to the sea at the rate of 20 inches to the mile.

Flooding used to be a great problem. In the broad valley of the upper Thames, where it flows through west Oxfordshire between the Cotswolds and the Downs, it is noticeable how the villages and towns are set well back from the river to avoid the disastrous flooding that was a common occurrence. Various efforts were made to bring the water under control, and pound locks were built in the 18th century under an Act of Parliament. These were designed both to help control the floods and to provide storage in the drier season for the increasing demand for water from the towns of the Thames Valley and, above all, London, which was the largest city in the world.

The creation of the Thames Conservancy Board in 1857 was the first real attempt to harness and control the whole river, and it is from that date that the system of weirs and sluices, locks and cuts that we now see began to take shape. In recent years the Thames Water Board has taken over responsibility for the river and all its tributaries, for its navigation and upkeep, and for managing the one billion gallons of water removed every day for domestic use, to say nothing of the 900 million gallons of cleaned water returned every day from hundreds of sewage plants.

Very slowly the river is recovering from the terrible pollution of the 18th and 19th centuries, when it was virtually an open sewer, particularly near London. One writer described it in the 1840s as 'a river of floating filth'; and it was only in this century that serious measures were taken to restore it to health. Some of the tributaries of the upper Thames, particularly the river Ock (which means 'salmon') near Abingdon (4/1C), were famed for their salmon in the Middle Ages and one

Opposite: The Thames at Goring

day, perhaps, they will return. The discovery of a salmon near Teddington in 1974 was the first recorded since the early 18th century. In 1980, the Thames Salmon Trust instituted a major breeding exercise and 176 adult salmon were recorded in 1986 returning from the Atlantic – a good omen for the future.

For centuries, of course. the river was as much a barrier to communication as an artery, particularly towards its mouth where medieval London Bridge stood alone until Putney Bridge joined it in 1730. On the narrower upper Thames, however, many small stone-arched bridges were built and rebuilt throughout the Middle Ages and contributed to the importance of towns like Wallingford and Abingdon. Because the roads were so poor, the Thames was one of the principal transport routes in southern England, used for handling stone, timber and grain and later, when the 18th-century canal network was opened up, coal and other goods carried in narrow boats from the Midland collieries. You can still see great steel barges hauled by tugs on the London Thames, but commercial traffic on the rest of the river is virtually extinct.

In the last quarter of the 19th century, boating on the Thames became an immensely popular pastime. In 1889 Jerome K. Jerome wrote his famous book *Three Men in a Boat*, which sold two million copies in his lifetime, and this amusing account of river adventures and mishaps between Kingston and Oxford added still more to the river's popularity. An easy railway journey took you to Windsor or Maidenhead (8/2&3 A&B), or further up river to Pangbourne (7/2B) or Goring (7/1A)–three shillings and ninepence (about 19p in today's currency) for a 3rd class ticket; Mr Salter's river steamers, still operating today, began in 1888 for those who did not wish to hire a boat themselves. Grand houses with tennis courts, riverside lawns and boathouses were built by Victorian tycoons; and smaller villas for the less well-off proliferated along the river, giving places like Wargrave (8/1A) and Shiplake (7/3A) an Edwardian air. Messing about in boats was all the rage.

Since these English counties or shires were formed in the Middle Ages, the boundary between Oxfordshire and Berkshire was determined by the Thames along the whole extent from Henley-on-Thames to just east of Lechlade. In 1974, however, this boundary was regrettably altered to a line below the Berkshire Downs, and is now marked by the river only between Wallingford (4/3C) and Henley (7/3A). It was along this short stretch, about a two days' leisurely journey, that the author sailed in a hired cabin cruiser with his two sons last summer.

From Wallingford bridge, a mixture of medieval and Georgian stone arches, it is a pleasant two-hour cruise to Goring, going at a fast walking pace, which is the maximum permitted speed on the Thames. The country on both banks is relatively flat, and villages like North and South Stoke (7/1A) and Moulsford (7/1A) are set well back from the river behind the broad river meadows. It is entirely pastoral, with very few houses to be seen, and you can take the opportunity to study the abundant bird life on the river.

The largest waterfowl, unquestioned Lord of the Thames, is the swan, or mute swan to give it the proper name. There are large numbers of these superb birds which are, however, quite pugnacious and best kept at a respectful distance. Moorhens and coots abound near the banks, engaging creatures with their restless jerky head movements seeming to propel them along on the surface of the water.

Memorial to two boys who drowned in the Thames, Lower Basildon churchyard (see p. 198)

'On the river you tend to measure your journey from lock to lock.'

Then there are many kinds of duck, coloured and plain, dabblers and divers, often so tame that they follow the boats in the hope of a discarded titbit.

Through Cleeve Lock, beautifully kept, you go down to Goring, a pleasing Edwardian riverside village now growing with commuters. A concrete and wooden bridge spans the Thames to Streatley (7/1A) on the Berkshire bank, where there is a famous river inn, The Swan. Centuries before any bridge or ferry, even before the Romans, the Icknield Way crossed the Thames here, continuing west along the high ridge of the downs.

A mile or so below Goring the river flows under the large railway bridge built to carry Brunel's Great Western Railway, and here the scenery starts to change dramatically. For this is the Goring Gap, where the Thames breaks through the high chalk hills that cross both counties. On the Oxfordshire bank the Chilterns rise steeply, with beechwoods clinging to chalk cliffs right to the water's edge. Opposite the hills rise more slowly, revealing the noble pile of Basildon Park (7/A&B), a splendid Palladian mansion built of golden Bath stone in 1776 and now owned by the National Trust; the view from its terrace across the valley is truly Arcadian in the best 18th-century tradition.

On the river you tend to measure your journey from lock to lock; and the four miles from Goring to Whitchurch Locks is one of the most beautiful on the whole river. Somehow, even in high summer, the Thames never seems crowded although there is occasionally a wait to get through the locks. The strict regulation of speed, with the blessed absence of waterskiers and speedboats, makes a wonderfully peaceful atmosphere in which to enjoy the woods and meadows on either bank.

Whitchurch (7/2B) and Pangbourne (7/2B) are a pair of riverside villages (Pangbourne almost a town) joined by a Victorian cast-iron tollbridge, one of only two such bridges remaining on the Thames. The little river Pang flows into the Thames from the Berkshire Downs. Along the riverside road in Pangbourne are a number of Victorian villas known as the Seven Deadly Sins. Clinging to the steep wooded bank, with the railway line just behind them, they are an evocative reminder of Pangbourne's heyday round the turn of the century. Jerome K. Jerome gives a moving account of the discovery just upstream from here of the body of a poor woman who had given up the struggle to maintain herself and her illegitimate child and thrown herself in the river. It is a powerful piece of writing, especially effective after the somewhat relentless humour of the rest of *Three Men in a Boat*. On the hill above Pangbourne is the famous Nautical College where generations of Merchant Navy Officers were taught and learned their boatmanship on the river.

The Thames now curves north in a loop away from the outskirts of Reading and along a particularly beautiful couple of miles to Mapledurham. On the Oxfordshire bank are two fine Tudor houses: Hardwick House, where Charles I once played bowls, is dimly glimpsed through the trees; and Mapledurham House (7/2B), ancestral home of the Blount family and of their descendants the Eystons. The latter romantic-looking house, described elsewhere in this book, was the home of Alexander Pope's 'scornful beauty' Martha Blount and her sister Teresa. When Teresa retired from London after George I's coronation in 1714 it was to Mapledurham that she went.

> She went to plain-work, and to purling brooks,
> Old fashioned halls, dull aunts and croaking rooks,
> She went from opera, park, assembly, play,
> to morning walks and prayers three times a day.

The old corn and grist mill at Mapledurham, powered by a waterwheel and partly dating from the 15th century, has recently been lovingly restored to produce wholewheat flour, which can be bought there.

Basildon Park, Berkshire (see p. 198)

Beyond Mapledurham the first signs of Reading (7/2&3 B) start to appear on the Berkshire bank in the shape of Tilehurst, which is Reading's western suburb; on the Oxfordshire side, however, it is still rural and undeveloped until the start of Caversham (7/2B). Reading's river frontage is surprisingly short considering the size of the town. There are only two bridges, which may account for the main spread of the town being to the south, away from the Thames. The only lock is Caversham Lock, beyond which the river Kennet flows in from Berkshire. Near the point at which the two rivers meet are the few remains of Reading Abbey, the large Benedictine house founded by Henry I in 1121, one of the greatest monasteries in England in the Middle Ages. More enduring than the abbey is the oldest song in the English language, 'Sumer is icumen in', first written down by one of the monks there over 700 years ago..

Unlike the drive through Reading, which seems to take for ever, the river leaves it very quickly and two miles later you reach Sonning (7/3B) a beautiful brick village with one of the most attractive locks on the Thames and a fine 11-arched bridge joining the two counties. Despite being so close to Reading, Sonning has managed to retain its old-world atmosphere – with mellow brick Georgian houses and a number of famous hostelries, including the White Hart and the French Horn, both near the bridge, and the Bull, just off the churchyard and much recommended by Jerome K. Jerome during his famous river trip. The old mill has been converted into a theatre and restaurant, and it is a pleasant thing to dine and see the play by boat, tying up at the adjoining landing stage.

We moored for the night a mile downstream from Sonning, amid wild flowers and overhanging trees. Although the yellow lights of Reading were visible on the skyline three miles away, the peace and quiet was total and only broken by the strange honking sound made by hundreds of Canada geese as they flew overhead at dusk and landed on the watermeadow opposite.

Shiplake (7/3A) church and college stand on a bluff above the river on the Oxfordshire side, opposite the Loddon river which joins the Thames at this point. Alfred, Lord Tennyson, married in the church in 1850 after a long engagement to his Emily, wrote a delightful ditty to the vicar in gratitude (see p. 146). More Tennysonian was his later comment: 'The peace of God came into my life before the altar when I wedded her.'

Lower Shiplake lies beyond the lock. This part of the river, with Wargrave on the Berkshire bank opposite, is charmingly Edwardian with handsome houses of every style from cottage orné to stockbroker's Tudor, well-trimmed gardens and wide lawns sweeping down to the water's edge, where boathouses and landing stages await the weekend's pleasure. Wargrave Manor, a splendid white Georgian house with a rather 'American Deep South' flavour, looks grandly across the river from a hill evoking thoughts of those leisured house parties from Friday to Monday at the turn of the century.

Between Wargrave and Marsh Lock, the last lock before Henley (7/3A), the steep hills and woods on the Berkshire bank are spectacular. Part of the area is occupied by the Park Place Estate where in the 18th century General Conway created fine pleasure grounds with grottoes, stone circles, rusticated bridges and all the trappings of rich Georgian fantasy, much of it still there. A later owner at the end of the century was the famous courtesan Georgiana, Duchess of Devonshire, the subject of one of Gainsborough's most celebrated portraits. The Oxfordshire bank is by contrast quite flat and we saw a fine pair of herons standing in a field. On our attempt at a closer inspection they lazily flapped their enormous wings and flew for a few yards before resuming their glassy stare towards the water.

A mile downstream from Marsh Lock you come to Henley-on-Thames. Of all the towns on the Thames between here and Oxford, Henley seems to be the most identified with the river, which is part and parcel of its very being in a way that is not true of, say, Abingdon or Reading. The town is largely on the Oxfordshire bank, and attractive houses and pubs of every period crowd along the waterfront behind the establishments where boats of all descriptions can be hired. On the Berkshire side it is less domestic, with the grounds of the Leander Club and the open fields that in June and July contain the tents and enclosures for the famous Henley Regatta. The new, brightly coloured brick and metal regatta headquarters is in strange contrast to the elegant 18th-century bridge next to it.

The great regatta, which has taken place annually at the beginning of July since 1839, is held on the 1½-mile straight stretch of river between Henley Bridge and Temple Island. Ten years before, in 1829, the first Oxford and Cambridge boat race was held here, but the venue was later moved to London. It is the loveliest stretch of water imaginable: unspoiled fields and meadows on either side with Temple Island, a graceful white Georgian folly designed by Wyatt, in the centre of the river and, beyond, a backdrop of Chiltern beechwoods. Coming upstream, as the competing oarsmen do, you see the much-photographed view of Henley Bridge and church tower.

During the summer, and particularly during the regatta, Henley is full of boats – skiffs, punts, dinghies, launches, narrow boats and houseboats (gin palaces, as they are usually known). There is a vital, festive and cheerful air about the place. It was well caught by John Betjeman, on a visit just after the Second World War, in his poem 'Henley-on-Thames':

> When shall I see the Thames again?
> The prow-promoted gems again,
> As beefy ATS
> Without their hats
> Come shooting through the bridge?
> And 'cheerioh' and 'cheeri-bye'
> Across the waste of waters die,
> And low the mists of evening lie
> And lightly skims the midge.

> *Collected Poems*, John Murray (Publishers) Ltd

Pageantry:
Windsor, Ascot and Eton

HUGO VICKERS

Windsor

Windsor Castle has loomed in its magnificence on a high chalk mound by the Thames for 900 years or more. Built by William the Conqueror as a stronghold to guard London from the west, it has been rebuilt and readorned by the generations of sovereigns that have followed. Its first purpose was to serve as a military fortress and as such it continues to serve to this day. For that reason there is always a flag flying over the Round Tower: the Union flag, or the Royal Standard which replaces it when the Sovereign is in residence. It is possible to observe the Union flag flying happily and then, almost surreptitiously, another little bundle making its way up the pole. This is explained by the simultaneous descent into the castle of a royal helicopter, the unfurling of the Royal Standard and the lowering of the Union flag. The observant will then know that the Queen has arrived. At this point the castle serves its second purpose – as a royal residence. It was first used as such by Henry I who felt he could best protect his somewhat shaky claim to the throne from a more strategically elevated position. Incidentally, the flags vary considerably in size. On special occasions a huge flag flies, at least 30 feet wide. It appears to drape the castle and is a sign that Windsor is *en fête*. But on days when fierce winds blow, the flag appears from afar no larger than a pocket handkerchief. Either way, one or other of the flags always flies.

Windsor Castle has other roles, too. It is the home of the College of St George. The Dean of Windsor and his Canons preside over St George's Chapel, one of England's finest ecclesiastical buildings, constructed in the Perpendicular style. The building of the present structure was begun by Edward IV in 1475 near the site of Henry III's earlier chapel. The door at the east end of the chapel, through which the Royal Family enter on Christmas Day, is Henry III's former West Door, with ironwork dating from the 13th century. A number of our monarchs lie buried in the chapel, including Henry VI, Henry VIII, the executed Charles I and all sovereigns (except Queen Victoria and Edward VIII) since George III. Edward VII and Queen Alexandra lie in a tomb to the right of the high altar. At the king's feet is an effigy of his beloved dog Caesar. King George V and Queen Mary lie in the nave; and in 1969 a special chapel was built beside the north quire aisle for the remains of King George VI.

St George's Chapel is not only the resting place of kings but the home of the Order of the Garter since its foundation in 1348. Thus the quire of St George's Chapel is also the Garter Chapel. Above the oak stalls of the knights hang their banners. Raised at the time of their installation they remain there until death. Likewise above the stalls there is a helm with the family crest above it. Below the helm is a half-drawn sword, symbolizing the fact that Knights of the Garter are ever at hand to defend their Sovereign. The Order of the Garter consists of the Queen, the Prince of Wales and 24 knights. In addition there are certain Royal Knights, Ladies of the Order such as the Queen Mother, and extra knights – sovereigns of

Church Street, Windsor

foreign lands. The Sovereign's stall is the one traditionally occupied by the dean in a cathedral, on the south side, and the Prince of Wales' is on the north. The fine multi-coloured banners hark back to the days of the Middle Ages. So too do the brass stall-plates, for each Knight's stall plate remains in his stall in perpetuity. The earliest is that of Ralph, Lord Bassett, appointed a Knight of the Garter in 1368.

Each June, the Order of the Garter provides Windsor Castle with its most splendid display of medieval pageantry. The Order was founded by King Edward III as a way of surrounding himself with the flower of European knighthood to assist him in his regular conflicts with France. In the forefront of his mind was the concept of King Arthur and the Round Table with its attendant ceremonies and jousting. The Garter itself is said to have been inspired by a dance enjoyed by the king and Joan, Countess of Salisbury. The countess's garter slipped to the ground and the king picked it up, tying it round his own knee. His courtiers deemed this amusing but the king was unabashed. 'Shame on him who thinks badly of it', he declared (*Honi soit qui mal y pense*). 'I will make of it ere long the most honourable garter that was ever worn'. The Order has gone from strength to strength, and since 1948 there has been an almost annual ceremony, the most colourful and at the same time the most intimate of all the annual pageants.

New knights are invested privately in the sanctum of the Garter Throne Room. The ceremonial garter is buckled below the left knee, and the blue velvet robe with its surcoat of red velvet and its collar of red and white roses, the George itself appended from it, is placed on the new knight in the presence of the Queen. Then a magnificent luncheon is served in the Waterloo Chamber, after which the knights emerge, in the words of one of the heralds: 'in a haze of cigar smoke and general euphoria'. The procession is then formed to walk down the hill through the cheering crowds and the bands for the installation service in St George's Chapel.

The procession is led by the Governor of the Castle, until February 1988 Marshal of the Royal Air Force Sir John Grandy, wearing his RAF uniform and the riband of a Knight Grand Cross of the Order of the Bath. He is followed by the Military Knights of Windsor, splendid old officers, some of them octogenarians, many sporting handsome white moustaches. They wear scarlet uniforms with white sword belts, cocked hats and red and white plumes. They live in the castle and represent the Knights of the Garter every Sunday Matins (the knights being too worldly to attend the chapel on a weekly basis). Thus every Sunday morning they can be seen coming out of their houses in the castle wall in the Lower Ward and walking over to the chapel. After the Military Knights come the Officers of Arms or Heralds, often described as resembling playing cards, their dark stockinged legs emerging from under their tabards emblazoned with the royal arms. All walk two by two. The Heralds are followed by the Garter Knights, the new men first, the old ones to the rear. Their dark-blue velvet robes shimmer in the June sunlight and the ostrich plumes on their bonnets bob and sway in the summer breeze as they make their stately progress to church. Among them field marshals, admirals, politicians, dukes, Lords Lieutenant, and others whose merit is less easy to pinpoint, they are often misidentified by the crowd. In the 1960s the arrival of the late Earl Stanhope was always greeted by a ripple of 'Attlee! Attlee!'.

After the Senior Knight, currently the Duke of Northumberland (appointed in 1959), comes the Duke of Kent (given the Garter on his 50th birthday in 1985), then the Prince of Wales escorting the Queen Mother, who still walked effortlessly

Garter Ceremonial 1987 with Sir James Callaghan (Syndication International)

in the procession in her 87th year. Next come the Officers of the Order, including the Gentleman Usher of the Black Rod.

Technically, should a knight misbehave, he can be demoted from the Order by the descent on his shoulder of the Black Rod itself. The only reason for demotion is high treason, an act given wide interpretation over the years. There is among the Order today Emperor Hirohito of Japan. First appointed in 1928, he was quietly removed from the Order in the Second World War. But in 1971, on the occasion of his state visit to Britain, his banner was once again raised above his stall. The Sovereign of the Order, the Queen, accompanied by Prince Philip, follows the Officers and the procession ends with a phalanx of the Yeomen of the Guard.

Overleaf: Windsor Castle, East Front

When they reach St George's Chapel, the military band atmosphere of outside is superseded by a solemn ecclesiastical atmosphere within the chapel. A fanfare announces the Queen's arrival at the great west door. The newly invested knights are then installed and there is a short service of thanksgiving.

After the service, the knights spill out down the great west steps, allowing their Sovereign to walk between them. The Royal Family leave in carriages and the knights in cars. Thereafter these medieval men revert to 20th-century life. The Prince of Wales can often be seen a while later departing in his Aston Martin for a game of polo at Smith's Lawn. Other knights, in shirt sleeves, battle with the rush-hour traffic between Windsor and London.

The only other time in the year when the knights gather in force is at the presentation of the banner of a deceased knight. This usually takes place at Evensong, and those knights present sit under their banners and wear their Garter stars. At a given point in the service, the Military Knights leave the quire to fetch the dead knight's banner. The silence of the service is broken by the distant stomp of their military boots. Presently they re-enter the quire, escorting the banner to the high altar rail. The banner is given to the Dean, who then lays it on the altar.

Windsor Castle continues to serve as fortress and home. There are also moments when it becomes the focus of the nation's attention. When a sovereign is buried, the body is brought from London by train, escorted from the station to the castle on a gun carriage and conveyed through the Lower Ward to St George's Chapel. Many foreign sovereigns, heads of state and the leading men of the nation will be present in the chapel. The coffin resting before the high altar will be lowered at a point in the service into the royal vault. The new monarch will scatter earth and, by ancient custom, the Lord Chamberlain will break his ceremonial white wand. The most recent service in which the royal vault was used during a funeral was that of Princess Andrew of Greece, Prince Philip's mother. Having been born at Windsor in 1885, she lived in many foreign lands, returning to Windsor in death in 1969.

Other members of the Royal Family are accorded private funerals at the chapel. On these days the castle is closed to the public and after the funeral the coffin is taken by car for private burial at Frogmore. The most recent such funeral was that of the Duchess of Windsor in April 1986, her coffin carried by men of the Welsh Guards (the Prince of Wales being by tradition Colonel of that regiment). The body of the Duke of Windsor lay in state in St George's Chapel before his private funeral in 1972. On the other hand, the funeral of the Queen's other uncle, the Duke of Gloucester, in 1974, was a military one. His body was borne through the streets of Windsor on a gun carriage. At the end of the service, as the coffin was carried out through the nave, a lone piper walked down the south nave aisle, playing a lament.

In recent years, partly to free London from unwelcome traffic jams, some state visitors have been received at Windsor. Normally they arrive at a specially constructed pavilion on the lawns on which the annual Windsor Horse Show takes place. There is a carriage procession through the town and up the Long Walk. Queen Margrethe of Denmark arrived at the Royal Naval College, Greenwich, for her visit in April 1974 aboard the Danish Royal yacht, *Dannebrog*. She was received by the Lord Lieutenant of Greater London, Marshal of the Royal Air Force Lord Elworthy. He happened also to be the Governor of the Castle; therefore he made a quick trip by helicopter to Windsor in order to greet her again at the steps of Windsor Castle. In the evening of the first day there is a magnificent banquet in

St George's Hall. The Lord Chamberlain and the Lord Steward walk in backwards, leading the Queen, her state visitors and other members of the Royal Family. These dinners are now occasionally televised. The Queen speaks in English and the guest sometimes speaks in his native tongue. The King of Spain and President Reagan have both been entertained in this way.

A state visit follows an established pattern. The Queen sends a member of the Royal Family to greet the visitors at Heathrow Airport and to bring them back to Windsor. When the King and Queen of Spain arrived on 22 April 1986, the Prince and Princess of Wales went to Heathrow with the Spanish Ambassador and his wife. They then travelled in a convoy of cars to the 'Royal Pavilion' in the Home Park. Here King Juan Carlos and Queen Sofia were greeted by the Queen and the Duke of Edinburgh. At this point important dignitaries such as the Prime Minister and the Foreign Secretary were presented and the King inspected a Guard of Honour. Meanwhile gun salutes were fired in the private part of the Home Park to the west of the castle and at the Tower of London (some way out of royal earshot). The carriage procession made its way through the town and up the Long Walk escorted by a Sovereign's Escort of the Household Cavalry with two standards, found (as the Court Circular puts it) by the Blues and Royals.

Within the Grand Vestibule of the castle other members of the Royal Family were waiting to be presented: Princess Anne, Princess Margaret, Princess Alice, Duchess of Gloucester, The Dukes and Duchesses of Gloucester and Kent, Princess Alexandra and the Hon. Angus Ogilvy. The Queen then gave a private luncheon party and invested the King with the Royal Victorian Chain. (She reserves the Order of the Garter for her return state visit a couple of years later.) Because it is Windsor, the King received addresses of welcome privately from the Chairman and Members of the Council of the Royal County of Berkshire as well as the Mayor and Councillors of the Royal Borough of Windsor and Maidenhead. It is traditional for the state visitors to call on the Queen Mother at her home. This time she awaited the King and Queen at Royal Lodge, a short drive away along the Long Walk. In the evening there was a state banquet.

On occasions such as these, when television cameras are needed in Windsor Castle, wonderful fake battlements are built, merging subtly with the ancient stone walls of the buildings. Behind them lurked television cameras so that the passing show could be transmitted back to Spain, and indeed to far corners of the globe.

On a more daily basis, Windsor is guarded by one of the Guards regiments, or occasionally the Gurkhas. Ceremonial Changing of the Guard takes place each day, and from time to time small bands of soldiers march through the castle to relieve the sentries. If the Queen is in residence the guard mounting ceremony takes place in the Quadrangle, but at other times outside the Guardroom beside the Henry VIII gateway. At Christmas and Easter the Royal Family are invariably in residence in the castle. Whereas the Queen normally worships privately in the Royal Chapel of All Saints in the Home Park, on these days, she leads her family to more public worship in St George's Chapel. Thus crowds flock to Windsor in the hope of seeing the Royal Family united.

The castle is also the setting for the annual Windsor Festival, founded in 1969. Artists from all over the world have come to perform in the Waterloo Chamber or St George's Chapel. The Dungeons of the Curfew Tower, where once prisoners languished in misery, became a club for festival members.

Ascot

The Garter Ceremony has been referred to, jokingly, as the 'Ascot Vigil', during which the knights pray for a winner later in the week. Garter Day is always the Monday of Ascot Week (the third week in June), when the Queen entertains a large house party at Windsor. For the next four days the Royal Meeting takes place.

The history of Royal Ascot goes back to the days of Queen Anne. In 1711, soon after the celebrated victories of the Duke of Marlborough in France, Queen Anne drove over from Windsor with members of her court to witness a day's sport. Ascot's next royal patron was the Duke of Cumberland, who bore the distinction of being the first member of the Royal Family elected to the Jockey Club. He bred the famous Eclipse, which won a Noblemen and Gentlemen's Plate at Ascot. The Prince Regent had a winner in 1785 and thereafter was as extravagant in his racing expenditure as in other matters. In 1822, when he had acceded as George IV, the first royal pavilion was built to a design by Nash, and in 1825 the King made his first ceremonial drive from Windsor Castle to the racecourse. Both William IV and Queen Victoria paid visits to Ascot, but after the death of the Prince Consort the Queen eschewed all such frivolous pleasures. As Prince of Wales, and later as King, Edward VII did much to promote Ascot as an important society event, and the year before his death, his famous Derby winner Minoru on the St James's Palace Stakes. Since then, in peacetime, Royal Ascot has been an integral part of the Sovereign's year.

The present Queen is a noted authority on equestrian matters. Early in her reign she had success with her colt Aureole, which won the Hardwicke Stakes and the King George VI and Queen Elizabeth Stakes in 1954, and there were further similar wins later in the 1950s.

It is the arrival of the Queen at Ascot that provides the pageantry of the day. The Royal party leave Windsor Castle by car and change to their carriages in Windsor Great Park. In the days of Queen Mary it was noted that she ignored the crowd until she was seated with dignity and comfort in her carriage. Only then did she acknowledge their presence with a royal wave. The Royal Procession consists of five Ascot landaus, which are kept in the Royal Mews at Windsor Castle. These are elegant postilion landaus with basketwork sides, a little lighter and smaller than the semi-state landaus. The Queen's carriage is drawn by four greys, preceded by two outriders, also on greys. The other four carriages are drawn by four bays and preceded by one outrider on a bay. The Royal Coachmen wear scarlet liveries, and the postilions a special Ascot livery. Boots and white breeches are surmounted by a short tunic, the coat of which is black, heavily braided in gold, and the sleeves of which are red. The Royal Procession makes its way up the racecourse past the Silver Ring, the Grandstand and the Royal Enclosure and then turns into the Unsaddling Enclosure, depositing the royal racegoers and their party before the front door of the Royal Box. The Queen's arrival is eagerly awaited by the spectators and press commentators. In the days before the Prince of Wales married, any young girl in the party would be scrutinized as a potential royal bride. Nowadays the fashion experts observe with fascination the latest outfits of the Princess of Wales and the Duchess of York.

During the course of the afternoon, the Queen makes occasional visits to the Paddock. Accompanied by HM Representative, she walks through the crowds to the Paddock. Such is the relaxed atmosphere of an essentially formal occasion that if the Queen wishes to alter her route slightly, she has but to point her umbrella and the racegoers part like an obedient Red Sea.

Until 1972 the Queen's Representative was the Duke of Norfolk who, among his many other qualities, was a master of ceremonial and timing. (He retained his mastery even towards the end of his life, when infirm and walking with a stick.)

Elegance and fashion have always been an integral part of the day. There are strict rules concerning dress in the Royal Enclosure. Gentlemen must wear morning dress and top hats or service dress. Ladies must wear formal day dress with hats that cover the crown of the head. In the 1960s one lady attempted to enter the Royal Enclosure in a trouser suit. She was duly turned away, upon which she removed the trousers and was allowed in in what became a mini-dress. Those admitted to the Royal Enclosure wear badges with their names on them. But the Royal Family wear no badges, thus occasionally an embarrassed official fails to recognize a Royal and attempts to turn him or her away. This has happened to Princess Margaret and Lord Snowdon, and to Prince Andrew.

Royal hats at Royal Ascot (Syndication International)

King Edward VII's death in May 1910 having just preceded the Royal Meeting, all the ladies wore black, and the event became known as Black Ascot. It was a series of photographs of this that inspired Cecil Beaton to re-adapt and re-create the scene in the celebrated musical play and film *My Fair Lady*. His black and white clad ladies, whom he described as 'the motionless frieze of ladies like magpies against a white drop' will forever epitomize all that is elegant at the Royal Meeting at Ascot.

Eton

Eton College lies almost within the shadow of Windsor Castle on the other side of the Thames. The school was founded by Henry VI in 1440, based on William of Wykeham's college at Winchester. Surprisingly, Henry was only 19. The king decreed that there should be a Provost, ten priest Fellows, Chaplains, Clerks and choristers, a Master, an Usher, 70 poor scholars and 13 poor infirm men. The foundation of 70 scholars was said to be based on the 70 disciples of Christ. Other boys were also admitted and allowed to share the scholars' education, but unlike the scholars they had to pay for accommodation and living expenses. Eton is spoken of as the most advanced grammar school in the land. The system remains essentially the same today as it has always done, although there are many improvements, such as language laboratories and less primitive dwellings. Over the years the college has benefited from generous patrons, notably Provost Roger Lupton who built Lupton's Tower, part of the Cloisters, the Long Chamber and Lower School (dating from the 15th century and said to be the oldest schoolroom still in daily use). Eton College Chapel is a twin to St George's Chapel and the Colonnade underneath Upper School is said to have been based on designs by Sir Christopher Wren. Around the college buildings have sprung up the houses of the Oppidans, some of which were built as late as the 1960s. In each one a Housemaster presides over some 50 boys ranging in age from 12 to 18.

The outside visitor to Eton is likely to be faced with a variety of conflicting atmospheres. For a third of the year the town sleeps. Its population of boys and masters is absent on holiday. Even in the working term there are hours of stillness. Then suddenly the division room doors open and for ten minutes or more boys stream out, heading from physics to classics, or from maths to divinity. Often described as resembling a penguin, the Eton boy wears a dark morning coat with a black waistcoat and pinstripe trousers. More often than not, he carries under his arm an impossible number of books, few of which can be vital to his morning class. His stiff white collar and white shirt are further embellished by a little white square of tie, just enough to cover the collar stud. Senior boys in positions of authority are further distinguished by 'stick-ups', the white butterfly collar and full bow tie. And then there is the select and self-electing group called the Eton Society, known more colloquially as 'Pop'. These figures wear sponge-bag trousers, their tailcoats have piping round the edge and the pockets, and they wear gloriously colourful waistcoats, many adorned in brocade. Sadly the day of the top hat is past, although the more enterprising take to them on the annual celebration of The Fourth of June. Interestingly, it is maintained that the boys wear black out of respect to their favourite monarch George III. It is his birthday (in 1738) that is celebrated with characteristic Etonian style.

'The Fourth of June will be celebrated on the Fifth of June' is a curious

Eton College boys

announcement occasionally spotted in the newspaper. Since the middle 1960s the Fourth of June has been a slightly diminished celebration; the fireworks that traditionally ended the day have been discontinued and many boys take the chance for an extra day away rather than a time of *fête* and celebration. However, the cricket match on Agar's Plough is still the scene for some good play and more leisurely picnics, and the procession of boats is the highlight of the day. A variety of impossibly thin old boats make their way down the Thames, their crews adorned in white trousers, short naval jackets and flower-crested boaters. As they pass the crowd of Etonians, parents and friends, they raise their oars and rise from their seats. The final gesture is to salute by removing their boaters. The operation normally proceeds smoothly, but occasionally a member of the crew shows the wear and tear of the picnic, his coordination falters and, to the delight of the crowd, the eight either sink or topple into the Thames. A sinking boat's crew was of course dealt with fairly ruthlessly in the old days back at the boathouse. But those were the days when the cane swung at the least provocation, a tradition happily on the wane.

Perhaps the most memorable Fourth of June took place early in the present Queen's reign. After the procession of boats had passed, the Queen herself sailed down the Thames on the Royal Barge manned by the Bargemaster and his scarlet-clad bargemen and disappeared into the evening mist.

OXFORDSHIRE

East St Helen's, Abingdon

Previous page: The City of Oxford from Hinksey Hill

Oxfordshire Gazetteer

Abingdon (4/1C) An ancient borough and market town south of OXFORD where the river Ock flows down from the Vale of White Horse to meet the Thames. A Benedictine abbey was founded here in AD 675 and for 800 years, until the Dissolution of the Monasteries under Henry VIII, it both created and dominated the town that grew around it. The abbey was completely destroyed by the Danes in the 10th century but recovered enough for William the Conqueror to spend Easter here in 1084. His son Henry I appointed the gifted Italian Abbot Foritius in 1100 and the abbey reached the zenith of its power and prosperity in the 12th century. At the Reformation the worldly Abbot Pentecost accepted the new order and retired on a pension to CUMNOR. There is little left now to be seen, but the impressive 15th-century gateway has survived, attached to the medieval church of St Nicholas off Market Square, and some interesting old buildings down by the river. Of the great abbey church not a stone remains, but there is a pleasant park on the site and some bogus Gothic ruins to help in the contemplation of what has gone.

Across Market Square is East St Helen's Street, a pretty and unspoiled street running down to St Helen's Church. This was always the townspeople's church, a not unworthy successor to the abbey. It was continually enlarged as Abingdon's prosperity grew and now has the very unusual distinction of being wider than it is long, having no fewer than five aisles. Only one other church in England can claim that. There are many monuments to worthy citizens and a rare medieval painted ceiling in the second aisle. The graceful 150 ft spire was added in the 15th century.

The almshouses round the edge of St Helen's churchyard are remarkable, particularly Christ's Hospital, originally founded in 1446, whose houses are connected by a long wooden cloister that gives them a rather Flemish look. Brick Alley and Twitty's Almshouses are also picturesque. Among the original functions of the Christ's Hospital charity was the maintenance of the old bridges over the Ock and Thames that were such a vital part of the town's economy.

Abingdon used to be the county town of Berkshire. However, the power and the glory went to Reading in the 19th century, leaving behind the splendid Town Hall in the market square, built in 1678 by a pupil of Sir Christopher Wren. It is a very fine example of English Renaissance architecture, unusually dignified and grand for such a small town, and a museum is now housed in the former Assize Court on the first floor. Another reminder of Abingdon's past is the gloomily impressive county gaol by the river, which has been converted into a leisure centre.

Much of the town's prosperity in the late Middle Ages was based on cloth manufacture and the antiquary Leland noted in 1549 that it 'standeth by clothing'. Later centuries added brewing, flour milling and agricultural machinery. The famous MG car factory was the biggest employer in Abingdon until it closed in the late 1970s, a decision that still seems inexplicable to many of its inhabitants.

Adderbury (2/1B) A large village south of BANBURY that owed its original prosperity to the wool trade. The Sor brook cuts the village in half as it flows down the hills into the Cherwell. East Adderbury suffers from the main Banbury–OXFORD road (A423) but there are an unusual number of large and fine houses, including the remnants of a great house owned by the dissolute wit and poet Lord Rochester, who was a favourite of Charles II and died at the age of 33 'worn out with sensual pleasure'. His house was much altered in the 18th century and a large part of Adderbury, east of the main road, was pulled down to make way for a park.

West Adderbury, down by the brook, is quieter, with winding lanes and paths. The parish church of St Mary is one of the glories of Oxfordshire. Exceptionally large, with a spire that is a landmark across the valley, it was mainly built in the 13th century and has a splendid chancel erected about 1415 by New College, Oxford. (The college owned the living, and still does.) Over the great east window is a bust and heraldic shield of William of Wykeham, the founder of New College and owner of Broughton Castle a few miles to the north-west (*see* Broughton). The interior of the

Adderbury

church is light and spacious, and there is fine medieval stone carving and an ancient screen. A large 14th-century tithe barn is near by.

Adwell *see* Lewknor

Albury (4/3B) and **Tiddington** (4/3B) are two small villages on the OXFORD–THAME road where the boundary with Buckinghamshire is marked by the river Thame. Albury has a tiny church surrounded by a handful of thatched cottages and approached down a remote road across a field. A few hundred yards to the east, but only approachable on foot, is **Rycote Chapel.** By car, the drive to the chapel is off the A329 road which leads south-west out of Thame.

The chapel was built in 1449 by Richard Quartermayne, a member of an old Oxfordshire family whose punning coat of arms (four hands) can also be seen in the church of CHALGROVE. To the chapel was attached a chantry with a foundation of three priests whose duty was to pray for their benefactor. About 100 years after its foundation, the Rycote property was bought by Lord Williams of Thame, who had become very rich after the Dissolution of the Monas-

teries. He built a great Tudor mansion here which was visited at least six times by Queen Elizabeth, later by James I and Charles I.

Although the chapel exterior is an interesting example of Perpendicular architecture, it is the extraordinary interior that draws visitors to it. Halfway down the church and virtually blocking the chancel are two very large, square wooden pews that are really wooden rooms with superbly carved screens and detailed fretwork. The family pew has a second storey approached by wooden stairs; the royal pew has a remarkable wooden dome over it, decorated inside with stars on a blue background. It is thought that they were constructed for the visit of Charles I in 1625, the family pew being possibly a little earlier.

The splendid wagon-vaulted roof of the chapel is the original 1449 one and also has traces of the later decoration with stars and blue background. There is nothing quite like this fascinating place anywhere else in the county, perhaps in all England. It is owned and maintained by English Heritage and is open every day.

The great house built by Lord Williams was destroyed by fire; only the stable block remains and is now a private house. The Oxfordshire

Rycote Chapel

Way runs through the park past the chapel and a venerable yew tree planted, according to tradition, to commemorate the coronation of King Stephen in 1135.

Alkerton *see* Shutford

Alveston *see* Brize Norton

Ambrosden *see* Bicester

Appleton (4/1B) To the west of OXFORD towards the Thames below Cumnor Hill, this is a mixed village of brick and stone, as if unable to make up its mind which material to use. The ancient stone wall around the manor has a mellow brick upper storey as its solution to the dilemma. The manor house itself is partly 12th century, one of the oldest in the county, and its Norman doorway can still be seen over the churchyard wall. A gateway leads to an attractive old church, basically Norman with a 15th-century tower and later additions elsewhere. There is a fine tomb to a Fettiplace Lord of the Manor who was knighted by Queen Elizabeth on her progress through WOODSTOCK in 1597. A shroud brass commemorates John Midrington, 'gent and his wife Dorothe', who 'toke relygyon in ye convent of Syon' after his death in 1518.

Eaton (4/1B) is a stone-built hamlet of cottages and an inviting pub a mile to the north. A lonely and narrow road leads across the fields down to the Thames at Bablockhythe.

Ardington (6/2A) The road leading east from WANTAGE towards WALLINGFORD is known as the Portway and was built by the Romans, probably because the older Ridgeway on top of the downs was too exposed. The first village east of Wantage is Ardington, with a school, old rectory and Boar's Head Inn grouped attractively around the squat spire of the little church. There are some very curious carved heads on the tower and a fine Norman doorway with a corbel over it of a pelican feeding its young, an ancient Christian symbol. The handsome early Georgian Ardington House has a faintly Baroque feel about it and is built in Berkshire blue and red brick. The rooms are quite small, except for the hall with its grand staircase of the kind known as 'imperial'. The house was once owned by Lord Wantage, one of the first winners of the Victoria Cross in the Crimean War, and is open to the public during the summer.

Lockinge (6/2A) is an estate village under the

downs with an old church in a valley among trees. Next to it was a big house pulled down after the Second World War – now only trees and stables remain.

Ardley *see* Fritwell

Ascott-under-Wychwood *see* Shipton-under-Wychwood

Ashbury (5/3A) The last downland village in the Vale of White Horse before the Wiltshire border. It is all that a village should be with its chalk and thatch cottages, cheerful inn, ancient manor house and large and stately church looking across the Vale to the distant tower of SHRIVENHAM church to the north. A steep hill leads to the top of the downs and **Wayland's Smithy,** a prehistoric chamber tomb flanked by sarsen stones in a clump of beech trees. Much later the West Saxons fought here on the border between Wessex and Mercia and named it after Wayland, the magical smith of Germanic legend. It was already known by that name at the Conquest and is a place of haunting antiquity.

Deep in the downs in the remotest spot imaginable is **Ashdown House** (5/3A), a 17th-century hunting lodge built by an Earl of Craven. It is quite a small house but very tall and well proportioned rather like a doll's house. There is a fine oak staircase lined by contemporary portraits and, for those with the energy to climb to the roof, spectacular views of the downs. It is now owned by the National Trust and is open from April to October on Wednesdays and Saturdays.

Asthall (3/2A) In a beautiful, little-visited part of the Windrush valley between BURFORD and MINSTER LOVELL, just north of the A40. A large Jacobean manor house built in 1620 looks across the churchyard and down the village street towards the old river bridge, near which the Roman road called Akeman Street crossed the Windrush. Above on the hill is Asthall Barrow, a Saxon burial place. The church of St Nicholas is a mixture of dates and was much altered in the 19th century, but the curiously lofty chantry chapel contains a fine 14th-century effigy of Lady Joan Cornwall and some interesting medieval stained glass. From the other side of the bridge the view across the willow-lined river Windrush to the village is quintessential England.

Ashton *see* Bampton

Aston Rowant (1/2A) A peaceful village down a cul-de-sac under the Chiltern escarpment where the M40 motorway breaks through to the plain of Oxford. A place of flint and brick walls and cottages around a pleasant green with chestnuts. Home Farm is an agreeable house behind its well-cut hedges. The old church, originally Norman, has atmosphere and some interesting monuments, especially the one to Lady Cecil Hobbee, a colourful Elizabethan lady at prayer. The Purbeck marble font is unusual and is about the same date as Rowland de Eston, after whom the village took its name in the 13th century. Aston Park is now a development of expensive houses on either side of a drive with many decorative trees and a lake. Rather American in feeling, it is well designed and attractive.

High above on the chalk hill is the Aston Rowant Nature Reserve run by the Nature Conservancy Council. Despite the M40 cutting through it there are some interesting walks and dramatic views towards Oxford.

Kingston Blount (1/2A), a short distance north-east along the B4009, is a larger modern village. The Ridgeway and a disused railway line run under the hills south of both villages.

Aston Tirrold (7/1A) Lying below the downs off the A417 near Streatley, Aston Tirrold is a village of great charm with its half-timbered houses, cob and brick walls and its thatched cottages. The flint church of St Michael is mainly 14th century but there are earlier details with a Norman doorway and an even earlier one, probably Saxon, leading into the vestry. The north aisle was built by a Victorian rector who held the living for 67 years, from 1845 to 1912. There is a fine Queen Anne manor house next to the church.

Aston Upthorpe (7/1A), or 'upper village', actually joins Ashton Tirrold and it is hard to tell which village you are in, although both parishes jealously guarded their separate indentity for nearly a thousand years. Both the Astons date from Saxon times and it is generally thought that King Alfred's great victory over the Danes at Assendune was fought near here. The plain, simple little church with its roughly carved wooden roof has a window to St Birinus, the Apostle of Wessex, who is much venerated in this area.

The little Presbyterian chapel should also be seen as a rare example of an 18th-century meeting house for Nonconformists – one of the earliest in the county and still in use.

Looking down on both villages is Blewburton Hill with a clearly visible Iron Age hill fort on top of it. This is good walking country with tracks leading to the downs and the Ridgeway.

Baldons, The (4/2B&C) **Marsh Baldon** (4/2C) is down a gated road just east of the HENLEY-ON-THAMES road at NUNEHAM COURTENAY and is a pretty jumble of thatched, half-timbered and modern houses around a large, open green with farms and fields beyond. The small church of St Peter on the edge of the green has a strange octagonal tower built about 1300 which was obviously intended to carry a spire – but whether one was ever added is not known. Inside the church is an enormous copy of Guido Reni's picture of the Annunciation, looking very incongruous. **Toot Baldon** (4/2B) (Toot means 'hill') has wide views across the valley of the Thame towards the Chilterns, and a very attractive Jacobean manor house and farm. The 13th-century church is hard to find down an avenue of chestnuts, but it is well kept and feels used.

Bampton (3/2B) In 1069, only three years after the battle of Hastings, William the Conqueror

Bampton Church

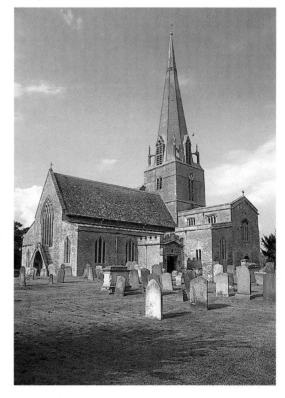

Ashdown House (see p. 68)

gave the manor of Bampton and all the land stretching south-east to the Thames to Leofric, Bishop of Exeter, and a copy of the splendid deed of gift can be read in the church. For over 900 years Exeter has kept this connection.

On the A4095 south-west of WITNEY, and sited well back from the Thames, which used to flood disastrously until brought under control in the 19th century, Bampton has a distinguished air with many elegant Georgian houses, a market place and a splendid church whose 170 ft spire is a landmark for miles around. Until the 18th century there was a weekly market here serving the surrounding villages; Bampton still has the feel of a small market town rather than a large village, with a town hall and many inns where

extensive restoration in the 19th century. The massive Early English arches supporting the central tower are impressive. The churchyard is surrounded by a stately manor house, old rectory and deanery (once owned by the Dean of Exeter), giving it a cathedral close atmosphere.

Ashton (3/2B) and **Cote** (3/2B) are hamlets of Bampton, part of the original grant to Leofric, lying to the east in flat meadowland. Cote has a beautiful early 18th-century Baptist chapel and a romantic-looking Jacobean manor house once owned by the Horde family, whose tombs are in a family chapel in Bampton church. A remote and lovely road leads down to the Thames at **Shifford** (3/3B) now only a farm and church, but supposedly the site of a great gathering of thanes and knights called by King Alfred in the 9th century, a forerunner of Parliament.

Banbury (2/1B) With its population of nearly 40,000, Banbury is the second largest town in Oxfordshire and undisputed capital of the northern part of the county (known to the locals as Banburyshire).

Since earliest times it has been the principal meeting point of roads from the Midlands to London and OXFORD, and the old salt road from Droitwich passed just south of the town. The wool trade brought great prosperity here in the later Middle Ages and communications were further improved by the cutting of the Oxford Canal, which reached Banbury in 1778, and the building of the railway in the next century.

An important castle existed here from the 12th century onwards and the town steadily grew under its protecting walls. In the great religious troubles of the 17th century, Banbury and its shire embraced Puritanism with great enthusiasm, an old rhyme speaking of a Banbury man 'hanging his cat on a Monday, for killing a mouse on a Sunday'. Naturally enough the citizens were 'hot for Parliament' in the Civil War, which caused great damage to town and castle: the latter was completely demolished in 1648 and the stone used for rebuilding.

There was a very fine and large medieval church here, looking from old prints like one of the Gloucestershire 'wool' churches, with the great windows and spaciousness characteristic of Perpendicular architecture. In the 18th century it was in a bad state of repair and the decision was taken to destroy it completely by blowing it up with gunpowder. It was replaced in 1793 by the present large, rather coldly Classical Georgian church.

the main roads cross. One of these is the Morris Clown, a reminder that Morris dancing has long been popular here; the annual festival brings hundreds of visitors and dancers.

There has been a church here since Saxon days, its size and quality a measure of Bampton's past. Mainly 13th century, but with fine windows and additions in the next two centuries, it is more interesting outside than in, due to

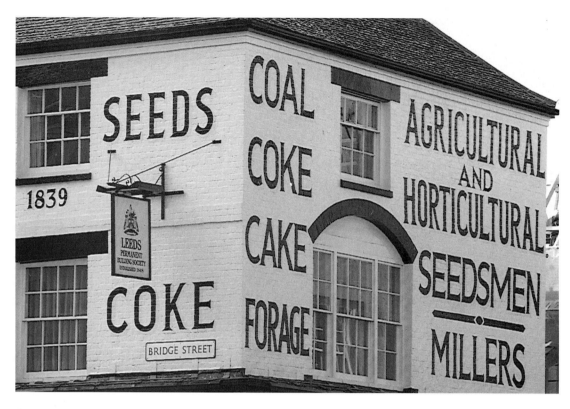

Banbury is still an important agriculture centre

Motorists passing through on the main road see Horse Fair and North and South Bar Street, which are wide and tree-lined with some attractive golden stone buildings on either side. The famous Banbury Cross at the crossroads is actually Victorian, for the original Banbury crosses (there were three) were destroyed by Puritan zeal. The 'Ride-a-Cock Horse to Banbury Cross' nursery rhyme is very old but owes its universal fame to an enterprising Banbury printer in the early 19th century.

The market place is large and has a busy air about it, but the famous cattle market has now moved to a site by the railway station. It is the largest cattle market in England, handling 600,000 head of livestock a year, and is a remarkable sight on Tuesdays, Wednesdays and Thursdays.

There is much new development in Banbury with modern engineering, food and hi-tech factories in industrial estates on the outskirts. Banbury has always been adaptable to change and this is neatly illustrated by the conversion of the façade of an Absolute Baptist chapel (there were three different Baptist sects at one time) of 1840 into a supermarket entrance.

An excellent museum by Banbury Cross is a good place to visit before walking around this interesting old town.

Barfords, The (1/3C) West of DEDDINGTON along the Swere valley are **Barford St Michael** and **Barford St John,** ironstone villages of character on either side of the river.

St Michael is the largest, with lanes running down a hill to the river and old golden brown cottages and houses. The George Inn is thatched and has a date of 1679. The church sits on a hill with a squat Norman tower and two doorways, the one near the road providing a very good example of zigzag decoration and beakheads. Across the river, St John is only a manor farm and a small church amid the farm buildings.

To the west along the Swere is **South Newington** (from Old English *nēowan tūne,* 'new homestead'), which is partly on the A361 CHIPPING NORTON to BANBURY road. The church of St Peter ad Vincula is much visited to see its famous medieval wall paintings, which are among the finest in the land. There is an excellent guide but only space here to note the martyrdom of Thomas Becket and a stunningly colourful depiction of the Virgin and Child, the paint still fresh and glowing after 600 years.

Milcombe (2/1B) is a farming village to the west of the main Banbury road with an attractive old dovecot in a field and an inn called The Horse and Groom. Just south of BLOXHAM on the Barford road is a modern housing development that is sadly noticeable for its use of pink bricks and brown windows in a part of England noted for its unique orange-coloured stone.

Bartons, The (2/1C) Three villages rolled into one on the B4030 CHIPPING NORTON to BICESTER road with the little river Dorn running through them all before joining the Glyme at WOOTTON. **Westcote Barton** (2/1C) has a Perpendicular church of great charm, painted in vigorous colours as it would have been in medieval times before such things were disapproved of. **Middle Barton** (2/1C) has old stone houses either side of a ford across the Dorn and much new development, mostly rather sympathetic in colour and scale. **Steeple Barton** (2/1C) by contrast is just a farm, cottages and, a large church with 15th-century tower some distance from the village. The interior is plain but there is some interesting stone carving and a floor slab to Sir Philip Constable complaining that 'his whole estate was confiscated by the usurpers for his loyalty to King Charles I'. From the churchyard you look across a lake to Barton Abbey, an ivy-covered house on the site of what was a cell of Osney Abbey before the Dissolution of the Monasteries.

Baulking *see* Uffington

Beckley *see* Otmoor

Begbroke *see* Yarnton

Benson (4/3C) A cheerful, bustling village just off the A423 HENLEY-ON-THAMES to OXFORD road, 2 miles from a large RAF station that houses the Queen's Flight. On entering the village the traveller is confronted with two rather grand 18th-century inns, the Castle and the White Hart, and there are other elegant Georgian buildings among the modern shopfronts. The most interesting, however, is the huge 18th-century barn in mellow red brick on the EWELME road. There are seven entrances and the tiled roof is over an acre in extent. The cavernous interior is still in farming use despite continual aircraft landings a few yards away. An unusual museum devoted to bicycles is opposite the scrapyard in the village.

To the north is **Berrick Salome** (4/3C) – derived from Old English *berewic*, 'barley farm', and Suleham, a Norman family name. The small church down a track was restored in 1890 in a curiously cottagey style and is rather engaging.

Bicester (2/3C) This has always been an important crossroads town and the centre of the flat plain that lies north-east of OXFORD towards the Buckinghamshire border. There has been much modern development in a haphazard manner, but the old market square retains the feel of a country town, with the parish church of St Edburg near by. This was built in the 12th century and dedicated to a holy nun, St Eadburga, the subject of a considerable cult in Saxon times. Three impressive Norman arches remain and many monuments, particularly to the Crocker family who lived here for 400 years.

There was a considerable Roman camp at **Ambrosden** (4/3A), a name that some have associated with the Romano-British general Ambrosius Aurelianus (or Emrys), who fought against, but was finally defeated by, the Saxons in the 5th century AD. The old village centre is hemmed in by the large military installations of the Ministry of Defence but the long, straight minor road south-west to OTMOOR is very peaceful.

Launton (2/3C), virtually a suburb of Bicester, has an attractive group of manor farm and old church with remarkable flying buttresses supporting the 800-year-old tower. Bishop Skinner lived here during the Commonwealth, having been turned out of the see of Oxford, and is said to have ordained 300 priests in defiance of the Puritans.

Binsey (4/1B) Although part of the city of OXFORD, Binsey is a rural oasis reminiscent of Normandy, with a thatched inn popular with undergraduates, farmyard smells and one of the smallest churches in England approached down an avenue of chestnut trees. There was once a much larger town here that was a centre for pilgrimages to St Margaret's Well, which is still in the churchyard. In the 8th century St Frideswide, a Saxon princess, hid in the woods near by to escape her amorous royal suitor, because she wanted to become a nun. When he was struck blind she prayed to St Margaret of Antioch and water gushed from the ground where the well is and healed him. St Frideswide founded an oratory on the site of the present 12th-century church and a nunnery in Oxford. It was in a punt on the river near Binsey that the Reverend Charles Dodgson (Lewis Carroll) first told the story of Alice in Wonderland to Alice Liddell, the young daughter of the Dean of Christ Church. From the towpath there is a fine view across Port Meadow to north Oxford.

Bix (7/3A) The name means 'boxwood' or 'hedge'. The fast road up the hill from HENLEY-ON-THAMES towards OXFORD was one of the first dual carriageways in England, much admired in the 1930s. The main part of this scattered village is round a very large common on top of the hill, marked on old maps as Bix Brand. There are fine views over the STONOR valley. Down a steep hill past Bix Hall is the romantic ruin of a small Norman church, abandoned in 1875 when the Victorian church was built on Bix Common. Beyond is the Warburg nature reserve at Bix Bottom, 250 acres of typical Chiltern woodland, chalk grassland and scrub imaginatively managed by BBONT, the Berkshire, Buckinghamshire and Oxfordshire Naturalists Trust, to conserve the remarkable variety of flora and fauna. Up the hill beyond the reserve you can walk to **Maidensgrove** (7/3A) and **Russell's Water** (7/3A), two remote and tiny hamlets on a wide Chiltern plateau.

On the other side of the dual carriageway a minor road passes an attractive Queen Anne house into Lambridge woods, where Grim's Dyke can be followed through the beechwoods stretching towards Henley.

Black Bourton *see* Brize Norton

Bladon; Blenheim Palace *see* Woodstock

Bletchingdon (4/1A) Village on a high ridge north of OXFORD on the B4027, with views across OTMOOR to the east and the Oxford Canal to the west. Stone cottages are gathered round a green in the centre of the village with the park gates – and a pub called the Black Head after a manservant at a nearby house. There are some fine-looking 17th-century houses on the ISLIP road. Bletchingdon Park, now a school, is a classical 18th-century mansion, on the site of a Royalist stronghold in the Civil War that was surrendered to Cromwell in person in 1645. On the edge of the park is the church of St Giles, rather over-restored in the last century but with some interesting memorials to former squires.

When the Oxford Canal was cut, about 1770, the hamlet of **Enslow** grew around its wharf and the picturesque Rock of Gibraltar Inn was built.

Blewbury (6/3A) A large and delightful village on the Berkshire Downs, between STREATLEY and HARWELL. The village forms a square, with a brook running through the middle, around the village church and is best seen on foot when the wealth of timbered buildings, thatched cottages and old cob walls can be really appreciated. Blewbury has always been a substantial place, since first mentioned as *Bleoburg* well before Domesday, and the fine parish church, with its wide aisles and long nave, reflects this. The stone-vaulted chancel and transepts are late Norman and once supported a central tower, but this has disappeared and been replaced by a west tower of the 15th century. Interesting details inside the church include a beautiful medieval door to the rood loft and a black letter Bible displayed in the aisle. An enormous Charles II coat of arms hangs over the door.

The downs rise south of the village up to Blewbury Down past Churn Knob, where St Birinus is said to have preached the gospel to the people of Wessex in the 7th century.

West the main road leads to **Upton** (6/3A), a small village with many new houses and a few older ones and farms. A little Victorian church hides behind yew trees with just a trace of its Norman origins visible.

Bloxham (2/1B) A large orange-coloured iron-stone village south-west of BANBURY, on two small hills, with winding lanes and thatched cottages. Bloxham School is a Victorian Gothic design by the architect G. E. Street. His buildings can be seen all over Oxfordshire where he was diocesan architect for many years. The school was founded in 1860 and dominates the Banbury end of Bloxham.

At the other end of the village is the great church of St Mary, one of the finest in the county with its wonderful 14th-century spire almost 200 ft high, and remarkable carvings of the Last Judgement by the west door. The cathedral-like interior is very impressive, with 13th-century arches and lively medieval carving. The Milcombe Chapel with its enormous windows dates from 150 years later and is thought to be by the mason who built the similar chancel at ADDERBURY. The Victorian east window is the

The Milcombe Chapel, St Mary's Church, Bloxham

Detail of the Last Judgment, St Mary's Church, Bloxham

work of William Morris and Burne-Jones.

Bloxham's position on the A361 road from CHIPPING NORTON and the wool-producing Cotswolds was responsible for its prosperity in the Middle Ages; and today being near to Banbury industry gives employment to its inhabitants. The lordship of the manor has been held since 1455 by the Lords Saye and Sele of nearby BROUGHTON and the patron of the church is Eton College, which acquired it in 1547 after Godstow Abbey was dissolved.

Boars Hill *see* Cumnor

Bourton *see* Shrivenham

Brightwell Baldwin (4/3C) A picturesque village west of WATLINGTON in rolling farmland. The whole of one side is taken up by Brightwell Park

with its fine cedars and the bright spring that gives the village its name flowing through it. The wall and gates survive but the big Georgian house has been demolished and the stables made into a house. The 14th-century church is quite plain inside except for the north aisle chapel, which is a mass of marble monuments to the Stone family who held the manor for 400 years. Earlier Stones are remembered who were buried in London before the Great Fire in 1666, but whose graves 'were not found after that dismal conflagration'.

Britwell Salome (1/1B) (pronounced 'Sallom') is near the Icknield Way under the steeply sloping Britwell Hill which leads to the top of the Chiltern escarpment. There is a pretty little church hidden behind Priory Farm, so called because a community of French nuns found refuge there after the Revolution.

Brightwell-cum-Sotwell *see* Wallingford

Brize Norton (3/2B) The enormous RAF transport base dominates this part of Oxfordshire, with VC10 aircraft constantly taking off and landing. It is a pleasant surprise therefore to find that the old grey stone villages round the perimeter seem to take it all in their stride and retain much of their original character. Brize Norton itself has a Norman church, the only one in England dedicated to St Brice, an obscure 5th-century French bishop. The road out to **Carterton** (3/1B) leads past an immense aircraft hangar, the biggest in Europe, with 5½ acres of space inside it. Carterton is named after a Mr Carter who bought 750 acres of farmland from the Duke of Marlborough before the First World War to create smallholdings. The scheme was not a success but the arrival of the RAF in the 1930s gave it a boost and it is now a prospering new town, the only one in this book with a 20th-century name.

Black Bourton (3/2B) is an ancient place on the southern perimeter, so called because the manor was held by the 'black' monks of Osney Abbey: one of the houses is still known as Bourton Abbots. The church with its Norman chancel and Early English nave contains some delightful wall paintings, executed about 1250 and covered in whitewash for four centuries. The charmingly naïve depictions of the Blessed Virgin, St Thomas Becket and St Richard give a real insight into the simple faith of the peasants who worshipped here 700 years ago. The Black Bourton brook runs through the village on its way to the Thames.

The village green at Kencot. The dragon and Sagittarian figure reflect the existence of a 12th-century carving of the same subject in St George's Church

Alvescot (3/1B) completes the airport circuit – more old stone houses and attractive farm buildings. The old, plain church is on a hill by itself. There is a grand memorial to an 18th-century rector, another to his poor wife who lost six children before they were five years old.

Broadwell (3/1B) Broadwell and its close neighbour **Kencot** are two of the prettiest villages in Oxfordshire, in the flat upper Thames Valley between WITNEY and Lechlade. Broadwell is a village of well-proportioned stone houses, an inviting-looking inn and a Gothic-windowed manor house behind the church, replacing one destroyed by fire. The old gate piers of the former house remain in the centre of the village. The church of SS Peter and Paul is surprisingly large, with a beautiful tower and spire untouched since it was built about 1250. The doorway is a fine example of Norman carving, but inside the church was severely restored in the 19th century. The great Norman arch that supports the tower is impressive. On a different scale the royal arms of James I are a

good example of the versatility of Stuart woodwork.

Kencot runs down to a small green and little church of St George, just as old but much humbler than its neighbour. Over the entrance there is a most extraordinary piece of 12th-century carving: a centaur, half man, half horse, shooting an arrow down the yawning throat of a monster with the word 'Sagittarius' crudely carved above it. It must have made a strong impression on the villagers 800 years ago – and still does today.

Broughton (1/3B) Coming from nearby BANBURY to this small ironstone village with old and new houses mingled together, the traveller is quite unprepared for the remarkable castle tucked away behind trees on the edge of the village. Built originally by John de Broughton in about 1300 as a small fortified manor house, it was acquired by the great William of Wykeham, Bishop of Winchester and founder of New College, Oxford, in 1377. Through his niece the manor came into the possession of Sir William Fiennes, 2nd Lord Saye and Sele, in 1450 and the 21st Baron lives there today with his family.

In 1554 Richard Fiennes entirely remodelled the old manor and built the Tudor house we can see now, although fortunately some of the medieval vaulted rooms and the private chapel are left. The interior is exceptionally interesting, with its Great Hall incorporating the older one, with fine rooms and splendidly decorative chimneypieces and plaster ceilings.

During the Civil War William Fiennes, 1st Viscount Saye and Sele, was a leading opponent of Charles I and prominent Roundheads met at Broughton to plot their next moves. William, however, thought the execution of the king was going too far and was eventually pardoned when the monarchy was restored in 1660. He was nicknamed 'old subtlety' with good reason.

Broughton Castle is open to the public during the summer and is one of the most fascinating places in the county. The fine 13th-century church outside the moat should also be visited; its tombs and memorials to the castle owners from 1300 to the present day are an informative essay in changing taste.

Henry James wrote of Broughton about a hundred years ago: 'it lies rather low and its woods and pastures slope down to it; it has a deep, clear moat all round, spanned by a bridge that passes under a charming old gate-tower and nothing can be sweeter than to see its clustered walls of yellow-brown stone so sharply islanded while its gardens bloom on the other side of the water.'

Broughton Poggs *see* Filkins

Buckland (3/2C) A compact and attractive village in the upper Thames Valley, well set back from the A420 OXFORD – Swindon road on a low ridge of Corallian ragstone above the Thames. All the houses are of stone and there have been few modern additions. Buckland House, now a school, was built by the Throckmorton family who owned the manor for 200 years until 1910. It was designed by John Wood the Younger of Bath and is described in Kelly's Directory (1928) as 'a handsome mansion in the Italian style'. Indeed it is, but its classical front and octagonal wings seem curiously alien to its particular surroundings. The older manor house behind

the church was turned into stables when Buckland House was built. It is now a house again; it has unusual Gothic windows.

The church is large with a sturdy tower and impressive Norman nave. Other points to note are the 13th-century chancel with its fine roof and the Jacobean pulpit with its 'perspective' carving. The rich and colourful mosaics that cover the whole south transept are a remarkable example of High Victorian taste. A tablet in the chancel to a Catholic priest who was chaplain to the Throckmortons in the 18th century is a monument to religious tolerance long before ecumenism was heard of.

Bucknell (2/2C) *Bukenhull* ('Bucca's Hill') was the origin of the name for this old stone village around a crossroads on slightly rising ground north-west of BICESTER. There are wide grass verges, a stream and an old manor house.

St Peter's Church has a massive Norman tower, but was remodelled in the 13th century and remains a remarkably unchanged church of that period, apart from some 17th- and 18th-century wall tablets to the Trotman family.

Burford (3/1A) This is always known as the gateway to the Cotswolds and is an ancient and picturesque wool town in a beautiful stretch of the Windrush valley, near the Gloucestershire border. The High Street leads down the hill between pollarded lime trees to the old river bridge at the bottom of the valley and consists of a remarkable array of golden stone houses, shops and inns. Virtually all are good to look at and range from the gabled 16th-century Court House, now a museum, to an elegant early 18th-century town house of great style that is now a Methodist chapel. Just off the High Street is Burford Priory, once an Augustinian hospice. It was acquired by Sir Lawrence Tanfield, Lord Chief Baron of the Exchequer to James I, who built himself a grand house and entertained his sovereign there. Subsequently owned by William Lenthall, Speaker of the Long Parliament of Charles I, it was reduced in size in the 19th century and is once again a monastic house – of Anglican nuns.

During the Civil War Charles I was here twice and stayed at the George Inn while his army extricated itself from encirclement by the Parliamentary forces; and Charles II stayed at Burford Priory 30 years later during a visit to Oxfordshire. Nell Gwynne was supposed to have been there, too, a legend given credibility by the

Typical Cotswold stone wall with Burford church in the distance

fact that her royal offspring was entitled Earl of Burford, a name still borne by the descendants of that union.

At the bottom of the hill past some medieval almshouses is the great church of St John the Baptist, with the Windrush curling round the churchyard. Originally built in the 12th century it has a superb Norman tower with a 180 ft spire added in about 1400. The added weight nearly proved disastrous, but extra buttressing and walling up of the transept arch prevented its collapse. As Burford's prosperity grew with the wool trade the pious citizens added further aisles and chapels to the existing building, giving it a somewhat complicated interior. The Lady Chapel, for example, sticks out at the west end at a strange angle because it used to be a separate building, before being incorporated into the main church in the 15th century.

The Tanfield monument of 1626 exemplifies Jacobean *nouveau riche* pomposity; the earlier Harman monument of 1569 in the nave has two Red Indians depicted on it, the earliest Americans commemorated anywhere in England. Christopher Kempster, a Burford master mason who worked with Wren on St Paul's Cathedral and also built ABINGDON town hall, is buried in the south transept.

The Victorian restoration of the church by G. E. Street was relatively mild but alarmed William Morris, who founded The Society for the Protection of Ancient Buildings in consequence. When he wrote to the vicar to remonstrate the reply was, 'The church is mine, Sir, and I shall stand on my head in it if I choose.'

Probably the newest thing in Burford is a simple plaque on the church wall, unveiled in 1979, by Anthony Wedgwood Benn, recalling three Levellers who were shot. Some regiments of Cromwell's army had mutinied in 1649, accusing him of betraying the principles for which they had fought. In a brilliant night march Cromwell took them by surprise and shot the ringleaders in the churchyard.

Just across the Windrush on the A361 is **Fulbrook** (3/1A), a small stone village almost overtaken by Burford. The simple Norman church, with its vigorously carved capitals and corbels and traces of 13th-century decoration on the chancel arch, contrasts nicely with the grandeur of Burford.

Buscot (3/1C) As you travel west on the lovely

A417 road from FARINGDON to Lechlade, Buscot is the last village before crossing the Thames into Gloucestershire. A long stone wall, fine trees and wrought-iron gates lead to Buscot Park, a large stone Georgian house that now belongs to the National Trust. It was purchased in 1889 by Alexander Henderson who had made a fortune in the City and became the first Lord Faringdon. He was a keen, if somewhat eclectic art collector and his fine collection of pictures from every period can be seen at Buscot. A patron of William Morris across the river at KELMSCOTT, he also bought Burne-Jones's four paintings of The Legend of the Briar Rose for a specially designed setting in the saloon.

Further west is the village of Buscot, small and much rebuilt by the Hendersons, with a pleasant footpath to the lock and weir on the Thames a quarter of a mile away. You can continue over the river and walk to Kelmscott through lush river meadows. Still further west in

The rectory at Buscot

this straggling parish is the old church with a superb Norman chancel arch, some exotic furnishings and a Burne-Jones window given by Lord Faringdon. The beautiful Queen Anne rectory next door is also National Trust property.

Eaton Hastings (3/1C) is hardly a village at all: just a few estate houses round Buscot Park and an ancient church, down by the Thames, with another Burne-Jones window.

Carterton *see* Brize Norton

Cassington *see* Eynsham

Caversfield (2/3C) The village itself has been largely engulfed by the spread of BICESTER, but the lovely church in the grounds of Caversfield House is one of the county's oldest. The saddleback tower is partly Saxon, with typical tiny windows set in it; the rest of the church is Norman and Early English, with a very early, simple font. On the floor under the tower is the

earliest inscribed bell in England, dating from about 1215. The Latin inscription can be clearly read: 'In honour of God and St Laurence...'. There is a charming brass to John Langston and his wife and 22 children, dated 1506.

Chadlington (2/2C) An elongated village stretching for about a mile along a slope in a particularly beautiful stretch of the Evenlode valley north-west of CHARLBURY. Stone cottages along the road and an old manor house of the 18th century are joined with a medieval church of some beauty externally, but restored inside in the 19th century. To the east is **Dean** (1/2C), a tiny hamlet with a handsome Georgian house and an ancient standing stone known as the Hawk Stone.

On the southern bank of the Evenlode are two enchanting hamlets: **Chilson** (3/2A), a single street of old stone houses and farms; and, a short walk east along the Oxfordshire Way, **Shorthampton** (3/2A), just a large farm and cottages and one of the most endearing little churches in the county with wall paintings, box pews and tiny Norman window.

This whole area, where the Evenlode flows through a gentle valley under the lee of Wychwood Forest, is remarkably unknown and unspoiled and has been praised by Hilaire Belloc in *Sonnets and Verse:*

> The tender Evenlode that makes
> Her meadows hush to hear the sound
> Of waters mingling in the brakes
> And binds my heart to English ground.
>
> A lovely river, all alone,
> She lingers in the hills and holds
> A hundred little towns of stone
> Forgotten in the western wolds.

('Dedicatory Ode')

Chalgrove (4/3C) Rather a surprise. Situated in the middle of the flat and fertile farmland to the west of the Chiltern ridge between STADHAMPTON and WATLINGTON, this is a large and almost entirely modern village except for a few old houses in the High Street by a stream. The big church with its handsome tower looking across the fields provides a contrast to the new houses surrounding it. Mainly 14th-century, it has a fine chancel notable for its medieval wall paintings, which are arranged in tiers, like cartoons.

The battle of Chalgrove Field in 1643 was won for Charles I by Prince Rupert's cavalry. It was not much of an affair, but is remembered because the great Parliamentary leader John Hampden was mortally wounded. He managed to escape to THAME, but died a few days later. A monument north of the village marks the spot.

Charlbury (3/3A) A delightful small country town in the Evenlode valley about 14 miles north-west of OXFORD. The manor was founded in Anglo-Saxon times and later it was owned by the Benedictines of Eynsham Abbey until the Dissolution. Narrow Sheep Street and Market Street cross the town with old stone houses and shops; Church Street, with some handsome houses on either side, is wider and is the scene of the annual Charlbury Fair held in September. St Mary's Church is large, and partly Norman, but mostly 13th and 14th century, with some beautiful window tracery and a fine tower looking out across the river valley. One of its Elizabethan vicars was President of St John's College, Oxford, and a translator of the Authorized Version of the Bible.

Lee Place, which used to be a dower house for the Lees of DITCHLEY, is an elegant Georgian house in a small park in the middle of Charlbury. The best way to visit Charlbury is to come by train along the Cotswold line to the station, designed by Brunel and hardly altered since it was built. An engaging little museum in Market Street gives a flavour of 19th-century activities (the key can be obtained from the pharmacy opposite). Since the 17th century Charlbury has had a Quaker tradition and the Friend's Meeting House in Market Street was built in 1779. The excellent *Town Trail,* published by the Charlbury Society, can be bought for a small sum at the local Post Office.

The 2000-acre estate of Cornbury Park and Wychwood Forest provide a backdrop to Charlbury on the western side of the Evenlode. Cornbury is one of the greatest houses in Oxfordshire, but is private and hidden in the thickly wooded forest. Partly Tudor, it was enlarged in the early 17th century. At the Restoration, Charles II gave it to the Earl of Clarendon, the Stuart statesman and historian whose daughter married James II. He built the fine Renaissance wing, best seen from the hill above Fawler on the STONESFIELD road.

A pleasant footpath leads from the lodge opposite Lee Place to FINSTOCK along the edge of the park, but the ancient rights of way through the forest have been discontinued.

Overleaf: Chastleton House

Charlton-on-Otmoor *see* Otmoor

Charney Bassett (3/3C) A Vale of White Horse village north of WANTAGE within sight of the downs. Charney comes from 'Churn', which was the name of the river here before it became known as the Ock in the Middle Ages. 'Ock' derives from a Celtic word for salmon: the river was famous for its fishing before the Thames became polluted. Bassett was a Lord of the Manor in the Middle Ages. There is an engaging little church with a quaint 17th-century belfry and some very good Norman carving: especially the tympanum in the chancel, which some authorities think could be Saxon. The manor house next door was once a grange for Abingdon Abbey, which owned so much land in the Vale before the Dissolution of the Monasteries. A footpath leads north to **Cherbury Camp,** an Iron Age fort that became associated with King Canute, who had a palace there.

Lyford (3/3C), barely a mile away across flat fields, is a peaceful and isolated place gathered round the church and manor farm. Near by is a picturesque group of tiny almshouses founded in 1611 by Oliver Ashcombe for the poor of EAST AND WEST HANNEY and Lyford.

Lyford Grange is very old and belonged to the recusant Yates family in Queen Elizabeth's reign. Here came the Jesuit Edmund Campion in 1581 to say Mass. Betrayed by a servant, he was arrested and subsequently martyred at Tyburn after a famous trial.

Chastleton (1/1C) On a high ridge of the Cotswolds on the borders of Gloucestershire and Warwickshire. A few stone houses lead up the hill, on top of which is Chastleton House, dwarfing the little church next to it. The house is early Jacobean, built about 1605 by Walter Jones, a rich wool merchant and Member of Parliament who originally came from Wales. It has five gables front and back, and each side has a tall battlemented staircase tower, which gives it a rather fortresslike appearance.

Unlike Walter Jones, succeeding members of this family never seem to have been very rich, so Chastleton has escaped the whims of Georgian or Victorian fashion and remains today virtually unchanged from the day it was built, and still with many of the original furnishings. Its most remarkable room is the long gallery at the top, which extends the whole length of the house under a coved plaster ceiling of great beauty. The room was designed for indoor exercises and games in bad weather, and has wonderful views from the leaded windows. The house is open to the public during the summer.

Chastleton has had a quiet history except for a day at the end of the Civil War when Arthur Jones returned from the battle of Worcester, where the Royalists were defeated. A troop of Roundheads followed him, suspecting he might be the escaping King Charles II. Arthur hid in a secret room over the porch and his indomitable wife Sarah put opium from her medicine chest in the soldiers' beer. While they were asleep he escaped on one of their best horses.

Checkendon (7/2A) St Birinus of Dorchester may have erected the first church here in the wooded Chilterns in the 7th century, as he built himself a retreat near by still known as Berin's Hill. The present Norman church is a gem. Two superb arches separate the nave from the chancel, at the end of which is a typically Romanesque apse with wall paintings of Christ and the Apostles from the 12th century. Two fine brasses are in the floor below. In the body of the church the interesting tablets include one to Admiral Manley, who as a boy sailed with Captain Cook to Australia. A beautiful modern window by the door commemorates the artist and sculptor Eric Kennington, who died here in 1960. It is by Laurence Whistler.

The village is typically Chiltern, attractively grouped around the church with several old brick and flint cottages, village hall and cricket ground. Checkendon Court is a fine Tudor house, approached by clipped yew hedges, which can be admired from a footpath leading out of the churchyard.

Cherbury Camp *see* Charney Bassett

Chesterton (4/2A) After crossing the Cherwell near KIRTLINGTON (4/1A), the Roman Akeman Street, still a road here, goes straight as an arrow for 4 miles to Chesterton, a neat and well-kept stone village surrounding its 13th-century church with its simple tower and chiming clock. Across the main BICESTER road some mounds and a bank in a field are all that remains of Alchester, an important Roman town covering 20 acres, which guarded this part of Akeman Street. To guard their empire the Romans needed good communications; the garrison here shows how they did it for 400 years and more.

Wendlebury (4/2A) is a village where new houses mix with old along the village street, on either side of a stream that runs down towards OTMOOR. There is an attractive 18th-century manor house and some old farms.

Childrey (6/1A) The Roman Portway below the downs west of WANTAGE goes through some of the most beautiful scenery in Oxfordshire. Childrey is particularly appealing with its old brick cottages, green, and duck-filled village pond. The splendour of the church is due to the fact that the Fettiplaces, one of the greatest local landowners in the Middle Ages, lived here until they moved to SWINBROOK in about 1500. It is cruciform in shape and mainly 14th century. The transepts were endowed as chantry chapels – the north by Sir Edmund de Chilrey, whose effigy lies below the window; and the south by William Fettiplace in 1526, just before chantries were abolished by the Reformers a few years later. Among other interesting things to see is the remarkable Norman font with its frieze of lead bishops, some fine old glass, and some unusual brasses. The Annunciation, with a beam of yellow glass shooting from God to the Virgin Mary, is a delightful piece of medieval imagery in the North transept window.

Opposite the church is the old manor house of the Fettiplaces where Charles I spent a night in 1644; and near the churchyard is the chantry house, built for the priest 500 years ago.

Chilson *see* Chadlington

Chilton *see* Harwell

Chinnor (1/2A) This large, mostly modern village lies south-east of THAME, on the border of Buckinghamshire under the Chilterns, which here rise steeply to Bledlow Ridge. A large cement works dominates the scene. It is not on any tourist route, but this is a pity as St Andrew's church, rather hidden away, is among the most rewarding in the county. A high, narrow 13th-century structure, it contains a most remarkable collection of brasses and pre-Reformation glass. The former are now set in the chancel wall (which is frowned upon by purists, but makes it much easier to see and appreciate them). The 600-year-old stained glass is even more fascinating. The windows to left and right of the altar have a colourful array of bishops and saints (including St Laurence with his gridiron), and pictures in the tracery depicting clothing the naked and giving drink to the thirsty are particularly touching. The large oil paintings hanging in the nave are a curious feature. Given by Rector Musgrove in the 18th century, they are supposed to be by Sir James Thornhill and badly need restoring.

Crowell (1/2A) is a hamlet south-west of Chinnor. Near the flint and chalk church is an old red brick house where Thomas Ellwood, Quaker friend and confidante of Milton, lived. There is a 70-acre nature reserve up Chinnor Hill run by the Berkshire, Buckinghamshire and Oxfordshire Naturalists Trust (BBONT). A mixture of grassland and woods, with many

The market place, Chipping Norton (see p. 86)

Beechwoods managed by BBONT

varieties of wild flowers and birds, it is open to the public.

Chipping Norton (1/2C) Very much a Cotswold market town ('Chipping' is from an Old English word for market) in the north-west corner of the county near Gloucestershire. The wide market place has some unusually grand buildings for such a small place (still only 5000 population) but wool was the source of the town's prosperity from the 15th century onwards, and 'Chippy', as the locals call it, has much of the feeling of a Gloucestershire wool town.

It is easy to miss the church, hidden in a side street down the hill. In 1495 a rich wool merchant called John Ashfield completely re-built the nave in the prevailing Perpendicular style, making it one of the most impressive in the area. It is very high and light due to the clerestory windows that run its entire length, and the church is notable for other windows of great size, including the enormous east window thought to have come from Bruern Abbey at the Dissolution of the Monasteries.

A path through the churchyard leads to a field where there are humps and mounds: all that remains of a Norman motte-and-bailey castle. Up the hill from the church are eight charming almshouses 'the gift of Henry Cornish, Gent. 1640', says the inscription.

The Roman Catholic church was built in 1836 by a chaplain from HEYTHROP, and is also architecturally distinguished.

Cholsey (7/1A) In flat countryside south of WALLINGFORD along the Thames, Cholsey is a straggling modern village with a station on the railway line to OXFORD and a pub curiously named the Brentford Tailor. Ethelred the Unready built a monastery here 1000 years ago which was sacked by the Danes. In 1171 Henry I gave the manor of *Celsea* to his new Abbey at Reading and the monks built the stately church that stands little changed outside the village. The great central tower, supported on four enormously strong Norman arches, and the fine monastic choir built about 100 years later, are very impressive. There is still a Benedictine feel about the church with the laity kept well away at the back while the monks sang divine office in the distant choir. This impression is heightened by the few monuments or tablets from later centuries. One, with commendable brevity, says of an 18th-century rector: 'to enlarge on his particular virtues decency declines yet justice requires this to be said that he died respected and esteemed'.

Manor Farm, next to the church, once had an immense medieval tithe barn that at 300 ft long (Great Coxwell barn is 150 ft) was the largest in England. Dismantled in 1815, it was replaced by the present barn, itself no mean size.

Christmas Common *see* Watlington

Church Hanborough *see* Long Hanborough

Churchill (1/2C) Appropriately named, as the church on this Cotswold hill near the Gloucestershire border is a famous landmark. It was built by the redoubtable Squire Langston in 1826 and the familiar-looking tower is an exact copy, but only two thirds the size, of Magdalen tower in OXFORD. Warren Hastings was born in one of the old stone houses in 1731. From relatively humble beginnings he rose to be the first Governor-General of India, but his eight-year trial at the bar of Parliament on charges of corruption was an 18th-century *cause célèbre*.

Another eminent Churchillian was William Smith, the father of English geology, whose memorial is a slab of uncut stone on the green. He produced the first geological map of England, using fossils to ascertain the age of rock strata.

Across the steep valley formed by the Sars brook is **Sarsden** (1/2C), a few houses and an ancient stone cross near Sarsden House, a handsome 17th-century mansion remodelled by the younger Repton in the early 19th century for Squire Langston. He also built the attractive rectory with its *cottage orné* lodge and its landscaped grounds looking over the valley towards Churchill. The Georgian village church is attached to Sarsden House.

Clanfield (3/2B) Long, attractive village on the fertile and watery plain of the upper Thames between FARINGDON and WITNEY. A stream runs the whole length of the village with many bridges to the houses along it. At one end of the village are two public houses opposite each other, one of them a striking Jacobean building. At the other end Friars Court is an old house on the site of a Knights Templar hospice. The church of St Stephen has a venerable tower with, halfway up it, a statue of Stephen himself, rather pop-eyed and holding a pile of stones, symbols of his martyrdom.

There is a lovely, lonely road to BROADWELL across the fields and a disused railway that used to go from Witney to Fairford.

Claydon (2/1A) The northernmost village in the county, north of BANBURY and well over 50 miles from the southern boundary and facing across the Oxford Canal into Northamptonshire. It is peaceful and remote farming country and the village reflects this with its Norman church and quaint saddleback tower. The Oxford Canal is particularly pleasant here as it flows out of the county and on to Coventry.

Mollington (2/1A) is south along the A423 BANBURY road, a pretty ironstone village on the side of a hill above the Mollington brook. It has won the award for best-kept village in Oxfordshire. The 14th-century church with some good monuments in it sits on a hill next to Church Farm, looking down on a Tudor manor and barn in the village street below.

The Oxford Canal at Claydon

Cleveley *see* Enstone

Clifton Hampden *see* Long and Little Wittenham

Cogges *see* Witney

Coleshill (3/1C) The narrow and hilly B4019 winds west out of FARINGDON past **Badbury Hill,** an Iron Age earthwork now owned by the National Trust. It is one of the highest points on the ridge of Corallian limestone that runs east to OXFORD from here, separating the Thames Valley from the Vale of White Horse. There are pleasant wooded walks and splendid views.

A mile further on fine trees, a long wall, impressive gates and what James Lees-Milne calls 'a sudden tautening of the landscape' suggest the presence of a great house. About 1650, the then squire commissioned his cousin Roger Pratt and Coleshill House was completed in 1662, with some help from Inigo Jones. An English Renaissance mansion on a grand scale, it had many original features inside and out, but was gutted by fire in 1952 and nothing, alas, remains. Pratt's other great house Kingston Lacy in Dorset, is very similar.

The Pleydell-Bouveries succeeded the Pratts and rebuilt some of the village on the side of the hill. They also re-ordered the old church, giving it an odd-shaped east window with some superb 16th-century French glass depicting the Nativity. There are some interesting Pratt effigies and a notable 18th-century Rysbrack monument of two Bouveries supported by plump cherubs.

Down the hill the river Cole marks the county boundary with Wiltshire. Just this side of the bridge is a small nature reserve run by the Berkshire, Buckinghamshire and Oxfordshire Naturalists Trust.

Combe (3/3A) On a steep slope above the river Evenlode west of Blenheim Park. The Glyme flows out of the great lake at Blenheim and the two rivers join just beyond the village. The church used to be down by the river, but the monks of EYNSHAM built the present one up the hill in 1395, presumably to avoid flooding. It is a particularly appealing church, virtually unaltered since the day it was built, with some faded wall paintings, an uncommon stone pulpit and beautiful old glass. Combe House next to the church is partly Tudor and used to belong to Lincoln College, which owns the living. There is a pretty village green with a cheerful-looking inn called The Cock and winding lanes leading from

it. In the valley, next to the railway, is a sawmill owned by the Blenheim estate. The splendid steam-powered early 19th-century beam engine is in full working order and is demonstrated occasionally in the summer.

Compton Beauchamp (5/3A) On the B4507 on the western edge of the county, where the Vale of White Horse enters Wiltshire, this enchanting place under the downs consists largely of a church, rectory and manor. **Knighton** (5/3A) adjoining it has chalk, cottages and farms.

The important Beauchamp family acquired the manor of Compton in the 13th century but held it only long enough to leave their name. Before the Conquest it was known as Compton Regis, being held by Edward the Confessor. There is a beautiful Tudor brick manor house with a grand Georgian wing in stone, all surrounded by a moat, which can be admired through wrought-iron gates down an avenue of trees. On the edge of the grounds is the little 13th-century church of St Swithin, built of chalk and richly decorated inside by an enthusiastic Anglo-Catholic squire. The decoration of vines and palms in the chancel was done in 1900. Those who enjoy fulsome epitaphs will appreciate the long one on the monument to Rachel Richards whose 'address was easy and unaffected and her conversation pleasant and engaging'.

Cornwell (1/2C). In a valley, west of CHIPPING NORTON, with a stream running through it, Cornwell is almost too picturesque. The small, stone-built village is beside an elegant Georgian manor house in beautiful grounds with a lake created by damming the stream; a convenient wrought-iron gate gives a lovely view of it. The house and whole village were beautified in the 1930s by Clough Williams Ellis, the architect who built the eccentric Welsh village of Portmeirion. The little church of St Peter is approached through the manor grounds; some Norman details remain but it was much restored in the 19th century.

Salford is a larger, less self-conscious village 2 miles north-east, on the A44 road to Moreton-in-Marsh. The partly Norman church and simple 18th-century rectory make an attractive group.

Cote *see* Bampton

Cottisford (2/3C) A small village sandwiched

between the wooded parks of Tusmore and Shelswell on the Northamptonshire border. Built around a ford over a stream, it has a small 13th-century church of great simplicity and an interesting manor farmhouse, parts of which are 14th-century: one of the oldest houses in the county. The manor used to belong to the great Abbey of Bec in Normandy, but Henry VI gave it to his new college at Eton in the 15th century. (College Farm was owned by Eton until quite recently.) Cottisford House, a fine early Georgian stone building next to the church, was orginally built for an Eton tenant.

At nearby **Juniper Hill** (2/3B) Flora Thompson was born in 1876, the daughter of a bricklayer. Her evocative descriptions of poor country life in *Lark Rise to Candleford* made her famous.

The road through the plantations and trees of Shelswell Park towards MIXBURY is particularly beautiful.

Cowley (4/2B) A forgotten village in an area that has been transformed since William Richard Morris founded his works in a disused military college in 1912 and brought the car industry to OXFORD. Before that Church Cowley was a separate village with its own smithy and a history stretching back at least to the 12th century, when the Augustinians from the Abbey of Osney, who then owned much of the land in what is now Cowley, encouraged the building of St James's Church. Part of the chancel arch and some columns, which still have their original paint, are Norman and so is the south doorway. The church was much restored in 1862-5 by G. E. Street. The nave roof was raised, making the 15th-century tower appear too small.

Cropredy (2/1A) An attractive and interesting village 4 miles due north of BANBURY on the Cherwell. There have been many variations on the name since the Domesday Book and no one is quite sure what the first element means; 'redy' probably comes from an Old English word meaning 'brook'. An ancient bridge first built in 1312 crosses the river and was the scene of a fierce battle in 1644 when Parliamentary troops under General Waller stormed the bridge and were beaten back by Royalists under Charles I in person who captured all their guns. The large and impressive 14th-century church built of ironstone has a number of interesting memorials, including one to the Labour Cabinet Minister and writer Richard Crossman, who

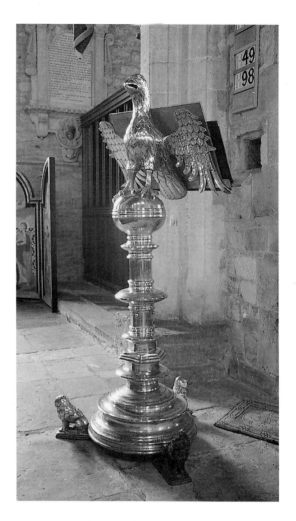

The lectern in Cropredy Church

lived near here and died in 1974. The pre-Reformation brass lectern is a great treasure. It owes its survival to being hidden in the river when the Puritans were getting rid of such things. It is a superb piece of craftsmanship and was also used for collecting Peter's Pence: coins were placed in a hole in its beak and came out in due course by its tail. There are pleasant walks along the banks of the river; it flows parallel with the Oxford Canal, which has a lock here. Brasenose College, Oxford, is the landowner and the Brasenose Arms has a colourful inn sign.

Crowell *see* Chinnor

Cuddesdon (4/2B) The village is about 4 miles east of Cowley, but fortunately rather cut off from it. It sits on top of a steep hill and is best approached along a narrow minor road over the

Thames from GREAT MILTON. For 400 years the Bishops of Oxford resided in a large house on top of the hill. It was burned down in 1960 – for the second time, as it had been purposely fired during the Civil War to prevent the Parliamentary army using it. Now the episcopal grounds are built over with comfortable houses behind well-kept hedges that contrast oddly with the gaunt and austere Theological College, founded in 1856. The training ground for generations of Anglican clergy, it is now called Ripon College.

The big church has a Norman doorway and later additions, including a fine chancel of about 1400. There are many Victorian windows and reminders of past bishops. The view from the churchyard across the plain of OXFORD to the Chilterns is magnificent. Further down the village is an inn called The Bat and Ball. It has an unusual cricketing inn sign.

Culham *see* Sutton Courtenay

Cumnor (4/1B) The Thames turns north after Newbridge and curves round Cumnor Hill and Boars Hill in a great loop before flowing south again through OXFORD. This is Oxford dormitory country, but Cumnor still retains an old village centre. Cumnor Place was once the home of Queen Elizabeth's favourite Robert Dudley, Earl of Leicester, and was the scene of one of the most famous dramas in English history when his young wife, Amy Robsart, was found dead at the bottom of the stairs. An accident? Or did Dudley organize it to leave him free to marry the Queen? Nothing was ever proved but the question has exercised people's imaginations ever since.

There is a large and interesting church that contains a life-size stone statue of the Virgin Queen which used to be at Cumnor Place and could well have been put there during Dudley's brief tenure. There is a marble monument in the chancel to Anthony Forster, who was Amy Robsart's host on the fatal night, and a much later tablet to a sailor who died during Anson's famous voyage round the world and was buried 'in the great South Sea in 1740'. But most memorable is the woodwork: some beautifully carved medieval pews, a Jacobean pulpit and clerk's desk, and a very unusual 17th-century circular staircase to the tower.

Boars Hill (4/1B) is very wooded still and from the top there is a celebrated view of Oxford's dreaming spires.

Dean *see* Chadlington

Deddington (2/1C) As you drive along the A41 from BANBURY to OXFORD (soon to be relieved by the new M40) the sight of Deddington's great church tower with its eight cheerful pinnacles lifts the spirit. Once it had the tallest spire in Oxfordshire, even higher than BLOXHAM, but one night in March 1635 the whole thing collapsed, taking a good part of the church with it. The new tower, put up 50 years later, has massive buttresses on each corner as if the citizens of Deddington were not going to take any more chances.

Over 400 ft above sea level, Deddington used to be quite an important market town and in the Domesday Book is twice the size of Banbury. There was a large castle looking over the Cherwell valley in which Piers Gaveston, the favourite of Edward II, was imprisoned before being beheaded in 1312. The castle seems to have been dismantled later in the same century, but there are huge mounds that can be explored east of the village, giving an idea of its size.

Over the years Deddington has declined in importance and today reveals itself as a large village of considerable charm with attractive ironstone houses in the market place and other interesting buildings in Church Street, Castle Street and the Bull Ring. The large 17th-century house next to the churchyard used to belong to the Dean and Chapter of Windsor, who acquired the living in 1358 and remain patrons to this day. Rising above its roof is part of a medieval peel tower, built for defensive purposes and more common in the North Country. The church is large and high with some fine windows but surprisingly few monuments. Two medieval statues of SS Peter and Paul look over the town from the tower. Survivors of the original tower, they have recently been given nice new heads.

Distinguished Deddington residents have included Sir Thomas Pope, founder of Trinity College, Oxford; Sir William Scroggs, arguably the worst Lord Chief Justice in our history; Mr Harris of pork sausage fame; and Mr Bowler who invented the hat.

Denchworth (3/3C) Deep in the Vale of White Horse north of WANTAGE, Denchworth has a pleasantly hidden feel about it. The Hyde family lived here for generations in the old manor, which can be glimpsed through a brick arch opposite The Fox, a cheerful-looking thatched inn. The Childrey Brook flows to the east, one of the many that rise in the downs and feed the river Ock and, ultimately, the Thames. The church is small, old and full of atmosphere. The large collection of brasses to the Hyde family is unusual in ranging from the early 16th century to a descendant killed just after the Normandy landings in 1944. The Cranmer Bible is in remarkable condition after 450 years.

The antiquary John Leland noted in the 16th century that the Vale of White Horse was 'frutefull of corne and in some parts marshy'. This is still true, although drainage is much improved. Due west, across more typical Vale country is **Goosey** (3/3C), houses and farms round an enormous green with a small church in one corner. The name means 'goose island'.

Didcot (4/2C) The town is dominated by an immense coal-fired power station erected in the 1960s. The six huge cooling towers, with their plumes of steam rising hundreds of feet in the air, bestride the upper Thames like a colossus and can be seen from every part of the Berkshire Downs, from the Cotswolds to the north and from the furthest part of the Chilterns to the west. The station is sited for ease of delivery by rail of the 20,000 tons of coal used every day and for access to water, but many wish a less highly visible site could have been found.

The rest of the town is mostly 19th and 20th century; the eastern part was previously North Hagbourne before being incorporated into Didcot. Old Didcot is on a hill to the west of the town centre, with one or two old houses left here and there and an old, although much restored, church with a huge yew in the churchyard which has survived all the changes around it. Inside the church is the battered effigy of Ralph de Dudecote, Abbot of Abingdon in the 13th century.

The railway station is an important junction on the Western Region main line where a branch goes north to OXFORD and the Midlands. The Railway Centre is delightful. Run by the Great Western Society, it has great sheds full of old steam locomotives of every kind, from express to the humble shunting engine. There is a stretch of line with engines steaming up and down next to the main line, which adds to the excitement as high-speed trains flash past at over 100mph. Old signal boxes, coaling points and advertisements for Mazawattee tea, Spratts Ovals and Virol for your Health will bring a wave of nostalgia to anyone over 50.

Ditchley (1/3C) Ditchley House and estate (there is no village) are situated on high ground east of CHARLBURY in a wooded area that was once part of Wychwood Forest. The ancient earthwork called Grim's Ditch or Dyke runs through the park and from it Ditchley derives its name. For 350 years it was the home of the Lee family, the last one dying in 1933. Another branch of the family are the Lees of Virginia in the United States, whose most famous member was General Robert E. Lee of the American Civil War. In the 1930s the house was in poor condition but an American couple, Mr and Mrs Ronald Tree, rescued and restored it. Now its final owner, Sir David Wills, has given it to the Anglo-American Foundation as a conference centre.

Of the four great houses within a few miles of here Ditchley is not as grand as Blenheim or HEYTHROP, or as historic as Cornbury, but it can perhaps claim to be the most beautiful. Designed by James Gibbs in 1722 and built of local grey stone, it is an early Palladian building with a central block with two smaller service wings, and its beauty lies in 'the proportion of the parts to one another and to the whole', as Gibbs himself wrote. Some of the rooms inside are very fine and the hall was designed and decorated by William Kent. It is usually open to the public for about ten days at the end of July.

Ditchley estate is within the parish of **Spelsbury** (1/3C), a pretty little village on the Charlbury to CHIPPING NORTON road. In the centre is a very curious, rather Oriental, drinking fountain and the church contains some very fine marble monuments to the Lee family, including a rather touching one to Sir Henry Lee who married the natural daughter of Charles II when they were 15 and 13 years old. They were happily married for 40 years and produced 18 children. There is an even more poignant brass to an old Lee servant, buried a respectful distance away, so as 'not to prophane, by a rude touch, the dust of his great master'.

At **Taston** (1/3C), a hamlet near by, has a name deriving from Thor's stone and the observant will notice a prehistoric monolith in a hedge near the centre of the village.

Dorchester (4/2C) On the A423 from HENLEY-ON-THAMES to OXFORD, Dorchester stands on the banks of the Thame just before it enters the Thames. It is the most historic spot in Oxfordshire. In AD635 the Benedictine monk Birinus, whom Pope Honorius had sent from Rome to convert the West Saxons, baptized King Cynegils and his court in the Thame. St

Birinus then built a church here and this became the cathedral of Wessex, until the see was transferred to Lincoln after the Norman Conquest. In 1170 the church was given to the Augustinians, who started building the great abbey that still towers over this small village.

The long barnlike roof is seen as you approach over the long bridge from the Henley road, its size accentuated by the stumpy tower. You enter through the west door into the aisle once reserved for the villagers' services and then into the nave with its uninterrupted view right down the church to the wonderful 14th-century east window, which fills the chancel with light and colour. Like most medieval churches it was built and rebuilt over a long period. The Norman nave is the oldest part, followed by the monastic choir in the 13th century, and about 100 years later the chancel or sanctuary was added.

The stained glass is still full of colour after 500 years and is rightly famous. There is an excellent guidebook to help decipher all the saints and scenes in the east window, the unique Jesse window to the north and the shields of the families who paid for it all on the opposite side. Among many other things to see is the remarkable lead font made about 1100.

Now that a bypass has relieved the main street of heavy traffic it is possible to enjoy the many attractive old houses there with overhanging upper storeys, painted and plastered in various colours, giving them a slightly East Anglian air. The George is a fine old coaching inn opposite the abbey and further up the street is a thatched wall made of witchert, a mixture of clay and limestone quite common in Buckinghamshire but unusual in Oxfordshire. A pleasant footpath leads across fields to the Thames.

Drayton *see* Steventon

Drayton St Leonard *see* Newington

Ducklington *see* Witney

Duns Tew *see* Tews, The

Easington *see* Lewknor

East and West Hagbourne (6/3A) The brook that flows through the two villages is first mentioned in a charter of King Alfred's time as *Haccaburna*, Hacca being probably a West

Opposite: The Jesse window in the Abbey, Dorchester

High Street, Dorchester

Saxon chief. Although so close to Didcot, East Hagbourne remains one of the prettiest villages in Oxfordshire with its venerable church and its main street running beside the brook, with timbered and plaster houses with oversailing top storeys. One end is known as Lower Cross, but only the stump remains as it was smashed by Cromwell's men in 1644.

St Andrew's Church is entered through a 600-year-old door, still on its original hinges and with its sanctuary knocker intact. The 12th-century chancel arch has curious grinning faces supporting it, and other parts of the church were enlarged later, but nothing much has changed since about 1450 or so. The medieval font is beautifully carved with the arms of the donors, some of whose brasses can also be seen. Another notable survival is the sanctus bell on the tower parapet. This was rung at the consecration during Mass and few in England survived the Reformation.

The road to the west leads under a disused railway past picturesque Coscote Manor to West Hagbourne. There has been more modern development here, but there are still enough old farms and cottages left to please the eye.

East and West Hanney (3/3C) Two old villages in the flat, rural countryside of the Vale of White Horse with the downs above WANTAGE in the distance. Although only separated by a few hundred yards they seem to have quite different characters. East Hanney has winding lanes and timbered houses typical of this area, intermingled with modern housing and rustic-looking barns and farmyards. Down a lane by the Letcombe brook, flowing from the downs to join the Ock, is a picturesque old manor house called Philberds, with a date of 1710 on one wall. It once had a very unattractive owner, Sir William Scroggs, Lord Chief Justice in Charles II's time. He retired to Hanney after accusations of bribery.

West Hanney is a more compact village, in the centre of which stands a handsome early Georgian brick house, with an exotic curved parapet giving it what its owner calls a dotty Baroque appearance. The large church near by had a tower once but this collapsed in 1946. It possesses one of the most remarkable collections of medieval brasses in the county. The oldest is to a priest, John Seyes of about 1370, and other brasses include Oliver Ayshcombe, who built almshouses in Lyford, and an Elizabethan adventurer called Sir Christopher Lytcot who was actually knighted by Henri IV of France. There is a wall tablet by the door to Elizabeth Bowles who died in 1718 at the age of 124.

East and West Hendred (6/2A) Both villages lie at the foot of the downs a few miles west of WANTAGE. East Hendred is the larger and is remarkably picturesque and rewarding. The wide main street and lanes leading from it have a wealth of old brick and timber-framed houses and the grouping of King's Manor, chapel and priest's house, and the Eyston Arms Inn, is particularly interesting. Hendred House in the centre of the village is a small medieval manor house belonging still to the Eyston family, who have held it since about 1450. They are an old Catholic family descended from Sir Thomas More, and the house contains relics of More and Bishop John Fisher, who was also beheaded in 1535 for refusing to recognize royal supremacy. Both men were canonized in 1935. The house

also contains a very ancient private chapel.

The large parish church is almost opposite the manor and has some fine 13th-century arches and a rare medieval lectern carved in wood. In fact the woodwork is generally interesting, particularly the comparison between the 15th-century screen to the Eyston Chapel and the Victorian screen to the chancel. But the most celebrated possession is the wonderful faceless clock built by John Seymour in 1525. It is one of the oldest clocks in England working as it was originally built, and still calls the hours and quarters as it has for 450 years. In the 17th century a musical carillon was added which plays Orlando Gibbon's 'Angel Song' every third hour. The huge weights that drive this remarkable timepiece are wound every day by a faithful villager.

West Hendred is a smaller and equally pleasant village with a humble and untouched 14th-century church by the Ginge Brook which tumbles from the downs above. There are some fragments of very old glass and a nice inscription on a window near the door 'C. Parker glazed this church and glad of the job 1784'.

From both villages there are lovely walks up to the downs, crossing Grim's Ditch to the Ridgeway.

East End *see* North Leigh

Eaton *see* Appleton

Eaton Hastings *see* Buscot

Elsfield *see* Woodeaton

Emmington *see* Towersey

Enslow *see* Bletchingdon

Enstone (1/3C) The name derives from 'Enna's stone' and there are still some ancient burial stones to be seen near a crossroads. The village, south-east of CHIPPING NORTON, needs relief from the traffic carried on the busy A34 trunk road. Even in 1800 there were 22 four-horse coaches going through every day on this old highway from London to Worcester, plus heavy stone wagons and other traffic. Church Enstone is the area by the entrance to HEYTHROP Park and has attractive old cottages. Near the Crown Inn an ancient barn has a date stone on it recording that it was built by the Abbot of Wynchcombe in 1382. It is still used and near the entrance to the farm is a medlar tree, a strange plant whose fruit is eaten when rotten.

The interesting old church is of many periods and dedicated unusually to St Kenelm. A fine Norman doorway and wide Tudor arch near the altar are noteworthy, also a curious monument to Stevens Wisdom staring rather wildly at his own tombstone.

There are four charming hamlets within the parish: **Lidstone** (1/3C), **Cleveley** (1/3C) and **Radford** (1/3C), all on the banks of the river Glyme, the last-named having a chapel designed by Pugin but no longer in use; **Gagingwell** (1/3C) is on the road to Middle Barton.

Epwell *see* Shutford

Ewelme (4/3C) The name comes from an Old English word meaning 'spring, source of a river'. It lies just below the Chiltern escarpment in rolling country to the east of, but quite hidden from, BENSON airfield. The spring still runs through the village, with watercress beds for some of its length and a trout farm. It is a pretty brick and flint village, and has some handsome Georgian houses and a most remarkable complex of medieval church, almshouses and school on a hillside at the western end. All three are virtually unchanged from their original construction between 1435 and 1450 by William de la Pole, Duke of Suffolk, and his wife Alice Chaucer, granddaughter of the poet Geoffrey Chaucer.

The church is a very fine example of the Perpendicular style and is particularly interesting as it was all built at one time, rather than developing over centuries like most village churches. Of the many things to see there, the magnificent wooden font cover and the wooden chancel screen are the most noteworthy.

It is, however, the famous tombs that most visitors will remember. In St John's chapel lies Thomas Chaucer, the poet's son, who was Constable of Wallingford Castle and Speaker of the House of Commons in 1414, and his wife Matilda. The two brasses on top show him in armour and her in wimple and veil and the sides have an elaborate display of heraldry showing their relationship to some of the greatest families in the land. A step away is the magnificent canopied tomb of their only daughter Alice, Duchess of Suffolk, whose full-length, superbly carved effigy is clad in a simple nun's habit with a coronet on her head. She wears the Garter on her forearm (the only other such representation is also in Oxfordshire, at STANTON HARCOURT). It is sad to remember, among the peace and beauty that Duchess Alice created at Ewelme, that her father-in-law was killed at Agincourt, her first husband fell in a battle near Orleans, and her second was murdered in 1450 in London.

As you leave the church by the old door under the tower the well-worn steps descend into the cloistered brick almshouses housing 13 Almsmen whose duty is to pray for the souls of their

Date stone in the 14th-century barn at Enstone (Viewing by appointment only)

Almshouses and church at Ewelme

Founders every day. They still do so, but are no longer required to wear a cloak with a red cross on the breast; the almshouses are still supported by the funds the duchess left in 1475. Through the churchyard a path leads to the old brick school. It claims to be the oldest primary school still in use for its original purpose.

There are few places where the atmosphere of medieval England is so strongly felt as at Ewelme.

Eynsham (3/3B) A small stone town 6 miles west of OXFORD, protected by the Thames and Wytham Hill. The Swinford tollbridge is one of only two left on the Thames and costs the motorist 2p. Eynsham belonged to the Anglo-Saxon kings of Mercia in the 8th century AD, but first came to prominence with the founding of a Benedictine abbey about the year 1000, when the place was called Egnesham. It was an important house, although not on the scale of READING and ABINGDON, and owned considerable estates. The site was west of the present church but there is virtually no trace left. The narrow main street leads towards the river with many old houses and inns, and a little town hall in the market square. A large and stately church occupies one side of the square with a handsome 14th-century tower and some 19th-century alterations inside. Eynsham Hall is a large house built early this century near Freeland. According to Kelly's Directory it 'commands a capital view of woodland scenery'. The A40 runs along the north side of the town.

Cassington (4/1B), a mile nearer Oxford, is in a watery landscape where the Evenlode river joins the Thames. The name means 'homestead where cress grew'. Houses and a pub are around the green and an avenue of trees leads to a Norman church of great dignity and interest, with rare pre-Reformation pews and a pretty 14th-century spire that lifts the heart as you drive along the ever-crowded A40.

Faringdon (3/2C) A pleasant, largely unspoiled country town of about 4000 people in the south-west of Oxfordshire on a high point of the low limestone ridge that runs from the Wiltshire border to OXFORD. It is sometimes called the Golden Ridge and from it there are fine views across the upper Thames to the north, and south towards the Berkshire Downs.

Fearndun, 'fern-clad hill', has an ancient history. It is known that King Alfred's son, Edward the Elder, died at his house here in

AD 920. There was a Norman castle here 200 years later, subsequently demolished by King Stephen. Being near a Thames crossing at **Radcot** (3/2B), the oldest bridge still in use on the river, and on an important crossroads for the Cotswold wool trade, Faringdon grew to considerable prosperity in the 15th and 16th centuries. The Civil War saw much activity as each side contended for the crossing at Radcot and the church spire was destroyed by a Parliamentary cannonade in 1644. A cannonball can be clearly seen on the east wall of the church, still lodged in the masonry after 350 years.

The market place, down the hill from the church, is an attractive jumble of mainly Georgian-fronted shops and inns, and a modest and pretty 17th-century town hall on stone columns. It has managed to retain its country town atmosphere, helped by a bypass which keeps the Oxford–Swindon traffic away.

The church looks down on the town from the top of the hill and is a massive Norman and Early English structure, oddly out of proportion since it lost its spire. The door still has its remarkable 13th-century ironwork intact and the interior is full of interest, although rather dark as the narrow lancets are filled with Victorian glass

and the great west window, inserted in the 15th century to give more light, is now blocked again by a recently installed organ. The Elizabethan monuments in the north transept are very grand and compare interestingly with the 18th-century marble tablets in the Pye chapel. Henry Pye was Lord of the Manor here when George III made him Poet Laureate. The lines he wrote on the loss of the church spire may explain why he is one of the least remembered of our Laureates:

Where once the tapering spire conspicuous grew,
Till Civil War the sacred pile o'erthrew.

Behind the church is the elegant 18th-century Faringdon House. Lord Berners lived there in the 1930s and commissioned the curious tower at the Oxford road entrance to the town – said to be the last folly built in England.

Fawler *see* Finstock

Fencott *see* Otmoor

Fernham *see* Longcot

Fewcott *see* Fritwell

Field Assarts *see* Leafield

Fifield Church (see p. 99)

Fifield (3/1A) In a remote part of the Oxfordshire Cotswolds north of BURFORD this is a
delightful stone village on the eastern slope of a
hill with fine views across the Evenlode valley.
The church has a most unusual 14th-century
octagonal tower and miniature spire.

A mile to the north and on the border of
Gloucestershire is **Idbury** (3/1A), on the same
ridge and even smaller. There is a timeless air
about it, with a small Tudor manor house gazing
down the valley and a poor and simple church,
with some crude medieval pews, that needs care.
In the churchyard is a strange memorial to Sir
Benjamin Baker, a great Victorian engineer who
built the Forth Bridge and the Aswan Dam. All
around are magnificent views out over three
counties.

In the Evenlode valley stands **Bruern Abbey**
(3/1A), once Cistercian, but now an 18th-
century mansion, hidden behind high yew
hedges. The old signal box by the railway is now
called Crossing House. The Oxfordshire Way
leads up the river to the 160-acre Foxholes
Nature Reserve, where the woodlands and water
meadows are controlled by BBONT, the
Naturalists Trust that does a remarkable job
preserving over 2000 acres in Berkshire,
Buckinghamshire and Oxfordshire.

Filkins (3/1B) Filkins and **Broughton Poggs**
(3/1B) are adjacent villages on the Gloucestershire border south of BURFORD. Only the
Broadwell brook lies between, but each has its
own character. Opposite Filkins Hall is the
home of Cotswold Woollen Weavers, who have
imaginatively converted an old threshing barn
into a traditional Cotswold weaving mill where
visitors can see ancient machinery and clattering
looms weaving fine woollen cloth, and buy the
finished products. There is also an interesting
exhibition of the history of wool in the Cotswolds
and the vital part it has played in the economic
and social history of the area. In other farm
buildings there are people busy rush weaving,
wood turning and stone carving, and an art
gallery. William Morris, who lived down the
road at KELMSCOTT, would have greatly
approved of all this. Sir Stafford Cripps, the austere
Chancellor of the Exchequer in the postwar
Labour Government, lived in the village for
many years.

The village street leads across a bridge to

*Richard Martin, proprietor and partner of the
Cotswold Woollen Weavers at Filkins*

Broughton Poggs. Its simple Norman church is
by a farmyard approached through the gates of
Broughton Hall. A notice in the porch regrets
that the church is locked but gives three names
and addresses in the village where the key may
be obtained. Many much larger villages would
do well to follow this example.

Finmere *see* Mixbury

Finstock (3/3A) Originally a forest clearing or
assart, Finstock is on the southern edge of
Wychwood Forest which lies between the village
and CHARLBURY. A growing village, it was described in 1978 by the novelist Barbara Pym,
who lived there: 'an interesting mixture of
carefully restored cottages and bright new
bungalows with broken dry-stone walls, corru-
gated iron, and nettles, and even the occasional
deserted or ruined homestead.' It has a delectable small manor house with a date of 1660
on it and a Victorian church in which T.S. Eliot
was baptized in 1929.

Down a hill to the Evenlode valley is **Fawler**
(3/3A) whose name derives from words meaning
'coloured floor' and remains of a Roman villa
with a mosaic floor have been found by the river
bank. There was ironstone mining here in the
19th century, and a brickworks, but now all is
peaceful in this tiny hamlet.

Freeland *see* Long Hanborough

Frilford *see* Marcham

Fringford (2/3C) Off the A421 BICESTER to
Buckingham road near the county border with
houses, farms and cottages scattered round a
series of attractive greens. St Michael and All
Angels church is basically Norman but has been
much restored, on the whole sympathetically.
There are no features of special note, except a
distinguished memorial to a Dr Addington who
died in 1790 and was physician to the Prime
Ministers Pitt the Elder and Pitt the Younger.
His own son Henry went into politics and
became one of our least-known Prime Ministers,
succeeding William Pitt for a short time in 1802.
He was not a success, giving rise to the cruel
rhyme 'Pitt is to Addington as London is to
Paddington'.

Hethe (2/3C) is on a high ridge above the flat
Bicester countryside with a thatched manor and
tiny church with a curious wooden turret. One
of the farms here was given to St Bartholomew's

Hospital in London by the Court Jester to Henry I and it remained in that institution's possession until this century. On the outskirts is a small Roman Catholic chapel and priest house built in 1830 after the Fermor family had left nearby Tusmore Park, which had its own chapel. Tusmore was one of Oxfordshire's finest houses, but it was unfortunately demolished in 1960. Between Hethe and Tusmore lies **Hardwick** (2/2C), in remote farming and hunting country, a peaceful hamlet with a 14th-century church and beautiful Elizabethan manor farm next to it.

Fritwell (2/2C) An interesting greystone village in the high flat country north-west of BICESTER. The Elizabethan manor house overlooking the Green has had a violent history. In 1665 a man was killed there in a duel and in the 18th century the owner killed his son and heir after a bitter row at cards. A more recent owner was Lord Simon, Home Secretary and Chancellor of the Exchequer in the 1930s and Lord Chancellor during the Second World War. A charming path leads to the church, which is rather unusually dedicated to St Olaf of Norway. There is a remarkable Norman doorway with beautifully carved tympanum, but much of the rest of the church was heavily restored by G. E. Street in the 19th century.

Two miles south-east are **Ardley** (2/2C) and **Fewcott** (2/2C), two joined-together villages with substantial modern developments and the A43 Brackley road along the edge. There is a partly Norman church and some earthworks near it, all that remains of a small castle.

Further east again is **Stoke Lyne** (2/2C), a small farming village with another Norman church next to the Victorian rectory. It is a plain and engaging little church with some tablets to local worthies and a statue of St Peter over the porch which has managed to survive for 800 years. All around is flat farming land interspersed with woodland.

Fulbrook *see* Burford

Fyfield *see* Kingston Bagpuize

Gagingwell *see* Enstone

Garford *see* Marcham

Garsington (4/2B) On a steep hill 2 miles east of the OXFORD ring road, Garsington has managed to retain a village atmosphere, despite new

housing and signs that new buildings are begining to creep up the hill from COWLEY. On the southern side is the beautiful stone manor house, principally Tudor but with some 17th-century additions. From the road you can admire the front, flanked by huge yew hedges that rise to the height of the roof. In the 1920s it was the home of Lady Ottoline Morrell, the celebrated hostess and literary lion hunter who used to entertain artists and writers here. T.S. Eliot, Virginia Woolf and other 'Bloomsberries' were frequent guests; also D.H. Lawrence who accepted the hospitality offered, then parodied Lady Ottoline mercilessly in one of his books. Her touchingly simple memorial is in the church, from which there are splendid views. It has a fine Norman tower.

Glympton (3/3A) Glympton and **Kiddington** (3/3C) are neighbouring villages on the river Glyme north of WOODSTOCK. Each is really a cluster of cottages and farms around a big house. Kiddington Hall was built by Barry in 1850 in an Italianate style; Glympton Park is an 18th-century mansion of classic proportions. Both houses are in lovely grounds said to have been 'landskipped' by the great Capability Brown during breaks from his labour at Blenheim Palace a mile down the road. Here, too, he created small lakes by damming the Glyme, as he also did on a large scale at Blenheim. Each village has a church in the grounds of the house, but the ancient St Nicholas at Kiddington, with its fine Norman chancel arch, is the more interesting. Glympton has some stylish almshouses built since the Second World War, which is unusual.

Goring (7/1A) The Thames cuts through the hills here, dividing the Chilterns from the Berkshire Downs, and Oxfordshire from Berkshire, as it flows through the Goring Gap on its way to London. The prehistoric Icknield Way crossed the river here to Streatley, where there was a ferry for centuries before the first bridge was built about 100 years ago. Brunel allowed the river to do his work for him and his Great Western Railway comes through the Goring Gap *en route* to DIDCOT. The coming of the railway and the popularity of the river developed Goring rapidly around the turn of the century and today it is a large and pleasant riverside village of

A 13th-century tithe barn at Great Croxwell (see p. 102)

Edwardian buildings, curiously named pubs and commuter residences. There was a medieval priory here of Austin canonesses and there are still traces of it visible in the Norman, but much-altered, church.

Goring Heath (7/2A) is reached by going east for about 4 miles through typical Chiltern beechwoods. There Mr Henry Allnut, Lord Mayor of London, founded eight almshouses in 1724. Built in pink and blue brick surrounding a Georgian chapel, they make a delightful picture and they are one of the most attractive, and least-known, buildings in the county.

A track beyond Goring station leads to the Hartslock Nature Reserve, managed by BBONT. Many interesting species of plants and butterflies flourish on the rich chalk grassland and there are excellent views to the Berkshire Downs beyond the Thames.

Great (3/1C) **and Little Coxwell** (3/2C) Seen from the A420 Swindon road west of FARINGDON, the great 13th-century tithe barn looms over the village like a cathedral. Beaulieu Abbey in Hampshire held the manor here and the

The Dormer tomb, St Peter's Church, Great Milton

Cistercian monks built the magnificent stone barn to hold the produce due to them from the rich soil. The huge stone roof, 150 ft long and 45 ft wide, is supported on slender oak posts resting on stone bases. Nearly all the timber beams, struts and posts are original and it is a tribute to the remarkable skill of the builders that the immense weight of the roof has been carried for 700 years. Now in the care of the National Trust, it is the finest medieval barn left in England and is open to the public every day.

The rest of this pretty, rather Cotswoldy village spreads down towards the small, many-windowed church, parts of which are older than the tithe barn – as a plaintive notice by the collection box reminds the visitor. The original 13th-century door is a beautiful example of woodwork.

Little Coxwell is the other side of the Swindon road with further old stone cottages and a small church with an ancient belfry. There are some Ancient British settlement remains to the south of the village.

Great and Little Haseley (4/3B) The Haseleys are situated in quiet, rolling farmland country south of the M40 and east of OXFORD. Great Haseley is a village of singular charm with old thatched cottages and stone houses, and a traditional group of manor, church and church farm with medieval tithe barn. The church is unusually large with a fine Norman door and high 13th-century chancel built by an unknown benefactor who is buried in the south wall. There are many interesting architectural details and a multitude of monuments and inscriptions. The glass is not old but there is an attractive memorial window in the south aisle dated 1925 illustrating Haseley Court, among other things. The famous antiquary John Leland, who wrote a sort of 'Shell Guide to England' for Henry VIII, was rector here, as was Christopher Wren, the architect's father. An impressive number of past rectors seem to have gone on to bishoprics. Preaching in such a long church must have been good practice for the cathedrals to come.

Little Haseley, a mile away, is remote and rural around a wide green. All around are splendid views towards the Chilterns.

Great and Little Milton (4/3B) To the east of OXFORD and south of the M40, Great Milton is hidden in the valley of the Thame which flows due south to join the Thames at DORCHESTER. The village has spread in recent years, but the

The King's Men, Rollright Stones

centre remains unspoiled with thatched cottages around the green and two inns, The Bull and The Bell. There are two large houses by the church: the much-altered manor house, now a famous French restaurant; and the Great House opposite, which has an elegant early Georgian façade. St Peter's Church is very large and light and was mainly built in the 13th and 14th centuries. It contains the most remarkable tomb in Oxfordshire. Sir Michael Dormer, Lord Mayor of London, who died in 1616, his wife and father, Sir Ambrose, lie on a marble tomb under a gilded canopy. Their alabaster figures are superbly adorned and all round the monument are marble reliefs, heraldic shields and other signs of earthly splendour. Above this *tour de force* of Jacobean family pride hang Sir Michael's helmet and sword. On the opposite wall are two pikes issued to the Home Guard in 1940 to stop the Nazi armoured divisions from entering Great Milton.

Little Milton is on the main road south to STADHAMPTON. There are two attractive rustic lodges to the manor and some older houses off the main road.

Great and Little Rollright (1/2C) North of CHIPPING NORTON, on the very edge of War-

wickshire, is a 700 ft high ridge of the Cotswolds with some magnificent views in every direction. On it stand the famous **Rollright Stones**, a prehistoric stone circle, the third most important in England after Avebury and Stonehenge. Although numerous theories have been advanced nobody really knows what they represent, or indeed exactly when they were put here, but informed opinion suggests an age of around 3500 years. There are about 70 pitted and weatherworn uprights in a 100 ft circle and a further five across a field that are thought to mark a burial chamber; the former are known as the King's Men, and the latter as the Whispering Knights. On the other side of the road, actually in Warwickshire as the border marches with the road, is the 8 ft King Stone, weathered into a fantastic shape, which looks straight down the slope to Long Compton below. For centuries they have exercised a powerful influence over men's minds, and local legends and superstitions abound. You can understand why, for there is still a very special atmosphere here.

Great and Little Rollright on either side of the stones are typically pretty Cotswold villages with churches that are well worth visiting.

Carvings in the church at Hanwell

Great Tew *see* Tews, The

Hailey *see* Ramsden

Hampton Poyle and Hampton Gay (4/1A)
North of the busy OXFORD–BICESTER road,
Hampton Poyle is a small and quiet village on
the Cherwell, cut off from Oxford by river and
railway line. Hampton is from an Old English
word for 'homestead' and Sir Walter de la Puile
left his Norman name here in 1268. Much of the
little church was built at the same period and
contains some old glass showing the symbols of
the four Evangelists, a Poyle brass and a
recumbent knight who may also be one of the
same family. There is a memorable view across
the floodplain towards KIDLINGTON.

A footpath leads across the watermeadows to
Hampton Gay, which can be reached also by car
down a narrow lane off the BLETCHINGDON road.
It might have been larger when Sir Roger Gait
(silent 't') owned it in the 12th century, but now
there are only three houses, including the 17th-
century Manor Farm where the key to the
church is kept. You must now proceed on foot
about half a mile over a field to the little church
of St Giles, passing the romantic ruins of the
manor house burned down a century ago. Both
church and manor are in a bend of the Cherwell

which 'winds with devious coil round Hampton
Gay and Hampton Poyle'. A lonely, beautiful
spot with its views across the river towards
Kidlington spire. There was a terrible railway
disaster here in 1874 when a train plunged into
the Cherwell and 30 people were killed and
many more injured.

Hanwell (2/1A) Two miles north of BANBURY on
the Warwick road, Hanwell is a beautiful village
of deep yellowy-orange ironstone houses around
a well-kept village green. There is a fine old
church with some vigorous stone carvings –
although not improved by the Parliamentary
soldiers who stabled their horses in it during the
Civil War. The interlocking arms depicted on
the capitals are typical of this area and the carved
animals in the chancel are most engaging.

The church sits on the edge of a spur looking
down on Hanwell Castle, which used to be much
larger: but a very imposing tower remains, built
around 1490. The surprising thing is that the
castle was built of brick in an area where stone
was plentiful and cheap. Sir Anthony Cope, an
enthusiastic Calvinist, lived there and became
MP for Banbury, but he was too fanatical for
Queen Elizabeth, who twice imprisoned him
and then released him.

A mile or so west lies **Horley** (1/3A), another
ironstone village on the same escarpment, which
runs for some miles on the Warwickshire
border. It is a long, thin village with the church
of St Etheldreda at one end, a Norman church
whose treasure is an enormous wall painting of
St Christopher probably dating from 500 years
ago. The saint says: 'What art thou and art so
ynge, bore I never so hevy a thynge.' The infant
Christ on his shoulder replies: 'Yey, I be hevy,
no wunther nys, for I am the kynge of blys.'

Half a mile south in a clump of trees near a
disused railway is a BBONT nature reserve,
located on some old ironstone workings. It is
open to the public.

Hornton is on the western edge of the
escarpment, which ends abruptly at Edgehill in
Warwickshire. It was famous for centuries for
the quality of its building stone, which was
extensively quarried all around this area. Nearer
Wroxton it was also dug out for iron ore.
Hornton marlstone, or middle lias limestone to
give it its full name, is a pale greenish colour
when cut but the iron veins contained in it
oxidize and permeate through the stone, giving
it the rich brown, sometimes orange colour, that
is characteristic of north Oxfordshire.

Hardwick *see* Fringford

Harwell (4/1C) West of DIDCOT and just off the A34 OXFORD to Newbury road. In flat country before the road rises to the downs, this is an apple- and fruit-farming area with extensive orchards all around. It is best known for the enormous Atomic Energy Research Establishment, which comprises over 700 acres of housing and laboratories about 2 miles south of the village, quite well concealed in a fold of the landscape. Despite much development on the outskirts, the old part of Harwell is remarkably unchanged, with cob and thatch walls and old brick cottages. Townsend, formerly the village pound, is very attractive. Two of the pubs are curiously named: the Kicking Donkey and the Crispin. St Matthew's Church is mostly late Norman with a fine 14th-century chancel. There are some interesting stone carvings and a pre-Reformation screen.

Chilton (6/3A) is a smaller village south on the A34 with an ancient church, but otherwise rather affected by the atomic establishment nearby.

Headington (4/2B) is a popular residential suburb above OXFORD and the home of numerous institutions such as the Polytechnic and the John Radcliffe hospital. From South Park, where the Parliamentarians camped in the Civil War, there is a commanding view of the city spires. Stone quarried in Headington was used to build many Oxford colleges. Before Oxford was founded Headington was the centre of an Anglo-Saxon royal domain with a palace where St Frideswide spent her girlhood. Henry I (1070 – 1135) was the last king to stay there.

Old Headington has considerable charm and an interesting mixture of old houses and well-designed new ones. A Breton knight built St Andrew's Church in the 12th century and the chancel arch dates from that period. The squat tower with its stair turret set diagonally was an attractive addition about 1500. The churchyard has some unusual tomb inscriptions, like the one in memory of John Young, a Royalist who 'liv'd to be old And yet dyed Young'.

Henley-on-Thames (7/3A) Very much the 'capital' of south Oxfordshire, Henley is famous for its beautiful position on the Thames and its great annual regatta. The approaches by road are

Below: Allotments and church at Hornton

Overleaf: Temple Island, Henley-on-Thames

particularly attractive, from OXFORD along the Fair Mile, or the approach from London where the road dips sharply down through the woods of Remenham Hill to reveal the oft-painted view of bridge, Angel Inn and Church.

The five-arched bridge replaced an earlier one in 1786 and is one of the noblest on the Thames, with sculptured heads of Father Thames and Isis. Beyond is what used to be the largest parish church in the county before the boundary changes brought ABINGDON into Oxfordshire. The best feature is the tall tower, built in the early 16th century in a chequer pattern of flint and stone and topped with pinnacles. It dominates the town, as a church tower should, and is particularly impressive seen from up river. The rest of the church has a late 15th-century flint exterior, but the interior was severely reorganized by the Victorians.

Hart Street and Market Place lead up from the church to the Town Hall. There are many pleasant Georgian and earlier buildings, notably Speaker's House, where Speaker Lenthall of the Long Parliament lived in the 17th century. The churchyard has attractive almshouses around it and probably the oldest building in Henley, the Chantry House dating from the 14th century. A passage leads through to New Street where there are many half-timbered houses.

Even before the coming of the railway, which made commuting to London possible, Henley was an important stop on the coach route from the capital to Oxford and there are a remarkable number of inns, including coaching stops such as the Red Lion by the river (where William of Orange once stayed), The White Hart and the Catherine Wheel. Many of the public houses are served by the Henley Brewery, whose pictur-esque premises in New Street have been owned-by the Brakspear family for many generations.

The famous regatta was started in 1839 and during the first week in July Henley attracts rowers from all over the world. The course is on one of the longest and widest stretches of the Thames from the bridge to Temple Island. Acres of tents and striped marquees cover the fields on the Berkshire bank downstream from the Leander Club, the rowing equivalent of the MCC, and the whole town is *en fête* while the regatta lasts.

Hethe *see* Fringford

Heythrop (1/3C) The comparatively small area between WOODSTOCK and CHIPPING NORTON

contains the four largest houses in the county: Blenheim, Cornbury, DITCHLEY and Heythrop, all within a circle of about 8 miles. Heythrop House is a magnificent Baroque mansion built in honey-coloured local stone in 1706 by Thomas Archer for the 12th Earl of Shrewsbury, who had spent many years in Italy. The Shrewsburys were here until the mid-19th century, when the interior of the house was gutted by fire, and the estate was subsequently sold to Albert Brassey, a Victorian millionaire. For most of this century it was a training college for Jesuit priests and is now owned by the National Westminster Bank.

An enormous park surrounds the house which, despite the varous institutional additions, still retains its grandeur and a certain air of restrained dignity, in marked contrast to the triumphal exuberance of Blenheim, which was built at the same time.

The estate village at the far end of the park was largely built during Mr Brassey's time. The church is large and Victorian but in a field near by is an older church, now disused. Only the 14th-century chancel can now be seen with a fine Norman doorway reset from the vanished nave. It is a haunting place with its Tudor glass and Shrewsbury tablets gathering dust. The key can be obtained in the village.

Hinkseys, The (4/1B) These are not mentioned as separate villages until 1316. At **North (Ferry) Hinksey** the first Saxon farmers are said to have forded the river with their oxen to found OXFORD. The present Norman church of St Lawrence may have replaced an earlier Saxon one. The ancient stone column in the church-yard was once topped by a cross and provided both a preaching and a meeting place. **South Hinksey** has a 13th-century church dedicated to another St Laurence. Under a yew tree in the churchyard is the grave of Sibylla Curr, who once kept the Cross Keys inn in the village and whom Matthew Arnold mentions in his poem 'Thyrsis' (1866).

Hinton Waldrist *see* Longworth

Holwell *see* Westwell

Hook Norton (1/3B) A large ironstone village about 6 miles north of CHIPPING NORTON in a relatively unknown area of beautiful hill country on the Warwickshire border. The manor was granted by William the Conqueror to his supporter Robert D'Oily in return for an annual payment of lace cloth (this has been suggested as the origin of the word 'doyley' for the piece of cloth or paper put under cakes).

From the centre of the village there are attractive lanes and steps leading down to a tiny stream which flows through the southern side and across a disused railway line. The railway cutting is now a nature reserve owned by the Berkshire, Buckinghamshire and Oxfordshire Naturalist Trust (BBONT) and may be visited, but the old railway tunnel is out of bounds. On the western edge of the village a road leads to the Hook Norton Brewery, an extraordinary Victorian pagoda-like building producing fine ales by traditional methods.

St Peter's Church has a commanding position in the centre of Hook Norton and its fine 15th-century tower is topped by gaily pennanted pinnacles. The interior is very impressive with a high clerestoried nave and unusual window over the chancel arch, flanked by 15th-century wall paintings of St Peter and St Paul. The Norman font is very endearing – primitive carvings of Adam holding a spade and rake and Eve with her figleaf and apple, and some of the signs of the zodiac carved with rustic enthusiasm 800 years ago. A wall tablet to 'Nathaniel Apletree, Gent' in 1786 has a neat solution to lack of space: 'He was, but room wont let me tell you what, name what a friend should be and he was that.'

Two miles south-east is **Swerford** (1/3C), a peaceful and pretty village over the river Swere. There was a Norman castle here built by the D'Oilys to protect their estates, but it was dismantled and the stone used to build the 13th-century church with its small stone spire and some curious heads with enormous teeth. Mounds showing the position of the castle can be seen in a field near the church. On the north bank of the river is a fine-looking 18th-century house and park, once a ducal hunting lodge.

The river flows east and 400 ft up the hillside above it is **Wigginton** (1/3B). Considerable Roman remains have been found south of the village near the Swere. There are some pleasing old stone houses and an odd-looking porch on the church.

Horley; Hornton *see* Hanwell

Horspath *see* Wheatley

Horton-cum-Studley *see* Otmoor

Idbury *see* Fifield

Iffley (4/2B) On a steep bank above the Thames, it has been a flourishing village for a thousand years and still retains its identity despite the surrounding postwar estates. Near the old lock a stone marks the site of Iffley Mill, a well-known beauty spot until it burned down in 1908. Parallel to the river is Church Way, which is winding and picturesque and includes a thatched school (1838) converted from a much older barn, and a house bearing the inscription 'Mrs Sarah Newell's School 1822'.

It is for St Mary's Church that Iffley is famous. The powerful Norman St Remy family paid for its building between 1154 and 1189, and it is considered the most perfect example of a small 12th-century parish church in England. Despite the addition of a chancel about 1270, and later modifications to some windows, it has a remarkable unity and simplicity. The black font is unusual and would have allowed infant baptism by full immersion. Notice in the magnificent carving of the choir a domestic bird guarding its nest. Outside, the south door is better preserved than the much-photographed west door, but it is unfinished because it is said the masons left to work on St Frideswide's priory in Oxford.

The enormous yew tree in the churchyard is very ancient and so, too, is the adjoining rectory, parts of which are 12th-century.

Ipsden (7/2A) On the eastern side of the Thames near GORING where the Chilterns slope gently down to the river and rise again on the other side as the Berkshire Downs. The lower slopes are open rolling countryside with splendid views across the county to the west; the top of the hill is beechwood forested in a typical Chiltern way. Prehistoric Icknield Way is clearly seen just west of Ipsden as it begins its long march the whole length of the Chiltern escarpment into Buckinghamshire. Just beyond the village it crosses Grim's Ditch, thought to be some kind of boundary or marker – although nobody really knows. The village itself is halfway up the hill and is scattered over a large area, from a farm with immense brick barns at one end to a simple little Early English church standing all alone at the other. It belonged once to the great Abbey of Bec in Normandy.

Up the hill through beechwoods leads to **Stoke Row,** which has been largely suburbanized. In the centre is the Maharajah's Well, given to the village by the Maharajah of Benares in 1863 as a compliment to his friend Edward

Reade of Ipsden House, who had been his engineering adviser in India. Apparently Reade had told him of the difficulty his village had in getting water, so the Maharajah at his own expense (£696) sank a well 346 ft through the chalk to solve the problem, and put a smaller one near Ipsden church for good measure. The chocolate-coloured Oriental dome adds an exotic touch to a small Chiltern village. Cars can be parked in Benares Road.

Islip (4/2A) Due east of KIDLINGTON near the OXFORD to BICESTER road. The river Ray meets the Cherwell here and the village looks out over OTMOOR (but is not one of the 'Seven Towns of Otmoor'). Islip has a place in history for Edward the Confessor was born here in 1004, the last of our English kings from Alfred the Great's lineage. He is best remembered as the founder of the great Abbey of St Peter at Westminster and gave the manor to his new foundation as his will proclaimed: 'I have given to Christ and St Peter in Westminster ye little town of Islippe wherein I was born.' The connection has lasted nearly 1000 years: the Dean and Chapter of Westminster are still patrons of the living.

There is a fine church in the centre of the village, its 13th century tower seen at its best from the Beckley road. The Ray was famed for eels in the 17th and 18th centuries and peasants used to come up from Otmoor to sell them on the big stone platform by the church gate. There was much skirmishing in the Civil War as either side tried to gain the bridge, which was an important river crossing. The chancel of the church was destroyed by a cannonade and rebuilt by Rector South, who also built the big stone rectory around which the traffic flows. The minor road east of the village leads to Otmoor.

Kelmscott (3/1B) Small, rural and remote, this stone village and its old manor house on the upper Thames floodplain will always be associated with the name of William Morris, writer, artist, craftsman and socialist visionary. He was born in 1834 and while at OXFORD formed a brotherhood devoted to art and poetry. Later, with Edward Coley, Burne-Jones, D.G. Rossetti and others, he founded Morris & Co, which produced metalwork and stained glass – examples of their work can be found just over the Thames at BUSCOT and Eaton Hastings. He also founded the Kelmscott Press, and its beautifully bound editions are now much prized. A Gothic Revival romantic, he dreamed of rural

England returning to a medieval utopia, with contented craftsmen weaving and printing in an aura of socialist brotherhood. It was impossible, of course. However, his writings, and particularly his textile designs, have had a great influence, which is still evident today.

Morris died in 1896 and lies in the peace of Kelmscott churchyard. The beautiful Tudor manor where he lived and worked is open on the first Wednesday of every month April to September and contains some examples of his work. On a cottage near by is a sculptured relief showing Morris sitting in his garden under a tree.

The little Norman and Early English church has great charm. The 17th-century velvet altar front was given by Mrs Morris and the side curtains are typical Morris designs.

Kencot *see* Broadwell

Kiddington *see* Glympton

Kidlington (4/1A) It sprawls in a shapeless way along the BANBURY road and is virtually a suburb of OXFORD. Most people drive straight through noticing only the ribbon development of the 1930s, and garages and shopfronts of the 1960s. This is a pity because tucked away down by the Cherwell is a delightful remnant of old Kidlington: some pleasing stone houses and one of the finest churches in the county, looking over the river valley towards BLETCHINGDON.

Before the Reformation the church was owned by Osney Abbey and in the 14th century when Thomas of Kidlington became abbot he rebuilt and enlarged it. It is very large and spacious with some fine windows and a superb display of medieval glass in the large east window. Some of the oldest choir stalls in the county are in the chancel, with beautifully carved emblems and tracery. The thin needle spire was also built by Abbot Thomas. Soaring to 170 ft, it is a very prominent landmark across the valley and was known in the Middle Ages as Our Lady's Needle.

Kingham (1/1C) A Cotswold farming village south-west of CHIPPING NORTON, on the eastern bank of the Evenlode near the border with Gloucestershire. The railway station south of the village is on the Cotswold line, which goes across country from OXFORD to Worcester. At one end of the village is a large green and the road leads from it between old stone houses to the church,

The Manor House, Kelmscott (By kind permission of the Society of Antiquaries of London – view by appointment only)

principally 14th century, although there have been many changes in succeeding centuries. The Victorian stone pew ends are very strange – possibly unique, at any rate in Oxfordshire. A memorial to a colonel in the 52nd Foot shows a soldier leaning on his reversed rifle. The 52nd Foot later became the Oxfordshire and Buckinghamshire Light Infantry, a distinguished regiment that played a notable part under Wellington in the Peninsular War and at Waterloo.

Rector Dowdeswell built the elegant house next to the church in 1688. His relations held the living until 1911 when 'the last of the hunting parsons of Kingham' died, so the church guide intriguingly tells us.

Kingston Bagpuize (3/3C) The village is joined to **Southmoor** (3/3C) on the A420 OXFORD to Swindon main road. A bypass is desperately needed. The curious name (pronounced 'Bagpewze') derives from Ralf de Bachepuise who came over with the Conqueror in 1066. The only notable building is Kingston House, a medium-sized, apparently early Georgian house of unusual design which may in fact be mid-17th

century, despite its later appearance. For 200 years it belonged to a prominent Berkshire family called Blandy. The house and garden are open to the public during the summer; there is fine panelling and plasterwork to see and a splendid staircase.

A mile east on the A420 is **Fyfield** (3/3C), fortunately bypassed, an attractive little village with a most beautiful manor house still retaining its 14th-century great hall and porch, to which has been added a narrow-gabled Elizabethan wing. It is now the rare book department of Blackwells, the Oxford booksellers, and the pleasure of browsing is heightened by the surroundings. The church next door was gutted by fire a century ago. There is a grisly tomb of Sir John Golafre, who owned the manor, and another to Lady Katharine Gordon, who was known as the White Rose of Scotland. One of her four husbands was Perkin Warbeck, the rather absurd pretender to the Tudor throne who was hanged in 1499.

Kingston Blount *see* Aston Rowant

Kingston Lisle (3/2C) Tucked under the downs in beautiful country west of WANTAGE, the manor was once owned by the Lisle family, to whom it was given by Henry II. Kingston Lisle

Park is a finely proportioned Georgian and Regency house in extensive gardens, with good views across the park to the downs and some fine beechwoods. The house is open to the public during the summer and is noted for its eccentrically designed flying staircase. The little church by the park entrance has an engaging wall painting of Salome perfoming a backward somersault, watched by Herod and Herodias dressed as a medieval king and queen. It is about 600 years old.

On the way up to the downs is the Blowing Stone which, men say, was used by King Alfred as a trumpet to summon his troops against the Danes. It stood on White Horse Hill before an 18th-century squire placed it in its present position. Thomas Hughes, who is buried at nearby UFFINGTON, tells in *Tom Brown's Schooldays* how a local publican blew a sound between a moan and a roar that could be heard for seven miles. Readers should remember, however, that this is legendary country and that St George killed the Dragon two miles down the road!

Kirtlington (4/1A) North of OXFORD on the east side of the Cherwell valley this was an important place in Anglo-Saxon times, a great Witan or assembly being held here in the year 977, attended by King Edward the Martyr and St Dunstan, Archbishop of Canterbury. The centre of the village is grouped around an attractive green and The Dashwood Arms recalls the name of the builders of Kirtlington Park. Set in 700 acre grounds, it is an 18th-century Palladian mansion described by Walpole in 1753 as 'Sir James Dashwood's vast new house which stands so high'. It still does, although showing its age somewhat. There is a pleasant footpath through the park, whose 'capabilities' were realized by the great Mr Brown, leading to Akeman Street, the Roman road that here forms the boundary of the park and is dead straight for about 4 miles.

There is an impressive church in the centre of the village, although much restored by Victorian Dashwoods. A mighty Norman arch supports the tower, which itself was completely reconstructed in 1853. The many memorials include one to three Dashwood brothers killed in the First World War.

Knighton *see* Compton Beauchamp

Langford (3/1B) in the flat, clay and gravel countryside of the upper Thames near Lechlade,

Langford seems just another stone-built farming village in this little-known part of Oxfordshire. And yet its lofty church tower, seen across the fields from every direction, beckons you to come and see the most remarkable Saxon building in the county. The large central tower is almost entirely pre-Conquest work and very impressive for such an early date. Inside, the high, wide nave is Norman with a narrow Saxon arch to the chancel and massive piers supporting the tower which have lasted for nearly 1000 years. The chancel itself is beautiful Early English Gothic.

As you walk up the path to the porch there is a headless figure of Christ on the wall with arms outstretched and flowing robe. Either late Saxon or early Norman, it is a beautiful and dramatic piece of sculpture, very modern in feeling, and could almost be by Epstein (*see* the picture of Epstein's Christ in Llandaff Cathedral in the *New Shell Guide to South and Mid Wales*).

Three miles away on the Gloucestershire border is **Little Faringdon** (3/1B), a small village in the shadow of an 18th-century house, whose humble and unpretentious Norman church, in a sheep-grazed churchyard, is the very antithesis of Langford.

Launton *see* Bicester

Leafield (3/2A) Village high on the ridge between the Evenlode and Windrush valleys, on the south-west edge of **Wychwood Forest** (3/2A). One of England's great medieval forests, there are only about 2000 acres of Wychwood left today, but it was once one of the largest royal hunting forests, stretching as far as WITNEY and BURFORD and covering at least 50,000 acres. Over the centuries clearances or assarts were made, often illegally, and Leafield and some of the surrounding villages grew from these. An Act of Parliament in 1857 officially disafforested much of the remaining area and the large Victorian farms and buildings around Leafield date from then. **Field Assarts** (3/2A), a mile south, has kept its descriptive name.

There is an attractive green in the centre of Leafield with a school in the middle of it. In 1860, a rich vicar commissioned Sir George Gilbert Scott to build the large and austere church in 13th-century Gothic style. Scott's milieu, however, was cathedrals and public buildings (like the Foreign Office) and the church here seems quite unsuitably grand for a country village. The ungainly spire can be seen for miles in every direction.

Ledwell *see* Sandford St Martin

Letcombe Regis (6/1A) 'Racehorses for two miles' says the notice at the entrance to the village, for this is downland country with gallops and wide downs stretching up to the Ridgeway 700 ft above and the Berkshire border beyond it. Passing an old mill on the Letcombe brook you come into a large village where modern houses mingle with old cottages and thatch, and a church that is of mixed periods, like the rest of the village. There are some fragments of medieval glass and a simple Norman font.

Letcombe Bassett (6/1A) (named after a Norman lord, but the king held Letcombe Regis) is one of the highest villages on the downs. The road leading to it follows the course of the brook, which carves a deep valley between the villages and is famed for its watercress beds (these can be clearly seen). The centre of the village is picturesque with thatched houses surrounding the church, small, plain and simple with a Norman doorway at the side and a tiny chancel arch. It has kept a very medieval feeling and you get an idea here of what a village church must have been like 800 years ago.

Even older is the large Iron Age Hill fort on top of the hill at Segsbury Down, with panoramic views over the Vale of White Horse. To reach it from Letcombe Regis there is a good walk up past Warborough Farm.

Lewknor (1/1A) The first Oxfordshire village to be seen as the M40 motorway from London cuts dramatically through the Chiltern ridge as it descends into the OXFORD plain. The village is tucked into the base of the hills and derives its curious name from Old English *Leofecanoran*, 'Lēofeca's slope, or bank'. Despite the M40 it is a quiet and peaceful place of cheerful brick houses and cottages, and an elegant Georgian former vicarage described in 1736 as 'a good mansion house with brewhouse and court attached'. Church Farm has a very fine late medieval barn. On the Icknield Way, which runs along the lower edge of the Chilterns, is a small nature reserve called Lewknor Copse; this is approached from the A40. Various of the helleborines, which are common in the Chiltern woods, grow there and spurge laurel flourishes.

Leafield Church spire

The flint and stone church of St Margaret is a basically Norman structure, but the chancel dates from 200 years later and higher than the nave, which gives it an odd appearance. Inside, the font is a particularly good example of Norman work and there are some Jacobean monuments. The north transept is full of memorials to the Jodrell family, from the 18th and 19th centuries. The clock in the tower has an enormous pendulum sunk into the floor at the back of the church and two of the windows are from William Morris's factory.

A good introduction to Oxfordshire, if you come in from the London direction, is to visit some of the charming and unspoiled hamlets in the rolling countryside west of Lewknor. A minor road leads through South Weston's (1/1A) brick and flint cottages to **Adwell** (1/1A) which consists of a fine late Georgian stone house, a few cottages under its wing and an earnest little Victorian church designed by Arthur Blomfield.

Half a mile away at **Wheatfield** (1/1A) a large park and fine trees presage the presence of a big house, but it was completely destroyed by fire on New Year's Day 1814, when the lake was iced over and the water froze in the firehoses. The stables remain as a farmhouse. The Georgian church also escaped the flames. Inside are box pews, pulpit, and coats of arms, much as it was when rebuilt by an 18th-century squire.

Next is **Stoke Talmage** (1/1A) where Petrus Talemasche owned land 700 years ago, and probably built the original church, but it was much altered in the 18th century, when the splendidly carved royal arms were installed. There are a few houses and farm buildings on the western slope of the hill. **Easington** (4/3C) can hardly be called a village at all. An unfenced road leads to a farmyard and, behind a barn, to a tiny, untouched 14th-century church, simple, rustic and quite delightful. All around are views of the rolling clay lowlands and up to the Chiltern scarp rising to 800 ft on Shirburn Hill.

Lidstone *see* Enstone

Little Coxwell *see* Great and Little Coxwell

Little Faringdon *see* Langford

Little Haseley; Little Milton; Little Rollright *see* Great and Little Haseley etc.

Littlemore (4/2B) Just outside the southern ring road, Littlemore is a suburb of OXFORD that is

noted for its connection with the great 19th-century churchman John Henry Newman. While vicar of the University church of St Mary he also had charge of the poor and obscure parish here, and built the Victorian Gothic church still in use today. With Edward Pusey and John Keble he was the leader of the Oxford Movement, but by the early 1840s was becoming more and more drawn to the Roman Catholic church. In 1843 he resigned his living and two years later was received into the Catholic church, an action that stunned his contemporaries in a way hardly conceivable today. Nearly 40 years later, an old man and a Cardinal, he came back to Oxford for the first time. The group of buildings where he lived near the church is now owned by the Oratory Fathers and you can see there a small exhibition, as well as Newman's spartan bedroom next to a small oratory.

Past the enormous hospital the road crosses a bridge over the HENLEY-ON-THAMES road to **Sandford-on-Thames** (4/2B), a fast-developing riverside village. The Thames splits in two here with weirs and a lock; and the country club on the right of the road is on the site of a Knights Templar hospice founded in 1274. The church porch was restored by Dame Eliza Isham in 1652 and carries the inscription: 'Thankes to thy charitie religious dame, which found mee olde and made mee new again'.

Little Tew *see* Tews, The

Lockinge *see* Ardington

Long and Little Wittenham (4/2C) South-west of DORCHESTER, over the Thames, are two beech-topped hills known as the Wittenham Clumps, familiar landmarks to travellers in this part of the county. The view from the top is magnificent and a Romano-British fort was built on one of them to command the river approach. Iron Age and Roman remains have been found here, and large numbers of Saxon graves further towards the village.

It is nearly a mile from one end of Long Wittenham (4/2C) to the other. A place of character, it has attractive timbered and plaster houses along the village street. The church stands at one end, approached past picturesque Church Farm, parts of which are medieval. St Mary's is ancient, with a fine Norman chancel arch and practically nothing later than the 14th

Box pews in Wheatfield Church

century. It contains one great treasure and a curiosity: the treasure is the 800-year-old lead font with a simple design of flowers and wheels and a row of bishops. According to Professor Ford (*Church Treasures in the Oxford District*, 1984) there are only 30 lead fonts left in England and it is remarkable that three of them are within 5 miles – DORCHESTER and WARBOROUGH being the other two. The curiosity is the tiny stone figure of a knight in the base of the piscina in the south transept. At least 700 years old, it is the smallest sculptured monument in England. At the other end of the village from the church is the Pendon Museum (landscape and transport in miniature).

Little Wittenham (4/2C) lies right under the Clumps – a few houses and cottages leading down to a rather uncared-for church near the river. A footpath leads across a bridge to the far bank and Day's Lock, one of the smallest on the Thames. Beyond is a pleasant walk across meadows to Dorchester.

North of Long Wittenham is The Barley Mow, a riverside inn made famous in Jerome K. Jerome's *Three Men in a Boat*. There is an elegant seven-arched brick bridge across the Thames built about 100 years ago by Sir George Gilbert Scott. The story is that he was dining with Lord Aldenham at **Clifton Hampden** (4/2C) who said that his servants from Long Wittenham were always missing the ferry. Scott thereupon designed a bridge on his shirt cuff and told him that the local clay was quite suitable for making bricks. He also designed the church, which is on a cliff overlooking the river, and the manor house.

Longcot (3/1C) A not particularly distinguished little village that used to belong to SHRIVENHAM, but there are superb views across the Vale to the White Horse downs. The pleasing little church, with lively Victorian glass has a fine Georgian tower that replaced an older one that collapsed while the bells were being rung one Sunday morning in 1772. The church guide does not mention the fate of the bellringers. A poignant brass in the chancel records the death of John and Lilian Carter who went down on the *Titanic* in 1912. He was a much-loved vicar of Whitechapel in London's East End; she was the daughter of Thomas Hughes, author of '*Tom Brown's Schooldays*'. When the *Titanic* hit the fatal iceberg she was offered a seat in the last boat but refused, and she and her husband sadly perished together.

Two miles east is **Fernham** (3/2C), with several thatched cottages, and the main road, called High Street, going past the church.

Long Hanborough (3/3A) It is indeed long, almost 2 miles, on either side of the A4095 road from Bladon to WITNEY. The only building of any distinction is an old manor house near the station end. A mile to the south is **Church Hanborough,** a small group of attractive stone houses and an inn called the Hand and Shears: this was sheep country once. The church of SS Peter and Paul is a delight. There is a very well-preserved Norman tympanum showing St Peter with his keys and the Lion of St Mark and, easily missed, the cock that crowed three times when Peter denied his Master. The nave was rebuilt about 1400 with unusually thin and elegant octagonal columns and above it all was placed one of the most delicate spires in Oxfordshire, a landmark down the Evenlode valley. The chancel screen, pre-Reformation, is in remarkable condition and still shows traces of its medieval blue, red and gold colouring.

A very narrow road leads across a valley to **Freeland** (3/3A), a small village of mixed old and new buildings. A pretty little Baptist chapel contrasts with the Victorian Gothic church opposite. Inside the latter there are some 19th-century wall paintings that entirely lack the freshness and vigour of the medieval art that they try to imitate.

Longworth (3/3B) In the upper Thames Valley on a low part of the limestone ridge running towards OXFORD known as the Faringdon or Golden Ridge. A prosperous-looking village, the centre is round the walled garden of the old Rectory, a mainly Georgian house but with an older part that housed a Tudor priest. Next to the many-windowed Manor House on the edge of the village is an attractive Perpendicular church with an unusual Jacobean screen. From the churchyard there is a fine view over the Thames Valley.

John Fell, Dean of Christ Church and Bishop of Oxford, was born here in 1625. His claim to fame rests mainly on the much-quoted rhyme written in the manner of a Latin epigram by a student he had reprimanded:

> I do not love thee Doctor Fell,
> The reason why I cannot tell.
> But this I know and know full well
> I do not love thee Doctor Fell.

The Wittenham Clumps viewed from the Thames

Hinton Waldrist (3/3B) is on the same ridge a mile to the west. The handsome 18th-century house next to the church stands on the site of a moated Norman castle built to defend the ford across the Thames at Duxford below the valley. It was built by the St Walery family who left their name here as Waldrist. The church has a venerable tower and two sad memories inside: a memorial to four sons of the manor killed one after another in the First World War; and a window to Airey Neave, local Member of Parliament, who was murdered by Irish terrorists at Westminster in 1979.

Lower Heyford *see* Upper and Lower Heyford

Lyford *see* Charney Bassett

Mackney *see* Wallingford

Maidensgrove *see* Bix

Mapledurham (7/2B) West of Reading the beech-covered Chilterns slope steeply down to the Thames and a narrow winding road leads to the tiny and picturesque village of Mapledurham. The brick and flint cottages and church are dominated by Mapledurham House, a large Elizabethan mansion built in 1588 by Sir Michael Blount, Lieutenant of the Tower of London. The approach is now from the back, with haphazard gables and immense chimneys seeming to support the whole structure, whereas the front is the more formal E-shape familiar in other Tudor houses.

The Blounts were here from the late 15th century, but Mapledurham has not had an eventful history, apart from being sacked in the Civil War. This may be partly because the Blounts were a Catholic family and therefore unable to take part in normal public life in the 17th and 18th centuries. The Catholic Relief Act of 1791 allowed them to build the charming Gothic chapel that is attached to the back of the house. There are some fine rooms in the house with family portraits going back to the 16th century, including a particularly attractive one of two Blount sisters. 'I see two lovely sisters, hand in hand, the fair-haired Martha and Teresa brown', wrote the poet John Gay. Another poet, Alexander Pope, was half in love with both of them.

Mapledurham House now belongs to the Eyston family, whose principal seat is at EAST

Overleaf: Mapledurham House

HENDRED. It is open to the public in the summer and you can also visit the old watermill, the only working one left on the Thames.

The little flint parish church at the back of the house has a great curiosity: an aisle actually owned by the squire and partitioned off from the rest of the building. A Victorian rector, Lord Augustus FitzClarence, who was one of William IV's ten illegitimate children by the actress Mrs Jordan, disputed the arrangement but lost in the High Court.

A nice way to visit Mapledurham is by boat up the Thames from Reading – only about 3 miles away – but it might be 300.

Marcham (4/1C) In the flat land around the river Ock just west of ABINGDON on the A415. Like so much of the Vale of White Horse it belonged to the great Abbey of Abingdon whose wealth derived from the tithes gained from the rich soil and meadowland. Marcham Park is a plain but handsome Georgian house that was the home of the Duffield family, but is now called Denham College and owned by the National Federation of Women's Institutes who run residential courses there. To the west is **Frilford,** scattered houses and a golf course, and further south, on the Ock itself, is **Garford,** a remote and pastoral village consisting of houses and barns and a little church approached through a farmyard. (A hen was laying an egg in the porch when the author visited it.)

Marsh Baldon see Baldons, The

Marston (4/2B) The name means 'marsh homestead' but today it is the suburbs of north OXFORD and New Marston which threaten to engulf it. Once the village was at the centre of the nation's history when in the Civil War the manor house, now divided into two, became the headquarters of the Parliamentary army. Oliver Cromwell visited it in 1645 and in 1646 the Royalist surrender was negotiated there. A cannonball fired from Marston hit the north wall of Christ Church where King Charles I and his court were residing.

St Nicholas' Church was much altered in the 15th century, but parts of the nave and chancel arches are Norman and the plate includes the oldest chalice still in use. In the porch is a memorial to Baron Florey of Adelaide and Marston who discovered penicillin.

Merton (4/2A) Not strictly one of the 'seven towns' of OTMOOR, but it has the feeling of an Otmoor village and looks across the river Ray towards it. St Swithun's Church is a very good example of the Decorated style of the early 14th century and is virtually untouched by Victorian restoration. But it has a sadly decayed air about it, with crumbling stonework, and an unlovely glass screen between the chancel and nave ruins the appearance. The fine Jacobean choir stalls have been replaced with modern chairs. A dead straight causeway road leads over meadows to Ambrosden. The battle of *Mertune* between English and Danes was fought hereabouts in AD 871. From the manor here the squire threw in his lot with Bonnie Prince Charlie in 1745 and went with him to his long, penurious exile.

Middle Aston see Steeple Aston

Middle Barton see Bartons, The

Middleton Stoney (2/2C) A few houses and an inn round a busy crossroads on the A43 OXFORD to Brackley road. The old village was demolished in the 18th century when the Earl of Jersey wished to enlarge his park. The church, however, remained. To see it you drive through the park entrance (the 'Private' notice applies to the grounds, not the church) and down a tree-lined drive. It is small, plain and isolated, and contains the Jersey memorial chapel, a study in Victorian gloom. The font was originally at ISLIP and spent some time as a feeding bowl for turkeys before being rescued. An inscription claims that Edward the Confessor was baptized in it, which is unlikely as the carving is 14th-century (but Pevsner says it might have been recut from an older one). The earthworks in the park near the church are the clearly defined remains of a Norman motte-and-bailey castle.

Weston-on-the-Green (4/2A) is south on the main road past an airfield. Modern housing, the Ben Jonson Inn and an old manor house among trees, now a hotel, can be seen, but the older and prettier part of the village is down a side road leading to BLETCHINGDON. The Berties held the manor here (until the heir was killed in the First World War) and rebuilt the church in 1743. It is unusual inside, rather chapel-like, with a huge Italian painting above the altar, said to be by Pompeo Batoni. The modern-looking iron cross by the pulpit actually comes from the masthead of a ship of the Spanish Armada.

Milcombe see Barfords, The

Milton (4/1C) Despite being almost in the shadow of DIDCOT power station, and near a large industrial estate, Milton retains a remarkably country air about it with old houses along its attractive village street. The Victorian church is dedicated to St Blaise, patron saint of woolcombers, and is situated just outside the wrought-iron gates of Milton Manor, a tall brick mansion built in 1663, supposedly to a design by the great architect Inigo Jones. The house and estate were bought by a successful London lacemaker in 1764 and his descendants still live there. The interior has a fine oak staircase over 90 ft high and some interesting Georgian rooms and furniture. It is especially noted for the delightful 'Strawberry Hill Gothic' library and the Catholic chapel on the first floor. During the summer the house is open to the public.

The pub in the village called The Admiral Benbow is on the site of a house where the famous admiral lived before he was killed in action in 1702 against the French. Tsar Peter the Great is thought to have visited him here to get ideas for modernizing the Russian navy.

Minster Lovell (3/2A) In a lovely part of the Windrush valley 3 miles west of WITNEY. In 1431 William, 7th Baron Lovell, returned from the French wars to settle at Minster and built a magnificent manor house on the banks of the river. It must have been one of the largest houses in the county judging from the size of the ruins. The 9th Baron was a prominent Yorkist and supporter of Richard III in the Wars of the Roses. With Catesby and Ratcliffe he was closely involved in many of Hunchback Dick's murderous plots and is remembered in the rhyme 'The Cat, the Rat and Lovell the dog, Rule all England under the hog'. After Richard's defeat and death at Bosworth Field in 1485, the Lovell lands were seized by Henry Tudor and Lovell disappeared. It was rumoured that he had hidden in a secret chamber at Minster to which a servant had lost the key and a skeleton seated at a desk was found during alterations 200 years later. Subsequently the house became ruinous and the remains, still considerable, are now owned by English Heritage and open to the public every day. A remarkable contemporary dovecot, in good repair, may be seen among the barns of Manor Farm.

The church, or minster, of St Kenelm was rebuilt at the same time as the manor and has some fine vaulting and a well-preserved tomb of one of the Lovells, almost certainly William.

The village street is pretty with its many thatched cottages leading past the Old Swan Inn to a bridge over the Windrush. Up the valley and across the Witney road is an area called Charterville, built in 1840 by Fergus O'Connor, Chartist MP for County Cork and champion of popular rights. Under a land settlement scheme he built about 80 houses with 2 or 3 acres each and put in North Country industrial workers who were supposed to be self-sufficient. The scheme failed and the workers drifted home, but some of the houses remain.

Mixbury (2/3B) In the north-east of the county where a portion of Oxfordshire pushes into Northamptonshire, the boundary being marked by the Great Ouse river. It is a small village with some Victorian housing and the remains of a Norman castle known as Beaumont, the site of which is marked by grassy mounds and a ditch near the church. At Fulwell House, 1½ miles to the east by the river, lived General Monck, one of Cromwell's finest generals who later helped to restore Charles II and was created Duke of Albemarle. Mixbury church is mainly 14th-century but has a notable Norman doorway.

To the east across a dismantled railway is **Finmere** (2/3B), an attractive village on two sides of a small valley. The ubiquitous architect G. E. Street laid a heavy hand on the church in the 19th-century, but it still has atmosphere.

Mollington *see* Claydon

Moulsford (7/1A) A riverside village on one of the most beautiful stretches of the Thames, upstream from Streatley and the Goring Gap. The downs stretch up behind the village to the west in great sweeps of hill and wood to Moulsford Downs with splendid views across the Thames Valley. The church is right on the river and was almost entirely rebuilt about 100 years ago. It is plain and simple inside with few things that are old, but a nice monument at the back to a West African 'merchant of note' who died in 1694. Also on the riverside is one of the best-known hostelries on the Thames, the Beetle and Wedge, where you may sit looking at the busy river traffic passing by, with Brunel's great railway bridge just visible in the distance.

Murcott *see* Otmoor

Nether Worton *see* Over and Nether Worton

Nettlebed (7/2A) Nearly 700 ft up in typical Chiltern beechwood country 4 miles north-west of HENLEY-ON-THAMES on the OXFORD road. The main street has some attractive 18th-century brick houses and inns, but suffers much from heavy traffic. An old brick kiln at the entrance to the village is all that remains of the local brickmaking industry that gave employment to the inhabitants for 500 years, Nettlebed being one of the chief sources of brick in the area. Joyce Grove, in the woods on the edge of the village, is a large Victorian house which was once the home of Peter Fleming, the author and explorer, and his brother Ian, who created James Bond. It is now a Sue Ryder home. The plain 19th-century church, built of grey brick, has two windows stained by the artist John Piper. All around are lovely walks through the woods, equally beautiful in the spring when the leaves are pale green and the autumn when they turn a brilliant yellowy-brown.

The next village towards Oxford is **Nuffield** (7/2A), small and scattered on the wide hilltop before the road descends into the valley at WALLINGFORD. From the old church there are splendid views across the river Thames to the Berkshire Downs. The strange prehistoric boundary (if such it is) known as Grim's Ditch or the Devil's Dyke climbs up the hill and through the village, just west of the church, and it is a good place to examine it and speculate on its origin. William Richard Morris moved live here when his car-manufacturing business at Cowley prospered and took his title from the village as Lord Nuffield. He belonged to the famous Huntercombe Golf Club which occupies part of the common.

Newington (4/3C) On the busy road from THAME to DORCHESTER you could easily drive through this small village without noticing it, were it not for Newington House, seen through a beautiful wrought-iron gate. Built by Squire Dunch about 1660 in grey stone, it is plain and well proportioned and must have been considered very modern in its day. The church next door is ancient and hardly altered since the Middle Ages, with a small 13th-century spire and sanctus bell. Inside, the monument to Walter Dunch and his wife of 1650 is fascinating in its own macabre way. They are represented wrapped in their shrouds with their faces showing and a knot over their heads.

Across the river in flat, fertile country between the Thame and the Thames is **Drayton St**

View across Otmoor from Beckley looking towards Charlton-on-Otmoor (see p. 126)

Leonard (4/3C), a cheerful village with a mixture of old and new houses, the Catherine Wheel and the Three Pigeons, and an old church much altered. St Leonard, one of the more obscure saints in the calendar, but unaccountably popular in medieval England, looks down benignly from one of the windows.

Noke *see* Otmoor

North and South Moreton (7/1A) The Western
Region main line goes through a cutting between these quiet country villages on its way to
DIDCOT, 2 miles west. You would call them
quintessential Berkshire if the bureaucrats had
not ruled them to be in Oxfordshire in 1974.
North Moreton has some attractive, mainly
17th-century timbered buildings mingled with
modern housing and a pub called The Bear with
a jolly inn sign depicting Rupert. The church is
quite outstanding; unaltered 13th-century nave
and chancel and a beautiful south chapel built in
1299 by Sir Miles Stapleton, who was later killed
fighting the Scots at Bannockburn.

The chapel east window is full of medieval
stained glass and is the finest to survive in a
village church in Oxfordshire. After 700 years
the rich greens, yellows and reds still glow with
all the glory of their original colour as they
illustrate various scenes in the life of Christ and
the saints. A wonderful sight and complemented
by the very fine modern window above the altar
in the chancel.

The bridge over the railway leads to South

The Perch and Pike at South Stoke

Moreton, a larger village with a wide main street leading to a fine-looking Georgian house with a buttressed wall round it. The Hacca brook goes past an old mill and farmyard and out into the flat arable countryside. A prehistoric mound is next to the church on the southern edge of the village, looking towards the downs. In the graveyard is an immensely ancient yew, completely hollow yet apparently still full of life.

North and South Stoke (7/1A) The ancient Ridgeway route goes through the tiny Thameside village of North Stoke before crossing the river near Streatley and over the downs. There is an old mill, a few cottages and a delightful church beside the farm in which time seems to have stood still. Once owned by the Norman Abbey of Bec, it has beautiful 13th-century work in the chancel including, very unusually, shafts of Purbeck marble. Apart from a rebuilt tower and a 17th-century pulpit, the interior is entirely medieval. The great contralto Dame Clara Butt was buried in the churchyard in 1936.

South Stoke, a mile down river, is a larger village of character with some elegant houses, and a pub called The Perch and Pike. At one end of the village a pleasant path leads across meadows to the river where there used to be a

ferry to the Beetle and Wedge at MOULSFORD on the opposite bank. The Western Region trains hurtle past the village over Brunel's river bridge, one of the largest brick bridges ever built. The church is old, although lacking the rustic charm of North Stoke. There is an enormous wall monument to Griffith Higgs, Chaplain to Charles I's sister Elizabeth of Bohemia, the Winter Queen: it is from her the Royal Family derive their claim to the English throne.

North Aston *see* Steeple Aston

North (Ferry) Hinksey *see* Hinkseys, The

North Leigh (3/3A) A large and growing village on a windmill-topped hill overlooking the Evenlode valley. There is much new housing near the A4095 WITNEY road, but the older part of the village lies on the northern slope of the hill towards the church, a particularly interesting one. There is something to see in it from every one of nine centuries: a Saxon tower of the 11th century, a simple Norman door of the 12th, and fine 13th-century pillars in the nave. In the 14th century many of the beautiful windows were inserted into older walls and the exquisitely fan-vaulted Wilcote chapel was built in the 15th as a chantry for the husband and sons of Lady Elizabeth Blackett. A monument in the chancel was erected to William Lenthall, father of the great Speaker Lenthall, in the 16th century and another to local gentry called Perrot in the early 1600s. A very unusual chapel was added by later Perrots in the 18th century to house their memorials and G. E. Street restored the church in the 19th century, adding the curious stone screen and rather heavy pulpit. A skilful addition of 1954 houses the organ and completes the litany of a remarkable church.

East End (3/3A), nearer the Evenlode, is a hamlet where there is a fine example of a Roman villa with a good mosaic pavement. The Roman road known as Akeman Street crosses the river here and there are many Roman sites in the area, but this one, known as the North Leigh Villa, is the only one that has been fully excavated. It is open to the public every day.

Northmoor (3/3B) At Newbridge, where the Windrush flows into the Thames, there is – paradoxically – one of the oldest bridges on the river. Built over 500 years ago it still carries a considerable weight of traffic on the A415 from WITNEY to ABINGDON and is well known for the public houses on opposite sides of the river: The Rose Revived and The Maybush. The single-track road to Northmoor along the river and through meadows and pasture is rural Oxfordshire at its most beautiful. The village matches the approach with old stone cottages by a brook, and Rectory Farm with its barns and Tudor dovecot flanking an unspoiled 14th-century church. It contains a beautifully carved wooden gallery built in 1710 and bearing the touching inscription: 'Richard Lydall gave a new bell and built this bell-loft free, and then he said before he dyed let ringers pray for me.'

Further on the road passes near the Thames where Matthew Arnold wrote of 'crossing the stripling Thames by Bablockhythe' on the old ferry, but his Scholar Gypsy would be surprised by the caravan site there now.

Nuffield *see* Nettlebed

Nuneham Courtenay (4/2C) As you drive from DORCHESTER to OXFORD massed rhododen-drons, azaleas and an elegant Georgian lodge give a hint of what is to come. The village that follows was built in the late 18th century by Lord Harcourt to replace the one he destroyed in order to erect one of the grandest mansions in Oxfordshire. The Harcourts had long been resident at STANTON HARCOURT when the first Earl, an enthusiastic patron of the arts, decided to create a classical villa in the fashionable Palladian style and set it in a 'Romantick' landscape. Having selected the site at Nuneham for its superb view across the Thames, he employed the architect Stiff Leadbetter from Eton to build an enormous house in a beautiful golden stone. The grounds were laid out by Capability Brown and the gardens were famed for the beauty of the site and for the temples, statues and follies that helped to set it off.

Contemplating his creation, his Lordship thought it 'as advantageous and delicious as can be desired, surrounded by hills that form an amphitheatre and at the foot the River Thames'. Two hundred years later the Harcourts have gone back to their old manor and Nuneham is a conference centre, but enough is left to understand why, when he saw it in 1780, Horace Walpole called it the most beautiful place in the world.

Otmoor (4/2A) Only 6 miles north-east of OXFORD, there is nothing else in the county, or indeed in this part of England, quite like Otmoor. This ancient fen formed by the river Ray and its tributary streams is a 4000-acre saucer-shaped area that has hills on three of its sides. Despite partial draining and enclosure in the 19th century – which led to fierce riots – it remains an empty, marshy wilderness with many unusual plants, migratory birds, and especially butterflies, a paradise for nature lovers in all seasons. The villages round the moor, known as the Seven Towns, have a special charm and character of their own.

A good place to start is **Beckley** (4/2A) on a 400 ft hill on the southern rim with good views over the moor. Pretty stone and thatched cottages cling to the hillside round the mainly 15th-century church which is dedicated to the Assumption of the Blessed Virgin. The medieval glass is very beautiful, that in the east window depicting the Assumption being particularly interesting, as are the wall paintings in the aisle.

East of the village was a royal hunting ground in the Middle Ages where Beckley Park, private and hidden, is an unspoiled Tudor house.

Noke (4/2A) is a tiny hamlet at the bottom of the hills on the edge of the moor itself, just a few houses and farms at the end of a winding lane

The Old School House, Noke

with a simple, lonely little church containing a splendid brass to Johan Bradshaw, her two husbands and eight children. Across the Ray is **Oddington** (4/2A), but you have to go by road through ISLIP in order to reach it as there is no river crossing here. It is a quaint little farming village with a church of great charm; a Maori princess lies buried near the porch. From the edge of the churchyard the view across Otmoor gives a good idea of the peace and beauty of it.

If Otmoor had a capital it would be **Charlton-on-Otmoor** (4/2A), a larger village with a wide main street and church whose tall 14th-century tower is a landmark seen from all parts of the flat fens surrounding it. The pre-Reformation rood screen and loft is a remarkable survival and the custom still persists of placing a large cross of flowers on top on May Day where it remains until September.

The name Charlton means 'freemen's village, or homestead' and the villagers fought bitterly for their ancient grazing rights when greedy landowners enclosed and drained the moor in 1830; finally the magistrates brought in troops and the old ways went for ever.

A narrow road curves round the northern perimeter through the churchless hamlets of **Fencott** (4/2A) and **Murcott** (4/2A), remote and rural places which are nonetheless two of the Seven Towns. A mile beyond the latter is Whitecross Green Wood, a nature reserve owned by BBONT, the Berkshire, Buckinghamshire and Oxfordshire Naturalists Trust. It covers 156 acres and there is evidence that a wood has existed here for at least 500 years. Public access is permitted along the paths and rides through the wood.

The circuit is completed by climbing the hill again to **Horton-cum-Studley** (4/3A), which combines the ancient parishes of Horton and Studley. There are fine views across Otmoor towards Charlton on the far side of the saucer. Studley Priory is a pleasant hotel on the side of the hill, once a priory of Benedictine nuns before being suppressed by Henry VIII, who gave the property to Sir John Croke. It is an interesting building, much of it 16th and 17th century.

A row of brick almshouses was built by a later Croke and the very odd little church in multicoloured brick was designed by William Butterfield, the architect of Keble College, Oxford.

Over and Nether Worton (2/1C) Over and Nether Worton (pronounced 'Werton') are small and delightful villages at the top and bottom of a hill in beautiful rolling country near Great Tew. Over Worton has a group of Georgian manor, rectory and little Victorian church, where John Henry Newman preached his first sermon in 1823. Two of the stone corbels are heads of Victoria and Albert.

A gated road leads through meadows down the hill to Nether Worton, where a stream runs through the valley. There is a castellated manor house and what must be the smallest church in Oxfordshire, joined to a schoolhouse.

Oxford (4/1B) No visit to Oxford should begin without a glimpse of the city from one of its hills. From Hinksey Hill, from Boars Hill, or even from the top of South Park in HEADINGTON, you look down into an amphitheatre of spires and domes, which Matthew Arnold called 'that sweet City with her dreaming spires' and Thomas Hardy's hero Jude likened to 'the heavenly Jerusalem'. You will notice how Oxford is hemmed in by a ring of hills, and by the river Thames and its tributary the Cherwell. With so little room to expand, the medieval street plan of the centre has hardly changed in a thousand years. Those who have wanted to build have first had to pull down, so that Oxford is a unique concentration of buildings representing every phase in English architecture, every stage in the nation's history.

The city's islandlike site gives it a poor climate, said to make for a long life but a rheumatical one. The damp probably kept the Romans away but the misty watermeadows with their lush grass attracted the West Saxon farmers, who by the 5th century AD had begun to ford the Thames at North (Ferry) HINKSEY, (*see* Hinkseys, The) with their oxen (hence *Oxenaford* and other early forms) and settle on higher ground near by. The real founder of Oxford is said to be the Saxon princess St Frideswide, who in 727 built a nunnery after a miraculous answer to prayer (*see* Binsey). It stood on the site of a later priory of St Frideswide, parts of which survive in Christ Church Cathedral, and around its gates the first settlement of Oxford almost certainly began.

Oxford is first mentioned by name in the *Anglo-Saxon Chronicle* of 912, which records that

Opposite: Detail of the St Frideswide window in the Latin Chapel, Christ Church Cathedral, by Sir Edward Burne-Jones, 1859 : (above) Prince Algar is struck by lightning; (below) the death of St Frideswide

King Edward the Elder had made it a fortified frontier position in his defence of Saxon Wessex against possible attack by the Danes to the north. Within its earthen ramparts there also lived the tradesmen and the craftsmen who clothed, fed and armed the soldiers. As the settlement grew, so did its trade and the surplus was exported by river to neighbouring towns like WALLINGFORD. Even a Viking incursion in 1012, which razed much of Oxford to the ground, could not slow down its rapid growth from a West Saxon fortified settlement into a flourishing trade and administrative centre.

After the Norman Conquest of 1066 King William appointed his comrade in arms, Robert d'Oilly, to be Oxford's governor. An enthusiastic builder, he not only rebuilt the walls and gates in stone, but added a motte-and-bailey castle on a bend overlooking the river and three stone bridges to provide yet more trading links. So by the 12th century Oxford was one of the nine most important towns in England with 5,000 inhabitants, a royal palace in Beaumont Street and 16 churches. It had, too, a powerful

Figure of Mercury in festive dress, Tom Quad, Christ Church

merchant class whose control of the town's trade was confirmed by the charter granted in 1191.

Exactly when the University began no one knows. At the beginning of the 12th century the Augustinians founded the priory of St Frideswide and the great abbey of Osney and Oxford had begun to attract scholars. Then in 1167 the University of Paris expelled its English scholars, who came to Oxford in search of new teachers; and soon afterwards the Dominican and Franciscan friars set up houses of study in the town. So by the early 13th century Oxford was known as a *studium generale*, a university, with 1500 students, each of whom studied for seven years under a Master (*dominus*, hence the abbreviation 'don') to become a Master himself. They were all in holy orders and the University's first headquarters was the church of St Mary the Virgin in the High Street, its first Chancellor the scholarly Franciscan friar Robert Grosseteste (1175-1253).

By the 14th century, however, Oxford was in temporary decline. The Black Death had killed many of its citizens, and houses stood empty or were destroyed by fire. The merchants were less prosperous and irritated by the students who complained about their lodgings or their food and ale. On 10 February 1355, the feast of St Scholastica, matters came to a head when a brawl in a Carfax inn developed into a two-day battle between town and gown in which 62 students died. As a penalty the leading citizens had to parade through the streets to the University church every St Scholastica's Day until 1825, and control of the town and its trade was seized by the University. By the end of the century most students were living not in lodgings, but in halls under a Master; and the first colleges had been founded by wealthy patrons or by the monasteries to provide accommodation for Masters studying for higher degrees. Then in 1379 William of Wykeham, Chancellor of England, opened his New College for both younger students and Masters.

Oxford did not escape the religious strife of the 16th century. Its monasteries and monastic colleges were suppressed by Henry VIII – although some, such as St Bernard's, which became St John's, and Canterbury, which became part of Christ Church – were refounded under new names. Churches were damaged and both Catholics and Protestants died in Oxford for their faith. In 1546 Oxford became a city and the chapel of Christ Church its cathedral.

The Quad at New College

More colleges were built and trade began to improve, especially for the stonemasons and the bookbinders, but then in 1642 the Civil War interrupted everything. The city was for Cromwell and Parliament but the University was for King Charles I, who made Oxford his capital and took up residence in Christ Church.

Charles fled the city in disguise in 1646 and Oxford surrendered to Sir Thomas Fairfax, the Parliamentary commander who wrote: 'I very much desire the preservation of that place (so famous for its learning) from ruin...'

Minimal damage was indeed done to the University but learning returned only briefly with scientists like Christopher Wren and Robert Boyle. And by the 18th century new buildings rated higher than academic achievements. Older medieval ones were pulled down to be replaced by some of Oxford's best-known landmarks like the Clarendon Building (1713), the Queen's College front (1735) and the Radcliffe Camera (1748).

The city, however, was in debt after the Civil War with dirty streets and disease rife. To meet expenses the city fathers were forced to sell off Oxford's parliamentary seats to rich landowners in the county, earning the nickname of 'the spaniels of Blenheim'. In time companies and committees were formed to rebuild the crumbling bridges and clean and light the streets. The Radcliffe Infirmary was built in 1770.

Most important of all, the bitter town and gown feud ended. The city was freed from its domination by the University and the St Scholastica's Day ceremony abolished. Dons were for the first time allowed to marry. In 1878 Lady Margaret Hall, the first college for ladies, was founded although women were not given full membership of the University until 1920. Today all but a handful of the 35 colleges accept both men and women.

In this century Oxford has been through a period of even greater change. In 1913 William Morris built his first car in a workshop in COWLEY. By 1938 the car industry employed 10,000 people and new housing estates had swallowed up old villages like CHURCH COWLEY and HEADINGTON. Today Oxford is an industrial and tourist centre as well as a place of learning and has a population of 115,000. Despite its traffic problems, its suburban sprawls and new shopping centres, Oxford will survive as it has done for a thousand years. This is part of its fascination.

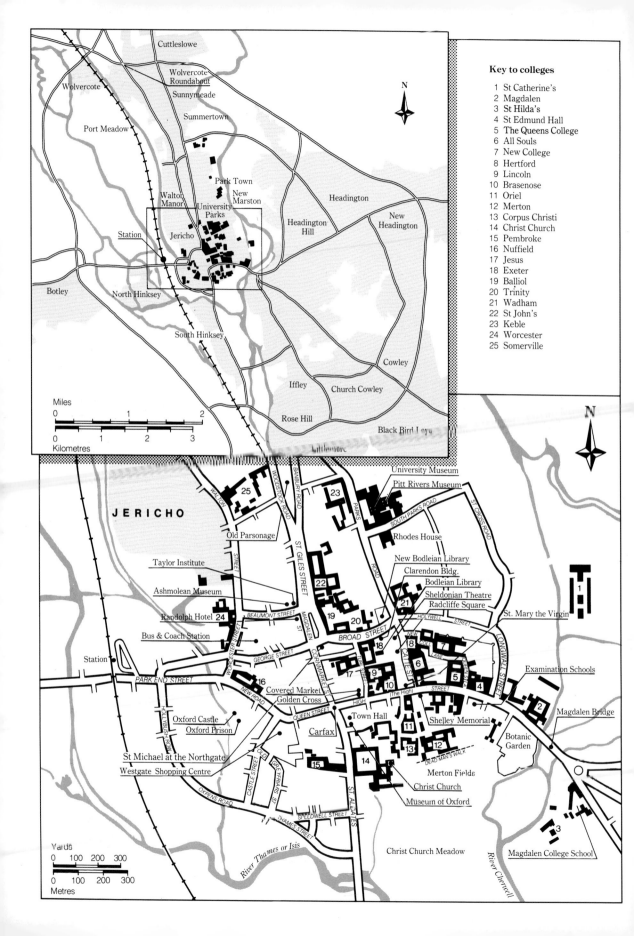

Key to colleges

1 St Catherine's
2 Magdalen
3 St Hilda's
4 St Edmund Hall
5 The Queens College
6 All Souls
7 New College
8 Hertford
9 Lincoln
10 Brasenose
11 Oriel
12 Merton
13 Corpus Christi
14 Christ Church
15 Pembroke
16 Nuffield
17 Jesus
18 Exeter
19 Balliol
20 Trinity
21 Wadham
22 St John's
23 Keble
24 Worcester
25 Somerville

Oxford Walks

WALK 1 St Giles' Street – Keble – St John's – St Michael at the Northgate – Balliol – Trinity – The Turl – New College
START   St Giles' Church
St Giles' Street makes an excellent starting point for a walking tour of Oxford. It is the city's widest street, traditionally used for processions and ceremonies. During the Civil War Charles I drilled his troops here and the ancient St Giles' Fair is still held every September.

Once St Giles' lay beyond the North Gate (churches dedicated to St Giles, patron saint of beggars and lepers, are often found just outside a city's walls). The original church dates from 1138, although much of the present building is 13th century. An attractive 17th-century parsonage around the corner in Banbury Road is now a hotel. A footpath north of the church runs through to Woodstock Road where almost opposite you will find Somerville College, founded for women in 1879 just after Lady Margaret Hall. It began with just 12 students. Past members include novelists Rose Macaulay and Iris Murdoch, politicians Margaret Thatcher and Shirley Williams.

Cross to the east side of St Giles', where a stream once flowed. In the 17th century it became fashionable for wealthy merchants to move out of the overcrowded city into elegant houses here. No.16, St Giles' House, was built in 1702 for an Oxford MP. Further on you come to the Lamb and Flag and beside it a very old chestnut tree and a passage leading to Keble College (1870), the first of the 'modern' colleges and intended for students of modest means. Bricks were used instead of stone to save money, but notice how effectively they are employed again in the 1970 new buildings designed by Ahrends, Burton and Koralek. Keble is best known for the painting *The Light of the World* by Holman Hunt, which hangs in a specially built side chapel, and for its association with the Oxford Movement. Opposite the college in Parks Road is the University Museum (1855) built in the Gothic Revival style. It has a magnificent soaring ironwork and glass interior, which makes a perfect setting for the dinosaur collection and a stuffed dodo. Behind it is the Pitt Rivers Museum of

View of Canterbury Quad from the garden, St John's

Ethnology and Pre-History, which includes material collected by explorers like Captain Cook.

Return to St Giles'. On the opposite side of the street note the Eagle and Child pub where the Inkling literary group, including C. S. Lewis and J. R. R. Tolkien, met for 30 years. Continue down the east side of the street to St John's College with a façade that has changed very little since it was founded in 1437 as St Bernard's College for Cistercian monks. After Henry VIII closed it in the 1540s it was bought and reopened by Sir Thomas White, a Merchant Taylor who named it after St John the Baptist, the tailors' patron saint. Above the main gate is a statue of St Bernard and on the inside of the gate tower a modern figure of *St John the Baptist* by Eric Gill. From the 15th-century Front Quad an arch leads to the more grandiose Canterbury Quad completed in 1636 with money given by Archbishop Laud, who was President of the college and later Archbishop of Canterbury. He placed bronze statues of King Charles I and Queen Henrietta Maria at either end of the quadrangle, then invited the royal pair to a banquet in the library to admire his work. An

Outside the Clarendon Building, Broad Street

archway leads to the garden, one of the most beautiful in Oxford.

From St John's cross to the Martyrs' Memorial (1841) on an island in the road. Designed by Sir George Gilbert Scott, it commemorates Oxford's 16th-century Protestant martyrs, Latimer, Ridley and Cranmer. Continue into Magdalen Street and over the crossroads into Cornmarket Street and on your left the church of St Michael at the North gate. Its Saxon tower (*c.* 1040) is Oxford's oldest building and was once linked to the city wall on one side and the North Gate on the other. Over the tunnel-like gate was the Bocardo prison where Latimer, Ridley and Cranmer were kept before their executions. The church includes the oldest stained glass windows in Oxford (1290) and a font where Shakespeare once stood as a godfather. The Church Treasury museum includes rare silver, early documents and prints and a chance to inspect the clock mechanism and the bells. From the roof there is a superb view of central Oxford.

Outside the church turn right and then right again into Broad Street. Now one of Oxford's most attractive streets. This was where Bishops Latimer and Ridley in 1555, and a year later Cranmer, were burned at the stake for their Protestant beliefs. There is a cross in the road and a plaque on the front of Balliol College to mark the spot. The heat from the fire scorched the gates that now hang in a passage in the north-west corner of Front Quad. Balliol's 19th-century façade has been unkindly criticized; however, the college is not famous for its buildings but for the writers and statesmen it has produced. They include Matthew Arnold, Gerard Manley Hopkins, Graham Greene, Edward Heath and the Earl of Stockton (Harold Macmillan). It is one of the three oldest colleges and was founded about 1263 by John de Balliol, a North Country baron who kidnapped the Bishop of Durham and as a punishment was whipped and ordered to pay for the education of 16 Oxford scholars.

Next to Balliol is Trinity College. It is set back from the road because it replaced a 13th-century monastery, Durham College, which was approached by a narrow walled lane. The gate tower is topped by the allegorical figures of Theology, Medicine, Geometry and Astrology and through its arch you reach Durham Quad, the site of the original monastery, and the entrance to the chapel (1694). A perfect example of 17th-century architecture, it was paid for by Dr Bathurst, then President of the college, and designed by Henry Aldrich, Dean of Christ Church – possibly with advice from Wren. The chapel's painted ceiling shows the Ascension by Peter Berchet and the magnificent carved screen and altarpiece are almost certainly the work of Grinling Gibbons.

The Norrington Room, Blackwell's Bookshop

Cross Broad Street to Turl Street and the site of the Twirl Gate, which let people but not cattle into the city. At the far end of the street is Lincoln College library, formerly All Saints' Church. A much older church stood on the spot until its spire fell down in 1699. On your right is Jesus College, officially founded by Queen Elizabeth I in 1571 for students from Wales; past students have included many eminent Welshmen. Across Turl Street is Exeter College with its beautiful chapel (1859) which Sir George Gilbert Scott based on the 13th-century Gothic style of the Sainte-Chapelle in Paris. To the right of the altar hangs a tapestry of the *Adoration of the Magi*, a Pre-Raphaelite masterpiece, designed by Sir Edward Burne-Jones and executed by William Morris, both honorary fellows of the college.

Return to Broad Street and continue along the south side past the History of Science Museum (*see* WALK 2). Opposite the Sheldonian Theatre (*see* WALK 2) is Blackwell's Bookshop, founded in one room in 1879 by Benjamin Blackwell. Cross Catte Street into New College Lane. You pass beneath the Bridge of Sighs (1914), a copy of its older namesake in Venice. This structure links the North and South quadrangles of Hertford College.

At the end of New College Lane you come to the gatehouse of St Mary College of Winchester in Oxford (New College). From his lodgings above the gate the Warden used to watch the comings and goings of his students. This was just one of the educational ideas of the founder, William of Wykeham, which other colleges followed. Whereas the first colleges had developed bit by bit, his New College completed in 1379 was carefully planned to provide for younger as well as older students. The Great Quad, based on a Carthusian monastery, has altered very little since Wykeham's day apart from the addition of a third storey. In the garden there is a section of the city wall that is particularly well preserved. Enter the chapel from the north-west corner of Great Quad. Epstein's remarkable statue of Lazarus is best seen from the altar. Notice the Founder's pastoral staff with its tiny figure of a kneeling bishop and the painting of St James by El Greco. New College has a distinguished choir and the stalls still have their original misericords. One has a carving of a gateway with portcullis which may represent the East Gate into the city, demolished in 1772.

Outside the Chapel turn right into the Cloisters, originally intended for prayer and ceremonial but used as a cannonball store in the Civil War. High up on the Bell Tower (1400) are some marvellously expressive stone faces.

WALK 2 Sheldonian Theatre – Bodleian Library – Divinity School – Radcliffe Square – Christ Church – Oriel Square – Merton College
START Broad Street in front of the Sheldonian Theatre

Broad Street was once a forbidding place in the shadow of the city wall, where small cottages huddled on one side and down the other the Canditch stream flowed. Later the street was used for horse trading. Today Broad Street is known for its bookshops, its colleges and its University buildings.

Until the 15th century the University church of St Mary the Virgin was the centre of University life, but in the next 200 years separate University institutions were built, many of them between Broad Street and the High Street. To make room for them a labyrinth of cottages and halls was pulled down.

To your left is the porticoed front of the Clarendon Building (1713), designed by Nicholas Hawksmoor for the University Press and partly paid for with profits from Lord Clarendon's *History of the Great Rebellion.* To your right is the History of Science Museum (1683), a perfect example of English Renaissance architecture with a

Opposite: Sundial in the Great Quad,
All Souls College
Below: The Clarendon Building and Sheldonian
Theatre from the roof of Blackwell's Bookshop

fascinating collection of early astronomical, optical, scientific and medical instruments in 17th-century surroundings. Until 1845 it was the home of the Ashmolean Museum (*see* WALK 3).

The Sheldonian Theatre (1667) was the first architectural work of Christopher Wren, then a young Professor of Astronomy. It was needed for important University meetings and ceremonies and was paid for by Gilbert Sheldon, Archbishop of Canterbury. Wren modelled it on a Roman open-air theatre and the ceiling painting by Robert Streeter is intended to give the illusion of an open roof. Notice the Roman touches like the tiered seats, the pulpits and the famous heads on the railings outside. From the cupola, which Edward Blore redesigned in 1838, there is a splendid view of central Oxford.

Through an archway enter the Schools Quadrangle (1613-24). Around you are the buildings of the Bodleian Library founded by Sir Thomas Bodley, a retired civil servant. It is now the second largest library in Britain with nearly 5 million books, but originally the lower floors were used for examination and lecture rooms. Each subject, known as a 'School', had its set of rooms and their names are above the doors. To reach the Divinity School, the oldest of them, enter the *Proscholium* through glass doors behind the statue of the Earl of Pembroke and it faces you. With its vaulted roof of 455 carved bosses by the master mason William Orchard, the Divinity School (1483) is considered

one of the most beautiful rooms in Europe. Orchard's initials appear in the ceiling and so do seven pub signs. At the far end a door leads to the Convocation House used for important University business and in 1666, during the Plague, the meeting place of the House of Commons. Above the Divinity School is Duke Humphrey's Library built in the 15th century to provide the additional space needed when Humphrey, Duke of Gloucester, gave his manuscript collection to the University. Between 1550 and 1598, at a time of national unrest, the library became so neglected that it was used as a pigsty until Sir Thomas Bodley saw it and decided to restore and extend it. Before you leave the Schools Quadrangle notice the unusual Tower of the Five Orders of classical columns.

Through an arch in the south side is Radcliffe Square and in its centre the Radcliffe Camera (1748), the first round library in the country, named after Dr John Radcliffe who left the money for its building.

On the east side of Radcliffe Square you can glimpse Wren's sundial through the wrought-iron gates of All Souls College, founded in 1438 as a memorial to the dead in the Hundred Years War. It has no undergraduates, just 62 Fellows, but an All Souls Fellowship is a great academic distinction. On the opposite side of the square is Brasenose College (1509), founded on the site of seven halls and called after Brasenose Hall, which in turn took its name from a brazen nose knocker: it still hangs behind the high table in the dining hall and there is a copy of it above the main gate.

Now cross to the north entrance to the University church of St Mary the Virgin. At its north-east corner notice the Congregation House, the first headquarters of the University. Until the building of Duke Humphrey's library the room above it was used as a library. Ceremonies, examinations and even trials were once held in the church and a damaged pillar marks the spot where Cranmer stood to receive his death sentence (see WALK 1). The original church was built c. 1300 but much of it was rebuilt in the 15th century in a stark Perpendicular style. For the stouthearted there are panoramic views from the tower of the 14th-century spire which rises to about 150 ft.

Leave the church by the south door and the Baroque porch, added in 1637 and recently restored. It was damaged by Puritan soldiers in the Civil War who objected to its statues. Turn right and along the High Street and at Carfax (see WALK 3) turn left into St Aldates' and walk past the Town Hall and the Museum of Oxford to reach Christ Church, the largest college in Oxford. Notice the cardinals' hats carved in the stonework of the outer walls and the statue of Cardinal Wolsey above the main gateway. He founded Cardinal College here in 1525. After he fell from favour, the king renamed it first as Henry VIII's College, then 'The House of Christ's Cathedral in Oxford', nowadays shortened to Christ Church or The House. To make room for his college Wolsey had to pull down much of the Augustinian priory of St Frideswide. The visitor's entrance from Christ Church Meadows takes you through the cloisters of the 12th-century priory. Then a shallow flight of steps leads into the Cathedral through the old priory entrance.

Much of the priory church, including its spire, survived Wolsey's rebuilding; but since 1546 it has served both as the college chapel and as a cathedral, one of the smallest in the country. Its massive Norman columns blend sympathetically with later additions like William Orchard's marvellous chancel vaulting and G. G. Scott's east end. In the Lady Chapel, with its windows by Burne-Jones and William Morris, a slab in the floor marks the approximate resting place of the Saxon St Frideswide. Near by her 13th-century monument has been reconstructed and opposite it is an unusual 'watching loft' where priests could keep an eye on pilgrims at her shrine. In the adjoining Latin Chapel the St Frideswide window, depicting 18 scenes from her life, is an early work of Burne-Jones. Charles I and his court lived at Christ Church during the Civil War and in the Lucy Chapel are memorials to Cavaliers killed in that conflict. Notice there, too, the Becket window (c. 1320). The saint's face was obliterated by order of Henry VIII. The Cathedral choir is famous and Evensong, at 6 pm every day except Mondays (Thursday: Sung Eucharist), is open to the public.

Leave the Cathedral by the west door and turn left into Bodley Tower and the spectacular staircase to the Great Hall (1529) with its original hammerbeam roof of Irish oak. Here Henry VIII held a banquet in 1533 and in 1644 Charles I called together those Members of Parliament who were loyal to him. The paintings include a portrait of the Reverend C. L. Dodgson, a Christ Church mathematics don who as Lewis Carroll wrote *Alice's Adventures in Wonderland* for Alice Liddell, daughter of the Dean.

The Great Quad was intended by Wolsey to have cloisters but he never completed it. Walk along its east side past the Deanery where Charles I lodged and enter Peckwater Quad built in 1705 in the classic style, on the site of the Peckwater Inn. Beyond is Canterbury Quad and the Christ Church Picture Gallery with a fine collection of paintings and drawings from 1200 to 1700.

From Canterbury Quad enter Oriel Square,

The Great Hall, Christ Church from St Aldates'

where suddenly everything is on a smaller scale. Facing you is Oriel College, the first to be founded by a king and named after Le Oriel, a house with an oriel window on the same site. Through the gate tower enter Front Quad (1620–42) with its grandiose entrance to the Hall. The words *Regnante Carlo* ('When Charles reigns') are a reminder that the quadrangle was rebuilt in the reign of Charles I. The statue on the left is Edward II, who founded the college for poor students in 1326.

Outside Oriel turn left into Merton Street with its medieval cobblestones. You pass Corpus Christi College (1517) which has the smallest quadrangle in Oxford and the ingenious Turnbull sundial; this can tell not only Oxford local time but even the day of the week on which any date in any year falls.

Continue to Merton College, one of the three oldest, which Walter de Merton founded in 1264 to provide an education for twenty scholars including his eight nephews. Above the gate is a statue of St John the Baptist (the college was built on the site of a church dedicated to him). Walk through a narrow archway opposite the gate tower and turn right into Mob Quad; no one knows the origin of the name. On its south and west side is the L-shaped library. Archway 5 leads to the chapel, planned on a cathedral scale but never finished. A *trompe-l'œil* by the organ shows how it might have looked. Return to Front Quad where in the southeast corner there is an interesting archway (1497) with the signs of the zodiac in its vaulted ceiling. During the Civil War Queen Henrietta Maria lived in rooms over the arch when King Charles lived at Christ Church.

Outside Merton turn left and then left again into Merton Grove, which leads to Merton Fields. Follow the path to the left known as Dead Man's Walk where a Royalist soldier was shot for treason in the Civil War. It leads to the Botanic Gardens and Magdalen Bridge.

WALK 3 Magdalen College – High Street – The Queen's College – University College – Carfax – Castle Mound – Worcester College – Beaumont Street – Ashmolean Museum

START   Magdalen Bridge

Oxford is built on a gravel bank between the Thames (Isis) and the Cherwell and since Saxon times its bridges have been vital. Robert d'Oilly, Oxford's first Norman governor, replaced an earlier wooden bridge here with the first stone one. In 1772 it was swept away by floods and the present bridge was built. In the Civil War Royalist soldiers defended the bridge by hurling rocks on to the heads of advancing Parliamentarians from the top of Magdalen College Bell Tower (1509). Nowadays only the beautiful and peaceful strains of a Latin hymn float down from the top each May Day morning when choir boys sing to huge crowds below.

Adjoining the river on the west side of the bridge is the University Botanic Garden. Its ceremonial entrance, the Danby Gate, commemorates the Earl of Danby who founded the first 'Physic Garden' in England here in 1621 on the site of a 13th-century Jewish burial ground. His head gardener was Jacob Bobart, who travelled Europe collecting many rare seeds.

Cross the High Street (The High) to Magdalen College, founded in 1458 by William of Waynflete, Bishop of Winchester and Lord Chancellor to Henry VI. Although dedicated to St Mary *Magdalen* it was first written down as *Maudelayn* and that is the pronunciation that has always been used. The college was built from Headington stone and replaced the medieval Hospital of St John the Baptist. Between the High Street entrance and the bridge is a blocked-up doorway dating back to the days of the hospital where beggars queued for food from the kitchen. Enter St John's Quad and in the south-east corner notice a pulpit where on St John the Baptist's Day (24 June) an open-air sermon is still preached.

Diagonally opposite is all that remains of a grammar school founded by William of Waynflete at the same time as his college. The other buildings were destoyed by fire in the 17th century but Magdalen College School still exists on the other side of the bridge. Next to the Chapel is the Founder's Tower, the entrance to the original college.

Outside Magdalen turn right up the High Street. Cross Longwall Street and then notice on the opposite side of the road the Eastgate Hotel, the approximate site of the city's East Gate, demolished in 1772. At No. 48 High Street

Punts at Magdalen Bridge

William Morris, later Lord Nuffield and founder of Morris Motors, ran a bicycle repair shop. In 1898 he opened a garage in Longwall Street and its façade is still preserved. Opposite 48 High Street are the Examination Schools, built in 1882 on the site of the Angel coaching inn and used for University examinations and lectures.

Pause to take in the sweep of the High Street, which curves from Magdalen Bridge up to Carfax and is arguably the most beautiful street in the world. Its grandeur depends partly upon the magnificent Baroque front (1735) of The Queen's College where Queen Caroline, wife of George II, presides under the cupola. The college is named, however, after Philippa, wife of Edward III whose chaplain, Robert Eglesfield, founded the college in 1341. It was for the education of 'Poor Boys' from the north of England but when one of them, Joseph Williamson, rose to become Secretary of State he offered to rebuild his old college on a much grander scale. To make way for it the modest medieval college was pulled down and Wren, Hawksmoor and Dean Aldrich of Christ Church contributed to the designs of the new one between 1671 and 1760.

Cross the High Street to University College, which also has a history far older than its buildings. The college claims to have been founded before Merton (1264) and Balliol (1263-8) because in 1249 William of Durham gave the equivalent of £200 for ten scholars to study theology, although the college did not officially open until 1280. The present buildings are much later and in 1700 the statue of Queen Anne over the gateway replaced an older one of King Alfred who may have founded the college at an even earlier date – about 872. At the 'thousand years' celebration in 1872 the Master was presented with a box of burnt cakes. In Main Quad a passage under staircase 3 leads to the curious Shelley Memorial (1893) in memory of the poet, who was sent down from the University for his atheism and drowned in Italy in 1822.

Return to the north side of High Street and continue past All Souls College (1438), built as a memorial to those who died in the Hundred Years War. The college has 62 Fellows, but has no undergraduates. On your right you come to the 14th-century University church of St Mary the Virgin (*see* WALK 2).

In medieval times to cross over Turl Street a little further up was to cross from gown into town territory. It was in this area that the St Scholastica's Day battles broke out in 1355.

The Mitre has been an inn since the 14th century and just past it is the entrance to the Covered Market, a delightful mixture of old-fashioned food shops and modern boutiques. Until

its opening in 1774 market stalls were erected in the surrounding streets, with a pig market at the end of Turl Street and the butchers in Butcher Row (now part of Queen Street). From First Market Avenue you can enter Golden Cross Walk, a picturesque development of small shops converted from a 13th-century coaching inn. At the far end turn left into Cornmarket Street for Carfax.

At Carfax, Oxford's four main streets meet (the name comes from the Latin *quadrifurcus*, 'four-forked'). This is the highest point in the city and has always been the centre of its life. The 14th-century Carfax Tower with its clock and quarter boys was the tower of the church of St Martin until 1896, when it was demolished. Outside the church was a 'Pennyless Bench' where beggars sat and women sold butter. The butchers had their stalls in Queen Street and in 1616 the massive Carfax Conduit was built in the middle of the crossroads bringing in piped water from Hinksey. On days of celebration it ran with beer or wine. Notice the plaque on the wall of Marygold House on the south-west corner marking the site of the Swindlestock Tavern where the St Scholastica's Day fighting began.

Walk down Queen Street, named after Queen Charlotte, wife of George III. Its medieval buildings have been replaced by nondescript shop fronts. At the point you join New Road is the Westgate public house, a reminder that the city's West Gate was in Castle Street to your left. The area in front of you used to be filled by Oxford's Norman castle, built by Robert d'Oilly in 1070. Its motte still stands and can be visited on application to the *Information Office* in St Aldate's Street. Adjoining it is Oxford Prison and St George's Tower (1074), all that remains of the chapel of St George in the Tower. A few yards down New Road is Bulwark's Lane which ran along the outer edge of the moat surrounding the bailey. The castle did not play a significant part in Oxford's history except one night in 1142, when the Empress Matilda was besieged there by her rival King Stephen and escaped in a blizzard wrapped in a white sheet. Opposite the castle mound is Nuffield College, completed in 1959 with money given by Lord Nuffield. Just past it turn right and continue into Worcester Street to Worcester College.

Like St John's and Trinity, Worcester College was first a monastery, founded in 1283 for student monks and known as Gloucester College. It, too, was dissolved in the reign of Henry VIII and nearly 200 years later it was refounded with money left by Sir Thomas Cookes, a Worcestershire

Right: May Week perambulations
Opposite: Tom Tower from Carfax

landowner, to build an 'ornamental pile' in Oxford. Its stately 18th-century façade is built like an open quadrangle with a library above the entrance and a chapel and hall on either side. Hawksmoor was probably consulted over the design. Worcester is best known for its extensive gardens, laid out in the 19th century with an ornamental lake. At the far side of the lake and blending perfectly with it is the Sainsbury's building (1983) by MacCormac and Jamieson, architecture that succeeds by combining medieval tranquillity and domesticity with modern materials and design.

From Worcester College cross to the north side of Beaumont Street and a tablet in the garden wall of No. 24 marking the site of Beaumont Palace, in 1157 the birthplace of King Richard the Lionheart. Beaumont Street was built between 1828 and 1837; with St John Street it forms the only complete Georgian development in Oxford.

At the end of Beaumont Street and facing the Randolph Hotel (1864) is the Ashmolean Museum, completed in 1845. The Museum was named after Elias Ashmole who inherited a collection of curiosities from John Tradescant, son of Charles I's gardener, which he gave to the University. It now includes a remarkable variety of exhibits ranging from Egyptian mummies and Greek sculpture to Impressionist paintings and the enigmatic Alfred Stone. Adjoining the Ashmolean but facing St Giles' is the Taylor Institute (Taylorian) dedicated to the teaching of modern languages at the University. Above its columned front are the allegorical figures of France, Italy, Germany and Spain.

Piddington (4/6A) On the Buckinghamshire border south-east of Bicester, Piddington was described by the poet John Drinkwater, who was buried there in 1937, as 'a plain, grey little village, neutral in design, ambling from cottage to cottage with no apparent sense of direction.' The church has a squat tower hardly higher than a nave, some elaborate 14th-century carving and a wall portrait of St Christopher.

Pusey (3/2C) The Pusey family held this manor in the Vale of White Horse well before the Norman Conquest, and traditionally obtained it from King Canute as a reward for entering the English camp and reporting the enemy plans back to the Danish king. It was a form of tenure called cornage or horn service and for centuries the Puseys possessed an oxhorn inscribed: 'I, King Knude give Vylliam Pewse thys horne to holde by thy londe'. The family sold their ancient lands in 1934 and the horn is in the Victoria and Albert Museum, London.

The grey stone village is a handful of cottages around a good, plain Georgian house built by a Pusey squire in 1753. The present owners have spent over 50 years creating a most beautiful garden. Its terraces, shrubberies, water garden and borders may be visited during the summer.

On the edge of the grounds stands a curious and attractive little Georgian church built at the same time as the house. Inside is a fine monument to Jane Pusey by the fashionable 18th-century sculptor the younger Scheemakers and another, earlier one to Whorton Dunch Esquire, which informs us that he was descended on *both* sides from families 'eminent for antiquity, opulence and noble virtues'.

Edward Bouverie-Pusey was a famous Victorian clergyman who was one of the leaders (with Keble and Newman) of the Oxford Movement which transformed the Church of England in the 19th century. His portrait is in the church.

Pyrton (1/1B) 'Pear tree place' is the meaning of the name of this small village near WATLINGTON, whose parish once extended to within 3 miles of HENLEY-ON-THAMES and included STONOR. Peaceful and rural, it is bounded on one side by the large park belonging to Shirburn Castle. There is an old manor house deep in the trees which belonged to the Symeon family, whose daughter Elizabeth married the Parliamentarian John Hampden in 1619 in the little church here. He struggled to get there after his mortal wound

Pusey House

at Chalgrove Field in 1643, but his way was blocked and he died at THAME.

Shirburn (1/1B) has a remarkable moated castle hidden by trees and walls, near the Watlington–LEWKNOR road. A castle existed here in Norman days but it assumed its present shape when licensed to crenellate in 1377 and was further 'improved' in the 18th century. Square, with corner towers, moat and drawbridge, it is an amazing survival. 'Private' notices abound but a visit to the gloomy church affords a glimpse through the trees.

The castle had many owners until an 18th-century lawyer, Thomas Parker, called the 'silver-tongued Parker', acquired the estate. He became Lord Chancellor and Earl of Macclesfield under George I but he was impeached for corruption, retiring to Shirburn in disgrace and dying in 1732. His descendants still live there.

Radley (4/2C) South of OXFORD, on the west bank of the Thames, Radley is known for its famous public school. St Peter's College was founded in 1874 by Dr Sewell, who bought the large Georgian manor house that had been owned by the Bowyer family. The house remains the nucleus of the school, but today the many newer buildings and playing fields cover a large area.

Upper Radley is largely modern, except for the old church, but Lower Radley runs picturesquely down to the Thames with attractive farms and cottages, and riverside meadows. There are views across to the landscaped grounds of NUNEHAM COURTENAY'S great house.

Away from the river and over the A34 is **Sunningwell** (4/1B), stone houses grouped round a pond and a pub called The Flowing Spring, a reference to the origin of the village name. The church is notable only for the remarkable seven-sided porch built c.1550, an early example of Renaissance influence in England.

Ramsden (3/2A) An attractive and well-mannered village down a side road 4 miles north of WITNEY. There is a single village street with well-kept houses and gardens, and a simple Elizabethan house set back slightly from the road. Although the village is old, it only became a parish when Wychwood Forest was officially disafforested by Act of Parliament in 1857 and Ramsden church was built at that time.

The Roman Akeman Street goes across the village to **Wilcote** (3/2A), pleasantly situated on top of a hill with views across the Evenlode valley. There are three large houses, an appealing little 13th-century church and practically nothing else. Wilcote House was originally a gabled Elizabethan building, but was greatly enlarged in the 19th century and has beautiful trees and gardens. The colour-washed manor near the church is unusual in stone country.

Further south towards Witney lies **Hailey** (3/2A), rather spread out on the main road. The north part of the village is called Delly End, pleasant houses around a green and a Georgian manor; the south part is Poffley End. Swanhall Farm once belonged to the ancestors of Gilbert White, the famous naturalist.

Rollright Stones *see* Great and Little Rollright

Rotherfield Greys (7/3A) Greys Court, about 3 miles west of HENLEY-ON-THAMES, was originally built as a fortified manor house by Walter de Grey, Archbishop of York, in the 12th century. Some towers and parts of his courtyard wall remain, but in the centre is now a flint and brick gabled Elizabethan manor house of exceptional charm, built by one of the Knollys family, who acquired the estate in the 16th century. Over the last 40 years the house and grounds have been carefully restored and were given to the National Trust by the late Sir Felix Brunner. An unusual feature is the Archbishop's

The maze at Grey's Court

Maze created by Lady Brunner on the theme of reconciliation. The puzzle includes the Path of Life and the overall plan represents the Crown of Thorns. The central cross is a combination of Roman and Byzantine design. The maze was dedicated by the Archbishop of Canterbury in 1981.

Open in summer, the combination of medieval ruins, Tudor architecture and grounds make it an agreeable place to visit.

The village is some way away across a wooded valley surrounding a picturesque green and cricket ground. The church is to the south of the village, rather over-restored by the Victorians but worth visiting to see the extraordinary Knollys monument.

Rotherfield Peppard (7/3A), or just Peppard as it is usually called, is spread out around a large common that goes down a steep hill into some woods. Beyond is SONNING COMMON, a fairly modern community spread over a wide area towards READING.

Rousham (2/1C) A small village in the Cherwell valley gathered round Rousham House, built in about 1610 by the Dormer family whose descendants still live there. The stone-built house has an engagingly fortresslike appearance and was indeed the scene of some Civil War exchanges. The Cottrell-Dormers, as the family became in the 18th century, had the unusual distinction of being Masters of Ceremonies to

A longhorn bull in the grounds of Roulsham House

Charles I and to every monarch until the end of the 18th century. As a result they moved in a more fashionable world than might be expected of a country squire, and in 1738 invited William Kent to remodel the house and grounds. It still contains some rooms designed by him; but Rousham's chief glory is its garden.

Until the early 18th century fashionable gardens were of the formal Italian type, but in the 1730s the idea of the picturesque garden took hold and Rousham was one of the first where the natural effect was skilfully used to create a Romantic landscape. Statues, follies and 'ruins' are used with leafy bowers to heighten the effect and Rousham garden is still much as Kent left it. It is open every day in the summer and is a most rewarding place to visit. A further delight are the longhorn cattle that graze contentedly in the park.

Russell's Water *see* Bix

Rycote Chapel *see* Albury

Salford *see* Cornwell

Sandford-on-Thames *see* Littlemore

Sandford St Martin (1/3C) In pleasant rolling countryside just west of the BARTONS, it is a small ironstone village through which the little river Dorn flows before eventually joining the Glyme near WOOTTON. There are a number of interesting things to see in St Martin's Church: an Elizabethan Royal Arms over the chancel, long hidden from view, possibly because of the Puritans; a fine memorial to a Georgian admiral; and a striking new stained glass window by John Piper. Under an oddly shaped grass mound in the churchyard is buried Lord Deloraine, son of the ill-fated Duke of Monmouth. Opposite the church is an elegant Queen Anne house in a small park.

A mile north is the tiny and picturesque hamlet of **Ledwell** (1/3C).

Sarsden *see* Churchill

Shellingford (3/2C) In the flat arable country of the Vale of White Horse south-east of FARINGDON, Shellingford has a Cotswold feel about it with grey stone walls and cottages and an attractively gabled 17th-century former rectory.

In the Middle Ages an annual fair was held here on the feast of St Faith, but a longstanding dispute with WANTAGE resulted in bloodshed in 1276, followed by a complicated lawsuit between the lords of the manor. The right to hold a fair was not to be surrendered lightly as it was a valuable asset.

St Faith's church has a graceful 13th-century tower and a spire that now boasts a fibreglass top – which has not spoiled it at all. A fine Norman doorway leads to a light and well-kept interior. The splendidly bewigged head on the north wall is Sir Edward Hannes, physician to Queen Anne; he must have been kept busy as she was constantly ill and had ten miscarriages. Lord Ashbrook, on the other wall, 'preferred the tranquillity of retirement to the tumult of business' and died at the age of 37.

Shenington *see* Shutford

Shifford *see* Bampton

Shillingford *see* Warborough

Shipton Court

Shilton (3/1B) A very pleasing village in a valley formed by the Shill brook south of BURFORD, not quite in the Cotswolds. From the south the steep hill runs past an unspoiled and modest Jacobean house down to a wide ford at the bottom of the valley. Manor Farm beyond the ford has an old dovecot whose occupants spend much of their time on the church tower on top of the hill. Still bearing the name of the Holy Rood, it is a most agreeable little church with fine Norman arches retaining traces of their original decoration. A pious Victorian replaced the rood or cross on the chancel screen again and the font has remarkable 14th-century carving. Griffith Gregory lived here in 1702, leaving 10 shillings a year to the vicar and 10 shillings a year to the poor, charged on a house in Burford for 1000 years. It is to be hoped it still gets paid.

Shiplake (7/3A) on the Oxfordshire bank of the Thames, near HENLEY-ON-THAMES, Shiplake is really two villages: the old village with church, vicarage and large house (now a public school) on a bluff above the river; and Lower Shiplake which is an area of Edwardian riverside villas and trim gardens that grew up around the railway station on the branch line to Henley.

Tennyson was married in the church in 1850 after a 14-year engagement, and composed an uncharacteristic ditty for the clergyman:

> Vicar of this pleasant spot
> where it was my chance to marry,
> happy, happy be your lot –
> You were he that knit the knot!

The 15th-century stained glass is a revelation. During the French Revolution the Abbey of St Bertin in St Omer buried its glass to preserve it from destruction by the mob and an enterprising vicar later bought it for Shiplake. There are wonderfully colourful pictures of saints and bishops, and some splendidly expressive portraits, possibly of the original donors. All have an air of bourgeois vitality, like the contemporary paintings by several Flemish masters. Not to be missed.

Shipton-under-Wychwood (3/1A) The Evenlode river turns to the east here to form the long valley that leads towards CHARLBURY and Wychwood Forest, which used to be much closer to Shipton before the clearances of the 19th century and earlier. The village itself is on the A361 north of BURFORD, on the west bank of the river centred round a large green on which is

The ford at Shilton

a memorial to 17 inhabitants who set off to make a new life in New Zealand in 1874. They were drowned with 470 companions when their ship sank off Tristan da Cunha. There are many fine stone houses, among them Shipton Court, a superb Jacobean house glimpsed from the main road down a topiaried drive. Among the inns are The Lamb and The Shaven Crown; the latter is 15th-century and was once a guesthouse for Bruern Abbey.

The large double-aisled church with its graceful 13th-century spire is on the edge of the green by the river. On the other side is the railway station, a stop on the Cotswold line, near an old-established family mill that produces a delicious flour called Cotswold crunch.

The best method of reaching **Ascott-under-Wychwood** (3/2A) is to walk the Oxfordshire Way footpath along the Evenlode. It once boasted two castles: one at the western end called Ascott Earl; one by the station built by the Norman D'Oillys who were prominent landowners in Oxfordshire. Manor Farm and its barns are on the site of Ascott Doyley Castle and the village High Street, really just a country lane, leads along the railway line past Priory House, which may have had a monastic connection in the Middle Ages. The High Street peters out in a farm but the footpath continues over the hills.

Milton-under-Wychwood (3/1A) is almost joined to Shipton on the western side. It is a large village with considerable new development and a Victorian church built by G. E. Street in about 1850.

Shirburn *see* Pyrton

Thatched and thatch near Shutford

Shorthampton *see* Chadlington

Shrivenham (3/1C) In the far west of the Vale of White Horse, on the A420 almost into Wiltshire. The entry from the east passes through a modern housing development serving the large establishment of the Royal Military College of Science. Once across the Bower brook, however, the old village reasserts itself, with stone walls, cottages and a wide main street with shops and at least four public houses. In its day Shrivenham was quite an important stop on the Swindon road and had a market in the Middle Ages.

The church in the centre is a curious one. Once owned by Cirencester Abbey, the tower was built about 1400 and has indeed a rather Gloucestershire look about it. In 1640 the rest of the church was rebuilt in a large 'preaching-box' manner so there is the phenomenon of an almost Wren-like church, but with the original medieval arches of the tower in the centre. There are memorials to the Barringtons, whose mansion is now part of the military college.

Bourton (3/1C) over the railway to the south, is a rather engaging Victorian estate village on a hill overlooking Wiltshire.

Shutford (1/3B) The countryside due west of

BANBURY as far as Warwickshire is remarkably beautiful, with richly coloured ironstone villages in the folds of hills that culminate at Edgehill on the border. The road runs through the tiny hamlet of **North Newington** (1/3B) and past Welshcroft Hill, tree-topped and picturesque, to Shutford. The 17th-century manor with tall projecting gable was supposedly where Lord Saye and Sele of nearby BROUGHTON trained his troops in secret for the coming struggle with King Charles. For many years the village was famed for plush weaving and a factory existed here until the 1930s. (Plush is a fabric, silk or mohair, woven in a special way to produce a rich velvety texture much in demand for Victorian interiors.) Fashions began to change after the First World War and the business declined, the final straws being the exile of the Spanish royal family in 1931 and the fact that the Shah of Persia was unable to pay his bill.

A couple of miles north are two delightful villages, **Shenington** (1/3A) and **Alkerton** (1/3A), facing one another across quite a deep valley. Shenington seems the larger, with a beautiful green surrounded by dark golden stone houses and the Bell Inn with a datestone of 1700 on it. The church on the edge of the green has a fine early Tudor tower. Alkerton clings in a haphazard way to the opposite bank, its tiny, hidden church with massive Norman arches all beautifully kept. At Shenington they have the ancient custom of strewing the church with freshly cut hay between Whitsun Eve and the first Sunday after Trinity.

Epwell (1/3B) is another village at the western end of this remote and hidden part of Oxfordshire. An old mill house stands outside the village itself which has thatched cottages and a little green near a ford. St Anne's Church is old and minute, like a Cornish church. Epwell Hill looms 700 ft above the village.

Due south along the hill are the **Sibfords – Gower** and **Ferris** (1/3B) – on either side of a brook. The Ferrers family held land on one side in the 11th and 12th centuries and a certain Thomas Guher on the other. Both are rustic, cottagey places with gardens and a duckpond. There is a large Quaker school at Sibford Ferris and a meeting house at Sibford Gower. Opposite the Wyckham Arms in the latter is the manor house, rebuilt in 1915 'into a riotous nightmare of the picturesque', says Pevsner.

Somerton *see* Upper and Lower Heyford

Souldern (2/2C) East of the Cherwell valley and just south of the county border, Souldern is down a No Through Road, always a good sign. It has a wide village street with some attractive stone houses including one with a beautiful 18th-century shell hood over the porch. The minor road west stops at the Oxford Canal, with a Constable-like view of the spires of ADDERBURY and BLOXHAM in a rural landscape. There is a dramatic Victorian railway viaduct near by.

On the edge of the village is a much rebuilt Norman church. William Wordsworth used to stay with his old friend Robert Jones, the rector, and wrote a sonnet for him called 'On an Oxfordshire Parsonage', including the lines:

Soft airs, from shrub and flower,
Waft fragrant greetings to each silent grave;
And while those lofty poplars gently wave
Their tops, between them comes and goes a sky
Bright as the glimpses of eternity,
To saints accorded in their mortal hour.

South Hinksey *see* Hinkseys, The

South Leigh (3/3B) A narrow road south from WITNEY leads to this lonely farming village:'only five farmhouses and labourer's cottages appertaining' a Victorian rector described it; it has

changed little. The late 15th-century church with wide, slender arches is notable for its wall paintings, heavily restored in the 19th century but none the less remarkable. The Doom, or Last Judgment, over the chancel arch, shows the saved looking rather smug as St Peter greets them while the lost are being dragged into the inferno by devils. Among the lost it is surprising to find crowned heads and a bishop! On the south wall is an enormous Weighing of the Souls, a subject much loved in the Middle Ages, with the Virgin Mary surreptitiously dropping her rosary on the scales to weight them in favour of the poor soul being judged. On another wall Pope Clement is shown with an anchor, the symbol of his martyrdom in AD 99.

It has recently been argued that the Weighing of Souls is actually a Victorian painting, although there is probably an original small painting underneath. Be that as it may, there is no better place in Oxfordshire to contemplate the fearful certainty of medieval religion.

John Wesley preached his first sermon here on 16 October 1725, when he was 21.

Southmoor *see* Kingston Bagpuize

South Moreton *see* North and South Moreton

South Newington *see* Barfords, The

South Stoke *see* North and South Stoke

South Weston *see* Lewknor

Sparsholt (3/2C) Another of the unspoiled rural villages on the Roman Portway below the downs near WANTAGE. It is a fairly wooded area, which may account for the probable meaning of the name: 'holt (or wood) where spear shafts were obtained'. The road due south leads to the top of the downs and a spectacular view from 700 ft near the Devil's Punchbowl. It is known that there has been a church here since before the Norman Conquest and the present one has a fine Decorated chancel from the 14th century. But the special interest is the woodwork, starting with an ancient door with its original ironwork intact. The simple screen to the transept probably dates from the 13th century, which is 200 years earlier than most surviving pre-Reformation screens. In the Middle Ages wooden effigies were relatively common, but not many have survived woodworm, Puritans, changing fashions and other depredations –

perhaps about 100 in the country. Sparsholt has three of them: a knight and two wives, beautifully carved with flowing robes and a wimple, all dating from the 14th century.

Spelsbury *see* Ditchley

Stadhampton (4/3C) A large village in the flat Thame valley country north-east of DORCHES-TER on the A329 towards Thame itself. Parts of the village are old. The church is much rebuilt, with a tower topped by four Georgian urns giving it a cheerful flavour. It looks across an attractive green to an unassuming 17th-century manor house. Along the CHALGROVE road some brooding gate piers and a magnificent avenue now lead to nothing, but there was once a great house, built in 1660 by Thomas Dormer and almost immediately burned down.

Over the Thame bridge – much fought over in the Civil War – lies **Chiselhampton** (4/3C), a tiny hamlet around the Coach and Horses inn. A handsome house sits on the hill where lived the Peers family, who also built the delightful Georgian village church in 1762. It remains exactly as they made it but it is now, alas, redundant. The key can be obtained at Church Farm next door, but go quickly for it is deteriorating. John Betjeman wrote a characteristic poem for its appeal fund in 1952, but it would sadden his heart to see it now. Here is part of it:

> Across the wet November night
> The church is bright with candlelight
> And waiting Evensong.
> A single bell with plaintive strokes
> Pleads louder than the stirring oaks
> The leafless lanes along.
>
> It calls the choirboys from their tea
> And villagers, the two or three
> Damp down the kitchen fire
> Let out the cat, and up the lane
> Go paddling through the gentle rain
> Of misty Oxfordshire.

'Verses Turned...', *Collected Poems*, John Murray (Publishers) Ltd

Standlake (3/3B) the Windrush divides into two streams north of Standlake before joining up again and entering the Thames at Newbridge. Extensive lakes and gravel workings are found near by with abundant bird life. One of the pits is now a leisure centre and Vicarage Pit, near STANTON HARCOURT, has become a Nature Reserve, managed by BBONT, where many species of waterfowl can be seen, among them

greylag, barnacle and snow geese.

The village itself, on the A415 south-east of WITNEY, has been much built over in recent years but a half-timbered, rather East Anglian manor house remains in the village street, and a pleasing old church dating from the 13th century with lovely Victorian wood carving inside. Gaunt House along the NORTHMOOR road was the scene of fighting in the Civil War, probably in defence of the river crossing at Newbridge.

To the north and west, across the main Witney road is **Yelford** (3/2B), which must be the smallest place in this book. In 1921 its population was eight and it cannot be much more now. From the narrow road you can see a small, simple timber-framed manor house and the equally small, unspoiled church of St Nicholas and St Swithun, built in early Tudor times. A time capsule if ever there was one.

Newbridge

Stanford in the Vale (3/2C) A substantial village, for centuries the market place and centre for the prosperous farming community in this part of the Vale of White Horse. Some time in the 16th century the market ceased, but the size of the village and the number of large and well-proportioned houses round the two greens shows that Stanford remained an important place well into the 18th century, before being overshadowed by neighbouring WANTAGE and FARINGDON.

The stately church in the centre of the village, mainly 14th century, is dedicated to St Denys, patron saint of France. This is uncommon and may be because one of the most famous relics of ABINGDON Abbey was a finger of St Denys, which it acquired in the 10th century. Tradition has it that the finger was displayed from time to time in the carved stone reliquary on the south

wall of the chancel for the edification and wonderment of the villagers.

Stanton Harcourt (3/3B) Between the Windrush and the Thames in flat watery country south-east of WITNEY. The Harcourt family gained the manor of Stanton by marriage about the year 1150 and have remained in possession of it ever since. Their manor house in the centre of the village has some remarkable features, including the great kitchen, unique in England, dating from about 1380 and the splendid tower, also medieval, which is always known as Pope's Tower: in the 18th century the poet Alexander Pope spent two years in the small room on the first floor working on his great translation of Homer's Iliad. He scratched his name on one of the windowpanes which can now be seen in the house.

In 1688 the first Viscount Harcourt decided that Stanton was too old-fashioned and built himself a fine house at Cokethorpe (3/3B), 3 miles away. Seventy years later the even grander mansion at NUNEHAM COURTENAY became the Harcourt home and Stanton declined, much of the ancient manor being pulled down. The wheel has now come full circle and the family have returned to their original seat, which they open to the public on various days (advertised locally) in the summer. It contains some fine paintings and furniture.

The church the other side of the manor wall is an impressive example of Norman and Early English architecture. The collection of Harcourt monuments and tombs ranges from the standardbearer to Henry Tudor at Bosworth Field in 1485 (his tattered standard still hangs above) to Sir William Harcourt, who was Gladstone's

Pope's tower, Stanton Harcourt

Chancellor of the Exchequer. The wooden chancel screen is one of the oldest in England.

Stone farm buildings, thatched cottages and a picturesque inn – the Harcourt Arms – complete a village that gives more of a feeling of feudal England than anywhere else in the county.

Stanton St John (4/2B) An attractive stone village off the B4027 west of OXFORD. Much of it is owned by New College, Oxford, which is responsible for the pleasing estate houses and the unusual village sign with the college arms on it. In an old house opposite the church in the early 17th century lived John White who founded the Massachusetts Company, which sent settlers to start the new colony in America. Woodperry House, on the Beckley side of the village, is a handsome Georgian mansion. St John's Church, set on a mound in the centre of the village, from which there are views to the distant Chilterns, has a justly celebrated Early English chancel with some beautiful medieval glass.

A little south-east on the B4027 is **Forest Hill** (4/2B) with old farms and some new housing. On a steep slope above the Oxford bypass, the little church has great character, with immense buttresses against one end to prevent it slipping down the slope. It is basically Norman but much redecorated by a Stuart rector with the Ten Commandments and other grave injunctions. The fragment of an old cope is fascinating; it dates from the 15th century when English needlework was famed all over Europe and known as *opus anglicanum*. Its colours of red and gold still glow after more than 500 years.

John Milton was married here in 1643, he an earnest and serious man of 31, she a local girl of 17. It was a disastrous match and she left him after a month, prompting his pamphlet on divorce. Two years later they were reconciled but she died in childbirth seven years afterwards.

Steeple Aston (2/4C) The largest of the three Astons on the west bank of the Cherwell, halfway between OXFORD and BANBURY. There are some fine houses and high stone walls on both sides of a narrow valley, and a prosperous air deriving originally from wool. The large church is a mixture of dates and styles and used to contain the famous 14th-century Steeple Aston cope, a needlework masterpiece now one of the treasures of the Victoria and Albert Museum. Lovers of Baroque pomposity will enjoy the splendid monument to Mr Justice Page. Superbly carved in marble in 1730 by

Weathervanes at Middle Aston

Scheemakers the Elder, the bewigged judge looks down on his scantily clad wife with an expression of mournful compassion. Known for his bad temper, in fact, he reduced the sculptor's fee by £20 for forgetting to put a wedding ring on Lady Page's finger!

The narrow road through the hamlet of

Middle Aston (2/1C) is delightful, with splendid views over the Cherwell Valley. **North Aston** (2/1C) is scattered around a green with a big Victorian house built about 2 ft from the small church it dwarfs.

Steeple Barton *see* Bartons, The

Steventon (4/1C) just off the A34 near DIDCOT, and cut in two by the Western Region main line, Steventon does not appear to have anything particular about it except an enormous green. However, it has one feature that is unique in Oxfordshire: the causeway or floodpath, built by Benedictine monks 700 years ago so that villagers might keep their feet dry from the flooding stream when visiting the priory and church. Nearly a mile long, the causeway culminates in the priory, now National Trust property, and the 14th-century church, after passing some timber-framed 17th-century houses. The causeway is still maintained, and the stream still floods. The contrast with the rest of the village, nearly all modern, is fascinating.

Drayton (4/1C), east of the A34, is another built-over village, although the High Street preserves some character. The plain little church contains a very interesting alabaster reredos made about 1450 with beautifully carved scenes from the Passion: a rare pre-Reformation survival, buried for safety and rediscovered only a century ago.

Stoke Row *see* Ipsden

Stoke Talmage *see* Lewknor

Stonesfield (3/3A) In the Evenlode valley, west of WOODSTOCK, Stonesfield was a rarity in Oxfordshire – a mining village, the source of most of the stone roofing slates used in the northern part of the county and on many of the Oxford colleges. The whole of the area in and round the village is pitted with mines and shafts from which the stone, or pendle, was hauled up and covered with earth to await a frost. When one was expected the whole village would turn out to uncover the stone and allow the frost to split it into slates, which would then be trimmed and shaped for roofing. If the frost was at night the church bells would be rung to wake the village up. The last mine closed before the First World War and demand for replacement slates is now met from demolished buildings – but they are becoming difficult to get.

The inhabitants of Stonesfield have now found other ways to earn their living and it is a growing village with much modern development. The western side with its winding lanes and slatters' cottages on the side of a hill retains its old character. St James's Church is in the centre with pleasing Early English arches and some 15th-century glass remaining in an otherwise plain interior. Opposite is an attractive early Georgian manor house behind a high wall. An ancient lane leads south to the river and Akeman Street, a Roman road clearly seen here.

Stonor (7/3A) A turning north off the OXFORD road a mile out of HENLEY-ON-THAMES leads

Below: Slate-miners at Stonesfield, 1881 (Courtesy Mr N. Godfrey)
Opposite: Stonor Park and chapel in November

you through Middle and Lower Assendon (7/3A) to the Stonor valley, one of the most untouched parts of the Chilterns. Stonor is a small village of flint and brick cottages and farms at the entrance to Stonor Park, which is set in a deer park of quite exceptional beauty surrounded by wooded hills. The core of the house is medieval, but it has been added to piecemeal over 600 years and reflects the changing fortunes of the Stonor family, who have lived there since at least the 12th century.

The 18th-century, many-windowed façade of warm red brick covers an E-shaped Elizabethan house with earlier work behind it. Inside is a maze of small rooms and staircases with some fine furniture and paintings, including some interesting Italian drawings. The Library has a celebrated collection of Catholic books and documents: Stonor was a centre of recusancy during the penal times after the Reformation. The Stonors have always been Catholic and in consequence suffered imprisonment and the loss of many of their estates in the 16th and 17th centuries. There is an ancient chapel, one of the earliest brick buildings in Oxfordshire, and a special exhibition commemorating the Jesuit martyr Edmund Campion, who had a secret printing press here before his capture and execution in 1581.

Stonor is intimate rather than grand or stately, but has that very special atmosphere a house acquires when the same family have lived in it for hundreds of years. The house, gardens and park are open to the public during the summer.

Stratton Audley (2/3C) A well-mannered, attractive stone village in hunting country, only 2 miles north-east of BICESTER, but it seems further. The noble Audley family built a castle here in the Middle Ages, but all that remains are a few mounds in a field near the church. Sir James Audley was one of the original Knights of the Garter appointed by the Black Prince. The church is a fine one, mainly 14th and 15th century, with large late-medieval windows. Inside is a splendid monument to Sir John Borlase, who lies incongruously in Roman warrior's dress, but with a full periwig. Stratton Park is a large plain house on top of the hill north of the village from which there are panoramic views across the county. Two miles away the small hamlet of Godington (2/3C) juts into Buckinghamshire.

Sunningwell see Radley

Sutton Courtenay (4/1C) A large, remarkably interesting village on a backwater of the Thames near DIDCOT. The Courtenay family held land here after the Norman Conquest and left their name and a fine manor house, whose pink-washed gables are just visible from the road. Opposite is a house known as the Abbey, but actually built by monks from ABINGDON in the 14th century as a grange to administer their estate. As if this was not enough for one village there is a large house opposite the church that is pure Norman and one of the oldest houses in the county, having been lived in for 800 years.

A walk down the wide street past smaller but still beautiful houses leads to a footpath along the tree-lined river bank, now a backwater since the main stream was diverted along the Culham cut in the 19th century. Small bridges cross weirs and sluices which help prevent flooding.

On the river is a house called The Wharf where H. H. Asquith, the famous Liberal Prime Minister in a great reforming government, lived in retirement after being ousted by Lloyd George in 1916. He occupied the premiership for eight years continuously: this was a record that stood for many years. Ennobled as Earl of Oxford and Asquith, he died here in 1928 and, with his wife Margot, lies buried in the churchyard.

The church here is very impressive, with some Norman details, but mostly of the 14th and 15th centuries. An unusual and delightful feature is the late-medieval brick porch. Eric Blair, better known as the writer George Orwell, is buried in the churchyard also.

Beyond Sutton Courtenay to the north an ancient bridge crosses the Thames to **Culham,** a scattered village around a wide green with pub, church and a splendid early Stuart manor looking back across the river towards Sutton. At the other end of the parish are the enormous Culham Laboratories which house the EEC Joint European Torus project (JET).

Swalcliffe (1/3B) In picturesque undulating country south-west of BANBURY, above the Swale, with lanes tumbling down to this brook past attractive ironstone cottages. Near the church is a magnificent medieval tithe barn, still in farming use, built by William of Wykeham in the 14th century; there are few finer in the county. The church is ancient, too, with two tiny windows left from its Saxon origins, but most of it is of the 13th and 14th centuries with Wykeham monuments and a 17th-century pulpit and reading desk. A mile north is Madmarston

Hill, a large and important Iron Age earthwork.

Due west is **Tadmarton** (1/3B); its name apparently meant 'frog pool' in Old English. It has a village street in the local orange-brown stone, and a pleasing group of church, small manor house and another tithe barn, this time thatched and not on the same scale as Swalcliffe. A stream flows through the village to Lower Tadmarton. It eventually forms the moat at Broughton Castle.

Swerford *see* Hook Norton

Swinbrook (3/1A) An idyllic place in the lush Windrush valley east of BURFORD. The minor road from the north follows the Swine brook through a deep valley, with old stone houses and cottages on either side down to the village, which is grouped about the church. Near by is a small stone manor house and an agreeable Georgian vicarage, one of the few still lived in by the incumbent. The church stands on a slight rise and at first glance only the strikingly large east window attracts attention. But inside are the extraordinary and famous Fettiplace monuments. About six generations of them recline on stone and marble shelves – of 'a rich and singular design' says Kelly's Directory – and they create a remarkable effect enhanced by the simplicity of the rest of the church. The Fettiplaces were among the greatest landowners in Oxfordshire and Berkshire and built a great house here at Swinbrook of which no trace remains. In the 18th century four brothers all died childless and the Fettiplaces disappeared from history, leaving tombs and monuments in many places, but nothing like the ones at Swinbrook.

In the churchyard the author Nancy Mitford is buried next to her sad sister Unity.

A footpath leads across the river meadows to **Widford** (3/1A) ('willow ford') and the medieval church of St Oswald, a hauntingly beautiful place with its box pews and wall paintings, including one thought now to be St Martin. It is on a Roman site and parts of a mosaic floor are visible near the altar.

Fettiplace monuments, Swinbrook

Sydenham *see* Towersey

Swyncombe (1/1B) Hidden and remote in the beechwoods on top of the Chilterns with splendid views across the plain of Oxford towards EWELME. There is an enchanting flint and stone Norman church of great simplicity with a tiny-windowed apse in a typically Romanesque manner. It is dedicated to St Botolph, an obscure 7th-century English monk who had a considerable following in the Middle Ages. The modern house near by is on the site of a large Victorian dwelling, which itself replaced a 16th-century one. The narrow road leading up the escarpment from Ewelme to Swyncombe is very delightful.

Thatching in Great Tew

Tackley (4/1A) Following the river Cherwell north from OXFORD, you turn with relief off the BANBURY road to Tackley's unspoiled village green. An unusually large church with a fine tower is on a slope overlooking the village and has many interesting features, including a large Jacobean monument to Sir John Harborne, his wife and 15 children, who lived at the manor house on the green. This is now demolished but an old gateway remains, and some 17th-century stabling and a dovecot. The key to the church may be obtained from Mrs Sims on the green. The Roman road known as Akeman Street crossed the Cherwell just south of the village.

Tadmarton *see* Swalcliffe

Taynton (3/1A) A picture postcard Cotswold village in the watery meadows of the Windrush near BURFORD. It has golden stone houses, barns, an old vicarage and a small, late-medieval church with splendidly carved corbel heads and an unusual font. Taynton stone is the most famous of all the Oxfordshire limestones, and the quarries north of the village have been worked for a thousand years. In the 14th century it was used in the building of Exeter and New Colleges in OXFORD and some 2000 tons were used in the great works at Windsor Castle in 1358–69. The stone was transported overland to EYNSHAM on the Thames and thence by water to Windsor, a tremendous undertaking. In later centuries it was employed at Christ Church, Eton College and Blenheim Palace, as well as countless other buildings.

Taynton stone is of the type known as freestone as it cuts cleanly and easily. It is famed for its long-lasting qualities, which can be well appreciated in the church here (and also in the Norman carving on the tower of Burford church, which has withstood the elements for 800 years).

Tews, The (1/3C) Great Tew is justly famous for its picturesque rows of thatched cottages, built of richly coloured ironstone on the slope of a hill, and surrounded by woodland that looks natural but was in fact carefully created in the early 19th century by a landscapist called J. C. Loudon. The Falkland Arms Hotel in the centre of the village is named after Lucius Cary, Viscount Falkland, who lived in the big house further up the hill. He was a poet and golden boy of the 17th century and died for King Charles at the battle of Newbury in 1643, aged only 33.

Great Tew

A classical arch leads down a beautiful shrub-lined path to the large church, originally Norman but now mainly 14th century. It has a fine light interior with some old bench ends and a moving sculpture by Francis Chantrey of young Mary Anne Boulton who died in 1829. The Boultons, descendants of the great Birmingham industrialist Matthew Boulton, bought the estate in 1815 and lived there until recently.

Little Tew (1/3C) is down a hill on the other side of the B4022 ENSTONE road. It is equally pretty, although in a less mannered way, with a small Victorian church and a perfect old manor house.

Duns Tew (2/1C) lies 4 miles east along a ridge with good views. It has quite a different feel to the other Tews, with a happy blend of old and new buildings and a pleasant church with a fine 17th-century tower.

Thame (1/1A) A prosperous market town of some 6000 people, 12 miles east of OXFORD on the Buckinghamshire border at the beginning of the Vale of Aylesbury. The High Street stretches for a mile and is perhaps the finest, and certainly the widest in Oxfordshire. The main impression is of colour, with brick houses and shops of every description, mainly from the 17th and 18th centuries, and an astonishing number of pubs (there used to be even more). The Spread Eagle is a particularly handsome building, a noted hostelry before the Second World War when it was run by John Fothergill, who wrote *The Diary of an Innkeeper*. A little Victorian Town Hall sits in the middle of the street. In a house nearby, the great Parliamentarian John Hampden died in 1643 after being wounded at the battle of Chalgrove Field a few miles away. Once a year in September the whole town comes to a stop for the Thame Show, the biggest agricultural event in this part of the country.

South of the town is Thame Park, a large Georgian house in an immense park. It is on the site of a Cistercian monastery founded in 1138 and there are traces of the older buildings contained in the present one. On the Dissolution of the Monasteries in 1540 it became the property of Lord Williams of Thame. He was an important Tudor official who was a considerable benefactor of Thame, founding a school still named after him.

The cathedral-like parish church is at the other end of the town by the river Thame. The oldest part is the chancel, built about the year 1200, followed by the nave with its fine arches and considerable length. As Thame prospered the aisles were added and the tower heightened in the 14th and 15th centuries with additional large windows in Perpendicular style. The church has many monuments and an astounding tomb of Lord Williams and his wife, right in the centre of the chancel in front of the altar.

Tiddington *see* Albury

Toot Baldon *see* Baldons, The

Towersey (1/2A) The flat country between
THAME and the Chiltern scarp is on the
Buckinghamshire border and it has a Vale of
Aylesbury feel about it. Towersey, in fact, was
in Buckinghamshire until 1939, when it was
transferred for some reason. It is an attractive
village round a crossroads with greens, farms
and a pond. St Catherine's Church is mainly
14th century, with a newer tower that seems to
blend well with the older work.

Two miles south is **Emmington** (1/2A), a tiny
farming hamlet down a No Through Road. A
simple oil-lit little church, with a saddleback
tower, sits lonely in a field. When the writer
called, the harvest festival had just been held and
the church was filled with flowers and produce.
It was the final act, the quintessence of country
faith, for the congregation of four people have
given up the struggle and the church is now
closed after 700 years of Christian worship.

Over the Thame road **Sydenham** (1/2A) is a
larger village, an agricultural place with thatched
cottages and well-kept gardens, a stream
running through the flat meadows, pubs and a
church with a Victorian belfry looking like a
witch's hat.

Uffington (3/2C) A large village with cottages
built of chalk and brick in a flat and rural part of
the Vale of White Horse, west of WANTAGE. It
takes its name from Uffa, or Offa, a common
Anglo-Saxon name. The large and impressive
13th-century church is a landmark for miles
around and is known as the Cathedral of the
Vale. The curious octagonal tower used to have a
spire, but on 2 December 1740 'the stepel was
beat down by a tempes, wind, thunder and
liten', so the registers tell us.

Within the parish is one of the most
fascinating prehistoric monuments in Britain:
White Horse Hill with its famous 360 ft long
horse carved in chalk, looking over the vale to
which it has given its name. Nobody is sure how
old it is; however, there is a long-held legend
that Alfred caused it to be put there after his
great victory over the Danes in the 9th century.
Experts, however, believe that it was the work
of a Belgic tribe, the Atrebates, who were
hereabouts in the first century AD. Thomas
Hughes, author of *Tom Brown's Schooldays*,
spent his youth in Uffington vicarage and called

White Horse hill the 'boldest, bravest shape for a
chalk hill you ever saw'.

On the crown of the hill, at 900 ft above sea
level, is an Iron Age hill fort known as Uffington
Castle from which there are tremendous views.
Sweeping away to the west is a curious gully of
undulating mounds called the Manger, and, at
the foot of the hill, a grassless mound called
Dragon Hill where St George is supposed to
have killed his dragon.

For centuries the White Horse and its legends
have exercised the imagination of visitors and
travellers, and accessibility has not diminished
the effect. Cars can be driven to within 500 yd
and you can walk all over the downs here, and
up to the Ridgeway, with panoramic views in
every direction. A wonderful place. (The car
park below the White Horse was runner-up in
the BBC Design Awards for 1987).

The little village below the hill is **Woolstone**
(3/2C) – 'Walfric's tūn' – with winding lanes, old
cottages and a picturesque 16th-century inn with
great boulders, or sarsen stones, by its door. By
Manor Farm is a small chalk-built church hardly
changed from about 1300, with a Norman font
made of lead and some beautiful 20th-century
Stations of the Cross, which make an interesting
contrast. Rather surprisingly in this remote
place, a German bomb blew out all the windows
during the Second World War.

North of Uffington, in the very centre of the
Vale, is **Baulking** (3/2C): farms, cottages and a
miniature church round an enormous, gated
common. Here bentonite is quarried: a form of
fuller's earth used by textile workers to scour the
natural grease from wool and cloth.

Upper and Lower Heyford (2/4C) The
Heyfords are two small villages on the east bank
of the Oxford Canal in the Cherwell valley,
about halfway between OXFORD and BANBURY.
They are both remarkably peaceful considering
their proximity to the enormous fighter base at
Upper Heyford, which is fortunately mostly out
of sight to the east. The road from STEEPLE
ASTON to Lower Heyford crosses a very old
bridge over the Cherwell, from which there is an
impressive view of the house and garden at
ROUSHAM. There was originally a 'hay ford'
here. The village street winds attractively from a
group of houses round the pub down past the
14th-century church to an old manor and farm
group near the Oxford Canal. Opposite the
church is an unusually grand-looking former
rectory.

Upper Heyford is a mile north. It is slightly larger, with wide stone streets leading down to the canal and views across to Steeple Aston. The Victorian church with its older tower is light and attractive for the 19th century. From its churchyard you can admire a massive stone tithe barn built for William of Wykeham in the 14th century. New College, Oxford, which he founded, still owns the living here.

Further north, still on the canal, is **Somerton** where bridges cross both river and canal with a delightful walk along the latter in both directions. The church is a very special one. The first thing to see is the 14th-century rood or crucifixion carved in stone on the outside of the tower, which has weathered its 600 years remarkably. Inside, very little has been changed and another unusual detail is the stone reredos of the Last Supper behind the high altar. This dates from the 14th century and few such survived the Reformation. If you think there are too few apostles, look closely to see St John with his head on Christ's lap.

The south aisle is full of tombs and memorials of the Fermor family who held the manor here before removing to Tusmore Park in the 17th century. Remains of their original house are in the manor farm buildings in the village. On the Ardley road is Troy Farm which possesses a Tudor turf maze.

The Cherwell valley runs more or less due north from Oxford to Banbury. The Oxford Canal was built in the 18th century and runs parallel to the river for nearly the whole 23 miles. The two are so close that it is quite difficult sometimes to tell which is which, and in parts river and canal merge completely. The canal is navigable the whole way and is one of the most beautiful in the canal network.

Upton *see* Blewbury.

Wallingford (4/3C) The Thames crossing here, near the HENLEY-ON-THAMES to OXFORD road, has always been an important one and a large castle to guard it was built in the 11th century at William the Conqueror's behest. It had many owners, mostly royal, and King John, Henry III and the Black Prince are known to have been here. It was noted for the strength of its defences, proved for the last time in the Civil War when it was the last Royalist stronghold in the county to surrender, after a resolute defence in 1646. Parliament ordered its complete destruction six years later.

Large grass-covered mounds of masonry remain, and from the top of the keep there is a peaceful view of the little red-roofed town, with the Thames and the Chilterns beyond.

Wallingford itself was granted a charter in 1155 and is a typically attractive small country town with market square, Corn Exchange and a delightful 17th-century Town Hall on four pillars. St Mary's Church in the market square is a large flint building with an impressive tower. Its many monuments to local worthies give it a rather civic feeling inside. There are some picturesque streets in Wallingford with many old houses and inns, but the traffic is a considerable problem as it streams through the town to cross the river on an ancient narrow bridge. The view of the town coming over the bridge from Henley is especially appealing.

Wallingford today is busy and prosperous with nearly 7000 inhabitants, and much new housing and industrial development to the west towards DIDCOT. **Brightwell-cum-Sotwell** (4/2C) has been nearly overtaken, although there are still some pretty thatched houses around the little church at the Sotwell end of the village. The flint and stone church of St Agatha has a pleasing red and blue brick tower added in the 18th century. Half a mile south, down a muddy road, is the remote and rural hamlet of **Mackney** (4/2C) with a delightful Elizabethan manor house built in stone, which is unusual in this part of the country.

Wantage (6/1A) Although situated on the Roman Portway below the downs, the town seems to be of Saxon origin and was well established by the 7th century. It is celebrated as the birthplace of King Alfred in 849. He was the first king to style himself Rex Anglorum, or King of the English, and his victories over the invading Danes and reputation for scholarship and justice have given him the title of Alfred the Great. There is a splendid statue to him, battleaxe in one hand and manuscript in the other, in the market square.

Wantage prospered in the Middle Ages and grew round the market, which was established in the 13th century. It became, and still is, the centre for the western end of the Vale of White Horse and by the end of the 18th century was known as 'black Wantage' for the behaviour of the citizens and the number of alehouses. The name and reputation have long since disappeared but the market is still held and the market square has an 18th-century flavour,

Statue of Alfred the Great sculpted by Count Gleichen (Prince of Hohenlohe-Langenburg), 1877 (see p. 161)

especially The Bear Hotel on the corner of it.

Church Street is old and picturesque with a delightful small museum, principally devoted to a display of downland life in the days when sheep and wool dominated the lives of local folk. Just beyond is the large 13th-century church of St Peter and St Paul whose central tower is supported on massively strong, pillared arches. There is much Victorian work inside, commissioned by the highly active W. J. Butler, who was vicar for 30 years. However, the lovely medieval choir stalls survived with their elaborately carved misericords and a tomb of Sir William Fitzwarin, who was one of the earliest Knights of the Garter and wears it on his leg.

The Reverend Butler was a notable High Churchman and founded the Anglican Sisterhood at St Mary's Convent on the FARINGDON road in 1848. They were the first order of nuns ever to be formed in the Church of England and initially much local hostility was aroused by this 'Popish' innovation. They are now a worldwide

order and until recently ran the famous girl's school of St Mary's, just off the market square.

Another famous school is King Alfred's, founded in Queen Elizabeth's reign, just south of the church.

Near Wantage, the village of **Grove** (6/1A) has been submerged by suburban growth as has **East Challow** (3/3C), although to a lesser extent. **West Challow** (3/3C) however, is tiny, peaceful and remote with winding lanes and hedgerows. Its little stone-roofed church has a 14th-century bellcot with the oldest bell in England to bear its maker's name: 'Paul the Potter made me 1283' it says in the English of those days. Manor Farm is a fine Georgian house in the same exuberant Baroque manner as West Hanney House and a house at STANFORD IN THE VALE. In the early 18th century there must have been a local builder with unusual flair.

Warborough (4/3C) In flat and fertile country where the Thame and Thames converge near DORCHESTER. The large green, with houses and cottages around it in a homely mixture of styles and periods, has great charm, as has the church with its chequered flint and stone tower with 1666 written large upon it. Inside there are a number of interesting details to look for: an 800-year-old lead font which is similar to, but simpler than, the one at Dorchester Abbey and a very unusual painting on the chancel of the Prince of Wales's feathers. The initials CP probably refer to Charles I who held land here before he became king. The lectern is in the form of a pelican feeding her young, an ancient Christian symbol not often seen.

Shillingford (4/3C) is the other side of the HENLEY-ON-THAMES road, with some pleasant houses by the river and one of the Thames' more elegant bridges.

Wardington (2/1A) A spreading village north of BANBURY near the Northamptonshire border with orange-brown ironstone farms and houses and wide grass verges. A delectable small Jacobean manor house in Upper Wardington can be seen through wrought-iron gates in the garden wall. St Mary Magdalen's Church is large and mostly of the 12th and 13th centuries, in a very well-kept churchyard with many flowers.

Waterperry (4/3B) A little way north of the A40, on the eastern approach to OXFORD, this

Opposite: Cogges Manor Farm Museum (see p. 165)

peaceful village sits on the floodplain of the river Thame. At the end of the village the Waterperry Horticultural Centre is in the grounds of a Georgian house. The beautiful gardens can be visited and plans bought at the garden centre – in the middle of which, rather incongruously, is the ancient parish church with its wooden belfry, a rarity in Oxfordshire. It is one of the most rewarding churches in the county. The Saxon origin can be clearly seen; there is a splendid 14th-century tomb; and the woodwork includes pulpit, reading desk and box pews. The palimpsest brass under a carpet in the nave is very well known. It was first used for a man and woman in London in 1440 and, at the Reformation, was sold, cut down and re-used for Walter and Isabel Curson. Finally, the medieval glass is outstanding.

Waterstock (4/3B) is a quiet and pretty village across the Thame from Waterperry, but to reach it requires a long detour by road across the Buckinghamshire border and back again through Ickford. Here is rural and unspoiled countryside, half-timbered and thatched cottages, and a quaint little church on the river's edge. The church contains beautiful glass and a monument to Mr Justice Croke looking sadly down on his wife who was 'the honor of her sex while she lived and scarce left her equall when she died'. The judge was an opponent of Charles I and declared Ship Money tax illegal.

Watlington (1/1B) A small and ancient market town lying at the foot of the Chiltern escarpment near the Icknield Way. There were five mills here in the Domesday Book and land was held by the D'Oilly barons and Preaux Abbey. Later a castle was built, which has quite disappeared, and a market was granted in 1252.

Watlington is as small as a town can be, with only three streets, a number of winding lanes and a wide variety of attractive brick buildings and shops from the 17th and 18th century. It used to be noted for its numerous number of inns, but a 19th-century Methodist bought six of them and closed them down. The town hall, around which the traffic flows, was built by Thomas Stonor in 1664 and also served as a grammar school and covered market. It is one of the oldest in Oxfordshire. The church, with old tower but Victorian nave, is tucked away on the west side of the town.

A steep climb leads up the scarp to Watlington Hill towards **Christmas Common** (1/1B), a heavily beechwooded hamlet on top of the Chilterns. Watlington Park is a Georgian house with magnificent views over the Oxford plain.

Wendlebury see Chesterton

West Challow see Wantage

Westcote Barton see Bartons, The

West Hagbourne; West Hanney see East and West Hagbourne etc.

Weston-on-the-Green see Middleton Stoney

Westwell (3/1A) It would be very hard to judge which was the most beautiful village in Oxfordshire but Westwell would surely be among the finalists. South of BURFORD, on a lonely plateau before the Cotswolds proper begin, this old stone village grouped around a green and duckpond has successfully kept the 20th century at bay. On the edge of the green is a simple church with a good Norman doorway and a mass dial scratched above it. Inside, it has changed little over the centuries. There is a fine effigy of a 17th-century rector holding his Bible, and an absurdly large but pleasingly provincial monument to Charles Trinder and his wife and 14 children. Around the green are old stone farms and barns, and a Tudor manor house. The war memorial is a block of limestone, set with a numeral from the clock of the Cloth Hall at Ypres which dominated that terrible battlefield of the First World War.

Holwell (3/1B) is to the east and consists only of manor farm and a Victorian church. Roman Akeman Street crosses the parish on its march towards the Fosseway. Bradwell Grove is a Gothic mansion on the Lechlade road that is now the Cotswold Wildlife Park; among the specimen trees and shrubs is a fine collection of animals, birds and reptiles from all over the world. It is open every day of the year except Christmas Day.

Wheatfield see Lewknor

Wheatley (4/2B) About 3 miles east of OXFORD off the A40, Wheatley has inevitably been somewhat overtaken by it. But the High Street has some pleasing stone houses, including the manor, and there are two 17th-century farms left in Crown Road. The church is a rather bleak design by G. E. Street with a heavy spire. The village lock-up is the most unusual building in Wheatley: a pyramid with a ball on top. Dr Johnson, attended as always by the faithful Boswell, came to visit the poet William Mickle who lived in Crown Road.

Shielding Wheatley from Oxford is Shotover Hill, now a public park from which there are splendid views towards the Chilterns and Berkshire Downs. Below the hill is **Horspath** (4/2B), the first true village east of Oxford, although it has attracted some new housing developments. The church is a gem. Heavy arches in the south aisle are a good example of the Transitional style between Norman and Early English. The stained glass window opposite the door commemorates an Oxford don who was attacked by a wild boar when walking on Shotover Hill. He defended himself vigorously with a volume of Aristotle he happened to be carrying saying, as he thrust it down the brute's throat, *'Graeca cum est'*. ('This is with Greek' or, more roughly translated, 'With the compliments of the Greeks').

Whitchurch (7/2B) Approached down a long steep hill through typical Chiltern beechwoods, this Thameside village is full of character with a mixture of brick and flint cottages, Georgian houses and Edwardian villas built when the cult of the Thames was at its height. A cast-iron tollbridge connects it with Pangbourne in Berkshire. The Whitchurch Tollbridge Company was established in the 18th century and charges cars 4p: twice as much as the only other Thames tollbridge at EYNSHAM.

The church building is Victorian but full of interesting monuments, including a brass to Thomas Walysch, trayer (wine taster) to Henry IV and V in the 15th century, and a memorial to Richard and Anne Lybbe who died after 50 years in wedlock and 'are once more joined within this peaceful bed, where Honour (not Arabian Gummes) is spread'. What can this mean? The Lybbes built Hardwick House, a fine Elizabethan house on a chalk slope leading down to the Thames.

White Horse Hill *see* Uffington

Widford *see* Swinbrook

Wigginton *see* Hook Norton

Wilcote *see* Ramsden

Witney (3/2B) A busy, thriving town of about 14,000 people, 12 miles due west of OXFORD along the A40. It has been celebrated for the manufacture of blankets since the Middle Ages, and as recently as the 1930s well over 1000 people were employed on 500 looms. Earlys of Witney are still making blankets here as they have done for over 200 years. The water of the river Windrush, which flows through the town, is said to possess particular qualities that contribute to the softness of the blankets.

The principal street threads from north to south for nearly a mile, with old shopfronts, houses and factories on either side. The road up a hill past the 17th-century Butter Cross leads to a wide and spacious green with some handsome houses and inns and the Henry Box school, an elegant building founded in 1660. At the far end is St Mary's Church, with its splendid spire, one of the earliest and finest in the county, a landmark in the surrounding flat countryside. Church and spire are on the scale of a mini-cathedral and are very good examples of 13th-century architecture. As Witney prospered in the 14th and 15th centuries on its woollen products, chapels were added and aisles widened with new windows of impressive size and beauty. The interior, however, is a little disappointing owing to severe Victorian restoration; but some interesting monuments to Witney citizens have survived, particularly to the Wenman family who were among the most prominent blanket makers 500 years ago.

Witney has nearly quadrupled in size in the last 50 years with many new houses, some of them built in unsuitable materials and colours. However, on the whole it has managed to keep the atmosphere and character of a country market town, despite the pressures of new industry and traffic; and the stone-built supermarket complex behind the market place has been very well designed.

Cogges (3/3B) is an ancient hamlet over the Windrush, now surrounded by Witney. It was the site of a medieval priory and contains the Cogges Farm Museum, established in the old manor house, and farm buildings that have miraculously survived untouched by the 20th century. It is a fascinating place where not only old farm implements and machinery can be seen, but also breeds that have almost disappeared, such as Oxford Down sheep and Berkshire pigs.

Ducklington (3/2B) is another small village just south of Witney which has managed to retain its rural atmosphere; it has pretty stone houses around a pond and a fine old church with exceptional 14th-century windows.

Wolvercote (4/1B) At its northern end it becomes an OXFORD suburb, but Lower Wolvercote remains a riverside village. The most picturesque approach is from Port Meadow past the ruins of Godstow nunnery. Little is left of this former Benedictine house except a rectangular enclosure with the remains of a chapel in its south-east corner. King Stephen attended the nunnery's dedication in 1138. It was a Royalist stronghold in the Civil War until the Parliamentarians burned it down in 1645. The nunnery is best known for its links with Fair Rosamund Clifford, the mistress of Henry II, who is said to have fled here to die of a broken heart after Queen Eleanor discovered her at the royal hunting lodge at WOODSTOCK. Across the river is the celebrated 17th-century Trout Inn with its peacocks and weirside terrace. The original inn was a rest house for visitors to the nunnery. Just over the next bridge, notice in the wall a plaque commemorating the deaths of two young airmen whose plane crashed near by in 1912. Behind the green is a papermill with a 300-year history.

The parish church of St Peter in **Upper Wolvercote** (4/1B) was almost rebuilt in 1859. The Saxon font carved from one piece of stone is from the original church. So, too, is the unusual monument to Sir John Walter, who once lived at Godstow Abbey. Near the south door is a striking John Piper window (1976) showing hands of all nations greeting Christ on his entry into Jerusalem.

Woodeaton (4/2A) It is hard to believe that this perfect country village around a green and ancient stone cross is only 2 miles from the OXFORD ring road. Above the village is a fine Georgian manor house built by Squire Weyland and further dignified by Sir John Soane, the great 18th-century architect who was born in Oxfordshire. There are good views of Oxford from here. Time seems to stand still in the little 13th-century church of the Holy Rood, with its squire's pew, clerk's desk, rood screen and old pews. One of the best wall paintings of St Christopher in this country shows him standing with his feet among fishes and promising in Norman French that those who looked on his image that day would not die ('Ki cest image verra le jur de mal mort ne murra').

Elsfield (4/2B) is another village even nearer to Oxford with farms and thatch and an old manor, with a Victorian wing, that once belonged to John Buchan. The plain, small, 12th-century church overlooking Oxford was dedicated to St Thomas of Canterbury in 1273.

Woodstock (4/1A) Long before the great palace of Blenheim was thought of, Woodstock, north-west of OXFORD, was a favourite manor and hunting lodge for English kings. Alfred the Great lived here for a time. In the 12th century Henry I stocked the park with deer, and put a wall round it, making it the first enclosed park in England. It was the favourite residence of King Henry II, whose mistress, Fair Rosamund, is

The north façade of Blenheim Palace

supposed to have lived in a bower in the park. Edward of Woodstock, the Black Prince, was born here in 1330. Later monarchs were frequent visitors and Woodstock remained a royal manor until the reign of Queen Anne.

Woodstock today is a small town of about 2000 people, with many attractive Georgian buildings and shops in the High Street. For nearly 300 years visitors and tourists have been attracted here and there are many inns and hotels, of which the Bear Hotel is probably the best known. Opposite the church, originally old but almost entirely rebuilt in 1878, is the Oxfordshire County Museum: it contains an excellent permanent exhibition on the county's development from earliest times.

At the end of Park Street, a triumphal arch leads to one of the most famous views in England: the great bulk of **Blenheim Palace** (4/1A) seen across the park and lake about half a mile away.

In the early years of the 18th century John Churchill, 1st Duke of Marlborough, was given the manor of Woodstock by Queen Anne as a reward for his great victory over the French at Blenheim and commissioned John Vanbrugh to build a house for him. The result, after 20 years of building – and furious arguments between Vanbrugh and the formidable Duchess Sarah – was a Baroque masterpiece on a heroic scale.

'Toad crossing' sign, Wootton

Detail of thatch, Wroxton

The sheer size of Blenheim, built of golden stone from the famous TAYNTON quarries and covering 7 acres, is breathtaking, as is the setting in the magnificent 2000- acre park landscaped by Capability Brown. Small wonder that King George III exclaimed: 'we have nothing to equal this'.

Inside, state room succeeds splendid state room, hung with Marlborough portraits and famous Blenheim tapestries until the library is reached, 180 ft long and one of the biggest rooms in England. A recent addition is the interesting exhibition of the life of Winston Churchill, grandson of the 8th Duke, who was born at Blenheim in 1875. He is buried in a movingly simple grave in the village churchyard at **Bladon** (4/1A), on the southern perimeter of the park.

The palace and formal gardens are open to the public every day in the summer; the lovely walks in the park can be enjoyed all year round.

Woolstone *see* Uffington

Wootton (4/1A) Off the A34 north of WOOD-STOCK, Wootton is an attractive old village in the valley of the river Glyme. After the toad (!) crossing, the road winds up the hill from the river bridge between stone-roofed houses to the plain, mainly Early English church with a 15th-century tower and a fine porch. Next to the church, the former rectory is a typical Georgian parson's house with a wall surrounding the large garden. Akeman Street runs through the parish, crossing the Glyme on an ancient bridge south of the village. On the GLYMPTON road is an inn called The Killingworth Castle, named after its

17th-century owner William Killingworth and his wife Silence.

Wootton was once part of the large royal forest of Wychwood but was cleared in the Middle Ages, Kings Wood on the CHARLBURY road in the hamlet of Woodleys being the only remnant. Grim's Ditch turns south here towards Blenheim park.

Wroxton (1/3A) Just off the A422 BANBURY–Stratford road, a large brown-coloured ironstone village of many thatched cottages. The Abbey is a grand Elizabethan house built on the site of an Augustinian monastery and subsequently owned for many generations by the North family, one of whom was Prime Minister to George III and lost the American colonies. The house is now occupied by an American university. Lord North is buried in the church, his splendid monument surmounted by Britannia and a rather glum lion. Thomas Coutts, the great 18th-century banker who started life as a clerk, is also buried there and another marble monument commemorates the three wives of Lord Guilford, who each 'raised their husband to a degree of happiness far beyond what man ought to expect'.

Wroxton is at the centre of the area of Oxfordshire where iron-mining once flourished. During the last 100 years it supplied huge quantities of local ironstone to the steel industries of South Wales and the Midlands, but its ore cannot now compete with bulk imports of higher grade material. It was extracted by opencast methods, and many fields in the area are up to 30 ft lower than the roads crossing them, giving the landscape a very unusual appearance.

Wychwood Forest *see* Leafield

Wytham (4/1B) Pronounced 'white 'em', this village is just outside of OXFORD beyond the western ring road, but is protected from that city by road, canal, river and railway.

It consists of old stone cottages, many still thatched, the attractive White Hart Inn and a great house with a 700-acre park under Wytham Hill. The house, with a fine Tudor front, is called Wytham Abbey, although there was never an abbey here, and is now part of Oxford University. There was, however, a nunnery in the 7th century. Offa, the great 8th-century Mercian king, had a house here. The endearing little church was completely rebuilt in 1811 with a plain whitewashed interior and some lovely old glass rescued from Cumnor Place.

Yarnton (4/1A) On the A34 between WOOD-STOCK and OXFORD, Yarnton is now virtually an appendage of the latter. To take the turning to

The Post Office, Wytham

Cassington, however, is to enter another world. Exeter Farm is a picturesque-looking house that used to belong to Exeter College, and beyond is the schoolroom built in 1817. An ancient thatched cottage with solar-heating panels is a very curious sight. The no-through-road to a farm ends at a very pleasing group of church, rectory and large Jacobean manor house, remarkably rural and peaceful after the A34. A branch of the Spencers of Althorp (from whom the present Princess of Wales is descended) built the manor, and their quite remarkable monuments are in the church. A certain Alderman Fletcher made a huge collection of early stained glass and donated it to the church in 1817, where it fills practically every window and is of great historic interest.

North of Yarnton on the A34 is **Begbroke** (4/1A), which has been overtaken by the 20th century. Norman church, Servite monastery and a high-tech factory make strange bedfellows down the road past an inn called The Royal Sun: the 'Royal' was added because various monarchs made stops there on their way to Blenheim Palace. Private aircraft buzz overhead from busy Oxford Airport beyond the village.

Yelford *see* Standlake

Above: The 'Aldworth Giants' in St Mary's Church, Aldworth

Previous page: Windsor Castle

Berkshire Gazetteer

Aldermaston (7/1C) West of READING along the A4 you turn south across the Kennet valley to arrive at this attractive old village with brick and timber houses along the main street. The Atomic Weapons Research Establishment is hidden behind the walls of Aldermaston Court, which once belonged to the Forster family, at the far end. There is a fine and ancient church which is kept locked, apparently with no notice as to where the key may be obtained. This is a pity, for inside there are some medieval wall paintings, including one of St Christopher with the infant Jesus; a rare Elizabethan pulpit; and an alabaster figure of Sir George Forster, who lived in the big house in Henry VII's reign.

The minor road to the west across the little river Enborne is extremely pretty and brings you to **Brimpton** (7/1C) with its cheerful, rather French-looking, church spire looking across the Kennet valley to the north. Manor Farm is on the left of the road leading down to the river. Among the farm buildings is a remarkable survival: a tiny flint chapel with a Norman doorway and Maltese cross carved above it. This indicates that it was a chapel of the Knights Templar, founded in the 12th century to protect pilgrims on their way to the Holy Land.

Aldworth (7/1A) High on the eastern Berkshire Downs, up the steep wooded hill (B4009) that leads from the Thames at STREATLEY, Aldworth is a small and scattered village with splendid views across two counties and a good access point to the Ridgeway. But what draws people here, and drew Queen Elizabeth 400 years ago, are the extraordinary stone effigies in the church known as the Aldworth Giants. There are nine of these huge sculptures, all made between 1300 and 1350, and all members of the de la Beche family who came to England in the wake of William the Conqueror. They built a great castle here of which only the site remains, near the Four Points Inn, where Grim's Ditch crosses the road. The de la Beches were a family of consequence; Sir Nicholas was Constable of the Tower of London and tutor to the Black Prince. Despite centuries of neglect, and partial defacement, the effigies are a remarkable sight and they

dominate the small church. The yew tree in the churchyard is over 600 years old and is 27 ft around the trunk.

Two miles south-east is **Ashampstead** (7/1B), another downland village around a large and attractive green. The little Norman church of St Clement has 13th-century wall paintings.

Arborfield (7/3B) An old parish in the Loddon valley about 3 miles south-east of READING. There is, however, little left to prove it and even the ancient Norman church was pulled down and replaced. This is now military country with a huge Royal Electrical and Mechanical Engineers (REME) complex south of the village. Off the WOKINGHAM road to the east is **Barkham,** granted to Abingdon Abbey in 941 and mentioned in the Domesday Book. The church, in farmland on the edge of the village, is much restored and contains an unusual wooden effigy of about 1350, placed now in the porch. The Ball family, ancestors of George Washington, held land here for many generations. The immense cedar tree in the churchyard was planted in 1788.

Two miles north, along a road lined on either side with rhododendrons, is **Sindlesham** (7/3B). On the left is **Bear Wood,** a vast Victorian mansion built in supposedly French style by John Walter in 1865. It is a monumental tribute to the power, wealth and influence of the Walter family, who founded and owned *The Times* from 1785 until early this century. The third John Walter was proprietor of *The Times* from 1847 to his death in 1894, inventor of the first steam-driven printing press and MP for Nottingham, and later for Berkshire. He and many members of his family are buried in a kind of communal family grave in the church he built at the gates.

The woods, which used to be part of Windsor Forest, are famed for cedars, junipers and rhododendrons and there is a 40-acre artificial lake in which the fourth John Walter was drowned trying to rescue his brother. The house is now the Royal Merchant Navy School.

Ascot (8/2B) South of Windsor Great Park the first racecourse was laid out in Queen Anne's

Lady Hoby's tomb, Bisham Church

reign; Ascot Week (the third week in June) is still a most popular sporting and social event. The country around about was once part of Windsor Forest and is still very wooded, with an abundance of evergreen and silver birch. Rhododendrons and laurel also thrive on the sandy soil of this part of Berkshire. Ascot, with neighbouring **Sunninghill** (8/2B) and **Sunningdale** (8/3B), are what might be termed 'High Suburbia'. Nearness to WINDSOR, suitable woodland made available and, above all, the arrival of the Southern Railway, which put London in easy reach, all combined to render this area attractive to the man of affairs at the turn of the century. Prosperous and comfortable villas abound, standing in their own grounds, with high hedges, well-kept gardens and drives marked 'Private'.

Sunningdale has a famous golf course and includes half of the great ornamental lake of Virginia Water built by the Duke of Cumberland in the 18th century. (The other half is in Surrey.) Sunninghill has an interesting Victorian church with a chapel in memory of Thomas Holloway, famed for his patent medicines, who built the incredible Royal Holloway College just over the county border.

Ashampstead *see* Aldworth

Aston *see* Remenham

Avington *see* Kintbury

Barkham *see* Arborfield

Basildon Park *see* Upper and Lower Basildon

Bear Wood *see* Arborfield

Binfield (8/1B) The village itself is just north-west of BRACKNELL and mainly suburban now but the wooded, rolling country to the north and east appears to have an unusually large number of 18th-century houses with small parks and home farms. The poet Alexander Pope had a happy childhood here where his father, a draper, had retired to a smallholding. In his 'Ode on Solitude' written in 1717, he refers to his father:

> Happy the man, whose wish and care
> A few paternal acres bound,
> Content to breathe his native air,
> In his own ground.

The 14th-century church to the north of Binfield is built of conglomerate, a mixture of Bagshot sand and ironstone mortared together which is unique to this area of Berkshire. Building stone was expensive to transport in medieval days and Berkshire has no stone of its own. Brick, so extensively used in the county, became available in quantity only in the 16th century. Seen from this churchyard, the gleaming towers of Bracknell's office blocks 3 miles away make a strange contrast.

Bisham (8/1A) Called Bustlesham or Bistlesham in early times, this is a small and pretty Thamesside village on the Berkshire bank nearly opposite Marlow. The elegant suspension bridge, built in 1836 and splendidly unsuitable for modern traffic, links them, beside the Compleat Angler Hotel, one of the most famous Thames watering places. Bisham Abbey, which overlooks a particularly picturesque stretch of the river, is a rambling Tudor brick house of great beauty, built on the site of an Augustinian monastery. Clear traces of the medieval priory can be seen in the fine 14th century entrance, but the rest is Tudor. It is now owned by the

Sports Council and there are squash courts and other facilities in the grounds.

The priory church disappeared at the Reformation and with it the tomb of Warwick the Kingmaker who was buried here in 1471 after the failure of his final bid for power at the Battle of Barnet. Half a mile upstream is the parish church whose famous white chalk tower has looked across the Thames for 800 years. Inside is the most remarkable collection of family monuments in Berkshire. The Hoby family (pronounced 'Hobby') acquired Bisham Abbey at the Dissolution of the Monasteries in 1540. Two finely carved alabaster effigies of Sir Philip and Sir Thomas lie side by side clad in armour with their feet on hobby hawks, a play on their name. The first was ambassador at the Court of the Emperor Charles V and the second Queen Elizabeth's ambassador to France. 'Philip the first in Caesar's court hath fame' and 'Thomas in France possessed the Legate's place' says the poem on the front, composed by Lady Hoby.

But it is Lady Hoby's own tomb, designed by herself down to the last detail, that is the most memorable. Kneeling at her prie-dieu in widow's weeds and coif, and attended by her numerous family, it is a *tour de force* of Elizabethan self-confidence and family pride.

Boxford *see* Lambourn Valley

Bracknell (8/2B) A few miles to the south-west of Windsor Forest in sandy, pinewood country. There is little left of old Bracknell, which is not surprising as the population has risen in two generations from 3000 to over 50,000. Some 40 years ago it was designated a New Town, the only one in Berkshire. There is an immense shopping and pedestrian precinct surrounded by multi-storey car parks and office blocks. All this is in a modern idiom that does not appeal to everyone, and the place is already showing signs of wear; but Bracknell appears to function efficiently and should be visited if only as a contrast to the other towns in this guidebook.

The houses of the New Town cover a large area, including **Easthampstead** (8/1B), and are well laid out with trees and green spaces. The absence of chimneys is very noticeable, which makes the roofscape perhaps less interesting than is usual in English towns. High-rise flats have been resisted, except for one 17-storey hexagonal block much admired by Pevsner.

The Victorian church has some fine stained glass by Burne-Jones and a tablet to Sir Walter Trumbull. He was the friend and patron who encouraged Alexander Pope to embark on his great translation of Homer in the early 18th century.

There is an 8-acre area of old woodland just off the CROWTHORNE road which is now a nature reserve run by the Berkshire, Buckinghamshire and Oxfordshire Naturalists Trust (BBONT).

Bradfield (7/1B) The river Pang runs through the village on its course through the hills until it joins the Thames at PANGBOURNE 4 miles to the north-east. The country around is wooded and pretty. The village is filled with the Victorian brick buildings of Bradfield College, founded in 1850 by the Reverend Thomas Stevens, a rich 'squarson' who both held the living and owned the manor. It is famous among other things for its amphitheatre where boys still perform Greek plays every year in the summer term. Stevens was nothing if not enthusiastic and he set about improving the old church with some curious results, although fortunately the 16th-century brick tower above was left. The old brick buildings by the church and river are attractive.

Sundial with painted fly, Bucklebury Church (see p. 176)

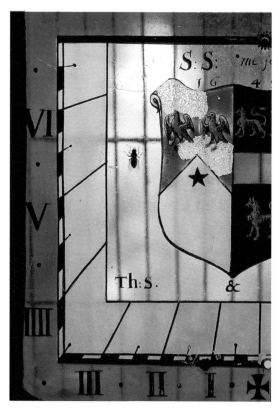

Bray (8/2A) The claim to fame of this village is the 16th-century Vicar of Bray. He was in turn Catholic and Protestant – whichever way the wind blew in the turbulent religious climate of Tudor times. He was called Simon Aleyn and, when taxed about his lack of principle, declared that his only conviction was to live and die the Vicar of Bray. The song celebrating such extreme flexibility is of a later date and setting. His anxiety to hang on is understandable, for Bray must have been a very desirable living with its large church, handsome vicarage and attractive Thameside village. Although so near to MAIDENHEAD and with much modern housing, the old village centre is protected by fields and is picturesque with old cottages and inns grouped around the churchyard with its medieval gatehouse.

The church is mainly of the 14th century and contains interesting old brasses. The Jesus hospital on the **Holyport** (8/2A) road is a fine example of Jacobean architecture built round a courtyard. Nearby **Monkey Island** has two fishing lodges built by a Duke of Marlborough in the 18th century. One of them is now a hotel and has some old murals of monkeys, hence the name. The road south goes under the M4 to Holyport, much built over but retaining an attractive green with cottages around it.

Brightwalton *see* Chaddleworth

Brimpton *see* Aldermaston

Bucklebury (7/1B) In the heart of the Pang valley where the river winds through unspoiled farming country a few miles east of NEWBURY. The road running down the Pang from Frilsham across a ford is a particularly pleasant approach to the cluster of cottages by the church and old rectory. St Mary's church is one of the most beautiful in this part of Berkshire. It is entered through a superb Norman doorway above which there are two unusual dormer windows, cut into the roof in the 17th century to give more light. Inside the box pews have survived and there are many interesting monuments and hatchments to various descendants of Jack of Newbury's son John, who was granted the manor when Reading Abbey, the previous owner, was dissolved in 1539. He rebuilt the church and is remembered on a wooden beam across the chancel.

The most modern thing in the church is the glass by Sir Frank Brangwyn. Put in just before the First World War, it is full of colour and power and an interesting change from much of the Victorian glass in local churches. The tiny window in the squire's pew has an extraordinarily lifelike fly, painted on it in 1649.

To the south is Bucklebury Common, over 5 miles of woodland and common where Oliver Cromwell once camped with his army. There are many footpaths across the common: it is a good place for a walk, with its fine trees and a profusion of wild flowers and butterflies.

Burghfield (7/2B) Burghfield and Burghfield Common are residential areas for READING, but are quite cut off from the big town by the river Kennet, which is very wide at this point, and the M4 motorway. It is pleasant, wooded suburban country. The church is a curious essay in Victorian Norman, but contains some interesting tombs. There are, for example, alabaster figures of Richard Neville, Earl of Salisbury, and his wife, the parents of Warwick the Kingmaker (*see* Bisham). **Stratfield Mortimer** (7/2C) looks across the Hampshire border towards Stratfield Saye. There are some old buildings around the impressive church, which houses a Saxon tomb slab, one of the oldest in England. It dates from about AD 1000 and the Latin inscription is still quite legible and contains the words: 'Ægelward son of Kypping was laid here'. It is strangely moving.

California *see* Finchampstead

Caversham (7/3B) On the other side of the Thames from READING and to all intents and purposes part of it. The bank slopes steeply, and along the road towards Mapledurham are many Victorian villas that were the homes of affluent Reading citizens. The church is older, although much rebuilt, and looks down on the gardens of Caversham Court and across the Thames to Reading proper. Caversham Park is an enormous house further up the hill. Now owned by the BBC, it was the scene of Charles I's sad farewell to his children before he was taken under guard to London and subsequent execution. A later owner was William Crawshay, the great Welsh ironmaster, who bought it in 1844 after leaving Wales because, it is said, one of his wretched workmen hurled a clod of earth at his carriage. His monument is by the church door.

Chaddleworth (6/2B) High in farming country on the Berkshire Downs in one of the most beautiful parts of the county, roughly halfway

Cookham

between HUNGERFORD and Wantage, and to the east of the A338. There is a pretty blue and red brick Georgian house in a small park next to the church and thatched cottages down the hill. The church is Norman, except for a Victorian chancel, and has two interesting and unusual 18th-century family chancels built out on the north side. The living is held by the Dean and Chapter of Westminster. This is because there used to be a monastery on the site of Poughley Farm in the south of the parish. This monastery was given by Henry VIII in about 1530 to the Abbot of Westminster in exchange for 100 acres of land in what is now St James' Park in London – a rather poor deal for the abbot. There is a memorial in the church to the Nelson family, one of whom 'fought two dragoons in the Civil War and was never well afterwards', says the church register.

A mile to the north is **Brightwalton** (6/2A) another downland village with large farms and pink-bricked cottages, many of them thatched. The church, school and rectory were all the work of G. E. Street, who built on an extraordinary scale in Berkshire and Oxfordshire during his 30 years as diocesan architect in Queen Victoria's reign. (He also built the massive Law Courts in the Strand in London, and much else besides.)

Chieveley (6/2A) Five miles north of NEWBURY where the A34 crosses the M4 motorway. It is a large village with some elegant Georgian houses and much new, but fairly sympathetic, building. The old church is heavily restored but retains a 13th-century tower and details. There is an old oak arch across the chancel. This was used to hang a curtain screening the altar during Lent, a rare survival from pre-Reformation days. A mile south, just over the motorway, is a large Iron Age hill fort in Bussock Wood and beyond is the little village of **Winterbourne** (6/2B) with its attractive manor house and church.

Combe *see* Inkpen

Compton *see* Hampstead Norreys

Overleaf: Detail of Christ Preaching at Cookham Regatta, 1953-9, by Sir Stanley Spencer (Stanley Spencer Gallery)

Cookham (8/2A) Although so close to MAIDEN-HEAD, Cookham is protected by a *cordon sanitaire* of farms and orchards to the south and the National Trust woodlands of **Cookham Dean** (8/1A) and **Pinkneys Green** (8/2A) to the west. As a result it has retained its own character with a broad green leading down to the picturesque High Street. Beyond, a winding road with many old houses crosses the Thames on a splendid Victorian iron bridge. Cliveden Woods, on the Buckinghamshire side of the river, form a backdrop with occasional glimpses of the Astors' great house (now a hotel, and owned by the National Trust) on the top of the hill.

Cookham church is large and basically Early English, but with additions in the 14th and 15th centuries. Among the many memorials is a fine sculpture to Sir Isaac Pocock who was drowned here in 1810. There is a gallery in the High Street where you can see pictures by Sir Stanley Spencer RA, who lived and painted here until his death in 1959. His *Resurrection*, showing the dead rising from their graves in Cookham churchyard, achieved notoriety in the 1930s.

Crazies Hill *see* Wargrave

Crowthorne (8/1C) In sandy, wooded, ever-green country in the south-east of the county, where once was only heath and Windsor Forest. The east of the village is cut off by Broadmoor Mental Hospital and its extensive grounds. Crowthorne itself has an undistinguished shopping street which leads south to Wellington College, a famous public school built as the nation's memorial to the Iron Duke in 1853. It is built, with conscious irony perhaps, in French château style and is very impressive. Throughout the various courtyards and passages are statues and busts of the military captains and statesmen who supported Wellington in his campaigns against the French. They are mostly by William Theed, one of Prince Albert's favourite sculptors.

The road south leads to the Blackwater Valley and the Hampshire border. It marks the beginning of a large military area centred round Camberley, which is just over the county boundary. The fine white classical building of the Royal Military Academy at **Sandhurst**, however, is just in Berkshire. The original officers' school was founded in High Wycombe in 1789 but moved here in 1807. It used to be possible to visit the RMA together with the chapel, the Indian Army Museum and the museum of disbanded Irish regiments, but now modern security requirements prevent this and you have to apply in writing.

Datchet (8/3B) The Thames forms the northern and western boundary of the Home Park of WINDSOR CASTLE and just across the river lies Datchet, which used to be in Buckinghamshire. It has houses and shops around a large green, and has managed to retain a personality of its own, although so close to Windsor. There are some pleasing riverside houses looking over the river towards the park.

East (6/3A) **and West Ilsley** (6/2A) The A34 comes over the crest of the Berkshire Downs on the county border and it is something of a relief to turn off into East Ilsley, now a quiet village but once an important sheep market where, until comparatively recent times, as many as 3000 sheep and lambs would be bought and sold on market day. Racehorses are more important here now, but the number of inns and larger houses still testify to the local importance of the village. It is one of the few where enclosures were never carried out and commoners' rights still exist on land in the parish. The 13th-century church is on a hill overlooking the village. Inside it is quite plain with some Victorian glass and a brass of 1606 to Katharine Hildeslea (Hildeslea was the old form of the village name). Church Farm opposite is partly Tudor.

West Ilsley, on the other side of the A34 road, lies in the lee of the downs with tracks leading to the Ridgeway on the crest. It seems a quiet and peaceful place with a small Victorian church. It has had some curious rectors. In 1616 the Italian Archbishop of Spalato (Split) fell out with the Pope and came to England, where he embraced the Protestant faith. James I made him rector here and later Dean of Windsor. Getting no higher in the Anglican church he went back to Rome on the promise of a cardinal's hat, but was thrown into prison instead. Another rector was made a bishop, but went over to Rome during Oliver Cromwell's Protectorate.

Eastbury *see* Lambourn Valley

East Garston *see* Lambourn Valley

Easthampstead *see* Bracknell

Eddington *see* Hungerford

Enborne *see* Hamstead Marshall

Englefield (7/1B) From the A4 just west of READING you can see the great 'Victoribethan' palace of Englefield sitting in its park above the Kennet. Originally Elizabethan, it was owned by the Englefield family until Sir Francis fled the country after plotting to rescue Mary, Queen of Scots. Queen Elizabeth gave the house to her Secretary of State, Sir Francis Walsingham, and is known to have visited him here when he built a special gallery for her; parts of this survive in the house. For the last 200 years the Benyons have been seated here and are responsible for the present appearance of the house.

The estate village in warm red Berkshire brick is in contrast to the grey stone of the big house and church. The latter is largely Victorian but contains some impressive monuments, particularly one to the Marquess of Winchester, who fought so bravely for King Charles in the Civil War. His monument has no name on it, but bears a poem by Dryden.

Eton (8/3A) A new addition to Berkshire after hundreds of years in Buckinghamshire. Perhaps it was meant as compensation for the Berkshire downland untimely ripped from the mother county in 1974.

Since the bridge across the Thames from WINDSOR was closed to vehicles a few years ago, the High Street has regained some of its 18th-century atmosphere and charm, and its old buildings, inns and shops can now be admired in relative peace. At the far end of the village from the river are the chapel, buildings and quadrangles of Eton College, the famous public school.

It was founded by King Henry VI in 1440 as the King's College of our Lady of Eton (King Henry was also the founder of King's College, Cambridge) and it consisted originally of a number of priests and 70 poor scholars. The first building to be constructed was the chapel. This is one of the great glories of Perpendicular architecture, smaller and simpler than St George's Chapel, Windsor, just across the river, but remarkably light and graceful. It is a great surprise to find that the beautiful fan vaulting, so typical of the 15th century, is in fact completely new; it was built in 1959 to replace the old timber roof which was beyond repair. The stained glass is also modern, the old having been destroyed by a bomb during the Second World War. The great east window above the altar was designed by Evie Hone in 1950 in rich red and blue colours in a basically conventional design,

whereas the windows either side of it by John Piper are strikingly original illustrations of parables and miracles, done in more muted shades.

The 15th-century wall paintings are among the finest in Europe. Whitewashed over by the college barber at the Reformation, they were rediscovered 300 years later and only fully restored in this century. Illustrating various legends and miracles associated with the Blessed Virgin they are wonderfully vigorous and alive, giving an extraordinary insight into medieval piety. There are many other points of interest in the chapel; the reason the floor is 13 ft above ground level is to avoid the Thames floodwaters.

The large quadrangle flanking the chapel is known as School Yard. This, and the College Hall beyond, are Eton's oldest parts after the chapel. In the centre of School Yard is a statue of Henry VI. Every 6 December bay leaves are laid upon it to commemorate his murder in 1471 by Edward IV, who also usurped his crown. Around the walls of the upper school, near the entrance, are the names of nearly two thousand Etonians who were killed in the two world wars, many of them within a few months of leaving school. Opposite is the stately Tudor brick tower, known as Lupton's Tower after the provost who built it in 1520.

Over 500 years there has been a steady increase in the reputation of Eton College and in its numbers, and its buildings have been altered and added to in every century since its foundation. In the summer certain parts of the college can be visited and there is an amusing exhibition of Eton life permanently on display in the Old Brewhouse.

Farley Hill *see* Finchampstead

Farnborough (6/2A) Over 700 ft up on the southern slopes of the Berkshire Downs, and off the B4494, this is the highest village in the county and also one of the most delightful, with its scattered farms and cottages and elegant 18th-century rectory seen across a ha-ha from the road. The tiny medieval church is quite plain inside and now has a new (1985) window by John Piper in memory of his friend John Betjeman, who lived in Farnborough for a time. Piper uses the old symbolism of butterflies to illustrate the Resurrection as he also does in his windows in Eton chapel. The view from the churchyard across rolling farmland is very beautiful.

Fawley (6/1A) Fawley and **South Fawley** used to be called Great and Little Fawley. They are two small villages facing one another and are among the most remote in Berkshire in wide rolling downland on roads that peter out into tracks across the hills. Fawley has a fine Victorian church by the architect G. E. Street and South Fawley has a romantic-looking Jacobean manor house. Down on the A338 Wantage road a granite cross commemorates a local squire who fell with his Yeomanry Regiment in Palestine in 1917.

Finchampstead (8/1C) In wooded, sandy country south of WOKINGHAM towards the Blackwater valley and Hampshire. It lies between the military country of ARBORFIELD and Sandhurst, and its list of residents in 1928 included nine colonels and three generals. It is a large village with trim Edwardian houses and well-kept hedges and gardens. The Norman church is built on an ancient earthwork and from the churchyard there are extensive views over the valley towards Hampshire.

Although the brick tower is 18th century, the inside of the church is much older with its Norman nave and windows and later chancel. There is an ancient brass of Mrs Blighe holding her daughter by the hand and a more modern plaque to General Watson, who won the Victoria Cross at the siege of Lucknow.

West towards SWALLOWFIELD a minor road goes through **Farley Hill** (7/3C), a small hamlet on a hill with fine views.

Signposts to the north lead to the strangely named **California** (8/1C), an area of bungalows and small houses developed in the 1920s.

Great Shefford *see* Lambourn Valley

Greenham *see* Newbury

Hampstead Norreys (6/3B) The name announces that this village on the B4009 north of the M4 motorway once belonged to the Norreys family, great Berkshire landowners in the Middle Ages. The river Pang rises just north of the parish and runs through the village, with its attractive old brick houses and barns, and past the ancient church. The church is mainly 13th century, although there are earlier details, and the oldest thing it contains is a remarkable

Opposite: Memorial window to Sir John Betjeman by John Piper, Farnborough Church

Norman carving of a knight on horseback. It is very rare but nobody knows who it is: could it be one of the Cifrewart family who held the manor before the Norreys?

Many of the memorials are very readable, particularly a rather poignant one to a young soldier who was killed at the siege of Badajoz, in 1812, while serving under The Marquess of Wellington in Spain which is interesting as Wellington was only a Marquess for a few months.

Travelling along the valley to the north you pass Perborough Castle on the left, an Iron Age hill fort, before arriving at **Compton** (6/3A), a large and quite developed village with a big research establishment. The church is Victorianized and homely. This is real Berkshire Downs country – great rolling hills to the north of the

Town Crier and Bellman, Mr Robin Tubb, with the 'Lucas Horn' and the two 'tutti poles' at the Hocktide Festival in Hungerford (see p. 184)

The 'tutti men' collecting tithes and kisses from house to house

village look towards Lowbury Hill, one of the highest points in the downs, where the Ridgeway crosses them.

Hamstead Marshall (6/2C) Going west along the A4 out of NEWBURY you can cross the Kennet here at one of the few bridges between that town and HUNGERFORD. The little Jacobean church stands all alone in a great walled park. An enormous house once stood here, built for the Earl of Craven in 1660 by the Dutch entrepreneur, painter and architect Sir Balthazar Gerbier. It was said to have been modelled on Heidelberg Castle, but was completely destroyed by fire in 1718. All that is left is a series of elegant but crumbling gate piers in the park behind the church: an evocative testament to a vanished past.

The small, mostly Norman church of **Enborne** (6/2C) on the other side of park has great charm and simplicity.

Holyport *see* Bray

Hungerford (6/1B) Since Roman times there has been an important stop here on the old Bath Road (A4). In the 18th and 19th centuries the Kennet and Avon canal, and then the Great Western Railway, also came through Hungerford. The most interesting approach, however, is south of the river from KINTBURY across Hungerford Common. The common rights and some fishing rights in the Kennet were given to the town by John of Gaunt 600 years ago and they are still jealously preserved.

Every year in Hocktide, the second week after Easter, the Town Crier blows an ancient horn to summon the Commoners and the rules relating to the fishing and grazing rights are read to the manorial court, presided over by the elected Constable. Meanwhile the tithing men, or 'tutti men' as they are known, go round the town demanding a penny and a kiss from every household. It all ends up with a banquet at the Corn Exchange and much quaffing of ale in John of Gaunt's memory.

The wide High Street is an attractive jumble of Georgian houses and shops, many built in the red and blue brick which is so typical of Berkshire. The Victorian Town Hall provides an interesting contrast to this 18th-century setting. There are pleasant walks along the canal bank past several locks towards St Lawrence's Church, which was built in 1815.

Eddington (6/1B), just across the Bath Road, is thought by some to be the site of the Danish camp that King Alfred visited disguised as a minstrel.

Hurley (8/1A) A riverside village off the A423 Henley-MAIDENHEAD road at the East Arms Hotel. Despite some modern development near the main road Hurley retains a strong sense of the past. Beyond the Bell Hotel, picturesque and medieval, towards the Thames was a Saxon church where Edward the Confessor's sister Editha is believed to be buried.

The Normans founded a Benedictine priory on the same site in 1086 and the present interesting church is essentially the one they built. Next to the church is the monastic refectory, now a private house, and across the road are old tithe barns and a monastic dovecot, still with its doves. It is rare to find so much remaining of a small Benedictine house after the Dissolution of the Monasteries.

The church contains a wooden Saxon cross and a spendid Elizabethan memorial to the Lovelace family who acquired the manor when the monks had gone. Hurley people seemed to be great travellers in the 19th century and there are tablets recording their deaths in Ootacamund, Borneo and Lucknow, and that of one young man who was 'wantonly murdered in Hong Kong by Chinese pirates'. The Reverend Florence Wethered was vicar here for no less than 35 years.

Up the steep hill on the other side of the main road is Hall Place, a grand red brick Georgian mansion now an agricultural college. The top of the hill has a superb view of the Thames Valley and heavily wooded Chilterns. Further towards Henley, opposite the Black Boy, a footpath leads to a delightful nature reserve of beechwoods and chalk grassland run by the Berkshire, Buckinghamshire and Oxfordshire Naturalists Trust (BBONT).

Hurst (8/1B) A large village north of the M4 just east of READING, but protected by the river Loddon which flows through the parish. It is flat, farming country with clumps of trees and some quite large houses dotted about in well-kept estates. Although the village has inevitably grown, the old part by the church of St Nicholas has a timeless air about it with old brick houses, an Elizabethan inn and some charmingly simple almshouses dating from 1682.

The church is built of flint with a brick tower and has some ancient things in it. The gaily painted wooden screen with its Stuart coat of arms is unusual and the 16th-century pulpit with its hourglass stand is a reminder of the lengthy sermons that were once considered *de rigueur*. Brasses and monuments abound, particularly in the north aisle which is entered through Norman arches with carved heads. Alice Harrison, who died in 1600 'in childbed', is depicted on a brass lying in her four-poster bed. Another large

Hungerford Common

Harrison monument records the sacrifices made for the King in the Civil War and ends with the rather endearing lines about the widow:

> A double dissolution here appears
> He into dust dissolves, she into tears.

Inkpen (6/1C) In the wooded Kennet valley in the south-west tip of Berkshire, a delightful village approached by narrow twisting lanes east of the A338, with old cottages hidden behind high hedges. There is a well-cared-for 13th-century church and a beautiful 18th-century rectory opposite. Inkpen lies directly under the dramatic chalk escarpment of Walbury Hill, a one-in-six climb to the highest point in Berkshire at 974 ft. The view from the top is immense, the Chiltern Hills far to the north-east and Wiltshire stretching away to the west.

A short walk along the ridge takes you to Combe Gibbet, which can be seen for miles. It

Below: Coot's nest on the river Kennet, near Kintbury

was put up in 1676 to hang an Inkpen man and a woman from **Combe** (6/1C) who had murdered their children. Down the hill in a hidden valley the tiny remote hamlet of Combe has its Norman church of St Swithin and an old manor house next door. Legend has it that Charles II stayed there once.

Further along the Hampshire border is a fine 17th-century house at **West Woodhay** (6/1C). It was built by Inigo Jones for Sir Benjamin Rudyard, a doughty Parliamentarian who sided against the King in the Civil War with much

reluctance. It can be seen from the road down a magnificent avenue of lime trees.

Kintbury (6/1B) Between HUNGERFORD and NEWBURY in the valley of the Kennet from which its name derives – Kennet bury or borough. For centuries it was known for the production of whiting which is used in the making of paint. The soft upper layer of the local chalk was ground into a pulp and allowed to settle in tanks; the resulting pap or slurry was then transported by barge to Bristol and

Above: Beech trees near Combe

READING. It was quite an important little place in its day and its citizens built an impressive church in the 13th century and added to it over the years. It has been very Victorianized but there are some interesting monuments.

A mile or so west, on the north bank of the Kennet, is **Avington** (6/1B). A few cottages, a pretty Georgian manor house surrounded by an ancient wall, and one of the smallest and most fascinating churches in Berkshire, hardly

Avington Church (see p. 187)

changed since it was built by the Normans not long after the Conquest. Entered through a porch built in 1594, which is the only 'new' addition, the inside is plain and simple, all the windows being Norman except one put in a hundred years later. The beautifully carved chancel arch, bowed in the middle with the weight of 800 years, and the font are outstanding examples of 12th-century craftsmanship.

Lambourn (6/1A) a cheerful small town on the river of the same name, and south of the Lambourn Downs. Alfred the Great lived here once and gave the manor to his wife Eahlswitha. There was a market here for centuries, when it was known as Chipping Lambourn ('chipping' is from an Old English word for market), but this was closed a hundred years ago. Breeding racehorses is the principal occupation now and the wide chalk downland for miles around has training establishments and gallops where horses are put through their paces. The parish church in the centre of the town is large and impressive with its late Norman arches and 15th century chapel. Near by are some very appealing decorated brick almshouses around a courtyard. Prehistoric earthworks and barrows abound on the downs near here, notably **The Seven Barrows** (in fact there are more) on the B4001 road to Wantage.

The views from the top of the hill on the Ridgeway are spectacular.

Lambourn Valley (6/1A) The Lambourn river rises in the downs near Lambourn and flows into the Kennet at NEWBURY 15 miles away. The river slowly widens along its course and the gentle valley it cuts through the chalk hills contains villages of great charm.

From Lambourn you come first to **Eastbury** (6/1A), with little bridges across the stream and a fine old brick farm surrounded by its barns. This was once the manor house of the Fitzwarines who were lords here in the Middle Ages. Barely a mile further on is **East Garston** (6/1B), where practically every house seems to have its own footbridge. (The name derives from *Esgars tūn*, so 'East' does not imply a 'West' village near by.) The church is somewhat set apart and is mostly Norman with a squat tower and fine doorway. There is a very handsome Queen Anne manor next to it.

The valley narrows as the main A338 Wantage road is approached and around the crossroads are the cottages of **Great** and **Little Shefford** (6/1B). Charles I spent the night in the manor next to the church, which has a round Norman tower making it look East Anglian. It is the only round tower in the county. Little Shefford (or East Shefford) was once held by the Fettiplace family who owned large areas of Oxfordshire and Berkshire in medieval days.

There is no trace of their house, but the little church by the river bank contains their tombs and is an enchanting spot.

The river widens considerably now and is perhaps at its most beautiful at **Welford** (6/2B) with wide pools and flowered banks, and great dark trees belonging to Welford Park, an imposing William and Mary red brick house which can be seen from the churchyard.

The road continues to follow the river to **Boxford** (6/2B), a picturebook village with its thatched cottages and rectory grouped around the stream and church with its brick and flint tower. The disused track of the Lambourn Valley railway also follows the road and river down through watermeadows and farmland to **Donnington** (6/2B), now really part of Newbury but retaining its own character and identity. On a steep hill just north of the river is Donnington Castle, a splendid ruin that was the scene of a heroic defence during the Civil War, when on three occasions Sir John Boys withstood everything the Roundheads could do, including the destruction of most of the castle. The impressive gatehouse still stands, with cannon ball damage clearly visible. It is open to the public.

The Lambourn river finally runs its course, before disappearing into the Kennet, through **Shaw** (6/3C), now suburban Newbury but with a fine Elizabethan house built by Thomas Dolman, a rich clothier, in 1581.

The Lambourn river

Cottages at Boxford (see p. 189)

Langley *see* Slough

Little Shefford *see* Lambourn Valley

Maidenhead (8/2A) In medieval times Midden-hythe ('Midway Wharf', a landing place) was the name of this prosperous Thameside town midway between Marlow and WINDSOR. The river crossing here has always been important and the old Bath Road (later the A4) crossed the elegant bridge built in 1772. The advent of the railway age and the popularity of the Thames brought great changes in the 19th century, and riverside villas and commuters' houses sprang up in quantity.

The motor car age of the 1920s and '30s brought night clubs and restaurants along the river and Maidenhead acquired a slightly 'fast' reputation. It also acquired monumental traffic jams, as the Bath Road ran through the old High Street, now much relieved after the construction of the M4 motorway in the early 1960s. Now the centre of the town is transformed again with supermarkets and multi-storey car parks, office blocks and ring roads. It is a restless, energetic sort of place, adapting itself to every passing phase, from the stagecoach to hi-tech.

If you enter the town from SLOUGH on the A4 there is a good view of Brunel's great railway bridge across the Thames, said to be the widest brick arch ever built. It was painted by Turner in 1844 in his famous picture of a railway engine called *Rain, Steam and Speed*. Further into the town there are some pretty 17th-century almshouses on the right, and one or two old coaching inns, but everything else is modern.

Beyond the town centre the road to the west goes up Boyne Hill past an enormous Victorian Church by the architect G. E. Street. Beyond are the National Trust woods and commons of Pinkneys Green (8/2A) and Maidenhead Thicket (8/1A).

Ockwells Manor House, found surprisingly between the M4 and modern housing estates, is a remarkable example of a medieval manor. It was built around 1450 by the Norreys family and its survival in almost its original state is a remarkable piece of luck. It is not open to the public but can be admired from the road.

Monkey Island *see* Bray

Newbury (6/2B&C) Newbury has always been an important crossroads town. The A4 London–

Bath road, originally Roman, goes just north of the town centre. The main Winchester–Oxford road (A34) crosses the Kennet and the Lambourn here, and the bridges across the two rivers played a strategic part in Newbury's history during the Civil War. In the 15th century the wool and cloth trade brought great prosperity to the town. Its richest inhabitant was John Smallwood, always known as Jack of Newbury, who was described in his day as 'the richest clothier England ever beheld'. He entertained Henry VIII and Catherine of Aragon in Newbury and provided a hundred soldiers for the battle of Flodden Field (1513) but refused a knighthood, asking instead for some special trade concessions. His house in Northbrook Street was on a site now occupied by Marks & Spencer: you feel he would have approved.

The parish church of St Nicholas is his monument and reflects the great prosperity of Newbury in the later Middle Ages and early Tudor times. It is very large and has the grandeur and spaciousness associated with the Perpendicular style. Unfortunately it is rather darkened by the masses of stained glass put in by pious Victorians. There is a modest brass to Jack of Newbury, who largely financed the building, and his initials JS can be clearly seen on the wooden roof.

The centre of Newbury, around the church and market place, retains some of its market town character, particularly Northbrook Street with its pink and blue brick houses above modern shop façades. The Cloth Hall is an old building down by the river with gables and an overhanging top storey which is now a pleasant little museum of local life and history. Further north on the London road are many Georgian inns from the time when Newbury was an important staging post on the road to Bath. One of the best known was the George and Pelican, said to be well-named because of the size of its bill!

The town's most historic event is known as the first battle of Newbury and took place during the Civil War. In 1643 the Parliamentary army under Lord Essex tried to force its way through to London and was opposed by the Royalists under King Charles I in person. A bloody action followed and, although the Royalists' line held, their casualties were so great that they had to withdraw and Essex continued on his way. The mounds where the dead were buried can still be seen on Wash Common on the Andover road and a memorial there remembers the death of Lord Falkland, the young Cavalier poet, at the

Newbury Lock

age of 33. The second battle of Newbury, a year later, was fought to gain possession of the little bridge over the Lambourn at Donnington.

Horse racing has been popular here since the 18th century and Newbury's famous racecourse is south of the Kennet on the eastern side of the town. Half a mile south again is **Greenham** with its large common and woodland area now covered by an enormous American air base.

Speen (6/2B), a residential suburb to the west on the Bath road, was the site of a Roman camp and has some elegant Georgian villas. In the large church there are some interesting monuments including, unexpectedly, a ponderous memorial by Canova, the famous Italian sculptor, to the Margrave of Ansbach who died in 1806.

Thatcham (6/3B), to the east on the A4, may have once had an identity of its own but is now to all intents and purposes part of Newbury. There is only one thatched house left to remind us of its origins, but a little medieval chapel on the busy road catches the eye.

Padworth *see* Sulhamstead

Pangbourne (7/2B) The Pang burn or stream enters the Thames here after its short journey through the downs. It is a small riverside town that still shows many signs of its heyday as a popular Edwardian resort when the cult of the Thames was at its height. The river here is particularly beautiful as it cuts through the steep and wooded hills from the Goring Gap upstream. Brunel's Great Western Railway rushes through, clinging to the bank of the Thames, and one of only two tollbridges on the river takes the motorist across to Whitchurch on the Oxfordshire bank. The river road (A329) towards Lower Basildon passes some curiously decorative houses known, for some reason, as the Seven Deadly Sins – echoes of the Naughty Nineties perhaps.

Opposite the church with its gaily pinnacled

*Lion commemorating the men of the Royal
Berkshire Regiment who died at the battle of Maiwand
in 1880, by George Simonds, Reading*

brick tower lived Kenneth Grahame, the author of *The Wind in the Willows*, the charming children's book that began as stories he told his son in the early years of this century. He died in Church Cottage in 1932.

At the top of a steep hill is Pangbourne College, founded in 1917, which used to train boys for a career in the Merchant Navy and beyond is Bere Court, once a summer house for the abbot of Reading.

Tidmarsh (7/2B) has cottages and houses along the Pang, in one of which the author Lytton Strachey lived in the 1920s. The church has a fine Norman doorway and Early English apse.

Pinkneys Green *see* Cookham

Reading (7/2&3B) There is virtually no trace now of the Saxon settlement by 'Reada's people' on the river Kennet from which Reading began. Apart from seizure by the Danes in AD 871, the first significant date is 1121, when the great Benedictine abbey was founded by Henry I – Henry Beauclerc, younger son of William the Conqueror. The huge church took 40 years to build and ranked as one of the most important in England, with over 200 monks in the abbey at the height of its fame. Reading Abbey lasted for four centuries until the Dissolution of the Monasteries in 1539, when the last abbot and two of his monks were hanged from the Abbey Gateway for refusing to accept royal supremacy.

The town, meanwhile, had grown around the abbey walls and continued to prosper on the wool trade and the manufacture of cloth. Queen Elizabeth granted a charter in 1560. William Laud, Archbishop of Canterbury, is Reading's most famous son. He was educated at Reading School, of which he later became a benefactor. Gradually, over the next two centuries, Reading asserted its claim to be the county town of Berkshire over that of its rival Abingdon (which is now in Oxfordshire).

The 19th century, and the coming of the Great Western Railway with its important junction here, gave another boost to Reading's economic growth. The Huntley & Palmers Biscuit Company was established in 1826 and grew to enormous size. Its factory in Reading was the biggest of its kind in the world, employing many thousands of people and exporting its products far and wide. When in 1904, the first British expedition ever to reach Lhasa arrived at the Dalai Lama's palace, the Tibetan monks offered

Broad Street, Reading, from the roof of Fountain House

them yak-butter tea and a tin of Huntley and Palmer's biscuits. Production here in its home town, however, has now ceased. Another famous company is Suttons Seeds, started in 1804 but no longer present in the town.

In recent years there has been an explosive growth of new office blocks as Reading has benefited from being near to London Airport and the M4 motorway.

Reading has often had a less than good press, but it has the kind of central area that is better seen on foot than from a car. If you walk about looking above the shop fronts at the buildings themselves there is much of interest.

A good place to start is in the Forbury Gardens, which is also the site of Reading Abbey; one or two walls of flint and mortar remain to indicate its size. The much-restored Abbey Gateway can also be seen, near the Old Shire Hall. In the centre of the Forbury Gardens there is a colossal lion of cast iron weighing 16 tons. It commemorates 300 men of the Royal Berkshire Regiment who were killed, fighting to the last man, by the Afghans at the battle of Maiwand in 1880. Reading Gaol, where Oscar Wilde wrote his famous *Ballad of Reading Gaol*, sits rather grimly at one end of the gardens and somewhere under the lawns and flowerbeds Henry I lies buried.

Leaving The Forbury past the 12th-century church of St Laurence with its fine tower you come to the Market Place, which still has a feel of old Reading about it. Beside the church, and quite overshadowing it, are the old municipal buildings, partly the work of the architect Alfred Waterhouse, who lived in Berkshire. They include the Old Town Hall, a symbol of Victorian municipal pride, now sadly run-down. Here, too, is Reading Museum, which contains the Silchester Collection, one of the finest arrays of Roman artifacts in the country, and the Art Gallery with some good modern paintings.

Walking west along either of the two main shopping streets – with some remarkable tiled façades still left – you arrive at the enormous modern shopping centre of The Butts with its attendant multi-storey car parks. Here also are the new Civic Offices, which are a most

Bestobell Mobrey, one of the 1920s buildings on the Slough Trading Estate

impressive piece of modern architecture. The old church of St Mary's Butts across the road with its striking 'chequerboard' flint and limestone tower makes an effective contrast.

Reading has signposted riverside walks along the Thames – with a stretch on the CAVERSHAM (7/3B) side between Reading and Caversham bridges – and the Kennet. Blake's Lock Museum, by the latter river and to the east of the central area, has displays based on Reading's 19th- and early 20th-century industries and trades (open Saturday and Sunday afternoons; all day Monday–Friday).

Finally, mention must be made of Reading University (7/3B), out at Whiteknights on Shinfield Road, a fine parkland site on a hill. Founded as a college in 1892, it achieved university status in 1926 and is especially renowned for its Faculty of Agriculture and Food. Also here is the Museum of English Rural Life (open Tuesday–Saturday, most of the year).

Remenham (7/3A) A scattered village on the Berkshire bank of the Thames opposite Henley. The road past the Little Angel Inn runs parallel to the Henley Regatta course to a small Victorian church. A footpath leads through a farm down to the Thames and a view of Temple Island, an elegant Georgian folly known to oarsmen as the start of the regatta course.

Remenham Hill is on the A423 leading up the hill through thick beechwoods to MAIDENHEAD. On the right, but not visible from the road, is Park Place, built by Frederick, Prince of Wales in the 18th century and once famous for its gardens and pleasure grounds.

Down by the river again is **Aston** (8/1A), a hamlet with a picturesque inn where there was once a ferry.

Ruscombe *see* Twyford

Sandhurst *see* Crowthorne

Shaw *see* Lambourn Valley

Shinfield (7/3B) Both Shinfield and **Spencers Wood** (7/3C) are on the west bank of the river Loddon and are really commuter villages for READING, about 3 miles away. Shinfield is the older of the two and has an ancient church with a fine brick tower built in the 17th century. It has been much restored but still retains some interesting tablets and memorials. All around is the agricultural research complex of Reading University. Spencers Wood is a modern place called after the de Spencer family of nearby SWALLOWFIELD, one of whom attended the first

Opposite: Scissor bracing in All Saints Church, Swallowfield (see p. 197)

parliament summoned by Simon de Montfort in the 13th century.

Shottesbrooke Park *see* White Waltham

Slough (8/3A) The town has only been in Berkshire since 1974, when the county boundaries were altered. The name is unattractive (from Old English *slöh*, meaning 'muddy place', 'mire'), but there are many points of interest in Slough, notwithstanding John Betjeman's famous lines:

> Come, friendly bombs, and fall on Slough
> It isn't fit for humans now

'Slough,' *Collected Poems*, John Murray, (Publishers) Ltd

Modern Slough is a collection of villages grouped together on the north bank of the Thames opposite WINDSOR and has a population of about 100,000. Transport is the key to Slough's past and present. In the 17th and 18th century it was on the busy Bath Road (the A4); and it was an important station on the Great Western Railway in the 19th century. Today it is skirted by the M4 motorway and is close to London Airport.

The Slough Trading Estate was formed after the First World War to make use of 600 acres of unwanted War Office land and workshops along the Bath Road and the railway. The idea of building factories before letting them was pioneered here and has been copied all over the country. Many of the factories are interesting examples of 1920s and 1930s architecture. The centre of Slough is largely modern with a shopping precinct off the High Street. It is very impressive and there are enough Victorian buildings remaining to give the town character.

Slough contains one outstanding treasure: the parish church at **Langley** (8/3A) on the eastern edge. Entirely surrounded by modern housing, but sheltered by an ancient yew, the medieval church of St Mary the Virgin is flanked by mellow brick almshouses built in the 17th century and still occupied (the key to the church is obtained from one of them). Inside the church the heavy Norman arches between the nave and aisle were removed in 1630 to make more room and replaced by oak columns. By this means more people would be able to listen to the sermons from the handsome Jacobean pulpit.

In the nave and aisle there are a large number of interesting memorials, including a rare wooden panel to Sir Richard Hubert, Groome Porter to Charles I, and another to his wife Dorothea, née King and 'descended from the ancient Saxon Kings of Devonshire'.

The Kederminster chapel on the south side has a most extraordinary carved screen behind which the family sat looking through window openings covered in leather strapwork. The effect is almost Islamic. This was built by Sir John Kederminster in 1623 – his monument is in the chancel. He also built the library next to the family pew which contains a unique collection of 16th- and 17th-century books and documents and is virtually unchanged since the poet Milton used it. It can be visited by appointment.

Sonning (7/3B) An exceptionally attractive village less than 3 miles north-east of READING. It was a Saxon bishopric before the see was moved to Salisbury about the time of the Conquest. The sturdy Tudor brick walls around the churchyard are all that remains of a palace once owned by the Bishops of Salisbury. Flanking the churchyard and behind one of the old palace walls is a large and interesting house designed by Sir Edwin Lutyens at the turn of the century. This is one of the newer houses in Sonning, which contains a rich variety of Georgian and of earlier architecture, and has remained remarkably unspoiled.

The Thames is crossed by a 200-year-old bridge with the White Hart Hotel beside it, and the French Horn Hotel on the opposite bank. Sonning Lock is one of the most famous on the Thames. It regularly wins the competition for the best-kept lock.

Sonning is a large and prosperous village and St Andrew's Church is on a scale to match it. Somewhat gloomy inside because of the Victorian stained glass, it has a wealth of monuments and tombs of local worthies covering five centuries – although the old brasses are now hidden under the carpet on the chancel floor. Under the tower behind the door there is a heavy marble table with two urns on top of it and all supported by dismal cherubs. It is a memorial in an eccentric classical style to two members of the Rich family who died in 1663 and 1667. Hardly beautiful, and certainly an oddity but it perhaps deserves to be more accessible.

The Blue Coat School, founded in Reading in the 16th century, is now just outside the village on a fine site near the Thames.

South Fawley *see* Fawley

Speen *see* Newbury

Spencers Wood *see* Shinfield

Stanford Dingley (7/1B) A small village as attractive as its name which comes from the Dyneley family, who held the manor here in the Middle Ages. The river Pang runs its short course from HAMPSTEAD NORREYS to PANGBOURNE where it enters the Thames; Stanford Dingley is in the centre of the wide valley the Pang makes through the Berkshire Downs. Old brick and timber houses look across the river meadows, and a handsome Georgian rectory can be seen behind a hedge. The church, with a weatherboarded turret, is mainly 12th- and 13th-century, but the 18th-century chancel is unusual and its wide plain windows do much to lighten the church interior. It is unusual because generally the 18th century was not a time when Englishmen altered their churches much. The church contains some very interesting medieval bricks with various designs, including the Star of David and the Paschal Lamb.

Stratfield Mortimer *see* Burghfield

Streatley (7/1A) *Stretlea* it was called when given by the King of Wessex to Abingdon Abbey in 687. Long before that the Icknield Way, or Ridgeway, crossed the river here. The Downs fall very steeply to the Thames here and Streatley is picturesquely situated on the Berkshire bank, around the junction of the A329 and A417 roads. It has not grown as big as Goring on the opposite bank, lacking room to expand up the hill. The High Street leading down to the wooden bridge has some gracious Georgian houses and the Swan Hotel is a famous riverside hostelry. Lardon Chase, high up on the B4009 road to ALDWORTH, is owned by the National Trust and has splendid views across the Goring Gap to the Oxfordshire Chilterns.

Sulhamstead (7/2B) In rural undulating country a few miles west of READING and south of the A4, but protected by the river Kennet, which has prevented the county town from spreading in this direction. It is a scattered place of winding lanes and farms, beechwoods and views over the Kennet, and takes in Sulhamstead Bannister and Sulhamstead Abbots. There is a tiny flint-built medieval church.

A mile or so west is **Ufton Nervet** (7/2B); the second word being the name of the Norman family who held it after the Conquest. Ufton Court, hard to find through woods and valleys, is a romantic-looking Elizabethan house with no fewer than 17 gables. It was for long the home of the Catholic Perkins family, and the house contains a hidden chapel and priest holes used during penal times. One of the Perkins married Arabella Fermor, a famous beauty. She was Belinda in Alexander Pope's *The Rape of the Lock*, based on an incident in her life. The poet wrote:

> If to her share some female errors fall,
> Look on her face, and you'll forget 'em all.

Padworth (7/1C) is another hidden and charming place near by with beautiful views and an unspoiled Norman church. It is hard to realize that Reading is only a few miles away – it feels more like remotest Devon.

Sunningdale, Sunninghill *see* Ascot

Swallowfield (7/3C) Just north of the Hampshire border and just east of the A33 in the peaceful and rural country where the rivers Blackwater and Loddon meet before flowing northwards and into the Thames just below TWYFORD. Swallowfield Park is a typical late 17th-century house set in a beautiful park with the Blackwater running through. It was a royal hunting domain for centuries: it is known that King John was here in 1205, and that Edward III and the Black Prince were also visitors. The Earl of Clarendon built the present house and it was subsequently sold to Thomas Pitt, known as Diamond Pitt because of the famous diamond he acquired while with the East India Company in Bengal. He sold it to Louis XV of France in 1719 for the then incredible sum of £135,000 and acquired the Swallowfield estate. He was the grandfather and great-grandfather of the famous Prime Ministers.

The church is tucked away in the corner of the park among yew trees. Much of it is Norman and it has atmosphere. The old bell tower is supported inside by a complicated wooden structure known as scissor bracing: very picturesque and effective, too, as it has stood for over 500 years.

The chapter of Hereford Cathedral owns the living, having received it in 1269 from an abbot in Normandy.

Thatcham *see* Newbury

Theale (7/2B) Since the Bath Road was diverted and the M4 motorway built, this old coaching village just west of READING has lost its noise and bustle, but the large number of inns still testify to its former role. There is an immense early Gothic Revival church built in 1822 by the venerable Dr Martin Routh, who was President of Magdalen College, Oxford, for 63 years. It looks out of scale but is worth a visit.

Tidmarsh *see* Pangbourne

Twyford (8/1B) First the Bath Road and then the Great Western Railway crossed the river Loddon, which divides here into two streams: hence the name, which means 'double ford'. It was the railway that made Twyford what it is today, an industrious little red-brick Victorian town with little trace of its more distant past.

Ruscombe (8/1B), on the eastern side of the town, still has its 17th-century church built of brick with an earlier chancel and some farmhouses round about.

Bricks are to Berkshire what stone is to the Cotswolds and a wide variety of bricks and tiles have been made in the county for 600 years since the lost Roman art of brick manufacture was rediscovered in the Middle Ages. The many different clays and gravels on or near the surface throughout Berkshire have proved very suitable for the purpose and the absence of building stone has provided the economic stimulus. The gravel beds in and around READING were perhaps the most important source and a flourishing industry was based on them.

Ufton Nervet *see* Sulhamstead

Upper and Lower Basildon (7/1A&B) Upper Basildon lies on the downs to the west of PANGBOURNE. Lower Basildon is on the A329 and the Thames between Pangbourne and STREATLEY. The old church is down by the Thames with a red-brick Georgian tower and 13th-century nave. The church, pink-washed old rectory and Church House Farm make a picturesque group with the river beyond. Just 100 years ago two young brothers were drowned here and their touching memorial, the boys in swimming costumes, is in the churchyard.

Basildon Park was described in Kelly's Directory of 1928 as 'a modern building with wings'. This seems hardly adequate for the grandest Georgian mansion in Berkshire, now beautifully restored by the Iliffe family and given to the National Trust. It was built in 1776 in Bath stone for Sir Francis Sykes, a friend of

Warren Hastings who like him had made a fortune in India. The architect was Carr of York, who created for Sir Francis a severely classical and elegantly proportioned Palladian mansion, seated in a romantic park with superb views across the Thames Valley to Oxfordshire. The interior is splendid and contains some fine 18th-century pictures and furniture, and an interesting exhibition of other 'nabob' houses, built in England on Indian fortunes. The house is open during the summer.

The Octagon room, Basildon Park

Waltham St Lawrence *see* White Waltham

Warfield *see* Winkfield

Wargrave (8/1A) The A321 road from Henley bridge to Wargrave runs along the bank of the Thames and is very picturesque. It goes through the grounds of Park Place (*see* Remenham) at one point and some of General Conway's 'improvements' on nature in the 18th century can still be seen. He is remembered by a very narrow bridge on the road known as Conway's bridge.

Wargrave itself is a picture of a popular riverside village with a pleasantly Edwardian air about it, although its origins are much older. There are a number of large and elegant houses with gardens leading down to the river and an attractive shopping street. There is a station on the branch line to Henley here, which has encouraged Wargrave's growth, and there has been considerable modern development up the hill away from the river.

The church has a strange story attached to it. It was completely destroyed, except for the tower, by a fire in 1914. There was evidence that the fire was started deliberately, but no culprit was ever found. It was thought that the Suffragettes burned it down because the vicar refused to omit the word 'obey' from the marriage service. The church was immediately rebuilt and is light and spacious inside with some quite pleasing 20th-century glass.

The steep hill behind Wargrave leads to the small hamlet of **Crazies Hill** (8/1A), with superb views across the distant downs and another pretty hamlet just beyond is called **Cockpole Green** (8/1A).

Welford *see* Lambourn Valley

West Ilsley *see* East and West Ilsley

West Woodhay *see* Inkpen

White Waltham (8/1B) Between the main line of the railway and the M4 motorway west of MAIDENHEAD is a stretch of flat and rural countryside with some quite unspoiled villages. White Waltham at the eastern end has a rambling farm group opposite the church where Prince Arthur, King Henry VIII's eldest son, is said to have had a house. After marrying Catherine of Aragon he died young in 1502 and his brother Henry married his widow, which caused no end of trouble when he became Henry VIII. The church has been heavily restored but the chancel is Early English.

Immediately west is **Shottesbrooke Park** (8/1B), an immaculate house that has both Tudor patterned brick and 18th-century 'Gothick' embellishments. The windows are exceptionally elegant. Shottesbrooke Park is the home of The Landmark Trust which has done such notable work in preserving some of the more unusual items in Britain's heritage. Next to the house is one of the most fascinating churches in Berkshire. A small religious college was founded here in 1337 and the church stands hardly altered since that time. Of cruciform design, in Decorated style, its beautiful spire soars skyward on a central tower. It looks like a miniature cathedral from outside. The interior is quite plain, with little church furniture in it, and it is still lit by candles. The 4 ft brass of a priest

and layman is especially noteworthy. The key can be obtained from a house in the stableyard at Shottesbrooke Park and anyone interested in church architecture should certainly do so.

Waltham St Lawrence (8/1B) completes this corner of the county. Apart from some pretty half-timbered cottages it has an unusual number of 18th-century houses with sash windows and resonant names like Paradise, Coltmans, Borlases. The Bell Inn is an inviting hostelry with some heavy medieval timbering. The church, dedicated to St Lawrence, looks straight down the village street behind an enormous yew planted by Rector Wilkinson in 1635. It is of mixed periods but dates mainly from around 1300 and some of the arches are made of chalk, which is unusual. The Elizabethan monument to the Nevilles is interesting.

Wickham (6/1B) An ancient village, south of Welford and just south of the M4 on the old Roman highway running west to Gloucester. Its recorded history starts in AD 686, when King Cædwalla gave it to Abingdon Abbey, and the monks were here for nearly 700 years. It is a true Berkshire village: a mixture of old and new, flint and brick, thatch and tile, with a fine old pub called the Five Bells. The church of St Swithin stands on top of a hill with splendid views across the Kennet valley towards Walbury Hill. The tower, although much repaired, is Saxon and the oldest in the county, and there are traces of Roman brick to be seen in it. By contrast the rest of the church is flamboyant Victorian with a spectacular wooden roof supported by enormous papier mâché angels and elephants with long curling trunks. They were placed here in 1860 and are quite absurd but great fun.

Windsor (8/3B) The old town of Windsor is attractively gathered around the foot of the castle walls on the west side: the eastern side of the castle is entirely taken up with the Home Park, which is mostly private. Near the Henry VIII gateway are some old houses in narrow streets, mostly restaurants and souvenir shops now, but still picturesque and interesting. Castle Hill, winding up past the Curfew Tower, has some well-preserved Georgian houses.

The old Town Hall in the High Street was partly built by Sir Christopher Wren (whose father had been Dean of Windsor) in 1687, and has great charm. The observant will note that some of the columns apparently supporting the ceiling do not in fact touch it. The councillors,

The Old Town Hall designed by Sir Christopher Wren

who were to meet in the room above, are said to have demanded more columns to support their weight. Wren agreed, but had sufficient confidence – justified so far – in his original design to build the columns an inch or so too short. The church of St John the Baptist near by is a large and rather plain early 19th-century building with some interesting monuments, including four large busts of the Hanoverian Georges near the sanctuary somewhat unlikely objects of veneration!.

The latest addition to Windsor's tourist attractions is the conversion of part of the 19th-century railway station into a tableau showing Queen Victoria's arrival at Windsor to celebrate her Diamond Jubilee in 1897. It has been done most imaginatively, by Madame Tussauds and it is very well worth visiting.

Windsor Great Park extends to about 5000 acres and covers most of the country south of the castle to ASCOT and Sunningdale. The Long Walk leads for a dead straight 3 miles south of the castle to a huge equestrian statue of George III. The view of the castle is very impressive. There are further walks in the park, much of which is forbidden to the car. The road leading from Windsor to Ascot gives a good idea of the park with its ancient trees and well-kept estate houses and lodges. The eastern side of the park is in Surrey and includes the beautiful Savill Garden, which is open to the public, and Smith's Lawn, the Guards Polo Club ground.

Overleaf: Interior of St Swithin Church, Wickham

The Long Walk, Windsor

Windsor Castle (8/3B) There was a West Saxon settlement here called *Windlesora*, but the story really begins with William the Conqueror's need to build a castle to protect these western approaches to London and the Thames. The sharp cliff and scarp above the river commands the flat country around and a fortress was built, probably of timber, in the late 11th century. By the time of Henry II in 1150 a stone castle had been constructed, which more of less followed the lines of the castle we see today.

Windsor is the largest castle in Europe and covers 13 acres within its walls – it is like a walled town in many ways. It consists of Lower Ward, which includes St George's Chapel and various buildings associated with it; Middle Ward is the area around the great Round Tower, which is the oldest part; and Upper Ward contains the State Apartments and the East and South wings, which are private apartments of the Royal Family.

A point to remember is that a good deal of the present appearance of the castle is the result of the great restoration in the early 19th century by George IV, which in turn was preceded by other work over the years, but the fundamental design is still 12th century.

Visitors enter through the Henry VIII gate

from the town and see in front of them what is arguably the most perfect late medieval Gothic church in England: St George's Chapel. It was started by Edward IV in 1475 as a celebration of his victory over Henry VI and the Lancastrians in the War of the Roses, and as a new chapel for the Order of the Garter. It took 50 years to complete and is a masterpiece of Perpendicular architecture. It is built of limestone from the famous quarries at Taynton in Oxfordshire which was transported down the Thames. This pale golden stone and the enormous windows characteristic of the exclusively English Perpendicular style combine to give the church a feeling of space and lightness. The great west window, one of the biggest in England, has nearly all its original glass left and is wonderfully colourful.

St George's is the burial place of the Royal Family and, with the exception of Queen Victoria and Prince Albert, virtually all members of it since George III in 1820 are interred there. Four earlier kings rest there, perhaps the saddest being the executed Charles I; the Parliamentarians denied him a funeral service in 1649 and his coffin was lost until 1813, when a workman discovered it by accident. One of the unexpected things about St George's is the large number of non-royal memorials and inscriptions, mostly to members of the household and to servants of the Royal Family in various capacities. Interesting exceptions are the tomb of Napoleon III's son, the Prince Imperial who was killed fighting the Zulus in 1879; and the memorial to the pathetic orphaned son of the mad Emperor Theodore of Abyssinia whom the British deposed about 100 years ago. Queen Victoria felt very sorry for him.

The choir contains the stalls for the Knights of the Garter, which were wonderfully carved between 1478 and 1485. The Sovereign's stall is the most impressive, as you would expect, but the carved statues and details on all the stalls are extraordinary. Above are the heraldic banners of the Garter Knights, each with crested helm, which hang there until their owner dies. Set in the woodwork behind are brass plates recording past knights' names and coats of arms: some were removed when knights were degraded, and some are missing, but over 700 of them remain out of around 900 knights created since the Order was founded c.1348: a fascinating historical record.

To the east of St George's is the Dean's Cloister, mainly dating from the 14th century

'On duty at Windsor'

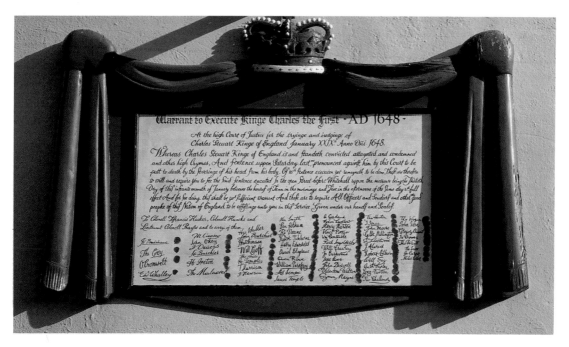

Warrant to Execute King Charles I, Church Street, Windsor (see p. 205)

and one of the oldest surviving parts of the castle. It is thought to be the earliest known example of a college built round a quadrangle, a pattern that later became common in colleges in Oxford and Cambridge. On two sides of the cloister are the Deanery and the canons' residences, both of which are private, and the south side is filled by the Albert Memorial Chapel. Originally built as a Lady Chapel and later intended as a mortuary chapel for Henry VII and Henry VIII, it fell into disuse in the 17th and 18th centuries. In the middle of the 19th century Queen Victoria decided to make it a memorial chapel to her beloved Albert. The walls and roof are covered in marble and mosaics and the result is overwhelming. Prince Albert's effigy is quite simple but is overshadowed by Alfred Gilbert's enormous memorial to the young Duke of Clarence, which fills the chapel like a ship in dry dock. He was the eldest son of King Edward VII and died in 1892.

Further up the hill, past the huge Round Tower, is the North Terrace from which there are dramatic views across the Thames Valley with Eton College Chapel in the foreground. This part of the castle, with the rest of the precincts, has always been freely accessible to the public; George III, who loved Windsor, used to potter about here in his old age mingling with

the Eton boys and chatting to visitors and townspeople. He is reported to have greeted the author of the monumental *Decline and Fall of the Roman Empire* with, 'Still scribbling eh, Mr Gibbon, still scribbling!'

It is from the North Terrace that access is gained to the State Apartments. After the Victorian Grand Staircase the next five enormous rooms were constructed for George IV in the 1820s. The two most interesting are the Garter Throne Room where the Queen receives her Knights and the impressive Waterloo Chamber with its remarkable collection of portraits of the Allied Sovereigns by Sir Thomas Lawrence. Lawrence's famous picture of the Duke of Wellington is above the door. George IV was very proud of the British victory at Waterloo in 1815, and eventually he even managed to delude himself that he had been present on the field.

The rest of the state rooms are part of the Baroque palace created for Charles II. They contain many items from the Royal Collection, wonderful tapestries, furniture and pictures; but perhaps above all it is the Van Dyck portraits of Charles I and his children that will stick in the memory for a long time.

From another entrance near the State Apartments Queen Mary's Doll's House is to be seen and also a – rather small – selection of Old

Opposite: Middle Ward, Windsor Castle

Master Drawings and Watercolours from the Royal Collection.

Windsor Castle is open to the public for virtually the whole year, but certain parts may be closed when the Queen is in residence, especially during April and June. There are excellent guidebooks available.

Winkfield (8/2B) Situated in unexpectedly rural country on the A330 just west of Windsor Forest and north of Ascot. The parish is one of the largest in the county: over 10,000 acres, as it includes **Winkfield Row** and parts of Ascot. A number of small country estates are dotted about with some fine-looking houses glimpsed mainly from afar. The heart of the village is around the church which is built of conglomerate, an unusual iron-coloured mixture of Bagshot sand and pebbles, only seen in this area. The tower is of 17th-century brick.

Two miles west is **Warfield** (8/2B), hardly a village at all but with a most remarkable church. Founded before the Norman Conquest from the priory at HURLEY, St Michael's is a large, mostly 14th-century church built of conglomerate like its neighbour. The barnlike wooden roof is of noble proportions. There are some fragments of medieval glass, but more interesting is the modern window in the north aisle with its unusual symbolism. Monuments abound and connoisseurs will enjoy the Walsh tablet in the aisle. Of Sir John it records: 'Few have passed through this transitory scene with less of the alloy of human infirmity'; while of Lady Walsh the author 'shrinks from the vain attempt to describe her elevated nature'.

The large chancel and impressive windows are a good example of the Decorated style and it may be wondered how such a small community came to support so large a church.

Winterbourne *see* Chieveley

Wokingham (8/1B) Queen Elizabeth granted this old market town east of READING its first charter in 1583, but its origins go back to Anglo-Saxon times. Like many towns in England it prospered in the late Middle Ages on weaving and the silk trade and also had a substantial brick industry from the 17th century. Perhaps, however, the most important single event in Wokingham's story was the coming of the Southern Railway in the 19th century; this transformed east Berkshire into the thriving commuting area it still is today. The M4

motorway with its huge intersection just north of the town has had a similarly galvanizing effect on Wokingham's economy.

There is all the more reason therefore to be pleasantly surprised by how much character the town retains. As you come in from the BRACKNELL direction past the church, the main street still has many old houses behind its modern shop fronts. At the end is the splendid multi-coloured Victorian Town Hall – a little out of place, perhaps, but Wokingham people are obviously fond of it, as it has been nicely cleaned and restored.

Broad Street, just beyond the Town Hall, has some attractive Georgian houses and shops; and the market place gives the impression that it could still serve its old function if required. At the Rose Inn, which stood in Rose Street, the poets Gay, Pope and Swift are said to have spent a wet day in the early 18th century composing verses on the charms of the landlord's daughter. Molly Mog they called her and she now has another inn named after her.

About a mile from the town centre, off the Sandhurst road, is the Lucas Hospital. It takes its name from its founder, Henry Lucas, and was established in 1663 for '16 poor men' who resided there. The mellow red brick and classic proportions of this beautiful building are like a miniature Chelsea Hospital and it includes a simple chapel of the same period. It is rather hard to find but well worth the effort.

Woolhampton (7/1B) Part of the village is on the A4 between READING and NEWBURY and the rest is up the steep wooded slopes north of the river Kennet. The Knights Hospitallers were here 700 years ago, as they were at Brimpton, south-west across the valley. Now there is Douai Abbey, the first Benedictine house in Berkshire since the great abbeys of Reading and Abingdon were suppressed by Henry VIII. It was established here in 1903 but its origins lie in an early 17th-century foundation for English Catholics in northern France. Douai Abbey church, started in 1928, is red brick outside and white stone inside.

Wraysbury (8/3B) North of the river Thames and about 3 miles from WINDSOR, Wraysbury and **Horton** (8/3B) are new additions to Berkshire since the boundaries were altered in 1974, set in a curiously cut-off area surrounded by enormous reservoirs. Despite the closeness of Heathrow Airport, Horton manages to keep quite a rural air, with some attractive old buildings and an ancient church with a Norman doorway. Wraysbury is more developed but still very watery, with flocks of wildfowl on the reservoirs and river.

Yattendon (7/1B) This old village with its mellow brick Georgian houses and cottages lies in heavily wooded hills about 8 miles north-east of NEWBURY and just north of the M4 motorway. Many believe it to be the site of the battle of Ethandune where Alfred the Great defeated the Danes under Guthrum in AD 878 and forced their surrender. There is a small attractive square in the centre of the village around an old well with the hospitable-looking Royal Oak Hotel and some shops.

Alfred Waterhouse, the great Victorian architect who built the Natural History Museum in South Kensington, was lord of the manor here and restored the church; his monument is inside. There is also one to a great Elizabethan, Sir John Norreys, who sailed with Drake and was ambassador to France. His ancient helmet hangs in the church and contrasts with the First World War one on the opposite wall above the war memorial.

Another notable resident was the Poet Laureate Robert Bridges, who lived here for many years before his death in 1930 and compiled the Yattendon Hymnal. Perhaps he had the woods here in mind when he wrote:

> Yet it was here we walked when ferns
> were springing
> And through the mossy bank shot bud
> and blade,
> Here found in summer when the birds
> were singing
> A green and pleasant shade.

His moving poem 'The Sleeping Mansion' refers to the manor house where he lived, having married Waterhouse's daughter.

The Round Tower, Windsor Castle

Detail of the choir-stall, St Mary's church, Swinbrook

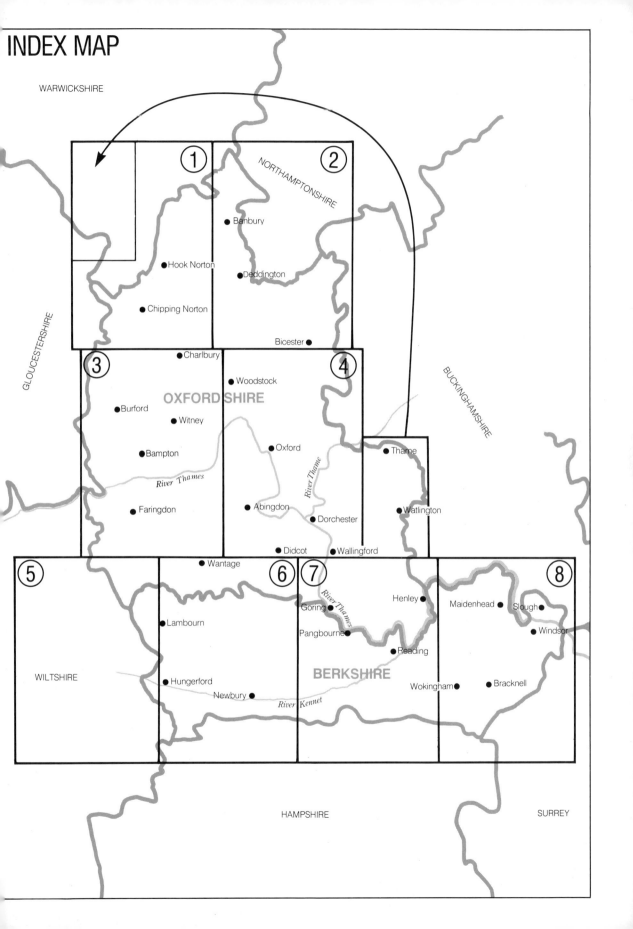

INDEX MAP

WARWICKSHIRE

GLOUCESTERSHIRE

NORTHAMPTONSHIRE

BUCKINGHAMSHIRE

① ②

● Banbury

● Hook Norton

● Deddington

● Chipping Norton

Bicester ●

● Charlbury

③ ④

● Woodstock

OXFORDSHIRE

● Burford

● Witney

● Oxford

● Thame

● Bampton

● Abingdon

River Thame

● Dorchester

● Watlington

River Thames

● Faringdon

● Didcot

Wallingford ●

⑤ ● Wantage ⑥ ⑦ ⑧

River Thames

● Henley

Maidenhead ●

● Slough

Goring ●

● Lambourn

● Windsor

Pangbourne ●

WILTSHIRE

● Reading

BERKSHIRE

● Hungerford

● Bracknell

Newbury ●

Wokingham ●

River Kennet

HAMPSHIRE

SURREY

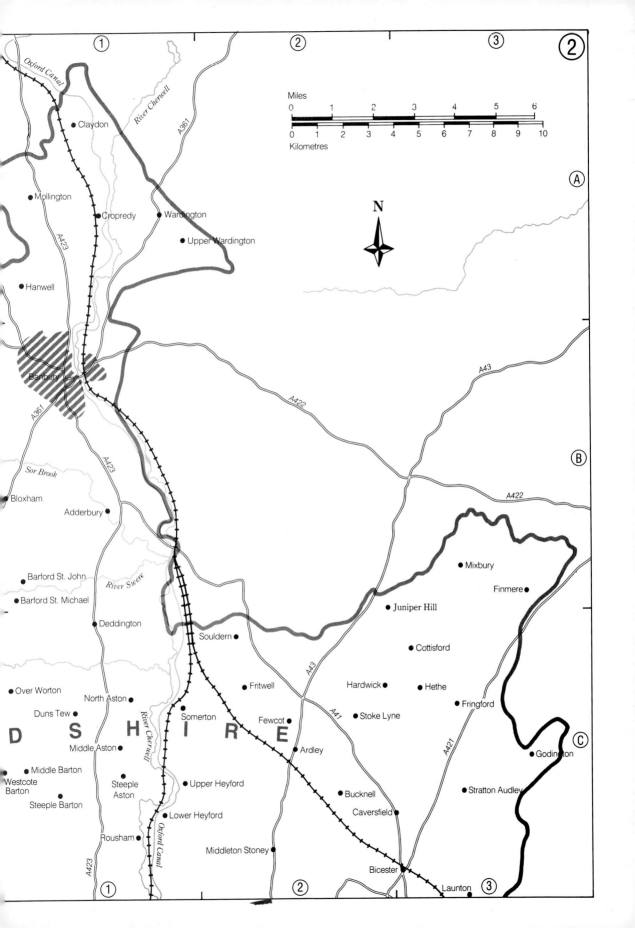

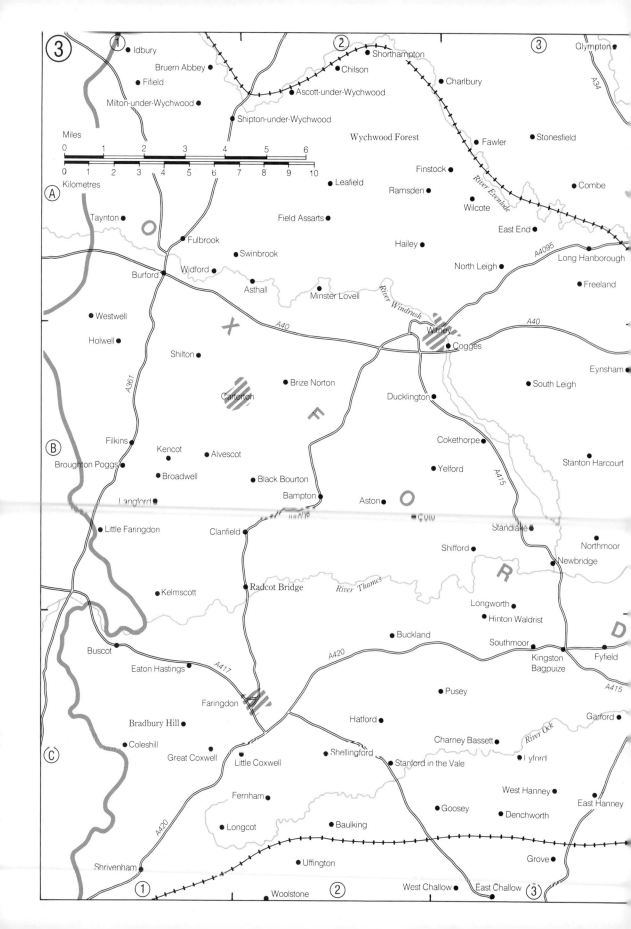

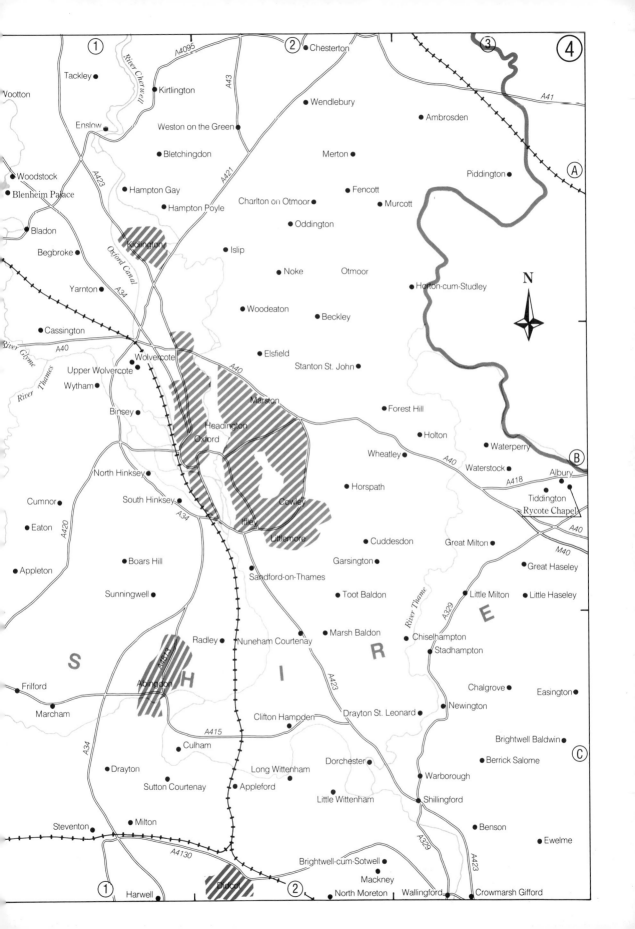

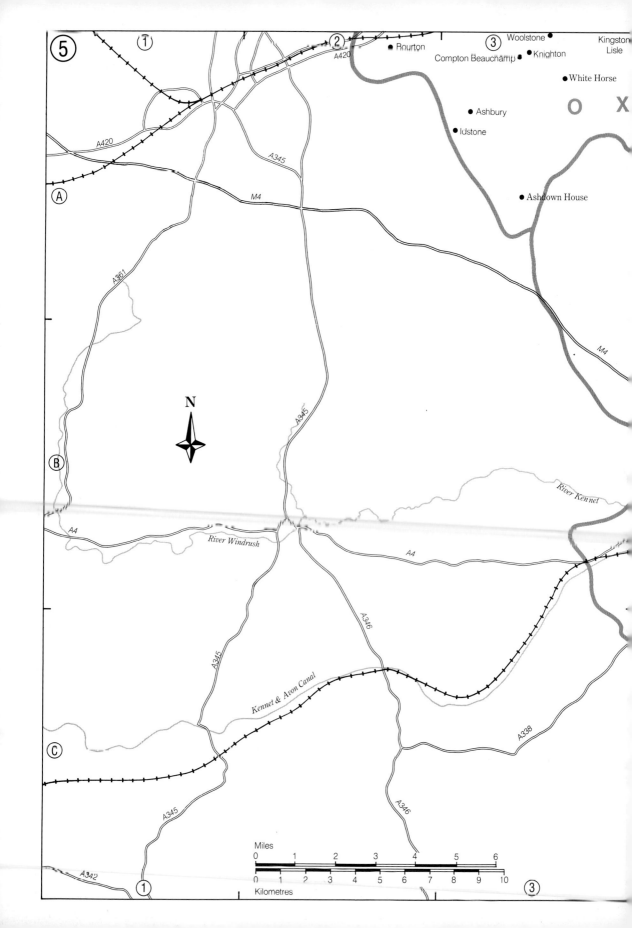

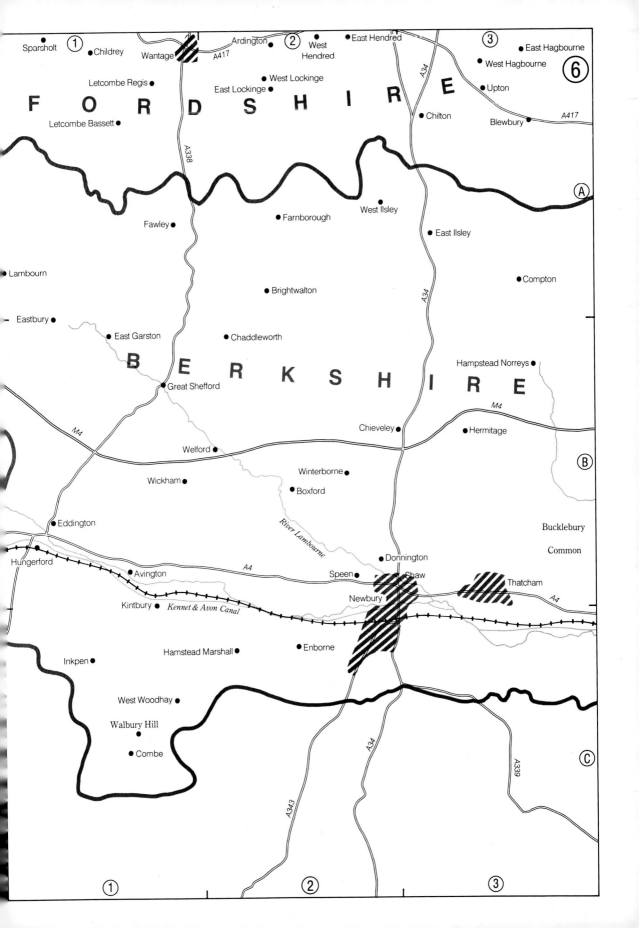

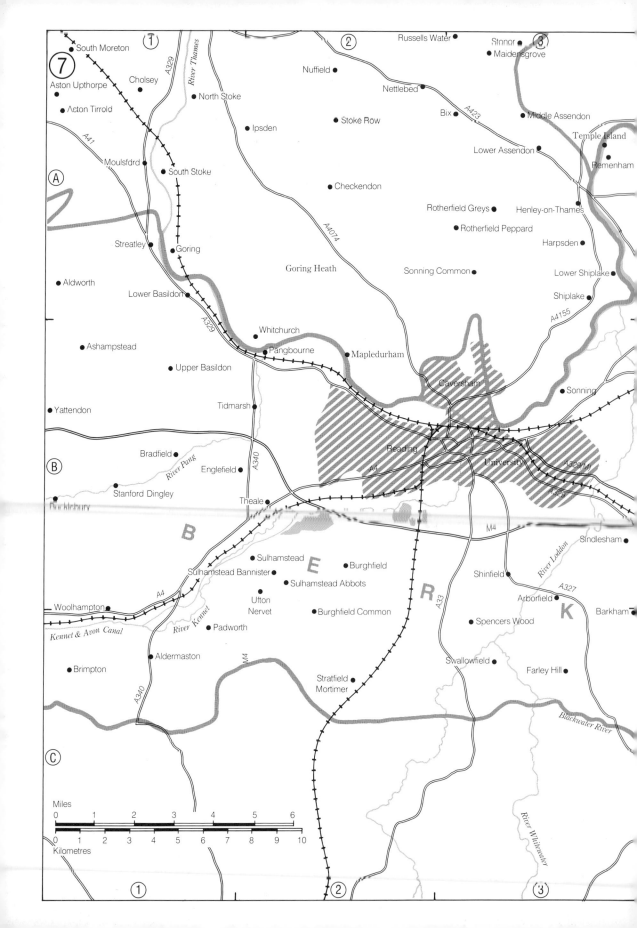

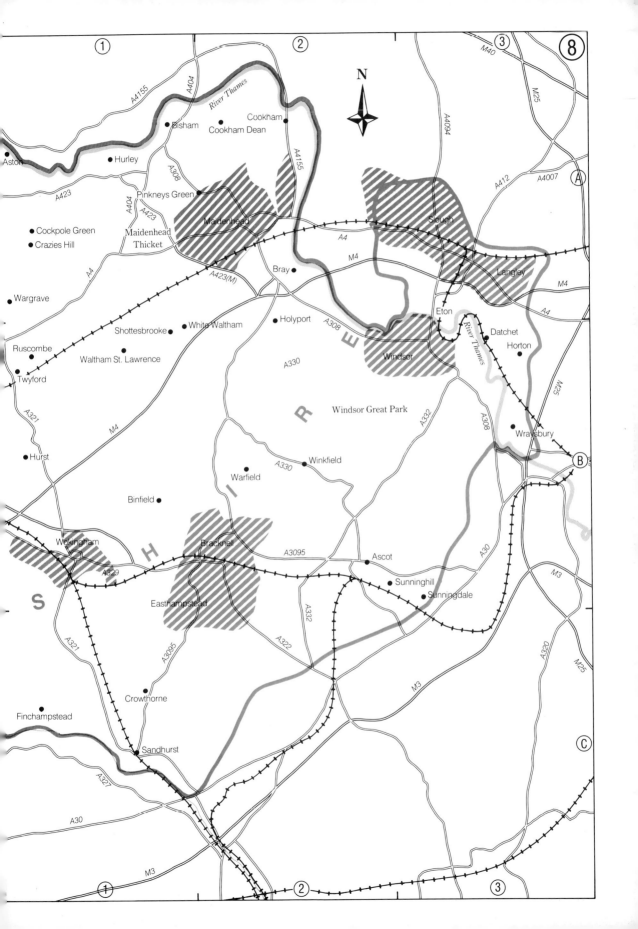

Bibliography

Alexander, H. *The Place-names of Oxfordshire*. Clarendon Press, Oxford 1912

Arkell, W. J. *Oxford Stone*. Faber & Faber, London 1947

Atkinson, M. *The Thames-side Book*. Osprey, Reading 1973

Betjeman, J. *Church Poems*. John Murray, London 1981

Betjeman, J., and J. Piper (editors) *Berkshire Architectural Guide*. John Murray, London 1949

Cameron, K. *English Place-names*. Batsford, London 1961

Carleton-Williams, E. *Companion into Oxfordshire*. Methuen, London 1935 (4th edition 1951)

Edwards, J. 'Wall Paintings', in *Oxoniensa*, Vols X/VII & X/VIII 1983

Ekwall, E. *The Concise Oxford Dictionary of English Place-names*, 4th edition. Clarendon Press, Oxford 1960

Emery, F. *The Oxfordshire Landscape*. Hodder & Stoughton, London 1974

Ford, E. B., and J. S. Haywood *Church Treasures in the Oxford District*. Alan Sutton, Gloucester 1984

Hadfield, J. (editor) *The Shell Guide to England*. Michael Joseph, London 1970 (also *New Shell Guide to England* 1981)

Hammond, N. *The Oxfordshire Village Book*. Countryside Books, Newbury 1983

Henderson, M. S. *Three Centuries in North Oxfordshire*. Blackwell, Oxford; Edward Arnold, London 1902

Hinton, D. A. *Oxford Buildings from Medieval to Modern*. Ashmolean Museum, Oxford 1977

Kelly's Directory of Berkshire, Buckinghamshire and Oxfordshire. London 1928

Levi, P. *The Flutes of Autumn*. Harvill Press, London 1983

Mee, A. (editor) *The King's England: Berkshire*. Hodder & Stoughton, London 1939

Mee, A. (editor) *The King's England: Oxfordshire*. Hodder & Stoughton, London 1942

Morgan, P. *Royal Arms in Oxfordshire Churches*. R. Pardoe, Runcorn 1987

Morris, J. (general editor) *Domesday Book* (translation): 5 *Berkshire*; 14 *Oxfordshire*. Phillimore Press, Chichester 1978

Oxfordshire Museum Service: various pamphlets and leaflets

Pevsner, N. *The Buildings of England: Berkshire*. Penguin, Harmondsworth 1966

Pevsner, N., and J. Sherwood *The Buildings of England: Oxfordshire*. Penguin, Harmondsworth 1974

Piper, J. *The Shell Guide to Oxfordshire* (reissue). Faber & Faber, London 1939

Smith, A. E. (editor) *Nature Reserves Handbook*. Royal Society for Nature Conservation (on behalf of BBONT) 1984

Utechin, P. *Epitaphs from Oxfordshire Churches*. R. Dugdale and Friends of Oxfordshire Churches, Oxford 1980

Victoria County Histories: *Berkshire* and *Oxfordshire*

Yarrow, I. *Berkshire*. Robert Hale, London 1952

Index

Numbers in *italics* refer to illustrations

The New Shell Guides
Oxfordshire and Berkshire